COLLECTED EASTER HORROR SHORTS

TALES FOR A TERRIFYING EASTER

Collected by Kevin J. Kennedy

Collected Easter Horror Shorts © 2017 Kevin J. Kennedy

Collected by Kevin J. Kennedy

Originally published in 2017 in the United States of America by Amazon and CreateSpace.

All rights reserved, including the right of reproduction in whole or in part in any form.

For information about special discounts for bulk purchases, please contact Kevin J. Kennedy at kevinkennedyez@hotmail.co.uk or at http://www.kevinjkennedy.co.uk.

Edited by Brandy Yassa

Print Production and Design by Weston Kincade

Cover Design © 2017 by Lisa Vasquez

He Has Risen © C.S.Anderson

Magic Awaits © Christopher Motz

It's Not All About Bunnies and Chocolates © Veronica Smith

Easter Gunny © Peter Oliver Wonder

The Rebirth © Mark Cassell

Trying To Write A Horror Story © Andrew Lennon

Mia's Easter Basket © Mark Lukens

SonnesHill © Lex Jones

Lord of The Dance © JC Michael

Echoes of The Bunny-Man © Steven Stacy

An Easter Prayer © Weston Kincade and David Chrisley

Hatch © Christina Bergling -

Killer Jelly Beans from Outer Space © James Matthew Byers

Paying It Forward © Jeff Menapace

Rotten Eggs © Jeff Strand

Bunny and Clyde © Lisa Vasquez

Sulphur © Mark Fleming

Last Supper © Suzanne Fox

Baby Blues © Briana Robertson

Easter Eggs © Latashia Figueroa

Lamb to Slaughter © Amy Cross

A Town Called Easter © Kevin J. Kennedy

First Printing, 2017

Manufactured in the United States of America

Summary: From the darkest recesses of some of the horror world's most chilling minds, Kevin J. Kennedy brings back together some of the authors that brought you Collected Christmas Horror Shorts, alongside several new authors, from upcoming indie stars to Amazon top sellers.

Whether you like Easter or not, you'll certainly have a different view of it after you read the stories contained within these pages.

Grab an Easter egg, dim the lights, get cosy and get ready for some chilling tales by some of the horror world's finest.

ASIN B06XSHD8G2 (eBook)

TABLE OF CONTENTS

FOREWORD

Nev Murray

Hello again!

Who would ever have thought that after writing the foreword for the *first* Christmas edition of this book, that they would actually ask me back!

Me neither! But here we are. It strikes me as odd though that they only contact me at holiday times. The rest of the year I'm just left to fester, but that is another story, for another time.

So, Easter. Did you know that as with Christmas, people fall under different categories when it comes to Easter? I surprised you with the categories at Christmas so thought I would make more up….sorry….explain the Easter ones to you.

Firstly, there is the part which I don't want to talk about, revolving around that thing called *religion*. For anyone that may be reading this that believes that is what Easter is all about, I applaud you for having faith. It's just not for me.

Next, we have the people who couldn't care less what happens at this time of year, they just want a few days off work.

Then we come to the two most popular categories. The people who love the whole Easter thing for a family get together, and those of us who worship chocolate!

I suspect there are many of you out there who, like me, don't go in for the big family get togethers. I mean why would.....you know what? Let's not even go there. My mum got a mention in the Christmas foreword for buying me something ridiculous and I thought it would be unfair to leave her out of this one. She did the same thing one Easter. We always used to get new clothes for Easter day. Ones to wear when we went to do the big family thing. Know what my mum bought me one year? Now, you have to bear in mind this was in the seventies; she bought me a cream shirt, with little brown images all over it of.....Laurel and Hardy. Yeah, I know. That is about forty years ago and I can still see it when I close my eyes.

The last category is all about the lovely scrummy chocolate. Chocolate is just the, greatest, thing, ever. I mean you can do so many different things to it and it still tastes bloody wonderful. I feel sorry for you American types though because any of your chocolate I have tasted is a bit meh. British chocolate on the other hand is just sublime.

But where is he going with this foreword I hear you ask? Well, I don't want to talk about any of the above categories. After all, you hold a horror anthology in your hand all about Easter. You want a horror foreword with horror things in it. Therefore, I am going to talk about............bunnies!

Yes, those beautiful little furry creatures with the little fluffy button tail and the floppy ears and the adorable chubby cheeks. Right?

Wrong!

Think about it. When was the last time you saw a cute rabbit? I reckon the last time any of you saw a rabbit was as it darted across a field or ran away from you in a forest. Maybe you even passed one at the side of the road on your way home today. Maybe you even brought one home for some stew recently. But when was the last time you saw a cute one?

In a movie? On TV? In a book? Wrong again. Let me give you some examples. You may have to go look these up on Google to see what I mean, but I will tell you the truth about bunnies.

Donnie Darko. I mean what the hell? Have you seen the bunny in that one? I have never seen a more frightening bunny skull face ever. Now I don't think that film was meant to be a horror but that bunny certainly scared the bejesus out of me.

Bunnicula: The Vampire Rabbit. Speaks for itself, doesn't it?

Easter Bunny, Kill Kill. Yeah OK that one is really a person dressed as a bunny but he wouldn't have been dressed like that if bunnies weren't evil in the first place!

Easter Bunny Bloodbath. *Kottentail*. Who could ever forget the cute little bunny, sorry, nasty beast with big pointy teeth that completely ravaged King Arthur's men in their quest for the Holy Grail. One of the most horrifying legends in English history. The list goes on and on and on. All of these films prove the point that bunny rabbits are evil and therefore you should be very afraid of the one that pops out at Easter. He isn't after your chocolate. He is after your blood!

Not surprisingly, there are a few bunnies in *Collected Easter Horror Shorts*. The people who wrote about them in this book have recognised the true evil that lurks under that fluffy white fur.

The people that wrote the stories in this book have also embraced the true meaning of Easter. It's not about the happy things. It's all about the horror.

Within this book, you will read stories that show the alternative side to Easter. While some families are having fun and frolics, many, many more are living through horrific times that are, sometimes brutally, exhibited in the pages you are about to read.

We have tales about the cute little bunnies morphed into killers. We have twists on the story of the resurrection involving zombies. We have a plethora of stories about the different kinds of eggs you can get at Easter. None of them will make you a nice omelette but they are all full of surprises. Some of those eggs may suck you into another world altogether and some may lead to copious amounts of blood being spilled.

You will read of mysterious caves that hide mysterious secrets and men who have hidden other secrets for two thousand years. You may hope that if someone gives you an Easter basket this year that it doesn't contain some of the horrors that the baskets in this book hold.

And the good old scavenger hunt for eggs? Be careful you don't win the grand prize. It may not be what you expected.

Intrigued? You should be. Once again, Kevin Kennedy has brought together a collection of authors, some from the Christmas Collection and some new, who have given their all in making sure that the stories you are about to read will entertain you, sicken you, and most importantly, scare you.

Easter isn't about family and fun times.

It's about horror. With chocolate.

And sorry mum, I can't forgive the shirt.

Nev Murray

March '17

LAMB TO SLAUGHTER
Amy Cross

On the last day, Father came to see me in the woodshed. I wanted to scream, to beg him for mercy, to ask him to explain why this was happening to me, but instead I kept quiet and stayed in the corner. I'd finally realized that nobody was ever going to explain, at least not in a way that my eleven-year-old brain could understand.

"Are you alright there, Oline?" he asked, standing in the doorway, framed against the allotments where my brothers had been working during the day.

I'd heard them through the locked door.

"Can I..."

The words caught in my throat. Somehow I felt as if I had to ask, even though I already knew the answer. I had to say the words, because if I didn't say them, what would that make me? Some pathetic thing that accepted its fate, far too easily? I didn't want to be like that. I knew I wasn't an adult, not yet, but I felt that I could hurry things along if I at least *acted* like one. So really, I had no option. I had to find my voice.

"Can I go back inside?" I managed to ask finally. "I mean, can I go back into the house?"

I waited.

His silhouetted figure did not respond. Only now did I notice that he was wiping something against a cloth. A moment later I saw a flash of metal, and I realized he was cleaning a knife.

"I have chores to do," I explained, hoping to make myself seem useful. I even began to sit up, although not all the way. I rearranged my damaged legs until I was kneeling in the corner. "I'm good at scrubbing floors. Do you remember? I was always the best at scrubbing floors. Mother said that no matter how ingrained the stain, no matter what else she'd tried, she could always rely on me to -"

"No."

"I'm very good at -"

"No, Oline. Just... No."

I swallowed hard.

There were tears in my eyes.

"Okay," I replied, but my voice was cracking now, and I was on the verge of breaking into full-throated sobs. I'd spent the whole day, and the night before too, trying to come up with ways to keep myself from sobbing. I'd tried digging my fingernails into the palm of my hands, I'd tried bending my little fingers back until I felt the bones strain, and finally I'd thought that by biting my bottom lip I might be able to summon enough pain. Enough to hold the tears back. All in preparation for this moment.

Now, however, tears were already starting to run down my face, and I knew Father could see them. I knew it was too late, so I let my body shake.

"Did you read the book I gave you?" Father asked.

I nodded, sniffing back more tears.

"So you understand?"

I nodded again.

"Well, then," he continued, holding a hand out for me to take, waiting for me to join him and go outside. "There's no need for any more of this chat, is there? Come on, girl. You're just wasting everybody's time now. You've got a job to do, little lamb."

***

"Oline!" Ronald shouted, grabbing me and pulling me tight; hugging me so hard that I feared he meant to burst me. "Look at you! No man ever had a better sister!"

I tried to pull away, but he put his arms around me and hugged me even closer, almost smothering me against the rough cotton of his unwashed work-shirt. Any other time, I would have pulled away and told him he was gross, but on that evening I took the deepest breath I could manage, inhaling the mix of sweat and motor oil and fertilizer until suddenly Ronald shoved me away and laughed. He took a sip of beer and leaned back, chuckling to himself, and already the smell of his shirt was fading from my nostrils.

I'd remember that smell, though.

I knew I would, and it turned out I was right. But that part came later.

"Eat!" Oliver said, sliding another plate toward me across the table. The younger of my two brothers, Oliver seemed less relaxed than Ronald, as if he hadn't quite come to understand the significance of the night's events. Still, he was making a good show of pretending. "This is still your favorite, isn't it? Mackerel in tomato sauce, on bread?"

I nodded, although I didn't remember ever saying mackerel was my favorite. Then again, I figured he was probably right. In that moment, I was so scared that I barely remembered anything of myself, and it took fully half a minute before I could even remember my name. Feeling a little dizzy, as if my body had become light and my head had become very heavy, I placed my hands on the edge of the table and gripped the wood tight, waiting for the sensation to pass. It *would* pass, I knew that, but the experience was still mighty unpleasant as I felt the table anchoring me to the world. And then, of course, it *did* pass, and I felt a little more normal again. And I remembered my name.

Oline.

I'm Oline.

I'm eleven years old and...

Suddenly I felt sick; it was the kind of nausea that strikes with no warning and pushes up through your gut like a fist. The kind of nausea that makes you think the bottom of your brain has become un-knotted and all the strings are hanging down into your neck. This, too, would pass in just a moment. I knew that. Still, after just a couple of seconds I felt pinpricks of cold sweat breaking out all across my face, and I leaned forward so that perhaps I could hide my face from the others. Now the sweat was running down from my forehead and I could feel more sweat in my armpits and my heart was pounding and I was starting to worry that I wouldn't be able to beat the feeling back.

But I did.

It passed, and finally I leaned back in my chair.

"What's up?" Oliver asked, nudging my right elbow. "Having second thoughts?"

I turned to him. "No."

"Are you sure?" This time his voice was much lower, as if he meant to keep Father from hearing. "I mean, are you really sure, Oline?"

I nodded.

He paused, and I could see that he wanted to ask again, but that he didn't dare. Or maybe he'd read the answer in my eyes, or he *thought* he had. Poor, sweet Oliver was always my favorite.

"Lamb," Father said suddenly.

I turned and saw him staring directly at me.

"Lamb," he continued, his dour face breaking into a smile that revealed his rotten teeth. "Are you not overjoyed by this feast we have laid out for you?"

I nodded, but I knew for sure that I didn't look happy. I couldn't remember how to smile.

"It's Easter," he added, keeping his eyes fixed on me, "and the door needs painting. God knows this. God knows that a new covenant is required, and He knows that our door needs painting. He's seen the chipped wood, and the flakes that fall to the floor every time that door is forced shut. God sees our front door, Oline, and He recognizes that it has become weathered and ruined. He knows that I'm not a lazy man. He knows I would have painted that door a hundred times over if I'd been able, but He knows that I've been waiting."

"God knows you were injured in the war, Stephen," Mother said hurriedly, as if she was keen to remind him. "God knows that the Third World War was -"

"Nobody calls it that!" Oliver sneered.

"God knows how the world is now," she added, turning to him. "He knows. He sees it all. He knows we make do with what we have, and He knows we're waiting for things to get better again."

Oliver shook his head and mumbled something under his breath. Ever the cynic.

"I won't have you arguing," Father said firmly. "Not on Oline's day. Her last day should be happy."

He paused, and those words seemed to linger in the air for a moment. I still heard them echoing in my thoughts, and I'm sure the others still heard them too.

Finally, Father placed his right hand on the table, half as if he wanted me to take it in his, and half as if he was merely resting for a moment. Still, he kept his eyes fixed very clearly and very carefully on my face.

"We're going to paint that door red, Oline," he continued finally. "Does that sound nice to you? We're going to paint it red tomorrow when the sun comes up. And then it'll dry as the day goes on. Doesn't that make you just a little proud?"

I nodded, because I knew he expected me to nod.

"How can she be proud?" Oliver whispered on my other side. "She won't be here to see it."

"Sshh!" I hissed, turning to him.

"You won't!" he continued, his eyes wide open with fear now. "Oline -"

"Quiet!" I said firmly.

"But how can you just sit there and take this? All these crazy religions of the world are all mixed into one and now this superstitious nonsense is -"

"Quiet!" I placed a hand on his arm, and I knew that this would silence him. He always stopped talking when I touched him. He was my brother. "You're going to have a new door tomorrow," I pointed out. "Bright red and shining in the sun. Just make sure not to touch it until nightfall. I wouldn't want it to get smudged, or to have your rotten fingerprints dried into it."

I waited for him to smile, but he simply stared at me. I suppose he was thinking of the fingerprints that appeared in the door shortly after it was painted eleven years ago.

"I wouldn't want any trouble," I continued. "Please, Oliver. I wouldn't want that at all, and if I can look down and -"

"Look down?" he spat back at me. "What -"

"Quiet!" I said again, and again he stopped speaking. I could tell that he wanted to say so much more, but instead he looked down at his lap, where his hands rested. Although he was a couple of years older than me, Oliver always listened to what I said. Not like the others.

Once I was sure he'd not speak again, I turned back to Father.

"I'm sure the door will look good," I said, hoping to steer the conversation back onto its proper course. "I'm sure the red will really stand out for miles around, and protect you all. Are you going to remove the locks and knocker, so you can paint under their edges? Or are you going to put tape on them? I think you should remove them. It's more work, but the end result will look so much better, and after all, this isn't something you do every day, is it? It might be *another* eleven years before you paint the door again. Well, longer even, because…"

My voice trailed off.

I was talking too much, and I knew it. Still, as I kept my eyes on Father, I felt certain that he was about to boil over with rage and send Oliver from the table, maybe even take him out into the yard and mete out some punishment. After a moment, however, I saw Father's face soften slightly, as if the weight of the evening was keeping him subdued, and he simply looked down at his plate. Father was usually a man quick to anger, and free with his tongue, yet now he seemed lost in thought. I supposed he was not used to thinking so much, and that perhaps he found it difficult.

The celebratory mood had faded now, and after a moment I heard Oliver whispering next to me, keeping his voice even lower this time.

"There should be another way," he was saying under his breath. "This isn't right. We should be better than this."

***

"It's coming, isn't it?"

As soon as those words left my mouth, I knew they had been a terrible mistake. I had sensed something approaching our forest, of that there had been no doubt. Still, there had been no need for me to speak of what I knew, no need to share the burden. Father was on his knees in front of me, and he had been buttoning my dark blue coat for the walk, but now he looked up at me with fearful eyes. I had stopped his thoughts, and his concern was my fault.

"I'm sorry," I continued, "I -"

"You feel it too?"

I paused, before nodding.

"Thundering through the air, Oline?"

I nodded again.

He turned and looked toward the window, and I did the same. Beyond the dirty and cracked glass pane, nothing was visible except the dark of night. We both knew, however, that the cold forest was out there, and we both felt something approaching at speed. Still many miles away, of course, but always coming. Soon, it would reach us. The house's new protection could not come soon enough. The Easter ceremony had to be completed, and the sacrificial lamb had to be offered.

"Please," I said finally, looking back down and seeing that Father's frail hands were still holding the buttons he'd been about to slip into their places, "carry on with my coat. Ignore me."

I waited, but he was still looking at the window.

"Father? Can you please -"

"You were too young last time," he replied suddenly, still not looking at me. "Just a baby. You heard your older sister's screams, but you won't remember them."

"No," I said with a dry throat. "I don't."

"You don't remember Anna at all, do you?"

I shook my head.

"Lamb of mine, she was," he continued. "As you are now. I knew that day that you would one day have to take her place, but I thought the years would last longer. Instead here we are, after eleven summers and eleven winters, and now I must button your coat the way I buttoned hers." Finally he turned to me again. "You know this is not my choice, Oline. You know that, don't you?"

"I know."

"If there were any other way -"

"I know."

"I was so certain I'd think of something; I had eleven years. I thought that over the course of eleven years I'd think of some way out for you, or that I'd find a way to move our family on from this wretched place." He seemed shocked now, as if he couldn't quite believe that so much time had passed. "I should have been smarter. What kind of father spends eleven years trying to save his daughter, and still doesn't come up with anything? I had all the time in the world, but I -"

He stopped suddenly, as if the words had caught in his throat, and then he looked up at me again. "Can you forgive me?"

I waited, trying to think of the right thing to say.

"Can you finish buttoning my coat up?" I asked finally. "I don't want to get cold."

***

"I can't go any further, Oline. I want to, but I just can't. You understand, don't you?"

I walked a couple more paces, before realizing that I could no longer hear Father's footsteps behind me. Stopping and turning, I saw that he was watching me from next to one of the huge old oak trees. I could barely make him out at all, since the light of the moon was mostly blocked by the dead branches overhead, but for some reason I could see the vapor of his breath in the night air.

"Do I just keep walking?" I asked.

He didn't reply.

"Is that what Anna did eleven years ago?"

Again, nothing.

"Is that what Anna did?" I asked one more time, but I already knew he wasn't going to tell me.

Turning, I looked straight ahead and saw vast, dead trees curling up from the forest floor, as if they'd died while trying to snatch something from the land. There was a hint of mist in the air, drifting through the slices of moonlight, so it was difficult to tell whether anything else was moving at all. After a moment I turned back to Father and saw that he didn't seem to have moved. He was still standing next to that big old tree, still silhouetted against the dark forest with the lights of our house still just about visible in the distance. We'd walked a long way, but maybe not as far as I'd expected.

"Does my suffering begin now?" I asked.

Again I waited.

Again, he said nothing.

"Father?"

I wished he'd speak. I wished he'd tell me that everything was going to be okay, the way he used to tell me over the course of the past eleven years.

"My little lamb," he said finally, his voice filled with regret. I couldn't see his face, not in the darkness, but he sounded as if he was crying. He couldn't be crying, though. Father never cried, I knew that. "Maybe there's another way. It's a twenty minute walk back to the house. In that time, maybe I can think of some other way for us to be safe."

"How can you do that?" I asked. "If you couldn't think of something in eleven years, how can you think of something in twenty minutes?"

He stepped toward me, reaching out a hand.

"Come."

"Where?"

"Home."

"Father, you said -"

"I know," he continued, coming closer and taking my hand by force, "but I was wrong." He looked past me, out toward the darker parts of the forest, as if he was watching and waiting to see something fearsome. "I can't let you do this, Oline. I can't let you wander off into the forest like your sister and sacrifice yourself just to keep the rest of the family safe."

"But eleven years of safety would -"

"There has to be another way!"

Gripping my hand tightly, he turned and tried to lead me back toward the house, but I stood firm. My hand slipped from his, and he managed a couple of paces before turning back to me.

"Oline -"

"I'm doing this," I told him.

"Child, you don't understand."

"It's what you need me to do, isn't it?" I replied. "You and Mother and Oliver and Ronald will be safe if I'm sent out into the forest. You've been raising me all this time, you've been treating me so well, because you knew that one day I'd have to come out here."

"I gave you everything I could," he replied, and now I could tell that he really had begun to cry.

"I know."

"I treated you better than any girl in the whole of human history."

"I know. I appreciated it."

"You're the lamb of our family," he added. "The devil can't take the form of a lamb, Oline. It's the only animal he can't become."

"Mother taught me about that," I replied. "Because the lamb is the only animal that's guaranteed to be pure, it's the only animal a God-fearing family can sacrifice. So you raised me to be happy and well, you called me your lamb, and now in return I have to do this."

"And I'm just supposed to let you go?" he continued, his voice trembling with fear. "No, I can't do that. I watched your sister walk away eleven years ago, when she was our lamb, and I've relived that moment every night since. I can't do that same with you, Oline. I just can't."

He tried to grab my hand.

I pulled free.

So he tried again.

And again I pulled my fingers free of his.

He tried yet again.

This time I took a couple of steps back.

"Oline, please, just listen to me. I know I've spent eleven years telling you that this is your destiny, but I was being foolish. I was letting the old religions cloud my judgment; I was allowing myself to fall into superstition. I'm your father and I'm ordering you to take my hand so we can go back to the house. You know you have to obey me."

Taking a deep breath, I realized that while I had always, *always* obeyed Father in the past, now I was going to have to break free. He was weakening; his resolve was crumbling, but our house and our entire family would be at risk if I went back there with him now. Every eleventh Easter, a sacrifice had to be sent out to the forest, and that simple fact was not going to change just because Father wished it were not so. He had spent so much time over the years teaching me to be strong. Now it seemed *he* was the one who was faltering.

"Oline," he continued, reaching for my hand again, "I cannot watch you walk away into the forest."

"Okay, then," I replied, taking another step back. "Then I shall run."

With that, I turned and bolted, racing between the trees and ignoring Father's cries. I knew he'd never be able to keep up; that his gammy right knee would surely bring him crashing to the ground. So I ran and ran and ran, until I knew I'd be out of sight, and then I clattered into a tree before turning and looking back the way I'd just come.

"Oline!" Father's voice called out from far, far away. "Come back!"

I wanted to go back, of course. I wanted to go home, but I knew that Father had raised me so that I might save the family on this very terrible night. I also knew that my sacrifice would guarantee eleven good years for the entire family. I turned and started walking between the trees. I felt my chest tighten and I realized my legs were aching from all the running; I stumbled a couple of times. It seemed as though my feet were sinking slightly with each step, as if the forest floor was becoming wetter and less stable. I kept going, simply because I knew that I had no choice. I'd imagined this night so many times over the years, wondering what it would be like, but now everything felt so normal and mundane. It was almost as if -

Suddenly my right foot caught in a harder patch of mud. I fell forward, landing hard on my hands and knees, and it took a moment before I was able to twist my foot free.

"Happy Easter, little lamb."

Startled, I turned and saw a familiar figure standing just a few meters away. Despite the darkness, I could just about make out her face, and I felt a rush of hope as I saw her smiling at me.

"Anna!" I gasped, struggling to my feet and brushing some mud from the front of my coat. "What are you -"

"Sshh!"

She placed a finger against her lips, to silence me.

"What are you doing here?" I whispered anyway, stumbling toward her. "Have you been here for eleven whole years, just waiting?"

"Not exactly," she replied, lowering her finger and then holding a hand up, gesturing for me to stop before I got too close. "So he really went ahead with it, did he? He really sent another lamb out here, hoping that he could buy himself eleven more years of peace and safety."

Still several meters from her, I squinted in an attempt to see her face properly.

"He looked after me," I told her cautiously. "What's wrong with your voice?"

"He fattened you up, you mean. His little sacrificial lamb."

"He changed his mind at the end. He wanted me to stay."

"He only *said* that so he could tell himself he *tried* to do the right thing," she replied. "He said the same thing to me, right at the end, and I took him up on it. Then he changed his mind again and pushed me forward, and sent me out here into the dark forest. If I'd protested again, he'd have found crueler, more unusual ways to make me keep walking. I thought the whole thing was a bluff, that the only danger out here would be wolves, so I walked anyway and I supposed I could just keep going until I reached another village. Then I thought I could go back to the house and rescue you. You were just a baby then, just a few weeks old, but I thought I'd make it back and save you." She paused for a moment. "I was wrong, Oline." The voice was getting louder all the time. "And eventually it..."

She hesitated, and now I could hear a faint gasp coming from her throat.

"You hear it, don't you?" she asked. "You hear the voice."

"So what happens to me now?" I asked, swallowing hard.

"What do you think happens?"

I opened my mouth to tell her that I had no idea, but at that moment something about her face caught my attention. I'd been too young when Anna left, so I didn't remember her at all, but I'd seen a few photos. Still, as I took a half-step forward and tilted my head again, squinting once more to get a better look, I noticed that her flesh seemed to be sagging a great deal, and that her eyes were merely dark holes in her face. A moment later, I realized I could see thick stitches running through her flesh, almost as if her face was simply a mask that had been attached to someone else.

And then I spotted a human skeleton nearby; its skin seemingly long since removed.

I turned to the figure in front of me. "You're not really Anna, are you?"

"No, little lamb," she replied."I'm not really Anna, though I wear her flesh for warmth."

"But I thought…"

I paused for a moment, as a cold shiver passed through my chest.

"I thought the devil couldn't take the form of a lamb?" I asked finally, even though I was scared I already knew the answer.

"Whoever told you that?" she replied, tilting her head slightly and smiling again, this time revealing the sharpest teeth I'd ever seen in my whole life. "You people really do believe the silliest things, sometimes.

To be perfectly honest, the lamb is my favorite form of all. So believe me, this is one sacrifice I intend to enjoy a great deal."

***

"Happy Easter!" Ronald called out, his voice sounding so loud even before I got too close to the house. "Can we eat now? I'm starving!"

"Help set the table first," Mother replied. "I've got to go and feed the new one."

As if on cue, a baby let out a brief gurgle. I stepped closer to the house, finally stopping to marvel at the beautiful, newly-painted, bright red front door. Evidently I had been away for a few days by this point, although I remembered very little of my time in the forest.

Reaching out, I found that the morning air had just about dried the door, although I felt a hint of stickiness against my fingertips. Pulling my hand back, I was surprised to see that I'd left five little bumps in the red, and I remembered at that moment that Ronald had once told me that similar bumps had been noticed eleven years ago, as if there was once another hand, long before mine. Perhaps Anna had once come back, just like me.

I could hear everyone celebrating inside.

The clink of plates.

Cutlery.

Glasses.

And I can smell all the wonderful food.

Reaching down, I turned the handle and gently pushed the door open. As it creaked, I slipped inside, just as Mother came over and slammed it shut again.

"I don't know when your father's going to fix this thing," she muttered, turning away from me and heading over to the table where Ronald and Oliver were getting things ready for the big Easter feast. "No matter how carefully I shut it, sometimes it just comes open like that."

"I'll take a look at it," Ronald said, clearly relishing the thought that he could start doing jobs around the house. "And don't worry, unlike Father, I actually *will* do what I say."

"How about starting with the table?" she asked, handing him a pile of plates. "You said you'd do *that* ten minutes ago."

"I meant jobs for men!" he protested, even as he started putting the plates on the table. "Not housework!"

I moved past him, then past Oliver too, and on over to the door at the far end of the dining room. All the clatter sounded so loud and frenetic, yet at the same time also distant. The house was beautifully decorated, with candles and candy, and everything a family could want for a proper Easter celebration. Over the hearth, a wooden sign had been hung proclaiming the family's thanks to God, and noting that they were grateful not only for their health and company, but for protection from evil.

And not one of them mentioned me.

Already, my chair had been pushed into the corner and used to store a pile of grain trays. There seemed to be no mourning period, no reflection. I had done my job, the family lamb had been sent off to be slaughtered, and now eleven years of peace and safety had been guaranteed.

And I had carried their sins with me as I walked to my death.

Stepping through to the corridor that ran the length of the house, I followed the sound of the crying baby, and finally I stopped in the farthest doorway. I immediately saw a baby wriggling in a nest of sheets, but to my surprise, I also saw that those sheets were being held by a young girl who looked no older than me. She was smiling at the child, but after a moment she turned to me and I realized immediately that this was Anna. The real Anna. My sister.

"You met her in the forest too, did you?" she asked, her voice soft and velvety.

I paused, before nodding.

"And did she..."

Her voice trailed off and paused for a moment.

"Does she wear your flesh now, the way she wore mine?"

Now it was my turn to pause, although eventually I nodded again. I still remembered then, as I still remember now, the sensation of my flesh being torn away in great bloody sheets.

And yes, I screamed.

How I screamed.

"She'll do the same to this little one in eleven years," she continued. "Unless we find a way to save her, that is. I tried to save *you*, but I couldn't come up with anything. Maybe with two of us, we'll have a better chance." She looked down at the girl. At our sister. "If we don't manage something, she'll end up the same way. She'll be sacrificed to protect the family, and that can't be allowed to happen. We have to think of something."

Sitting next to her, I peer over at the baby, who still has her eyes shut. A moment later I flinch as I feel something touch my shoulder, but then I realize that it's just Anna putting an arm around me.

"You're cold," she says calmly.

"So are you."

"We're dead," she points out. "This little one isn't. Not yet. Eleven years ago I swore to protect you, Oline, and I failed. Now we have to swear to protect little Emily. Together."

"We will," I reply, reaching over and brushing a hand against the child's face. She doesn't respond. Perhaps she doesn't even know that I'm here. "She won't end up as an Easter sacrifice. I swear."

"Do all families do this?" I asked. "Sacrifice a daughter, I mean."

"I don't know. I think a lot do, these days at least. They didn't before the war, but now people are getting very superstitious again. The old religions are being dredged up, and in some cases merged. Easter in the year 2025 is very different to Easter back in 2015 or the late 1990s. People take it more seriously now. Or a version of it, at least." She paused, looking down at the crying baby in her arms, and then she set her down in her crib. "I don't know what that thing is. The thing in the forest, I mean. Not really. But the sacrifice seems to work. What's that old saying? Even a stopped clock is right twice a -"

Suddenly she fell silent as Mother came into the room. Ignoring us, Mother went straight to the crib and picked up little Emily, and then she began speaking to her in a silly voice as she carried her back out of the dark bedroom and toward the light of the hall.

Anna and I sat in silence, each of us trying to think of some way that we might save that little girl in eleven years' time. And now, with those eleven years having passed, another baby is cradled in Anna's arms, and another little girl is standing in the doorway, staring at us after her encounter with the creature in the forest.

It's Easter again.

The End

SONNES HILL
Lex H. Jones

Brendan watched the steam rising from the kettle, as the orange power light switched itself off. In his mind, he could hear it whistling, just like it had in his grandma's old tin kettle when he was a child. The memory made him smile, taking him away for a moment, but the glint of the knife in his hand brought him immediately back to the present.

"No sugar in mine, please, Bren," Milo called from the living room. His voice sounded the same as it always had, which made Bren's skin crawl.

"All right," Brendan called back, gripping the knife tightly and glancing towards the door that would take him into the room the voice had come from. Milo always used to take sugar. One more thing that had changed. One more way in which Brendan didn't really understand who he was married to anymore.

"You're missing the film. Should I go back a scene?" Milo's voice came again.

"No, I'm coming in now," Brendan replied. He looked at the knife in his hand and closed his eyes for a moment.

Three Months Ago

The cottage that greeted the two men, as they walked up the stone path, was not at all what they'd been expecting. The advertisement had said it needed work, which was to be expected for a property as old as this, but on the outside, at least, it looked perfect. No collapsed windows, no loose roof tiles, no visible rot or decay on the brickwork. The garden was a little overgrown, and weeds had started sneaking their way through the gaps in the stones beneath their feet, but these things were easily tended. Cosmetic fixes, nothing structural.

"What do you think, Bren?" Milo asked, as they looked up at the cottage.

"It's nice. Beautiful, even," Brendan replied.

"I sense a 'but'…"

"I'm just holding off my excitement until we see the inside. There might be a gaping hole where the floor's meant to be."

"Always Mr.Cynical, aren't you?"

"Mr. Realistic. Remember that last place? Seemed perfect, until we turned the taps on, and that lovely brown juice dribbled out."

"You're right, that was a lesson learned, but we have to have sensible expectations. If we're wanting an old property with some history and character to it, as we discussed, then we need to have sensible expectations. Of course, that will also mean there will be faults—little ones, or even big ones—that a new build just wouldn't suffer from.'

"Like a big gaping hole in the floor?" Brendan suggested, earning him a playful elbow jab to the ribs.

"Sorry about that gentlemen, just another client," the accompanying estate agent explained as he walked over, placing his phone in his back pocket.

"Are you fake-phone-calling us?" Brendan laughed.

"I'm sorry?" said the agent, looking genuinely perplexed.

"Pretending to get a call from someone else interested in the property to make us just a bit more eager?"

"Erm...no, that genuinely was a client, but not about this property."

"Ignore him," Milo insisted. "He's a bit jaded; we've been screwed over a lot on this little journey to becoming home owners."

"Understandable," the agent smiled. "There are some snakes out there, and it makes my job that much harder. But no, I assure you my firm doesn't play any games like that. There's a degree of integrity that we like to maintain, but besides that, the regulatory bodies are on us like sharks since the 2008 Crash. We put a foot wrong, and we can get both fined and sued, then end up paying out more in compensation than we do in shareholder dividends."

"Good to know," Brendan said with a smile, earning him another jab to the ribs.

"Shall we go inside?" suggested the agent, opening the door.

"That'll plane off easily enough," Milo commented, noticing how the door jammed a little upon opening.

"Ah yes, the previous owner put this new wooden floor in, but then, didn't adjust the doors quite enough. There's lots of little things like that here and there, which is what you get when someone tries to fix up a house to sell it. Everything's done in a rush to sell, rather than at a leisurely pace, for your own pleasure."

"Why did they sell? This place is beautiful," Brendan commented, noticing the open-plan living room with dark, wooden floors. Alongside, was a door to the kitchen and a short hallway leading to the bedrooms and bathroom.

"Old age, to be honest. A place like this, as I'm sure you can appreciate, has a lot of years in it. Things will go wrong that you wouldn't get with a new flat, or something in the cities," explained the agent, almost repeating Milo's own words. "The owner lived alone, and he just couldn't take care of the house, anymore. So, he had as much fixed up as he could, then put it up for sale. He's with relatives, but he wants the house sold, so he can move to a place of his choosing."

"It's cheaper than I'd have expected."

"That's because he wants it sold quickly. He's not greedy, and he knows selling to anyone in a property chain would take longer. So we advised to sell a little lower, and it would then appeal to first time buyers, like yourselves."

The agent led them through the house: showed them the bathroom, kitchen and the impressive, if overgrown, garden outside. The master bedroom was bigger than either of them were used to, and the guest bedroom was perfect for visitors.

"Oh, Bren, I think I'm falling in love," Milo gushed.

"I know, it's pretty perfect, isn't it?"

A knock came at the front door, followed by a cheery "hello", as an older couple let themselves in. Brendan guessed they might be in their early sixties.

"Don't mind us, we're the neighbours. I'm Jonathan, and this is Judy. We thought we'd come and say hello. I know what it's like buying a new home; who you might be living next to can be a big factor in the decision, so we thought we'd come and show you we weren't monsters or anything."

Brendan smiled. "That's nice of you, thank you. I'm Bren, and this is Milo, my husband."

"Pleasure to meet you both," Jonathan shook both their hands firmly. "If you decide to settle in Sonnes Hill, Judy here will, no doubt, make you her famous chocolate cake as a welcome present. Not that I'm trying to persuade you, or anything."

"That sounds great. Neither of us can bake at all, to be honest," Milo beamed.

"It's a dying art, but that TV show just might get people baking again," said Judy.

"I've got to say, you guys aren't quite, erm...that is, we were worried that..." Bren fumbled over his words.

"Oh, I get it," said Jonathan, with a wry smile, turning to look at his wife, then giving her a playful wink. "You thought that, in a little old country village like this, we'd all be a bunch of old-fashioned types, who hate anyone who wasn't a straight, white, church-going couple?"

"Well, 'hate' is a strong word, but basically, yes," Bren replied, his cheeks flushing.

"Ha! Well, relax, you're fine. We're not that type of village. In point of fact, those villages die out. People stop going to visit, stop moving there, and they dry up and decay. We're all about change and renewal, and frankly you won't find anyone here who cares about race, or sexuality, or anything like that."

"That's mighty refreshing. Mixed-race, gay couple welcomed into little English village. It should be a news article," Milo commented, then turned to Bren. "So, are we going to put an offer in, or what?"

Two Months Ago

"I just don't think a modern couch, like that, would suit a home like this," Brendan protested, as Milo held up his phone to display the furniture in question.

"Why not? The colour is neutral, it doesn't clash with anything."

"It's not the colour, it's the style - far too modern."

"Just because this is an old cottage, doesn't mean everything in it has to have a look of 'grandma's house' about it," Milo sighed, then winced and rubbed the left side of his head.

"Another headache?"

"They keep coming and going. I think I must be coming down with something."

"Go and have a lie down. I'll bring you some tea and tablets."

Brendan entered the kitchen and flicked the kettle on, rolling his eyes slightly at the garish, red and black design that would look more at home in a high-end, London hotel suite than it did a rural, olde-English cottage. Milo had picked it, and Bren had decided against starting an argument over something as simple as a kettle. Living room furniture, now that was different. That might well be an argument on the horizon, if Milo didn't see sense.

"Only us!" Judy called, as she and Jonathan knocked, then opened the front door. Bren wasn't quite used to people just coming in this way, and wasn't entirely sure he liked it. However, these were nice people, and their neighbours, and he didn't want to cause upset by trying to change what was, no doubt, the local custom.

"Hi, you two," Brendan replied, walking back into the living room to greet the guests.

"Hope we're not intruding. We just brought you that cake we promised," said Judy, placing a large cake tin on the coffee table.

"Oh! That's fantastic, thanks so much."

"Where's your husband? Is he in?"

"He's just gone to bed for a while; he's been a bit under the weather lately."

"Oh, dear. Well do save him some cake, won't you?" asked Jonathan.

"I can't promise anything," Brendan responded playfully.

"We wanted to invite you both to dinner tonight, if you're interested. I know you're probably not unpacked yet, and probably getting sick of takeaways, so thought a nice, home-cooked meal would be a bit of a treat," Judy suggested.

"You're an angel; that would be amazing."

"Wonderful! Well, just come over about 6ish, and we look forward to having you over."

***

"I'm taking him to the doctor's tomorrow," Bren explained, as he enjoyed the perfectly cooked roast beef Judy had prepared. "He won't like it. He'll say I'm fussing, but he'll just have to live with it."

"You're right. It's better than worrying, isn't it?" agreed Jonathan, sitting across from Bren at the round, dark oak table.

"Jonathan is terrible about going to the doctor's. He could have nearly lost a limb, and he wouldn't go."

"It's a male pride thing," Bren shrugged. "But, pride or not, Milo's going to that clinic tomorrow, if I have to drag him there."

"Does he usually suffer from headaches?" asked Judy.

"He has for as long as I've known him. Migraines, too, sometimes. But, lately, they've been getting more frequent. And this one today; he's so out of it….I've never seen him that bad."

"Hopefully, they can get to the bottom of it. He's probably come down with something nasty. It sometimes happens when people first move house, doesn't it?" Judy suggested.

"True, the whole thing can be quite stressful, I suppose. I think the decorating will be the most stressful of all. We can't seem to agree on much."

"Well, in my experience, the best way to resolve those arguments is, to nod politely, and let the woman have her way," Jonathan teased. "I don't really know how that works with a gay couple."

"I'm sure Milo would love me to adopt that approach with him," Bren laughed. "But he's not having it all his way. I have to say, I like the carvings in the wood around your home." As he spoke, Bren glanced at the dark oak beams on the ceiling and walls, noting the carved pictures and patterns. "Did you have those done?"

"Actually, they were here when we moved in. They tell a story, apparently. Local myths and legends, that kind of thing," explained Judy.

"Or history, depending who you ask," noted Johnathan.

"You see that one there?" asked Judy, pointing at a carving on the beam just above their heads, her tone slightly exasperated as if she'd been forced to point this out repeatedly in times past.

"It looks like…I don't even know what that is. Some sort of dinosaur, or something, standing next to a man?" Bren suggested.

"Exactly. Local history, Johnathan calls it, where we have pictures of unknown beasts talking to people."

"This is why she won't let me answer phone-in quizzes on the radio," Jonathan winked at Bren, his voice a pretend whisper that was more than loud enough for his wife to hear.

"There'll be similar carvings in your house, I suspect, but they might be painted over," said Judy.

"I'll have to take a proper look in the daylight. I love things like that. It'll be something to look forward to, once I get Milo back from the doctor's."

"Do you need us to drive you there? The roads can get quite muddy, with all the rain we've had lately, and we've got the stupid off-road thing Jonathan insisted on buying," Judy suggested, with a slight frown in her husband's direction.

"I think we'll be alright, but that's very kind of you to offer," smiled Bren.

"Just let us know if you need anything, anything at all," replied Judy.

One Month Ago

"I don't understand," said Bren, his voice scarcely loud enough to be audible. "How can it be this bad?"

"We were late catching it. The location of the tumour meant that, for the first months of its growth, there were no symptoms. When they finally started to manifest, they didn't appear any worse than a usual migraine, or severe headache, yet all the while, it was growing and spreading," explained the doctor.

"You said it was inoperable?"

"Yes, I'm afraid so. The location of it, the way it's attached itself, makes surgery impossible. He wouldn't survive it."

"And you can't shrink it with radiotherapy, or chemo?" asked Bren, his voice breaking.

"Again, the location, the spread...you'd be causing such severe damage, so quickly, that the fact is, it would kill him more quickly than the cancer would," replied the doctor, sombrely.

"Jesus fucking Christ." Bren hung his head in his hands.

"We've already spoken to Milo, of course, but he asked that we explain it to you, rather than him."

"How...." Bren's voice caught in his throat, and he took a deep breath. "How long?"

"That can vary on so many things, but I think half a year might be realistic."

"What?? Six months??" Bren cried, incredulously.

"It's not finished growing. He's going to get worse, his health will start to decline, rapidly now that the symptoms have begun."

"I need to take him home," Bren told the doctor, tears in his voice.

"I'd advise against that; with how ill he's going to become, his best place..."

"His best place is at home, doctor. If you're telling me he's going to die, anyway," answered Bren, his voice laced with anger.

"That's his choice, and yours. If that's what you decide, then we'll get him discharged with whatever he needs to make him comfortable."

***

Bren sat watching Milo sleep, not really able to rest, himself. These past few nights since leaving the hospital, he'd been afraid to fall asleep for more than a few hours. He was afraid that he might wake up, to find that Milo never would. Milo, himself, was trying to keep his spirits as jovial as usual—for Bren's benefit, more than his own—but, he was clearly exhausted. Bren could see it in his eyes. Even the effort of getting out of bed, and walking around the house, was difficult for him. He seemed to have gotten rapidly worse since getting the news, and Bren wondered how much of that was psychological. Not that he judged this negatively; how could anyone not feel crushed, under the weight of such news?

Leaving Milo to sleep, Bren quietly made his way to the living room, and sat on the armchair. The room was open, and still largely empty; the two of them never having gotten around to agreeing on a couch to order. The armchair had been a recent purchase, before Milo had moved out of his flat, so it had been brought with them, and given a place in the new living room. Though it was comfortable—and Bren liked the design—as he sat stroking the fabric, he already doubted that he'd be able to keep it. Would he even stay in this house? He honestly didn't know; he couldn't even properly think that far ahead.

There was a gentle, quiet knock at the door. It opened very slowly, followed by Jonathan leaning his head round.

"Hello, Bren," he whispered. "I saw the lamp on, I thought you were probably up."

"Can't really sleep lately," replied Bren, despondently.

"Of course you can't, son," replied Jonathan, stepping closer and putting a comforting hand on Bren's shoulder. "I'm just going to take the dog out; she's been a bit restless. Would you like to come for some fresh air?"

"I don't know, I don't want to leave him," answered Bren, glancing back down the hallway, in the direction of the bedroom.

"He won't know you're gone, and we won't be long. I have something to show you," said Jonathan quietly, inclining his head towards the door.

Bren wanted any excuse to get out of the house, and enjoy the outdoors air, even for just a half hour. It would do him good, to see something beyond the walls of the house, and try to think of something else, for just a little while. Even for half an hour. That was why he agreed, more than any kind of curiosity about what Jonathan wanted to show him. He put on his jacket and boots, followed Jonathan outside, and quietly locked the door behind him. Jonathan's dog, a spry-looking sheepdog, waited obediently outside on the path, wagging its tail fervently at its master's return.

"I don't remember seeing the dog before," Bren remarked.

"Only got her this week; her name's Bess. The wife wanted a new one, but I said we were too old to be messing around with training a puppy, so we got her instead."

"That's nice. It's always harder to find homes for grown dogs."

"I'm just going to walk her up by the old marshes; I know a safe path. What I want to show you is up there, too."

"All right," responded Bren, agreeably.

The night was dark and still, and the cloudless sky meant that much of the ground was lit by moonlight. The torches Jonathan had brought for them both, were strong enough to help clearly light the path. Jonathan kept Bess on her leash, until they were away from the village. Once they reached the open fields, he let her run free. Bren watched the dog at play and smiled softly to himself. He and Milo had spoken about getting a dog themselves, but they wanted to finish decorating the house first. Bren wondered if everything he saw might make him feel like this now: a memory they'd never get to make

The area ahead was darker, where the ground was now swampy and growing muddier, with a few barren and twisted trees that pushed up from the ground. Bren almost lost his footing, until Jonathan grabbed his arm, pulling him back towards firm ground.

"It's basically a bog round here; just follow me because I know the path."

"Is Bess safe here?"

"She's not as stupid as we are," Jonathan pointed at the dog, who was happily, and confidently, traversing the path ahead.

"Seems an odd walking route," observed Bren.

"You only come here with purpose, son."

The two men walked on, now approaching something greyish-white that protruded from the marsh. At first, Bren thought they were trees, but the shape was all wrong. They looked more like bones; like the broken ribcage of something massive that had laid in the marsh, and never climbed back out.

"Is that....are they from a whale??" Bren asked, as they walked beneath one of the bizarre arches that rose above the path.

"Not exactly." Jonathan paused for a second, and turned to Bren. "Can I ask you a personal question?"

"Um, sure. I guess," responded Bren, hesitantly.

"Do you believe in God?"

"No, not at all," frowned Bren.

"I should have anticipated that. You assumed I meant the Christian God, right? Or, the Jewish one, or whatever denomination you want to give it. Whatever colour or creed you put on it, the fact is, that people generally have a similar sort of being in mind when they say God, don't they?" Jonathan explained. "And given your sexuality, I can see why you'd have no faith in such a being. How could you possibly find time, or love, for something that is supposedly responsible for everything in the world, and yet purportedly hates you for something you can't change?"

"That's about the size of it," said Bren. "Why do you ask?"

"Well, there are other gods, you know. Older ones. And they don't claim to be responsible for every little thing, either. That kind of belief came much later, with the Middle Eastern God. Prior to that, each god had their own little patch of land, so to speak. Maybe they'd bring rain, or wealth, or healing."

That last word caught Bren's ear, as he suspected it was meant to.

"Oh...ok." He sighed, stifling a laugh. "This is the bit where you try to convert me to some religion or other, isn't it? I mean it's a bold pitch, bringing me out here like this, to avoid doing it in my own home, where I can just shut the door in your face. And I appreciate that you probably think you're genuinely helping, but..."

"Brendan, it's all right," Jonathan laughed. "I don't believe in all that spiritual nonsense, either. I believe in what we can see, what we can feel. I'm just saying that there was a time, when the gods people worshipped, were just that."

"And that's what you believe in? Something you've actually seen?" asked Bren, doubtfully.

"Well, I've seen results, put it that way. Many around here have. We don't usually show people as new to the village as you, but with Milo's situation being so desperate, I couldn't not try and help."

"I'll be honest with you, whatever it is you're wanting to show me...herbs, or spring water you think is magic, or something...I'm willing to give it a go. Usually, I would just laugh in your face at something like that, but there's quite literally, nothing medical science can do for him, so I guess that forces me to be more open. Nothing to lose, I guess," muttered Bren, scuffing at the ground with his boot.

"No, there really isn't, unfortunately. And, like I said, I'm not trying to convert you to anything. I just want to help."

"I believe you, so lead on," Bren said, as he gestured ahead with his arm.

The path through the marsh grew more narrow, the air was getting thicker, with a hazy, greenish mist hovering in it. The water seemed to have a sort of current to it now, Bren noticed. It wasn't a current quite like any he'd observed in still bodies of water. It was rising slightly and then falling, almost like the earth below was breathing.

"Jonathan, this place is creeping me out a little," Bren admitted nervously.

"It did me, as well, when my father first brought me here. It's just old, Bren. Older than anything most of us will see in our life," stated Johnathan.

"You're not taking me to see some giant wicker statue are you?" Bren asked suddenly, trying to use a little humor to cover his nervousness.

"Ha, no. We save that for tourists; you actually live here," Jonathan replied, with a wink and a smile. "Although, if we're referencing films and such, I suppose what I'm showing you is more 'Pet Cemetery', than it is 'Wicker Man'."

"You have an Indian burial ground that raises the dead?" asked Bren, incredulously.

"No, but we have a cave that heals," said Jonathan, putting the leash back on Bess, and pointing the light from his torch at something up ahead. The beam hit a sunken stone structure with a low opening at the front. The darkness inside seemed impenetrable by their torch light.

"Erm…ok?" Bren scratched his head nervously.

"Not really clear what to say, is it? I understand. I was the same. I'd broken my arm playing on a rope swing, and my dad brought me here. I went in that cave, sat for an hour or so, fell asleep, and when I woke up my arm was fine. No pain, nothing."

"Seriously?" Bren's eyebrows shot up.

"Your husband is on his death bed, son. I wouldn't lie to you about something like this," Jonathan replied, the look in his eyes every bit as sincere as the tone of his voice.

"And how do you explain it? Some sort of gases in that cave, or…" Bren's voice trailed off in wonder.

"My father told me that there are places in this world, where the earth is older than in other places… and, in those places, we can be touched by the things that are a part of the old way. I don't really know too much about that part; I'm a cynic like you. But real is real, and I know for sure, that I went in there with a broken arm, and came out healed," Jonathan stated emphatically.

"And have other villagers been healed too?" asked Bren.

"It's used sparingly. It's not even spoken of, except by a very few," Jonathan replied, stroking Bess, who had fixed her eyes on the cave, and started to shiver. He went on: "None of us fully understand it, and you don't want to be abusing something like that. Enough people know about it to keep it fed with our belief, but we don't want people coming up here each time they graze a knee or get a sniffle, " Jonathan said, looking Bren in the eyes sternly.

"And you think, if I take Milo there...?" Bren's eyes had a hopeful, watery look to them.

"I don't know for sure. You can't, with things like this. But, is it worth not even trying?"

"I know exactly what he'll say when I suggest it," said Bren, mournfully.

"You don't." Jonathan shook his head. "People find faith in desperate times. Usually they put their faith in the wrong things, but they still find the need to put it somewhere."

"What's the process? Do I just go in there with him and..." Bren began.

"He has to go in alone, and he has to sleep. You have to wait for him to come out. That's about it."

"Why does he need to sleep?"

"Your mind goes elsewhere when you sleep, maybe that makes it easier to make the connection to whatever does the healing," Jonathan suggested. "I'm not a theologian, Bren. Not an occultist or whoever else might know more about this. I was a PE teacher for years, then retired when my back couldn't quite take it anymore. And, no, I didn't go to the cave to fix that, before you ask. Old age isn't a thing to cure, it just happens. But a young man dying, not long after getting his first home with his new husband...I can't stand by and not try to prevent that," said Jonathan, shaking his head.

"Thank you. I'll bring him. We have to try," Bren said firmly.

***

"I still can't quite believe that you agreed to this," said Bren, his arm wrapped tightly around Milo's shoulders, to steady him as he walked.

"Doesn't hurt to try, I suppose. And when it doesn't work, I can mock you for convincing me to sleep in a cave," Milo replied, shivering beneath the blanket that covered his head and shoulders.

"Deal," Bren said with a smile.

Bren looked ahead, and saw Jonathan had stopped, and was waiting for them to catch up. Milo could only manage a slow pace, but, still, he kept moving. The mid-afternoon sun made it much easier to see the safe path through the marsh, but Jonathan had still insisted on coming. That fact had actually been instrumental in getting Milo to take this even halfway seriously, as the presence of someone besides Bren, had made this seem less likely a ridiculous joke.

"I'm going to be right outside, and when you come back out I'll be there," Bren assured him as they approached the cave.

"What are you going to do? There's no signal out here for your iPad," Milo joked.

"I'm sure I'll survive," replied Bren, giving Milo a gentle squeeze.

The two men joined Jonathan at the mouth of the cave, the inside of which could be seen to slope gently downwards into a much wider interior.

"So I just go down there, find somewhere to sleep for a bit, and then come back out?"

"I know how it sounds," Jonathan noted. "But we have to try."

"Well, I've come this far," Milo agreed, glancing at the cave. "Big, scary opening with a cold wind blowing from it….this must be what it's like sleeping with Madonna."

"You know a gay man dies every time you mock Madonna," Bren reminded him.

"Not a fan?" Jonathan asked, smiling.

"Overrated. I much prefer GaGa." Milo responded.

"We're not starting this now. Get in the damn cave," said Bren, then pulled Milo into a warm embrace and kissed him, softly. "I'll be here when you wake up."

Bren and Jonathan watched Milo descend into the cave, wrapped snugly in his blanket, and taking a wrapped duvet and pillow with him. Bren clenched his fists tightly at the sight of his husband disappearing into the darkness, fighting the urge to join him.

"This can work, stranger things have happened, this can work," he chanted under his breath.

"I'll wait with you, if you want," offered Jonathan.

"Thank you, that'd be nice. If I stay alone, I'll probably lose my willpower, and run to join him in there. I don't want to do anything that might mess up…whatever this is," Bren declared.

"I'll stay as long as you need me, son, it's fine," said Jonathan, unfolding the two collapsible chairs he'd brought.

The two men sat down, and Jonathan handed Bren a can of beer. It wasn't his usual brand, but he wasn't feeling particularly fussy, and was frankly glad for anything that might calm his nerves.

"You know what's funny, is that whilst we're here, this whole thing seems a little less mad," admitted Bren.

"I know what you mean. If someone tells you something like this, whilst you're standing in the middle of a city, with all the trappings of the modern world around you, it couldn't seem more ludicrous. But here, now, it seems that little bit more possible, with the old world surrounding us out here."

"I'm willing to accept anything that might make him well," said Bren in all seriousness.

"Good. Then, once he's home safe, you can help me build that Wicker Man," remarked Johnathan.

"As long as you don't mind my shoddy craftsman skills," chuckled Bren.

***

"Bren? Bren, wake up." Jonathan was shaking him by the shoulder.

"Hmm?" murmured Bren, groggily.

"We fell asleep, it's morning. The sun's just come up."

"What? But that's impossible! How could we..." Bren cut his sentence short when he saw the slowly rising sun over the distant hills.

"Something's happened."

"Where's Milo? Has he come out? He can't have stayed there all night, he'd have frozen!" Bren jumped out of his chair, and turned to face the cave. Except there wasn't a cave. Where the mouth had been, was now a wall of ancient stones. Not stones that could have been moved, but high and moss-covered, as though they'd been there forever.

"We haven't moved. I checked, in case we sleepwalked, or something. But we haven't moved an inch," said Jonathan, running his hands through his thin, grey hair, and pacing back and forth.

"Has the cave sunk? The entrance could have...." began Bren.

"I thought that too, but surely we'd have heard it? Unless the gases from the marsh really put us under deep."

"Milo!" Bren yelled, slapping his hand against the rock, where the cave entrance had been. "Milo!"

"I'm going to go and get some pickaxes, shovels; whatever I have. And I'll bring the dog; she might be able to find a scent, or something, that could help," Jonathan announced with a snap of his fingers.

"Good, great. Check our house, in case he went back before....before whatever this is, happened," suggested Bren

"Of course. I'll be back as soon as I can." With that, Jonathan ran quickly down the safe path through the marsh, leaving Bren anxiously shouting his husband's name, and clawing at the stone with his hands.

***

"Fucking dammit!" Bren roared, tossing the pickaxe to one side. There were scratches and minor indents all over the surface of the rock before him, but no real damage had been done. He turned to his left to see Jonathan had dug a hole that was now nearly three feet deep, but facing him was still the sheer wall of rock. It just went down, however deep he went.

"It can't have sunk this much in one night, it just can't," said an exasperated Jonathan.

"I'm going to try the sledgehammer again," said Bren, wiping dirt and sweat from his brow. "Where's the emergency services??" he asked Johnathan, irritably.

"Probably trying to scare up a helicopter. They're not getting a vehicle through this marsh." Jonathan took out his phone. "I don't even have a single bar. I can go home and call them again if you like."

"I don't know, I don't know what's best." Bren sighed heavily, then frowned slightly, looking just over Jonathan's shoulder. "What's wrong with Bess?"

"She won't come any closer. I don't know why, but I've never tried to bring her this close to the cave before."

"You think she can sense whatever the fuck is wrong with this place?" asked Bren, as he watched the dog.

"I was thinking the same," said Jonathan.

"Maybe she's the smart one."

***

Bren awoke on the couch, for the second morning in a row. The first night, he'd spent outside the cave again, but, at Jonathan's insistence, he'd eventually gone home. The emergency services had arrived, surveyed the situation, and had rather quickly decided against the use of any explosives for fear it might make the suspected 'landslide' even worse. Jonathan had pointed out that a landslide wouldn't have had such a localised effect, but they had refused to budge on the matter. Instead, they'd insisted they needed to bring in some specialised drilling equipment, and would return as soon as it arrived.

Three days. It had now been three days since Milo had entered that cave. In the meantime, Bren hadn't eaten properly, or slept anywhere near enough. His mind constantly veered back and forth between anxiety, blind panic, and then, utter disbelief at the situation. Sometimes, he almost felt as though he wanted to laugh at the ridiculousness of it. He needed some air, he decided, knowing he might well end up going back to the cave, but not seeing any need to fight the urge. Throwing on his shoes and coat, he left the house and walked briskly down the garden path.

"What the hell?" cursed Bren, as his foot caught on something. Looking down, he saw a thick green vine had grown across the pathway, and started spreading up the old stone wall that ran parallel to the garden. There were tiny flowers on the vine, unlike anything he'd ever seen. Weeding was the last thing on his mind, so on he went.

Bren's walking route took him alongside several other cottages, and as he walked by the final garden, before he reached the clearing, he noticed a woman carefully pruning some unusual flowers with a pair of shears. This only caught his eye, because he recognised the flowers, and the vine they were growing from, as the same type he'd noticed on his own path.

"Unusual looking thing, isn't it?" the woman remarked, noticing Bren studying her work.

"Yeah, there's one in my garden. Never seen anything like it," responded Bren.

"You wouldn't have. They're extinct," the woman smiled.

"What?" exclaimed Bren.

"These plants, dear. They're prehistoric. Simply put, they don't exist anymore. Or shouldn't, at least," she replied, gazing at the flowers that shouldn't be.

"How do you know that?" Bren challenged, as politely as he could.

"Botany is something of a passion of mine. I used to teach plant biology at the school. The same one your neighbour, Jonathan, taught at, actually," she answered, bringing her gaze back to bear on him.

"Right. So, do you know why we might be seeing these plants all of a sudden?" Bren asked.

"Not a clue, but these vines aren't the only ones. Since last night, I've also found extinct species of Cycad, Davallia Solida, and Protea in my garden alone. Lord only knows what other people might find in theirs," she said with a little amusement.

"I don't know what any of those are, so I'll take your word for it," Bren smiled, then thought for a moment, and said, "Hang on, since last night? They've all grown since then?"

"That's right. Bizarre, isn't it?"

"Yeah. Yeah, it is." Bren felt queasy, a chill filling his bones, and making him sweat and ache at the same time. There was a compulsion to run, to immediately get back home. It wasn't logical; wasn't a feeling that came from anything resembling rational thought. Rather it was like a tug on his gut; like a rope around his innards had been pulled. "I, um, I have to go," he muttered awkwardly.

Bren turned and ran, back past the neighbouring cottages, and up the slight hill that led to his own place. He hadn't run that far—or that fast—in years, yet he managed to find the energy to not stop once. The door to his home was wide open, as he had a feeling it would be. He steeled himself, and entered, then came close to fainting when he saw who was waiting for him.

"Well, you took your time. Here I was expecting a big, grand welcome party, and there's not even a banner!" said Milo, standing stark naked in the middle of the living room. His skin looked healthy and bronzed, his physique was its old gym-honed self, his hair thick, and his eyes were sparkling. He looked better than Bren ever remembered him looking.

"Milo?" was all Bren could get out.

"That's what my underwear says. Or, it would, if I was wearing any."

"I don't understand," Bren stood there with a dumbfounded look on his face. It almost made Milo want to laugh.

"Neither do I. My clothes were all gone when I woke up. Weird isn't it?"

"That's not what..." Bren's hand came up to his face, covering his mouth.

"I know. And, I don't even know if *I* can answer your questions. I have as many myself as you do. But hey, I'm here, I feel great; what's to worry about? Things don't have to make sense, right? I mean, none of this did," Milo flung his hand out dismissively.

"No, I suppose not."

"And, I'm hardly the first person to wake up healthy, after three days in a cave," Milo joked. "Although, I think He at least got to keep his clothes. Seriously, what is this about, with the nudeness?"

"I can't believe you're here," said Bren, steadying himself against the armchair, for fear he might still faint. "Is this real? Am I dreaming this?" he wondered aloud.

"I hope not. Do you usually dream about me, nude?" Milo teased.

"Not just standing there, no," smiled Bren.

The two men embraced, and Bren burst into tears. Milo cried, too, his tears running onto Bren's shoulder. He could feel the warmth from his husband's body, as he held him close, so glad to have him near this way. But, deep in Bren's mind, something was screaming. Some long-forgotten instinct that warned of things the logical mind couldn't explain. He ignored it, and kissed his husband once more.

***

Bren sipped his coffee, and looked out the French doors, onto the rear garden. It had been tidy when he and Milo had first moved in, which was something of a blessing as grounds-keeping was hardly a task that either of them relished. Now, however, it was thick and overgrown. Those same vines Bren had noticed in the village, grew everywhere, as well as various other colourful flowers, the likes of which he hadn't seen before. He didn't fancy himself any kind of expert, but the flowers and plants filling his garden just seemed out of place. It was all too tropical, too wild.

"Going to have to buy some weed killer, or something," he commented, hearing Milo approaching him.

"Oh, I don't know, I quite like it. It's like we live in a jungle," Milo replied, sliding his arms around Bren's waist, and holding him close from behind.

"I don't even know what flowers they are. There was a lady in the village who said that she'd been seeing extinct flowers. Can you believe that? "

"Some of those in our garden, right now, are prehistoric," Milo commented, kissing the back of Bren's head, and then moving away to get his own mug of coffee.

"How do you know?" Bren asked.

"I know all sorts of things," shrugged Milo.

"OK…" Bren frowned slightly, knowing that Milo had never shown the slightest interest in horticulture.

"It's lovely out there, let's go outside," Milo beamed, opening the doors, and walking out barefoot. Bren put his slippers on, and followed him, more wary of stones and sharp thorns, or branches, than Milo now seemed to be.

Milo walked into the middle of the lawn, and took a deep breath, closing his eyes and exhaling loudly.

"Isn't it beautiful?" he exclaimed.

"Untidy, more like. There was a nice lawn here before this sudden growth," groused Bren.

"A neat, formulaic little square, with defined rows of plants around it, in their little boxes. You can't have nature that way, Bren. It needs to be free, wild. Like it used to be."

"Since when you do care about things like that?" Bren seemed perplexed

"I'm a new man," Milo shrugged.

Bren forced a smile, but couldn't stop himself from feeling edgy. He'd heard plenty of people undergoing personality transformations after a near-death experience, so perhaps that's what this was? It was certainly a possibility, but Bren felt a newfound uneasiness around Milo that had refused to disappear, once he noticed it.

"Erm...Milo?" asked Bren, his eyes widening. "Don't panic, just stay still, OK? There's a snake near your foot." Bren put his arm out, as if to shield Milo from the danger.

"Hm?" Milo looked down, and saw the brownish-green snake slithering around his foot. He smiled, and seemed to beckon it slightly with his hand, at which point the snake slithered up around his leg, over his back, and wrapped itself around his arm like a flowing scarf.

"Milo, what the fuck??" Bren shouted.

"It's alright, he's harmless," Milo replied calmly.

"You're not panicking."

"No, I suppose I'm not," said Milo, distractedly, as he gazed at his new friend.

"You're afraid of snakes, Milo. Don't you remember? We had a talk for hours about this area; you made me Google it to see how common they were because you were afraid of...well...something like this happening!" Bren finished in a rush of near-hysteria.

"I remember. I guess they just don't bother me, anymore."

"Well....great. That's good," smiled Bren, backing away as he spoke. "I'm going to get dressed."

"I'll be out here, having breakfast," Milo replied, as several other animals started to approach him. A few mice scuttled his way from the undergrowth, a bird landed on his shoulder, and worms were pushing their way up from the ground around his feet.

Bren dressed quickly, and then slipped quietly out of the house, checking once to see that Milo was still in the garden with his odd new friends. Once past the front gate, Bren's footfalls turned into a run. He had to go back there; he had to see.

***

The cave mouth was open again, as Bren had suspected it might be. He'd settled on the idea that the cave had, in some manner, swallowed Milo, and then spat him back out. Now that he was returned, the cave would appear as though nothing had ever happened. The appearance of the cave, as he stood before it, proved him right on this; but that wasn't enough. Bren stepped forward and steeled himself, clenching his fists tightly, and then ducked his head to enter the cave.

It was dark, damp, and very quiet. There was a light breeze outside, but in here it was still. Quiet and empty, but nothing else. When he'd come here before, Bren had felt a vague discomfort, even being close to the cave, but now he was standing inside it and felt nothing. He cursed himself for not bringing Bess with him, as he was fairly confident that the dog would now have walked right into the cave with no qualms. Anger grew inside him, and Bren reached down and took a sharp-edged rock from the floor, then cut his hand with it. Grimacing in pain, as he sliced it open, he held his hand up, staring at the wound in the muted light. Nothing. No change. He wasn't entirely sure how the process worked in any case, and couldn't be certain that it would have healed, anyway. But, with what he already suspected, what he increasingly felt about the cave, this only served as further proof. Whatever had been in this cave, wasn't here anymore. Which meant, of course, that it was now somewhere else.

***

"Jonathan, are you there?" Bren called, banging on the door for the third time.

"I'm here, son, hold your horses," Jonathan replied from behind the door, before opening it and asking, "What's the matter?"

"It's Milo. A couple of days ago, he came back. I would have come and told you, I should have, but…"

"Calm down Bren, it's all right. We already know," Johnathan reassured him.

"You do?" Bren's eyes widened.

"He came and saw us on his way back home. I wanted to call you, but Judy said we should let him reveal himself," said Johnathan.

"That's fine, you're not at fault. I just…has anything like this happened before? I know people have been healed in that cave, but he was gone so long. And the way it closed…" Bren trailed off.

"I was worried, too. You saw me…I was frantic. But, we don't know how that cave works, and even though it took longer this time, it still worked its wonders," he offered.

Bren smiled and nodded. A growing unease spread within him, as he looked into the smiling faces of his neighbours. His friends. They seemed themselves, nothing was overtly wrong, but something was just slightly 'off'. As though something barely noticeable, but still real, had been taken from them. Or added. The smiles were a little bit too warm, the eyes sparkled a little bit too brightly.

"We should all be happy. Milo was returned to us," said Jonathan, another overly-happy smile filling his face.

"Yeah. I guess he was," Bren reluctantly agreed.

***

"Mind your step." Bren pointed at the thick, flower-filled vines that now littered the walkway on their walking route. In fact, for the past week, the vines and other ancient flora, had seemed to grow daily. Now every wall of the village was starting to possess its own creeping sheets of ivy.

"I'm not as clumsy as you think," Milo frowned.

"You used to be," Bren said under his breath, remembering countless broken dishes and banged table edges.

"What's wrong, Mr Grumpy? You've been out of sorts all week," complained Milo.

"I just have a question to ask, I suppose," Bren responded rather reluctantly.

"Ask away," said Milo, throwing his arms up and out in a welcoming gesture.

"Who the fuck are you?" asked Bren, turning in the middle of the path and staring directly at Milo. He hadn't been going to broach this yet, but the silence of the fields around them seemed to press down on him, forcing the words outwards. He couldn't wait any longer.

"It's me, your husband," Milo answered, looking a little hurt.

"No it isn't. I don't pretend to know about this kind of thing. I didn't even think it was real, so I'm probably not making any kind of sense. But, I know the man I loved, the man I married, and you're not him. You do a damn fine impression, but I can tell the difference," Bren challenged.

"All right, Brendan," said Milo with a heavy sigh, his voice taking on a slightly different tone. Bren noticed it actually sounded as though it were an echo of itself, deeper and yet in some way calming. "You're right, I'm not Milo. It was wrong of me to deceive you, but the guilt affected my judgement," he confessed.

"Guilt about what?" demanded Bren.

"That I couldn't save him,"

"What are you saying?" asked Bren, swallowing the icy lump in his throat.

"Your husband died, Bren. I'm truly sorry."

"He's dead?" Bren yelled.

"Bren, you left a man with late stage cancer in a freezing cold cave. What did you think was going to happen?"

"You were supposed to heal him!" Bren roared.

"I was?"

"You're whatever was in that cave, aren't you?"

"That's right. And, perhaps, I'm not being fair. I did try to heal Milo, but he was too far gone. There was no way he was making it out of that cave alive."

"So he died cold and alone?" Bren's hand covered his mouth in dismay.

"No, he wasn't either of those things. I kept him comfortable, took his pain from him, and spoke to him. His final thoughts were of you."

"Then why seal him inside?"

"Because I needed him."

"For what?"

"This is a physical word, Bren. To walk here, one needs a physical form. I can fabricate them if needed, and have done so in the past, but times have changed. My previous forms would be far too large and cumbersome for the modern age," explained Milo.

Bren remembered the bizarre wood carvings in his neighbour's house, and whale bones in the marsh, and shuddered.

"This handsome man's form was left right there for me, and it was perfect. The last time I walked amongst you, people worshipped things that didn't look like them. Things they feared. But, now, they want familiarity, like that carpenter on the cross."

"Are you God? The Devil? Just what the fuck are you?" Bren demanded angrily.

"I'm neither of those. But then, what do you mean by the word 'God'? A divine being with power over everything? No, that's not me. In my time, people worshipped different gods for different things. We each had our own patch of land, so to speak."

"And what was yours? What did you do?" asked Bren angrily.

"Healing."

"You healed people?"

"Bodies, minds, the land. Whatever was wrong that needed correcting."

"When was this, what's even your name?" Bren demanded.

"When? Always, I've never stopped. I just operate on a smaller scale now because people forgot. I can't do as much when people don't believe I'm there. And as for a name, I suppose I don't know. Not in the modern English language, anyway. The last name I had was a picture, not a word."

"Are there others like you?" asked Bren.

"There were. I'm not so sure now."

"What do you look like, really?"

"My original, true form, wouldn't fit on your world. And your mind couldn't cope with seeing it."

"Fuck...Jesus fuck, am I going insane??" Bren paced back and forth, running his hands through his hair.

"Bren, I'm answering all your questions as honestly as I can. I know it's a lot of information to take in, but I wouldn't feel right lying to you. You're my husband, and also my midwife. I'm here again, because of you. And now I can resume my work," said Milo

"Work?" asked Bren, incredulously.

"Healing the world. Have you seen it out there? There's a lot to do. I've been considering a return for some time, and then Milo was brought to me, and it all fell into place. Now is the time, thanks to you," Milo smiled.

"I didn't do this for you," Bren frowned.

"You were trying to help your husband. Out of love, passion, devotion. All things I admire and cherish, Bren. I apologise, again, for my deception, but I couldn't predict how you'd react, and I didn't want to push you over the edge."

"I think I'm already there."

"But, you're not, Bren." Milo, grasped Bren by the shoulders in a firm, but not aggressive, manner. "I know you believe me; everything I just said. You know it's true, and you don't fear me. Perhaps that's because I wear his face, but I don't think it is," said Milo.

"Everything you've said made all of this make more sense, not less." said Bren, shaking his head in amazement.

"That's the power of truth, Bren. It heals. It cleanses. It rebuilds."

"The prehistoric plants are your work, I assume?" asked Bren.

"Just a bit of decorating. Making things look the way I remember," Milo shrugged. "I have a lot to do, but I need to start small.

I'm new to being back here, but the longer I stay, and the more people hear me, the stronger I'll grow. Then we can make a real difference," Milo said emphatically.

"We?" queried Bren.

"I want you at my side, Bren. I can't be your Milo, and I will never again pretend to be. But I still want to be yours, and for you to be mine,"

"You mean I get a choice?" Bren scoffed.

"It's true that the minds of men and women are…pushed…towards acceptance of me. But not yours. Your love for Milo is the reason I'm here. That makes you special," Milo smiled warmly at Bren.

"You understand I can't make a decision like that immediately?"

"Of course. I wouldn't rush you."

***

Bren stood at the back of the ancient church, the rows of pews illuminated by flickering green flames casting an eerie glow over the whole place. He wasn't sure what manner of powder had been used to create this effect, but it certainly provided an atmosphere. Milo, or the thing that wore his face, at least, stood at the front of the church, arms spread wide as he spoke. The pews were full of villagers, all smiling and grasping each other's hands in sheer joy at the words of their forgotten god.

"Go, tell more to come here. Your families, your friends. Film our sermons and put them on the internet, let everyone know the good news." Bren beamed, walking down the aisle and touching the foreheads of all he passed. "And, if any of you get sick, or you hurt yourself, come and find me. I'll be in my wonderful home with my husband."

Now

Brendan watched the steam rising from the kettle, as the orange power light switched itself off. In his mind, he could hear it whistling, just like it had in his grandma's old tin kettle, when he was a child. The memory made him smile, taking him away for a moment, but the glint of the knife in his hand, brought him immediately back to the present.

"No sugar in mine, please, Bren," Milo called from the living room. His voice sounded the same as it always had, which made Bren's skin crawl.

"All right," Brendan called back, gripping the knife tightly, and glancing towards the door that would take him into the room the voice had come from. Milo always used to take sugar. One more thing that had changed. One more way in which Brendan didn't really understand who he was married to anymore.

"You're missing the film. Should I go back a scene?" Milo's voice came again.

"No, I'm coming in now," Brendan replied. He looked at the knife in his hand, and closed his eyes for a moment. Taking a deep breath, he replaced the knife in the drawer, lifted the mugs of tea, and then re-joined his husband in the living room.

The End

EASTER EGGS

Latashia Figueroa

Sitting on the cold, hardwood floor of his bedroom, Brian could feel small specks of dirt beneath him. Ramming his already ragged toy cars into one another, he knocked the tiny wheel right off the blue and white Chevy. But this time, it was all right. His mom had noticed her son's worn matchbox cars, and promised to bring home something new that night. It was also the Friday before Easter, which meant his mother would walk in the front door with bags full of groceries.

This Easter, the plan was to visit Brian's grandmother, and a few other relatives. Grandma Margret's was the gathering place for the holidays. Brian smiled at the thought of getting that big hug from his grandma, playing with his cousins, and eating potato pie until his stomach couldn't fit anymore.

Pete never went to the holiday gatherings. And Brian liked that just fine. Because the trip to grandma's was more than a two-hour drive, he and his mom would spend the night, sleep in his mother's old room and cuddle up together. His mother would tell him about the dreams she had in her childhood room, and sometimes, Brian would catch her wiping away a tear.

He knew those dreams didn't have a man like Pete in them. Brian thought about his real dad, the little he could remember. "What was he like?" Brian often asked his mom.

She'd smile. "Kind, funny, gentle."

"Not like Pete," Brian would reply.

Angela didn't respond.

Pete just happened.

Folding his hands into the sleeves of his sweater, Brian checked the thermostat. It read sixty-nine degrees. Pete must have turned down the heat, again.

"Turn that goddamn heat down; we don't need a sky-high electric bill this month," he'd often say. Although it was April, there were still patches of snow on the ground, and the chill from the outside seemed to settle into Brian's home.

The night Pete beat Angela with a rolling pin, she ran outside crying and screaming, and old Mr. Eldridge called the police. They handcuffed him, pushed him into the backseat of the car and Pete spent a month in jail.

It was a great month. Angela allowed Brian to watch his favorite anime shows, and she watched the cooking channel. Not those reality police shows Pete liked to watch. Angela invited Mr. Eldridge over for dinner a few times; something she couldn't do when Pete was around. Laughter visited the house once again, and Brian wished it could always be that way.

When Pete got out of jail, he promised Angela he'd be better; he wouldn't drink as much, and he'd try to get a better job. "You know I don't mean the things I do, Angie," he cried, his head in Angela's lap. "I don't mean it," he kissed her hand. "I'll never touch you again, baby."

He sniffed a few times, though Brian didn't see any tears. Then Pete sat up straight and called Brian over. Brian shuffled over, hesitantly.

"You take good care your momma while I was gone?" Pete asked him. Brian nodded.

"Yeah, you're almost eleven years old. I was working on my daddy's farm by the time I was twelve." Pete rubbed Brian's head and then pushed him away.

Pete had never hit him. Angela swore she'd leave if he did. But, there were always those threats Pete had made to Brian when they were alone together. Threats that Brian shared with his friend, old Mr. Eldridge.

"Just stay out of his way, kiddo; just stay clear. You know I'm here if you need me," Mr. Eldridge told Brian.

Mr. Eldridge had his leg shattered in the Vietnam war. He walked with a limp and needed the assistance of a cane. He frequently wore his old Vietnam uniform, or battered teeshirts and fatigues. His beard was scruffy and wore his grey hair back in a ponytail. He had little, even less than Brian, but his heart was large.

When the arguing between Pete and Angela became too much for Brian, he'd go over to see Mr. Eldridge, who left his back door open. "This is your home too, son."

They'd play chess until the arguing would stop. Sometimes Mr. Eldridge would share stories, secret stories that Brian could hardly believe. But old Mr. Eldridge swore they were true.

Brian's Batman clock read 6:35 p.m.. His mom would be home soon. The smell of cigarette smoke began to travel to his room. Pete.

Brian covered his nose and mouth with his teeshirt, and walked slowly downstairs. Pete sat on the plaid La-Z-Boy recliner, his thin face seemed to glow, hauntingly, from the television screen.

Brian coughed, "Mom says you're not suppose to smoke in the house, 'cause of my asthma."

Pete turned his face toward Brian, his eyes narrow, his mouth working the cigarette in between his teeth. He stood, walked toward Brian. Brian found it hard to catch his breath, more because of fear than the toxic nicotine. Pete kneeled in front of him, took a long pull from his cigarette, and blew smoke in Brian's face. Brain began coughing harder, the air in his lungs getting tighter.

Pete grabbed Brian by the back of his neck, catching a few strands of his hair in between his fingers, held it tight, "If you tell your mom, I swear I'll cut out your tongue, throw it in the bottom of the lake, and let the fish eat it. You understand me, boy? Asthma will be the least of your problems when I'm through."

Jerking away, Brian ran up to his room, grabbed his inhaler from his dresser drawer, and inhaled deeply. Then he opened his bedroom window, and breathed in the fresh air.

Mr. Eldridge stood on his back porch, leaning on his cane. His eyes focused on his young friend in the upstairs window,

"You all right there, Brian?" his voice a thick whisper.

Brian nodded his head slowly.

Mr. Eldridge looked to his right, and smiled, "You're mom's home." Then he gave Brian a weary wave, and walked back inside his house.

Brian ran downstairs to catch Pete spraying air freshener around the living room. He gave Brian a sideways glance. Angela carried in two large grocery bags, "You boys wanna help me with these?" she sounded winded.

"Sure, baby." Pete grabbed both bags, kissing Angela on the cheek.

"And, how's my best little man?" Angela held out her arms. Brian wrapped his arms around his mothers waist. "I missed you, mom." Angela held her son's face, observing him closely, "You sound phlegmy. You been wheezing?"

From the corner of his eye, Brian glanced quickly at Pete, who was staring at him.

"I'm OK, mom. Just running around outside."

"Hmmm, well, be careful. You know this weather is tricky. It's still a bit cold out there." Angela walked over to the thermostat. "And speaking of cold, why is it only sixty-nine degrees in here, Pete?"

"Ah, hell Angie, it's not that cold. The bill last month was a hundred and ten; that's a lot of goddamn money." Pete watched Angela turn up the heat and rolled his eyes.

"If Brian gets a cold, it triggers his asthma, I told you that." Angela turned towards Brian, "There's another bag in the truck for you; go get it, sweetie."

Brian rushed out the door and outside, coughing still, excitement filling his irritated lungs. He opened the door of the pickup. There in the front seat there was a large, red plastic bag.

Brian pulled out the package, wide-eyed. Licking his dry lips, he lifted out the cardboard box inside: Three Hot Wheels Monster Jam Trucks.

"Whoa, cool!"

Brian ran back inside the house to find Pete and his mom kissing.

"Thanks mom, these are awesome!"

Brian's face felt hot as he saw Pete's expression change. His eyes tightening together, his jaw working from side to side. He released Angela, and snatched the cardboard box with the Monster Trucks still inside, from Brian's hands.

Pete turned to Angela, "I can barely afford to keep the heat on, and you're buying him more goddamn toys?"

Brian swallowed hard, the taste of thick phlegm caught in the back of his throat. His stomach began to feel nervous, the way it always did when his mom and Pete fought.

Angela grabbed the box from Pete's hands, "Here sweetie, put your coat on and go play outside for a bit."

Brian observed his mother's eyes; he knew that look. The look of sadness and anger. She took a lot from Pete, but not when it came to Brian. He was the cause of many of their arguments, and Brian felt guilty, helpless. He wasn't big enough to stop Pete from hitting his mom, he wasn't big enough to throw him out.

"Go on, honey." Angela said, with a fatigued smile.

Brian walked to the hall closet, retrieved his tattered wool coat, and watched Pete walk into the kitchen. He opened the refrigerator and got a beer. Angela shook her head, her face red, her lips pursed together.

Once the drinking started, things got worse, much worse.

Just before he stepped outside Brian could hear Pete say, "You keep spoiling that boy, Angie, and he's gonna grow up to be a pussy."

Brian shut the door, and heard his mom say, "Not as big of one as you."

There were shouts, and Brian could hear furniture moving. He sat on the porch, looking at his new trucks, still encased in the box, no longer having the urge to open it.

He walked to Mr. Eldridge's back porch and opened the door. Brian smelled something cooking, the aroma filled the small house. And, he was reminded how hungry he was. He hadn't eaten since lunch, but he didn't dare ask Pete to fix him anything.

"Come on in, kiddo." Mr. Eldridge stood by the stove, stirring a large black pot, heating on a burner, that made a bubbling sound.

"You hungry?"

"Yes, sir."

"I figured as much. Take off your coat and grab two bowls."

Brian left the Monster Trucks box on the table, and took the bowls from the cabinet.

"You ever had rabbit stew?" Mr. Eldridge asked.

Brian held the bowl next to the pot, "No, sir."

Mr. Eldridge dipped a large, ladled spoon into the pot, and poured the stew into the bowl, "Careful, it's hot."

Brian had two bowls of the stew, the warm meal settling nicely in his belly. He began to relax.

Mr. Eldridge picked up the box with the Monster Trucks. "I used to have a big truck like this, a long time ago."

"Really? Did you live here?" Brian asked.

"No, back when I lived in Tennessee. Yeah."

"Where else did you live, Mr. Eldridge?"

"I told you to call me 'Max'. I lived all over the world, kiddo; seen some great stuff, met some interesting people. Some good, some not so good," Mr. Eldridge's voice drifted. Brian noticed that Mr. Eldridge seemed to drift a lot when he talked about the past. His eyes would glaze over, his voice sounded distant. It was like he was seeing his past all over again.

"Let me open this for you," he said.

Brian watched Max Eldridge smile, as he took out each of the trucks, examining each one, before handing them to Brian.

"These are beauties; you should start a collection. It's nice to collect things."

"You have any collections Mister, I mean, Max?"

Brian watched Mr. Eldridge get that far away look in his eyes, again. He sat back in the kitchen chair, absently scratched his beard. Finally, he said,

"I sure do."

Brian sat on the thick blanket Mr. Eldridge had given him. The basement was small, smelled like mildew, and very cold. In the corner was a large beat-up trunk. Brian had the feeling that whatever was inside was special, and he felt special because Mr. Eldridge was allowing him to see it.

"You wanna see a collection?" Mr. Eldridge reached into his pocket for the key; it looked just as old as the trunk. He carefully opened the lock. "Here's a collection," Mr. Eldridge said, letting out a sigh as he maneuvered his way down to the floor, his cane assisting him. Each time he moved, he squinted, and Brian wanted to help him, but knew there was nothing he could do.

Finally on the floor, his legs stretched on the side of the trunk, Brian didn't move. He wasn't sure what was in there. Pete always called him a 'crazy old man', and told Angela she was just as crazy, for allowing Brian to be friends with him.

"He's harmless, and kind." Brian's mom said.

Something Pete was not.

Mr. Eldridge glanced behind him, toward Brian, a grin on his face, and suddenly Brian could feel butterflies in his stomach.

Mr. Eldridge began placing items on the floor, saying, "I got these from India." They were small vases: different colors, six of them, all differently designed. "I haggled with a street merchant over these. Barely paid anything for them."

Brian crawled closer. "Wow, these are cool." He picked one up, and asked, "You were in India?"

Mr. Eldridge stroked one of the vases. "Careful, don't drop it. Yeah, I lived in India for a couple of years."

Then, Mr. Eldridge pulled out a brown cloth bag. He turned it upside down, letting the item inside, fall into his hand. A pocket watch: gold, shiny. He reached for Brian's hand, and placed the watch in his palm. Brian couldn't believe how heavy it was.

"Is this real gold?" Brian asked.

"Yep. Got this from England. A lady friend of mine gave it to me." Brian observed his old friend blink back a tear, and he felt sorry for him.

"Bet she was just as pretty as this watch," Brian said.

Mr. Eldridge smiled and nodded.

Mr. Eldridge sniffed, and pulled out a wooden, rectangular box. "Here's something you'll be interested in, kiddo." Inside the wooden box, was an old, silver car.

"Wow!" Brian had never seen a toy car like this. Mr. Eldridge handed it to him. It was heavier than the watch.

"That, my boy, is a 1929 Studebaker, in pure *silver*," Mr. Eldridge touched the wheels gently.

"How much did you pay for it?" Brian stroked the car with his finger.

"Eh," Mr. Eldridge waved his hand, "won it in a card game in Italy."

Brian placed the car on the floor, and rolled it back and forth.

"No, no," Mr. Eldridge said, "It's not for playing. You can't bang this up like those others you've got. This one is just for display." Brian nodded, then held the car in his hand, observing the details.

"And if you promise to treat it well, Brian, you know, not to crash it up, it's yours."

Brian felt his chest get tight; he wasn't sure if it was due to the excessive dust in Mr. Eldridge's basement or excitement.

"What? Wait, I can keep this? You're giving this to me?"

Mr. Eldridge chuckled, "Only if you promise not to bang it up."

"No, I won't, really, I won't."

"Well, than its yours, kiddo."

Brian grabbed the old man around the neck, hugging him as tight as he could, "You're my best friend, Mr. Eldridge. I mean, Max."

Brian felt Mr. Eldridge's dry lips on his cheek, and then he sat back, pulled a handkerchief from his back pocket and wiped his eyes. Brian felt like crying, too. He'd never met anyone like Max Eldridge. Just plain kind. Brian imagined his father would've liked him. He pictured the two men, sitting at the table together, laughing, exchanging stories, while his mother cooked, and Brian sat at ease, listening to them.

"You've been all over, huh, Max?"

"Yep, sure have."

Brian leaned over, looking inside the trunk, "You really have a treasure, don't you?"

Mr. Eldridge grinned, "You could say that."

Brian noticed a bright blue velvet box, at the bottom of the trunk, almost the same length as the trunk.

"What's in there, Max?"

Brian reached for the box, the material swished beneath his fingers.

"No, don't touch that." Brian jumped at Mr. Eldridge's response.

"Uh, nothing; it's nothing, kiddo."

Brian began to cough, phlegm settling into his chest again.

"Brian, let's get you upstairs. It's too dusty for you down here."

Brian wiped the dust from his pants. He helped Mr. Eldridge up, and they walked up the stairs. Brian tightly gripped the silver car in his hand.

Up the stairs, they entered the kitchen to find Pete standing there.

Brian could feel his breath become heavy. Holding the silver Studebaker behind him, he took a step back.

"What the hell were you two doing?" Pete's voice was flat, his stance confrontational.

"I didn't invite you into my home. You're trespassing." Mr. Eldridge said.

Pete walked towards Mr. Eldridge, until he was inches away from his face, "You having fun down there with your little playmate? What? You like little wee-wee's?"

Brian took a breath, "Stop it, Pete." Cough.

Brian could feel his body go cold as Pete turned towards him, "Is that why you like coming over here?"

"You need to leave, *now*, Pete. Before I say something this boy shouldn't hear." Mr. Eldridge shifted his weight to his left leg, and then stood tall, holding the cane slightly in front of him.

"You feeling strong, old man?" Pete chuckled.

A heavy silence fell over the dimly lit kitchen. Brian could feel his heart beat harder.

"Pete, Brian, come on, dinner's ready!" Angela's voice shattered the silence, carrying a welcome relief to Brian.

"Let's go you, little shit." Pete pulled Brian forward.

"Don't forget your trucks, kiddo." Mr. Eldridge handed Brian the Monster Trucks and gave him a wink.

"I'll see you tomorrow, Max." Brian said, defiantly.

Brian sat on his bedroom floor, on his new Star Wars rug his mother had bought him. He told her he'd already eaten at Mr. Eldridge's and wanted to go to his room to play with his new trucks. But the Monster Trucks sat on Brian's dresser, while he observed the intricate details of his beautiful old silver car.

There was a new respect for the old man, his friend, Max Eldridge. Brian had no idea he'd been so many different places in the world. He wondered if he'd ever be able to do the same.

"You're not going, Angela. You're staying here, and you'll cook Easter dinner here."

Pete's voice rose to Brian's bedroom. Brian could feel his back tighten.

"I'm going to see my family. You're welcome to come." Brian's mother's voice was firm.

"I said you're not going, Angela."

Their voices a slow progress to becoming shrill, the butterflies returned to Brian's belly.

Soon, it sounded like all out war; the sound of dish ware and chairs moving filling the downstairs.

Brian left his room and stood at the top of the stairs.

"Stop it, Pete, let me go!" Brian took two steps forward, and what sounded like a clap reverberated through the house. Brian stumbled back, as his mother ran up the stairs pushing Brian into his bedroom, and slamming the door closed.

The left side of her face was bright red, her blouse disheveled and loose.

"Mom, are you OK?"

"Shhh!" Angela pushed Brian's chair under the doorknob. Pete's footsteps were quick and heavy. Three loud bangs and the chair jammed beneath the door moved violently.

"I'll kick this door in on your face!" came Pete's angry voice. Brian's mother held him close to her, "Go away! I'll call the cops, Pete!"

One kick, and the chair seemed to fly across the room, as Brian's door flew wide open. Pete moved in quickly, pushing Angela to Brian's bed.

"Don't you touch my mom!" Brian grabbed and threw the closest thing to him: the solid silver Studebaker. Brian's aim was off, and the antique only nicked the side of Pete's head, but there was blood.

The look on Pete's face stopped Brian from moving or breathing; his body shivered involuntarily. If the Devil existed, he was staring at Brian.

"If you touch my son, I'll knock your head off." Brian looked and saw his mom holding his bat like a pro baseball player.

It was after 11:03 p.m. when Brian heard the soft cries, and low voices coming from his mother's bedroom.

They were making up. Brian could tell by his mother's tone.

By 11:33 p.m. Brian could hear moans coming from behind their closed door. His mother wasn't mad anymore.

Brian wondered what Pete had said to convince his mom that he wouldn't hurt her, or him. He wondered why she didn't just throw Pete out, like she said she would so many times before. By midnight, Brian was in bed and a gentle knock rapped at his door.

His mother came in and closed the door behind her. Her smile was faint, her eyes misty.

"How you doing, honey?"

Brian shrugged, "OK, I guess."

Angela sat on Brian's bed, her leg slipped from between her robe and the bareness embarrassed Brian.

"Honey, I want you to know, that I'd never let Pete hurt you—not ever."

Brian sat up, "Why do you stay with him, mom? He hurts you. Did dad ever hurt you?"

"No, your daddy was very different from Pete. And I miss him everyday, sometimes, too much. Maybe that's why..." she looked away, brushed back a tear.

"Anyway, he's promised to do better, Brian."

"Yeah, he's promised that before, mom." Brian couldn't hide his frustration.

His mother sighed, "Well, we'll be having Easter dinner here this year."

"We're not going to grandma's?" The disappointment in his tone, clear.

"No, Brian. We'll have dinner here, as a family. Just me, you, and Pete."

Brian lay back on his pillow; he could feel the tears welling up and swallowed hard.

"We're all going to try a little harder around here, honey."

Brian tried not to move his leg as his mother stroked it.

"Can we have Mr. Eldridge over for Easter dinner, too? He's alone."

"Well, I'll check with Pete and …"

Brian turned over, his back to his mother, "Never mind."

Brian could feel someone in his room. Staring at his clock, it now read 1:43 a.m.. He sat up quickly, the glow of his Batman clock capturing Pete's silhouette leaning on Brian's dresser.

Brian felt so small, in the darkness, "W- What do you want?"

Pete sat on Brian's bed; Brian recoiled. With his back against his headboard, there was nowhere for him to go.

"Where'd you get this?" Pete's voice was light, as he held the antique silver Studebaker in front of Brian, donning a teasing grin.

With all the commotion, Brian had forgotten about his new treasure. He reached for it but, drawing it closer to his chest, Pete's grin widened, "I asked you a question. You don't want me to tell your mom that you're being difficult. Especially since we're trying to make a fresh start."

Brian sat up straighter, his hands clutching his sheets, "She'd wanna know what you were doing in my room in the middle of the night."

"I heard you coughing and wheezing, and looked in on you. Now, were'd you get this, you little shit?"

"Mr. Eldridge," the moment Brian said his name he wanted to take it back.

"Really?" Pete's face brightened in the dark.

"Is that what he was showing you in that basement... all his crap?"

Brian sat still, feeling a prisoner in his own bed.

"Yeah, I bet he's got a lot of good crap." Pete whispered, his eyes focused on nothing.

Brian bit his bottom lip, the smell of cigarettes resting on Pete's teeshirt. He could feel his chest getting tight.

"He's probably got some money hidden somewhere, too," Pete said. His eyes now focused on Brian, and Brian didn't like the way Pete's thin face looked in the glow of his Batman clock. It looked... skeletal.

Pete stood slowly, walking towards Brian's bedroom door, his eyes on the solid silver Studebaker.

Brian leaned forward, "That's mine. I'll tell mom you took it from me."

Pete's tall thin frame stood still. Brian thought he resembled a shadow.

Placing the Studebaker gently on Brian's dresser, Pete turned to Brian, "Yeah, well, I'm sure there's plenty more where that came from."

Brian realized at that moment, Pete was going to do something bad to his friend, Max Eldridge.

Brian's mom made his favorite breakfast but, he barely touched it. Pete was in a very good mood, humming as he ate his pancakes.

"You coming with me to the store this morning, right hun?" Angela asked Pete.

Licking his fingers Pete sat back in the chair. "I got a better idea. You've got a lot to do around here for tomorrow's Easter dinner. I'll run to the store and pick up what you need."

"Really, hun? You sure?"

Brian hated when his mother called Pete 'hun'. He cringed.

"Yep, I got a few errands to run anyway; just write me out a list."

"Oh, that's great, thanks so much." Angela kissed Pete's cheek and Brian couldn't help but role his eyes.

This was the man who had slapped her the day before, and had beat her with a rolling pin a few months ago. Pete stood, and before walking out the front door, he winked at Brian.

Brian sat at the kitchen table with Mr. Eldridge. He drank hot cocoa, Mr. Eldridge drank black coffee. Brian told him about the night before, about the solid silver Studebaker, the questions Pete had asked, and how scared he was for Mr. Eldridge.

Brian tapped his feet nervously on the floor. "He's going to do something, I know it, Max. He thinks you've hidden money in here."

Max Eldridge sipped his coffee, his eyes staring down at his wooden kitchen table.

"Max, I don't want anything to happen to you. I'm scared."

"I'll be ok, kiddo," Mr. Eldridge said, but Brian could hear the uncertainty in his voice. Brian watched Mr. Eldridge sip his coffee, his hands shaking each time he lifted the cup to his mouth, his lips working each time he swallowed.

Brian imagined all the terrible things Pete could do to his friend. He imagined the awfulness of it, the hopelessness of the situation and began to cry.

Brian couldn't contain the pain and fear anymore."I don't want you to die, Max. I don't want my mom to die."

Mr. Eldridge pulled his chair closer to Brian's."What do you mean? Did Pete hurt your mom again?"

Brian met Mr. Eldridge's eyes, and he saw the concern there. Brian opened his mouth, but the words get stuck in his throat. His attention was no longer on Mr. Eldridge, but on Pete, who was standing in the frame of the backdoor.

Mr. Eldridge turned around quickly, and Pete chuckled.

"I didn't mean to scare you guys, I just wanted to have a word with you, Max."

Mr. Eldridge gripped his cane and stood, "What about?"

"Well," Pete stepped inside, "I think I owe you an apology. That wasn't very neighborly of me yesterday, talking to you the way I did."

Mr. Eldridge shrugged, "OK."

"You know, we've been neighbors for a while now, and I think Brian knows more about you than Angie and I do." Pete walked slowly around the kitchen, his eyes on everything.

"There's not much to know." Mr. Eldridge said.

Brian shifted in the chair. His heart rate had gone up; his chest was once again tight. He reached into his pocket for his inhaler.

"I think there's a lot more to know than you let on, Max." Pete sat at the table, "So, Max, that old Studebaker you gave Brian. That is a nice piece. Where'd you get it?"

"I don't remember." Mr. Eldridge said, staring at Brian.

"Really? Well, it's pretty cool, and pretty expensive. Am I right?" Pete laughed, but no one else did. And, Brian wished he hadn't thrown the Studebaker at him.

Pete and Brian sat at the table while Mr. Eldridge stood in the middle of his kitchen, leaning on his cane.

Brian couldn't stop his feet from tapping on the floor. The sound irritated him, but he just couldn't stop. He felt like he was about to have a bowel movement.

Finally, Pete rose from the chair, "Well, I'd love to hang out with you guys, but, I promised I'd help the little woman. But, Max, maybe when I come back you can show me what's in the basement."

When Pete walked out the door, Brian saw Mr. Eldridge lock the back door for the first time.

"I need you to come down to the basement with me, Brian." Mr. Eldridge said.

The bright blue velvet box lay across the cold concrete floor, Brian couldn't take his eyes off it. Mr. Eldridge told Brian that it was a gift from a man, whose life he'd saved back in Vietnam all those years ago.

"It can only be used once," Mr. Eldridge said, and then he opened the box.

Six eggs, all of them different shades of red. Larger than the average egg, Mr. Eldridge had to use both hands to pick one up.

"You're right, Brian. Pete's a very dangerous man." Mr. Eldridge rubbed the egg gently, "But, there's a solution."

Brian brought the bright blue box back to his room. Mr. Eldridge told Brian all had he had to do was get a few strands of Pete's hair. That was all. While Pete drank beer and watched television, and his mother seasoned the ham, Brian took Pete's comb from the bathroom. Brian pulled out the strands from the comb and placed them in the box. Just like Mr. Eldridge told him to. Then he placed the bright blue velvet box containing the eggs under his bed, and waited.

The hum and rattle of the baseboard heater surrounded Brian's room. His bedroom door open, he could hear his mother brushing her teeth. 11:07 p.m., and Pete is still in the living room, watching television. But Brian knew they were both waiting for his mom to go to bed, and both for different reasons.

Brian lay in bed, listening anxiously to his mother's stride. She walked quickly down the stairs, moving a few things in the kitchen. Brian heard her say goodnight to Pete, then she ran back up the stairs.

Leaning over, her hair brushing Brian's face, he could smell the soap on her neck. Her lips landed full on his cheek.

"Love you, honey. Get a goodnight's sleep," Brian's mom said.

But he wouldn't.

12:46 a.m. Brian could hear Pete moving around downstairs. What was he doing? And what was going on with those eggs under his bed? He could hear nothing out of the ordinary. He could hear footsteps coming up the stairs. Brian closed his eyes. The footsteps stopped just outside his room. It was Pete. Brian lay still, trying hard to control his breathing. When the footsteps walked away, Brian opened his eyes and heard Pete walking down the stairs. And then, there was a sound beneath his bed, cracking and sharp.

Brian could feel the temperature in his body drop; the coolness of his sweat ran across his forehead. The crackling sound became louder, and then the smell of rotten eggs filled Brian's room, causing him to gag. The sound of popping and sizzling filled Brian's room and his legs moved involuntarily; his nerves getting the best of him.

"Remember, they're not here for you. They only go after the one whose hairs have been placed in the box," Mr.Eldridge had told him. And Mr. Eldridge, Max, was his friend; he wouldn't lie to him. Still, Brian wished he'd closed the door to his mother's bedroom door.

Next, the sound of something oozing, bubbling and then faint chirping. Brian could feel movement beneath him. There was the urge to look, to see what they were, but Brian's body felt like it didn't belong to him.

He could hear Pete open the front door, and then it closed. A loud screech and Brian could feel a bouncing movement beneath him. Little steps could be heard heading towards his bedroom door. Released from fear's power, he sat up, catching a glimpse of the creatures.

Both excited and terrified, Brian swung his legs over the bed; his feet landed directly on top of a clear, jello-like, slime that was warm and slippery. Multi-hued, red shells had been expelled across the floor.

The chirping sound seemed to descend down the stairs. Brian widened his eyes, trying to get a better look at the creatures that had just been unleashed.

They were brightly colored—whatever they were—yellow, and red. They were small, not quite as big as chickens, but larger than baby chicks. They left slime on the steps, and Brian stopped, realizing he didn't have on his shoes, or coat. By the time he put them on, the creatures were out the door...the opening of the door's mail slot still swaying.

Pulling back the living room window curtain, Brian watched Pete walk stealthily across the yard, heading to Mr. Eldridge's house... a pillow case in his hand. He'd been right. Pete *was* going to hurt Mr. Eldridge. And eventually he would hurt his mother, or worse. What they were doing was right. The fear seemed to flow from him. Brian opened the door slowly; the moonlight cast a dim glow across the ground.

Where were they?

Brian couldn't see Pete, either. Walking across the yard, he saw Mr. Eldridge's back door was open.

"Oh no!" he breathed.

Tiptoeing to Mr.Eldridge's back porch, and unsure of the situation, Brian could do nothing but stand still.

If Pete was already inside, Mr.Eldridge was in trouble. The thought was overwhelming. Brian began to breathe heavily, his asthma threatening to flare. He couldn't let his friend get hurt. Brian searched the ground for a large rock; large enough to hurt Pete with, but not too large for Brian's hands.

Searching diligently for his weapon, Brian tripped, landing on his hands and knees. Passing quickly, less than a foot away from him, all six creatures bounded up on Mr. Eldridge's back porch. Brian was able to see them, now, the moonlight accentuating their features.

Their beaks were pointed and sharp-hooked, like a sickle. Their pointed teeth looked too large for their small heads. Brian held his breath and his lungs began to hurt. Their claws were long and sharp like an eagle. Their bright yellow coat almost too bright to look at, and Brian could see that the bright red color pulsated; then realized it was their veins. And they had just one eye in the center of their head: dull, pink, and large.

They went inside Mr. Eldridge's house, hopping quickly.

Brian followed.

Some clanking noise and a groan came up from the basement. Brian walked slowly down the stairs to find only a low beam light above Mr. Eldridge's head. His hands and feet duct-taped, and a bruise on his forehead. Pete was holding one of the vases from India, when he noticed Brian standing at the bottom of the stairs."Well, well, well. Looks like we've got company, Max."

He walked over to Brian; grabbing him quickly, he threw him down next to Mr. Eldridge.

"I'll have to figure out what I can do with you, once I'm done here. And you know what?" Pete knelt in front of Brian, "I'm going to enjoy it."

A high-pitched squeal at the top of the stairs interrupted Pete. They stood together, all six of them, heads moving quickly, their teeth gnashing loudly. Pete lost his footing and stumbled back, falling on his back, "Holy Christ!"

As the creatures hopped down the stairs, Brian worked on ripping away Mr. Eldridge's duct tape.

"What the hell are they? What the hell is this?" Pete shouted.

Walking to the other side of the basement, Brian said, "They're here for you, Pete. Just for you."

Mr. Eldridge held Brian close, as the newly-hatched creatures made their way to Pete.

They surrounded him, at first. Pete tried throwing something, anything at them, but the creatures didn't move.

"Brian, please, get them away from me!" Pete pleaded, while he tried scooting away on his forearms. But the creatures were now on him. Two on his leg, one on his chest, one on his stomach and two directly above his eyes.

"No, no, oh God, please!" The moment Pete tried swiping them away, it began. It was like a feast for the creatures, each taking a part of Pete's body. They tore into his belly first, one working its way to his intestines, and then slowly pulling them out, eating them as if it had just pulled a worm from the ground. The creatures pulled out the veins inside Pete's leg, each of them working their beaks through the flesh. Pete's screams were loud, excruciating.

"Someone will hear," Brian whispered to Mr. Eldridge.

"No, not down here," Mr. Eldridge whispered back.

Then, they pecked away at his eyes, and Brian thought Pete would scream so hard, that he'd scare the creatures away. But they weren't scared away. They were there to do a job.

Brian and Mr. Eldridge held on to one another watching Pete's limbs flail, and his head rock from side to side, while his blood covered Mr. Eldridge's basement floor.

Looking down at Pete, Brian couldn't believe he was afraid of him, he seemed so helpless laying there covered in his own blood. The screams became less, as the creatures were working their way through the flesh pretty quickly. Soon, bone was exposed, and Pete's body shivered every now and again. In the end, it was just reflex...until he moved no more.

Brian thought he would feel something: remorse, or sadness. He thought about Pete beating his mom, Brian thought about the threats Pete had made, and what he'd done to Mr. Eldridge that night. He was capable of this, and so much more. How much more? Brian was thankful they wouldn't have to find out.

When the creatures were done, they walked in a circle, on top of Pete's body and then they began to shrink, slowly. Their heads folded into their necks, their legs became brittle and turned to dust. Eventually, only six balls of fur lay on Pete's bloody body.

Mr. Eldridge's basement was a mess.

"We better start cleaning up." Brian said, pulling his inhaler out of his coat pocket, he took a deep breath.

"No, you go home. Your mom will be looking for him. You would've been in your bed all night, you know nothing," Mr. Eldridge said, "You understand?"

Brian nodded.

"Go on, now go home, get into bed. I'll take care of this."

Brian did just that. He walked out into the night, the air cool against his face. He opened his door, locked it and walked quietly upstairs to the bathroom. His mother was still asleep; he could hear her snoring. Brian washed his face and hands. Went into his bedroom, hung up his coat, and changed his pyjamas. He cleaned the slime from his room and picked up the cracked, bright red egg shells on his floor. Then he got into bed, and slept. For the first time, in a long time, he slept without fear, and he slept hard.

He was awakened by the smell of ham and the sound of clanging pots.

Brian rubbed his eyes. The morning sun radiated through his window and seemed to engulf him.

His mother ran up the stairs and entered his room. "Hey, you're finally awake," she observed, kissing his cheek, "Happy Easter, honey."

"Happy Easter, mom. The ham smells great."

"Hey, do you know if Pete got up this morning to run to the store or something?"

Brian shrugged his shoulder, "No, I don't know."

"Hmm, OK, well, take a shower, come downstairs, and help me, OK?"

Brian did as he was told.

The night before didn't seem real, but it was. As Brian helped his mother set the table, she checked her cell phone occasionally, made a few phone calls, but no one had seen Pete.

"That son of a bitch." Brian could hear his mother say.

Mr. Eldridge sat on his back porch. Brian sat next to him. Neither of the two said a word for a while.

"How are you feeling today, kiddo?" Mr. Eldridge asked.

"I-I guess I feel OK." Brian looked down at his sneakers, and noticed two blood spots on the right one. "I don't know if that's the way I'm supposed to feel, you know?"

Mr.Eldridge nodded. "I understand."

"How bout you; everything, ok, Max?"

"Everything's fine, kiddo. No need for you to worry anymore."

Brian's mom walked up to them, "Hey, Mr.Eldridge, Happy Easter."

"I can smell your meal from here, smells wonderful, Angela."

"Thanks, umm, have you seen Pete around today? He seems to be missing in action."

Mr. Eldridge shook his head, "No, sorry."

"Mom, we have plenty of food. Can Mr. Eldridge come over for dinner?"

"Oh, no, no, son." Mr. Eldridge stood to go back inside his house, "I don't want to impose on the family."

"But, Max," Brian grabbed his hand, "you *are* family."

Brian could see the mist reaching Mr. Eldridge's eyes.

"Yeah, Mr.Eldridge, we'd love to have you, really," Angela said.

That Easter Sunday, they enjoyed their dinner, they enjoyed one another's company, and they enjoyed peace.

Later that night Angela held out a couple of bright red shards, "Brian, I found these underneath your bed. What are they?"

Brian looked at them, "Just shells."

"Shells? Shells from what?"

Brian took a piece out from his mother's hand, "Easter Eggs."

The End

THE REBIRTH

Mark Cassell

Kelly placed the mug of hot chocolate on the table and scowled at the front door. Who the hell was knocking at this time of night? Tomorrow was Monday, when she'd have to face a class of ten-year-olds; right now, she just wanted to relax.

Again, two knocks.

And, why weren't they ringing the doorbell?

"Hang on, for bloody hell's sake," she whispered. Pulling her cardigan tight, she walked to the door. Her bare feet shuffled across the carpet.

The wooden panel was cold on her cheek as she squinted through the peep-hole. A magnified circle of gloom revealed only the neighbour's door across the hall. No one was there. Although having lived on the sixth floor for the past two years, she hadn't really spoken with any of her neighbours. Certainly, there was the occasional exchange, brief and polite, though often forced on her behalf. Never had any come to her door, nor she gone to theirs.

Nope, definitely no one out there.

She unfastened the security chain and opened the door. She thought she heard something out in the hall, something flapping, but the chain rattling against the wood obscured whatever it was. Cold air blew into her face as she peered around the frame and her breath made a cloud. Someone had evidently left a window open in the hallway. The other three doors were closed. No more sounds, if she had, indeed, heard anything in the first place.

There had definitely been a knock. Twice. Two raps, both times.

She went to close the door and saw a wooden egg on the mat. It was about the size of a typical chocolate egg, yet carved from solid wood. It had to have been a neighbour. She picked it up. It was cool to the touch, and pretty weighty. It had been carved with an impressive weave of vines and leaves. Intricate, not one part of it the same, clearly handcrafted. No way was it machine made.

She closed the door with her hip, without taking her eyes off the egg. Beautiful. Without a doubt, she would take it into class tomorrow. She'd organised for the kids to make their own eggs based on things they love. This was her first Easter as a qualified teacher, and she was looking forward to seeing their efforts. Already, she suspected what some of the children would make. There'd be Star Wars characters, superheroes and villains, and Pokemon, for sure.

She stood the egg upright in an empty glass she'd left on the table earlier that morning. It made a perfect stand.

Why would a neighbour have given her the egg? She went to the window and looked out, wondering if she could possibly see a friend who'd given it to her as a prank. She could only think of Liz, who'd always been the joker. Maybe it was her.

Clouds, like phantoms, streaked the night sky that stretched downward to touch the knife-edged horizon of the sea. Further to the west, Hastings Pier clawed out into the still expanse of water. A twisting row of streetlights illuminated the winding road, where a couple of cars shot past. Several pedestrians dotted the promenade. Some hand in hand, others alone.

It wasn't the view that she was interested in.

Closer to her block of flats, the orange haze of a nearby street lamp flooded the area below. A lady stood beside a dog as it pissed up against the car park wall, and further along, through a row of winter-stripped trees, a man wearing a fisherman's cap shuffled past. He was more a silhouette in the gloom of the alleyway. For a moment, it looked like something fluttered in the bare branches above him, shifting with the shadows. Perhaps it was a late-night seagull.

Kelly allowed the curtain to fall back in place.

Back on the sofa, after a quick glance at the egg, she lifted her mug and took a sip. The hot chocolate slid down her throat, energising her taste buds. Where did the egg come from? The remainder of the evening, she watched TV; a half-arsed effort where she kept thumbing the remote, her gaze repeatedly wandering over to the egg.

Soon, her eyelids drooped and she fell asleep.

***

"So," Kelly said, having waited for each child to sit in their seats, "all your eggs are in, and waiting to be judged."

The room of twenty children sat alert, eager for the winners to be announced. She had a sheet of stars ready, so those who failed to make it in the top three did not go empty-handed.

Between herself and those expectant eyes, she'd arranged a table and covered it in straw. She'd dipped into her own pocket to buy a bag of the stuff from the local pet store. It looked great with the decorated eggs lined up. They were all hardboiled – at least she hoped, because if not, things could get messy. Some sat in painted egg cups or cartons, others simply cradled in straw or strips of paper, all of varying colours. Some were simple, others were impressive. One, thought Kelly, looked like the kid had scribbled over it with a permanent marker. There were, of course, superheroes and Pokemon just as she'd predicted. Parents had helped with a few, that was evident.

Her wooden egg lay on its side, next to the stapler she kept at hand on her desk. Her coffee sat there getting cold. Perhaps she'd been too excited for this, herself.

"They are all very, very good," she said.

So many wide eyes stared back.

"And," she added, "you know I can only pick three."

So many grins.

"This one is good." She picked up an egg that was painted black and had pointy ears. "Batman."

At the back of the class, a blond boy, named Jeremy MacDonald, clapped and the other children turned to look at him. "That's mine!" he shouted.

She nodded, knowing that it would be his. He always ran around the playground pretending to be Batman. Often, she'd have to tell him to be quiet in class because he'd be talking about a Batman comic, or the Batman cartoon, or the new Batman movie.

"This one is clever." She pointed to one that sat in a crushed egg cartoon that had been painted green and brown. The egg itself was painted grey, and pierced through the top of the shell was a small plastic cocktail stick shaped like a sword. She read the banner along the edge of the carton. "Eggscalibur."

Frizzy-haired Sarah Jenkins waved. "Daddy said that would win."

"Did he, now?" Kelly smiled, and moved further along the table. "You all have made my job very difficult."

The children started to talk at once, the classroom becoming an uproar of excitement. She picked up several others in turn, moved them around in their nests, pointing and smiling, all the while the cacophony increased.

"Okay, okay," she eventually said, "quiet now, please."

All eyes shifted back to her and the eggs, and their voices quieted. Soon, most of them were silent. A few whispers lingered, but that was fine.

"Which of these will be the runner up?" she asked.

"Mine!" shouted Joey Frank, a pleasant kid; indeed, the class jester. Intelligent, if only he applied himself to the work given to him, rather than trying to be the centre of attention. "You gotta pick mine as the winner!"

As it was, Kelly had no idea which one could be his. Perhaps it was the octopus, or the Teenage Mutant Ninja Turtles. She really had no clue.

There was even an egg covered with cotton wool, shaped into a rabbit. She picked it up. One of the cardboard bunny feet hooked a piece of straw. No way had a ten-year-old made this. Did the parents really think they'd pull the wool – or rabbit fur – over her eyes? She placed it back down and picked up one that had been painted with a steady hand. Nothing fancy, just circles and lines of dark blues and purples, reds and yellows. Very pretty. This certainly could've been painted by one of the more artistic kids.

"This is good," she said. "Perfect angles."

Bethany Simmonds, seated at the back in the far corner, smiled and lowered her eyes. Always a shy one. She'd get far in the creative arts should she pursue it, Kelly was certain. This wasn't the first time she'd thought such things of the girl's talent.

Kelly brushed her fingers over several others.

"I think—"

Something fell behind her, cracking as it hit the floor.

***

The wooden egg lay in pieces. A frothy, grey-green mess oozed between the sections, splinters of the intricate design floating as the mess spread. It ate into the floor, hissing. Tiny wisps of smoke curled upwards. Stepping back, Kelly's arse hit the table. She yelled. The kids began chatting animatedly, some getting out of their seats. But she didn't look at them, she only heard the clatter of chair legs, their frenzied voices. All she could do was watch as that bubbling goo spread and burnt into the floor.

"Get out!" she screamed. A putrid stink stung her nostrils. It was like rubber, vegetation, and something rotten. "Now!"

The stuff frothed and spat, peppering the front panel of her desk. From the spreading mass, thick tendrils of what looked like vines hooked out and shot across the floor. Tiny veins crackled along their lengths, splaying outward like a growing fungus. It looked like the creepers you'd find in a forest, only sentient, reaching, searching...

"Move!" she shouted at the class. She backed up, further away from her exit. "Get out!"

Amid scattered chairs and shunted tables, the children were funnelling towards the open door. Shouts echoed from the hallway.

More vines crept outward and Kelly backed up further, stamping and kicking at the creepers. One becoming five, becoming ten, becoming twenty, unfurling. She scrambled backwards, yelling. Her desk jolted, tilted into the sagging mass of creepers. Pencils and pens rolled first, then several notebooks slid forwards, everything sank into the nest—it *was* like a nest, for God's sake. This was insane.

Last to fall was the laptop and telephone.

She staggered further back, kicking at a thrashing vine.

The contest table jerked and shifted sideways. In a tangle of straw, all the children's eggs fell into the widening expanse of stitched vines. The centre of the nest deepened to become more a pit. The seething mass rustled and snapped as twigs and sticks wound around each other, reinforcing the whole damn thing. More vines branched out, shooting outward, clutching table legs. A thin veiny fungus coated everything like a kind of webbing.

Kelly had now backed up to the wall and shimmied around a cupboard. She had to get out of there. Most of the children had scrambled from the classroom, but some of the littler ones scuttled behind. Some slipped on the pens and pencils and rulers and books that littered the floor. Their cries echoed in the near empty room.

As Kelly rounded a number of upended desks and chairs, she kept glancing at the growing nest.

Bethany and Joey were the last children running towards the door.

A vine shot out and caught the girl's skinny leg. She crashed to the floor and shrieked. One shoe flew from her foot. Tiny creepers slithered around her ankle and dragged her back... towards the nest.

Joey scrambled for the door, but tripped over his classmate.

Kelly darted towards the pair of kids. Their screams filled her head. The room had darkened, the nest now expanding even further, swallowing tables and chairs. More vines slithered out, making wispy noises as they slid against the dry creepers that lined the nest. With her breath coming in gasps, she tasted foliage and vegetation.

A vine had now coiled around Joey's ankle, and both kids shouted, scrambling uselessly as they were dragged closer towards more eager vines.

"Joey!" Kelly leapt forward. On her knees, she grabbed the vine that clamped his leg. Its rough bark scratched her skin as she tore it free. "Run!"

The vine blindly slapped the floor.

He scrambled for the door and she watched him head for the hallway. Further away, Bethany flailed. Tears streamed down her red cheeks. Her hands raked the floor, now closer to the nest. The vines stitched around her legs, then her body vanished into the spreading nightmare.

"Bethany!" Kelly yelled.

Screams and shouts dwindled far out in the hallway, beyond the classroom.

Kelly wanted to get out, to run the hell away from this madness but—

What the hell was she doing?

She leapt over a thrashing, stumpy vine and launched herself towards the girl, arms outstretched. Her chest thumped the thatched vines and sticks. Her breath rushed from her lungs. As she gulped air, that stink poured down her throat. A miasma of light fizzed across her vision and soon the darkness closed in. She clambered through the tangle of scratchy vines, kicking and punching as they grabbed for her. She wriggled further into the nest.

Darker and darker.

She focused on Bethany's pale face, keeping the poor girl in sight as the nest dragged them both into its heart...

***

Joey hugged himself as his mum drove him away from school, leaving behind so many blue flashing lights. He'd never before seen so many policemen and police cars. He didn't know if he should feel excited or scared. Again, he thought of Bethany and his teacher, Mrs. Laurence.

He still felt as though the branch thing held his ankle.

His mum said to him, "Let's get some chips, shall we? We can eat them while we walk between the fisherman huts. You always enjoy looking at the boats."

He did. He liked the way they sat on the beach, out of the water. Sometimes he'd even seen the little yellow tractors pull them from the sea.

When his mum got to a red traffic light, she put her hand on his head. She always smelled of coconut. His head didn't hurt anymore from when he'd smacked it on the floor after tripping over Bethany. He wondered if she was still inside that giant bird's nest. Ever since managing to run away, all he thought of was how all those weird branches and sticks had swallowed Bethany. And Mrs. Laurence. He liked Mrs. Laurence. Bethany, too.

He hoped they were okay.

When the traffic light turned to green, his mum squeezed his neck a bit too tightly and let go. His ankle still itched a little. Nothing was there, though, and the nice man from the ambulance had said he was okay.

The drive down to the seafront was no different than usual, and Joey squinted into the red lights of all the cars in the traffic. His mum had recently told him that the sky was darker because in winter the sun was further away, and now in spring, the sun was getting closer. He pictured the sun as a tiny yellow marble far away in space. Mrs. Laurence had once explained that the Earth evolved—or was it revolved?—around the sun. It was dark in space. Like the middle of the nest had been, before it closed in on his friend and teacher, like dirty water rushing down a plughole. It had vanished. He remembered how some of the desks and chairs were broken, but the nest had gone. Like it had never even been there.

He was hungry.

Soon they walked across the car park, both with a bag of chips in hand. His mum had got a large bag for herself and him a small bag, although their portions looked the same. They ate them while walking between the fishermen's huts, where it always smelled of salt and grease, and of course fish.

Somewhere nearby, plastic rustled on the wind.

Beneath his shoes, pebbles and pieces of wood clicked and crunched. There was some string on the ground, too. They walked past chunks of white stuff that looked like lumps of snow. He knew it wasn't; it was actually broken bits of the packing that came in boxes to stop things from breaking. It was called 'polystylean' or something. There was always rubbish laying around there, but Joey liked it. Further down, closer to the beach, he'd see some boats up on stilts. He liked that word: 'stilts'.

The cold air numbed his fingers and he wanted to put his gloves on, but he knew he couldn't eat chips that way, he'd get tomato sauce on them. Seagulls circled overhead, some landed on the pebbles and hopped nearby. Several watched him from the flat roofs. Most likely they wanted one of his chips. He was glad he wore his woolly hat and scarf.

"Maybe afterwards we can go and get you a chocolate egg," his mum said to him.

That made Joey think of those eggs he and his friends had painted… and the way Mrs. Laurence's wooden egg had split open to spread the branches and sticks around the classroom.

And he again thought of how one had grabbed his ankle.

His mum walked further ahead of him. She passed a stack of red and white baskets that leaned against a hut with walls of peeling black paint. Usually there would be smelly fish in them, but these were filled with the worn and smooth planks he sometimes saw washed up on the beach. Green-black seaweed wrapped around them and draped down onto the dusty pebbles.

A fisherman stood in a doorway, his face hidden in the shadows of both the gloomy hut and his cap. He wore a long coat that reached down to his Wellington boots.

Joey saw the man's cap tilt as though he watched him approach. He dropped the chip he was about to eat.

The man also held something.

He stopped and stared while his mum kept walking, rounding the corner of the hut. His mouth went dry.

The man—was he a fisherman?—held an egg.

Joey heard his mum's shoes get fainter as she walked further away.

The egg that the man held was like the one Mrs. Laurence had on her desk, the one that had cracked and all that horrid stuff had come out. It was almost the same; the top was still smooth, yet to be carved.

Suddenly Joey was no longer hungry.

Behind the man, a bird flew around inside the hut. But it was too dark to see what type of bird. He didn't think it was a seagull, it was too black and had a long straight beak.

Joey wanted to run, yet he didn't dare.

The man stepped forward and gravel crunched beneath his wellies. His jaw moved behind his beard as though he said something, but Joey couldn't hear. In the man's other hand was a knife. It gleamed in the daylight.

Joey felt his stomach jump.

The man lifted the knife and began carving the egg. Tiny slivers of wood curled away and fell to the ground. He wasn't even watching what he was doing, instead he continued to stare at Joey, those tiny eyes squinting beneath bushy eyebrows.

"What is it, Joe-Joe?" His mum's voice drifted back to him, seeming far away.

Joey knew she stood somewhere nearby, but he didn't look at her. He watched the man raise the egg above his head.

She asked, "What's he doing?"

***

Kelly Laurence slid through the suffocating muck of slippery vines, further into the cloying darkness. It was as though she tumbled rather than being dragged, and by now, the creepers had become wetter, slimier. Still, her determination kept her pressing onwards. It was all she could do to keep upright, often slipping onto her chest. Her arms, shoulders and legs were killing her. She clambered through what was like the dense undergrowth of a forest floor, with tangled branches and brambles catching her now-drenched hair.

As for Bethany, Kelly could barely see the girl as those vines continued to drag her deeper into the nest. However, the surrounding creepers had long since receded enough to allow Kelly more leverage, more manoeuvrability.

How long had she been scrambling through this hell?

Her knees and feet slipped, and her hands grasped at the slick creepers. It reminded her of the time she'd fallen down a river bank and landed in the thick mud at the water's edge. Clumps of reeds had snatched her and the more she'd struggled, the more she sank, the water soaking her to the skin. Although that water had been cold, this insane place was warm, its atmosphere sweaty.

A rising fog had also started to curl from the glistening vines.

And the stink. It was incredible. Raw, meaty, like sewage. It clogged her nose, filled her throat, tasted like shit. Her teeth clenched so tight her jaw ached. How much longer could this go on?

She scrambled over a mound of splintered creepers. They were soft rather than sharp. For the umpteenth time, she cried, "Bethany!" and ended up coughing. That stench filled her lungs.

Why were those vines dragging the girl and not her? It was almost as though they were sentient, recognising that Kelly was in pursuit. Not only that, where were they taking her?

Kelly slid downwards, still scrambling after the girl, and twisted awkwardly to land on her arse. Water or filth or slime, whatever the hell it was, soaked straight through to her underwear. This was even warmer, hot in fact. Several creepers whipped her face and then recoiled. She swatted them away and she pushed herself sideways and sat up, hoping to not have lost sight of the girl.

"Bethany!"

Just ahead, the child hung suspended in the cross-hatch of thick vines and tangled creepers. These glowed purple, a strange luminescence in the gloom. They creaked as they tightened around her, squeezing. Her eyes were closed; she looked so peaceful, even though she was caked in black, glistening muck.

"Bethany!" Kelly yelled again and gulped the foul air. She choked.

As though relaxing, the vines released the girl and she fell. Her tiny – lifeless? dear God, no! – body slapped the ground. The black stuff splashed Kelly's face. She lurched forward, knee-deep in fog and filth. Bethany's eyes were closed but she breathed softly. Black bubbles dribbled over her lips.

Cradling the girl, Kelly gently slapped her cheek. "Bethany?"

Her eyes fluttered, opened, and widened. She screamed. Sharp and shrill. It was a flat echo.

"It's okay," Kelly whispered.

A rustling noise made her look up. Overhead, something shifted in the thatch of dripping creepers. Her heart pulsed in her throat, and she held her breath. What was it? She squinted. Nothing. Had something been there? She listened, yet heard nothing more.

Bethany mumbled and wriggled, and still Kelly looked up, her neck stretched. She felt as though she knelt on a forest floor, peering into a desperate twilight that leaked through dense branches. And somewhere in those branches... was that a pair of eyes reflecting the strange luminescence of fog and purple vines?

Her breath caught in her throat, and she coughed.

The filth around her started to froth, more of those purple vines churning the muck and creating clouds of billowing fog.

Kelly and Bethany clutched one another. The girl sobbed, coughed, and choked, her tiny arms and legs twitching. All the while the fog thickened. A bitter taste filled Kelly's mouth and she coughed again: great chest-rattling whoops.

More trunks thrashed in the muck, spraying them both. And the fog swirled and snaked around them, the darkness closing in...

Still Kelly felt those eyes watching them.

***

The fisherman hurled the egg across the yard and it smashed into the wall of another hut. Black and green filth spattered the brickwork. Immediately, sticks and twigs and branches shot out, whispering and rustling, snapping and cracking, splaying outward. It was another nest— exactly the same as Joey had seen in the classroom that morning—and it filled the area between him and his mum. It deepened as it spread.

The ground rumbled, the pebbles clinking against one another.

"Joe-Joe!" his mum yelled. "Get back!"

Joey didn't realise he'd dropped his bag of chips. The paper shivered on the pebbles as the ground shook. He staggered away.

A fog drifted up from the middle of the nest.

Followed by a hand.

Black slime caked it, the fingernails like claws. Another hand reached out, then someone's head, again slick with that disgusting, gloopy mess. Fog clouded the sky and with it a nasty stink that was like rotten vegetables, and farts.

Joey watched as out came…

***

…Kelly gulped fresh air. She smelled the sea, fish, and even grease. But thankfully, no more tasting the cloying fog and shit of decay and vegetation from the hell she'd just endured. She pulled Bethany free from the clutches of the vines and their rough bark. The poor child had cried herself into twitchy robotic movements.

Together they emerged, dripping filth, and squinting into the daylight.

Where were they?

The vines and creepers settled as she clutched Bethany tightly and clambered up and out of the nightmare. No longer were those vines trying to keep them in; it was as though they'd given up trying to imprison them.

Black walls and blue barrels, red and white crates and—how did they get here? They were all the way down by the sea, at the Fisherman's End. She'd expected to emerge back in her classroom, but why here?

Every one of her limbs screamed at her, her skin raw, her clothes saturated.

How long had she been in there, dragging both Bethany and herself through the embrace of slime and jungle-like foliage?

She coughed and spat. The stuff tasted foul.

Around her, the wood began to crumble, dust pluming, replacing the fog to drift upwards to an overcast sky. The ground levelled out, eventually flattening. No more vines, no more creepers, no more of that foul stink.

Everything was normal.

Apart from the taste.

She spat again.

Kelly then saw a woman crouch and take Bethany from her. For a moment, she was reluctant to release the girl... yet the woman smiled. She recognised her as one of the mums. Couldn't place a name, though. Behind her was Joey Frank. Of course! The woman was Mrs. Frank.

Kelly coughed.

Joey stared at one of the huts. A fisherman stood watching them, although he had his head tilted as though speaking with someone behind him. He held a woodcrafter's knife. Something dark inside the hut shifted, something large.

The man stepped aside.

Mrs. Frank said something, but Kelly didn't hear. The sound of the shrieking winged *creature*—it was most definitely not a bird—clawed its way around the door frame. The wood splintered beneath its talons.

Its eyes burned yellow in a head that was nothing more than a twisted mess of blistered flesh and fur. Its beak was as black as its charred flesh and as long as a bread knife. And just as serrated. Leathery wings slapped against its wrinkled body as the thing scrambled past its master. Extending great wings, it launched into the sky. Its cry drilled into Kelly's brain and she clamped hands to her ears. Mrs. Frank and her son both did the same.

Bethany was hunched over, clutching her stomach. She coughed, choking, and spat green filth onto the pebbles.

The fisherman stepped aside, arms folded. He nodded and watched the winged demon—that was what it was, surely, considering the hell she'd just climbed through—circle above. Its impressive wingspan thumped on the air to create a wind that froze her wet scalp.

Kelly shivered and coughed, and agony spiked in her stomach. She hugged herself. A dizziness swept over her, black and white flashes blinding her. The pain raged in her stomach, up into her chest.

Bethany was sobbing and coughing, and—

The little girl spat out a glistening egg as black as onyx. It clattered across the pebbles and rolled to a stop. The poor girl's eyes widened, and she staggered back, screaming.

A bitterness rose into Kelly's throat, and she heaved. Breathing sharp, hissing through the nose, she again coughed, wracking, thundering through her chest. Dear God, the pain... and she buckled over. Her palms hit the uneven ground and she slipped, her nose inches from the ground.

Absolute agony tore up her throat...

And she, too, spat out an egg.

Followed by vomit.

The stink clawed up her nostrils.

Overhead, the sound of those flapping wings got closer and that freezing wind strengthened.

Something thumped into Kelly's ribs and the air rushed from her lungs. She smacked into a blue barrel and it threatened to topple. It didn't.

The demon-bird-thing had both eggs clutched in its chipped talons and it rose higher, its shriek now an intermittent chirp. Like the damned thing was happy.

It had offspring, why wouldn't it be happy?

Kelly actually laughed at the insanity of it.

Mrs. Frank had both Bethany and Joey in her arms, cradling them tight. The children sobbed. Tears glinted on the woman's cheeks, her eyes moist and wide.

Kelly watched the creature as it flew over the boats, out over the sea and towards the horizon, to become a black dot. Its sporadic cries echoed, dwindling the further it went. When she finally looked away, she noticed the fisherman was no longer there.

The End

BABY BLUES

Briana Robertson

"Roxy? Roxy. Roxanne!"

I barely glance away from the television. "What?"

"Can't you hear Josiah crying?"

"Oh, Josiah's crying?" I roll my eyes. "Of course, I can hear him crying. That's all he's done all day."

I feel my husband's gaze, heavy with shock and disapproval, but I don't turn to meet it. Instead, I stare pointedly at the TV screen, watching, but not really seeing, the rerun of *Dark Angel.*

"So, you're planning to just sit there and let him cry?"

"He's fine, Eli. He's been fed, he's been changed, and he's been played with. He's worn out and fussy, and he needs a nap. It's not going to hurt him to cry it out."

"He's only nine months old, Roxy."

"That's old enough to start breaking bad habits. Besides, I needed a minute."

"Where's Addison?"

"In her room, I'm assuming."

"Assuming? You mean you don't know?"

I grab the remote, hit the pause button, and flop around to face my husband of nearly eight years. "Where else would she be, Eli? You act like I'm being irresponsible."

He says nothing; rather, he simply lifts a brow.

Suddenly, I'm infuriated. "You know what? Screw you. You're not the one who stays home with the kids every day. You have no idea what's it like to have them crawling all over you, every second of every day, always crying or whining or begging for something. You get to go out into the world. You get to see people over the age of five. You get to hold intelligent conversations with rational people whose favorite response isn't always 'why?' You have moments alone. You have twenty-minute drives home where no one bothers you. You know who *doesn't* have any of that? Me! So, excuse me for trying to take fifteen minutes for my damn self!"

I fling the remote onto the seat of my recliner, stand, and stride toward the door. Eli reaches out and tries to stop me.

"Roxanne, wait. I'm sorry, I—"

I swing around, my eyes blazing. "Just leave me alone." Marching down the hall, I enter our bedroom, and slam the door. Somewhere deep inside my brain the thought that I'm overreacting nags, but I shut it out.

He has no idea, dammit. No fucking clue. He thinks it's so easy to be a stay-at-home parent; that I've got it made not having to work like he does. What I'd give to be able to leave the house for eight hours straight, just once, and not have to worry about changing a dirty diaper, or wheeling and dealing with my overly picky five-year-old just to get her to eat, or doing whatever happens to work on any given day to get both of them to nap at the same damn time.

I pace around the bed, fumes pouring off me. Catching a glimpse of myself in the mirror on the wall, I come to a halt and take a long, hard look at myself. My hair is thrown into a sloppy ponytail; strands have come loose and hang in tangles around my face. Dark circles ring my eyes, and I still have the double-chin caused by the baby weight I put on with Addison over five years ago.

This isn't me.

I'm still two months away from thirty, for chrissakes. I should not look like a forty-six-year old hag. Before I can stop myself, I grab the first thing I see, which happens to be a coffee mug still bearing the dregs of this morning's joe, and fling it as hard as I can against the wall. It shatters with a satisfying crash, and the leftover coffee splatters the wall like a burst paintball.

Suddenly overcome with horror and exhaustion, I collapse into a heap on the floor, tears streaming down my cheeks and sobs ripping from my lungs. Pulling my knees up to my chest, I wrap my arms around them and rock, back and forth, a come-to-life seesaw that has apparently lost its fucking mind.

Eli bursts through the door. "Roxy? Roxy!" He drops to his knees beside me and pulls me close, murmuring words I either can't hear or don't understand. All I comprehend is his arms around me; tossed around in a raging sea, I've been thrown a life jacket, and I latch on to it for dear life.

"I'm sorry. I'm sorry. I'm so sorry. I didn't mean it, Eli. I'm sorry." The sobs come even harder now, as though they're trying to wrench my lungs free. I try to breathe, but the air in the room seems to have evaporated. I bury my head deeper into his chest, which makes no sense given the breathing situation, but I've given up on shit making sense anymore.

"Shh. It's okay, Roxy. I know."

"I'm sorry. I shouldn't have yelled at you, it's not your fault—"

"You don't have to apologize—"

"He was fine, Eli, I swear. I wouldn't have left him alone if I thought he wasn't okay. You have to believe me."

"Roxy. Roxanne. I know. Okay? I know you wouldn't. And he is fine. He's asleep. You were right. He was just tired. I'm sorry. I shouldn't have jumped on you about it."

"I know I'm not the best mom, but—"

"Hey. No. Don't even say it. You're a great mom, Roxy. Our kids couldn't ask for a better one. You hear me?"

When I don't immediately respond, he nudges me. "I'm serious. You hear me, right? You understand what I'm saying to you?"

I nod, but I'm still not convinced. Not completely. I try so hard. I do. And I want to believe I'm a good mother, but so many times—all the time, if I'm being completely honest—I feel like I'm failing my kids. I just don't know what to do about it.

"Good." He leans me back to kiss my forehead, then pulls me close again. "I love you, Roxy."

"I know. I love you, too."

When he releases me to stand, I don't have the strength to support my head; I simply fall forward until I run into my knees. "I … I'm just so exhausted, Eli."

The next thing I know, he's lifted me off the floor and is setting me down on the bed. "I know, sweetheart. Just lay here and rest for a while, okay? I've got the kids."

"Okay. Except, I need to pull something from the freezer. I forgot to do it earlier, and if it's going to have time to thaw …" I glance around, looking for the clock. *1:15*. Shit. At this point, it probably won't. Not if we want to eat at a decent hour.

"Don't worry about it, Roxy. We'll order takeout. You want pizza or Chinese?"

"But—"

"No buts. Just relax, and let me handle things today. Okay? Now, pizza or Chinese?"

"Chinese."

"Orange chicken and crab Rangoon?

"Sounds good."

"Good. Now stretch out, close your eyes, and get some rest."

He pulls the comforter over me, then heads for the door. I can hear Addison calling, and I have to fight the instinct to immediately get up. *Eli says he has things under control. Take the break and say thank you, Roxy.*

So I do. I send a mental note of thanks, then snuggle into the comforter's warmth. Within moments, I'm fast asleep.

***

"That's the best you can do? Six weeks? Yes, I'm sure you have a lot of patients … No, I don't think that, I just … Look, I'm just trying to help my wife, and six weeks is a long time. What? No, she's not suicidal! What do you mean, 'am I sure'? Of course, I'm sure! Because she's my wife. Look, I think I of all people would know if my wife was having suicidal thoughts. What? No, the kids aren't in any danger. What the hell is wrong with you? No, no. I'm sorry. I didn't mean to be profane. It's just … sir, please. I just want to help my wife. She's going through a really tough time, and I think she needs to talk to somebody about it. Yes, I understand that. Yes. Yes. Okay, fine. We'll take the first appointment available. Yes, alright. We will. Thank you."

I hear my husband muttering angrily, and I assume he's ended whatever conversation he was having. I raise my arms over my head to stretch, grimacing as I hear my spine pop, then settle back against the pillows. A moment later, Eli comes through the door, then stops short.

"Oh, you're awake. How are you feeling?"

"A bit groggy, but better, I think. What time is it?

"Just before six."

"Are you serious? Shit, Eli, why didn't you wake me?" I throw the covers back and swing my legs over the side of the bed.

"Hey, Roxy, relax, okay? You obviously needed the rest."

"Yeah, but the kids—"

"Are fine. Addy fell asleep a little after two and slept 'til nearly four. Josiah woke up just after her. They both just finished dinner—he had squash, and I cooked up some mac 'n cheese and green beans for her—and now they're sitting in the play room watching Disney Junior. Addy wanted to color eggs, but I convinced her to wait until tomorrow so Mommy could help out."

"How'd you manage that?"

"I bribed her with an extra dozen eggs and told her I'd see if I could use my powers of persuasion with the Easter Bunny, see if he might come before church instead of after."

"That's quite the deal."

"I thought so."

We both turn our heads when the doorbell rings.

"And that'll be the Chinese. Meet you in the kitchen?"

I just nod and watch him walk out the door. God, I love that man. I don't know what I'd do without him. Standing up, I walk into our adjoining bathroom, splash some cool water on my face, and run a brush through my hair.

When I get to the kitchen, Eli is already unpacking plastic containers and dishing food out onto plates. Trying to sound nonchalant, I bite into a crab Rangoon and shuffle my feet.

"So … who were you on the phone with?"

He glances up at me and winces, then turns back to the food.

"You heard that, huh?"

"Was it Dr. Allen's office?"

"Yeah. Look, Roxy, if you don't want to go, we can cancel the appointment. I just thought it might be good for you to talk to somebody … if you wanted. I mean, if you don't, obviously, I don't want to force you. I mean, I won't force you, you know that. But lately, you've been … well …"

"It's cool, Eli."

"What is?"

"That you called. You're right. I've been …" I gesture, and without words, we both know what I mean. "It's worse than when Addy was born, isn't it?"

The look on his face tells me he doesn't want to agree with me. But there's no point in denying it.

"Yeah. It's worse."

I nod. "Then I'll go see Dr. Allen."

He tries to hide his sigh of relief, and I pretend not to see it. I've obviously been putting him through hell lately, and that's the last thing I want. I've never liked the idea of going to a shrink, but if that's what it takes? I might not do it for myself, but for my husband? My kids?

I can do it for them.

"Oh, I meant to ask you earlier. You were home earlier than you said you'd be. Everything okay?"

"Yeah, everything's fine. A couple of my appointments got rescheduled and I didn't have any laboring moms today, so I came home early. The nurses know to page me if something happens. Guess we got lucky, huh?"

I think of the nearly four-hour nap I just had and smile. *Damn lucky.*

***

The scent of lilies permeates the air as we step into the church, and I have an instant headache. Josiah squirms in my arms, pulling at the tiny, purple bowtie around his neck and fighting to get down. I tighten my grip and grind my jaw. The morning's already been trying, and so far, it's not looking to get any better.

Despite Eli's persuasive powers, the Easter Bunny didn't show before church, and Addison has done nothing but whine and complain and cry about it since she got up. Now, she is pulling at Eli's arm, adorable in a lilac and pink flowered pinafore, already asking if it's time to go home.

It's going to be a long service. *Fuck.*

A stray thought pricks, warning it's probably not the best idea to mentally curse in the house of the Lord, but given how the day's gone so far, I'd like to believe He'll forgive me. That's what He does, right?

Although, I should probably feel sorry for it first.

Whatever. I'm too exhausted to traverse the nuances of theology right now.

We find a seat near the back. Eli turns and engages in conversation with the couple behind us, exchanging "good mornings" and "Happy Easters" and "how 'bout this sixty-degree weathers." I let Josiah's diaper bag slide off my shoulder and nudge it beneath the pew in front of us, then set him next to me. Immediately, he tries to climb down. And by "climb" I mean he leans forward into a headfirst dive toward the floor. I grab him and pull him back, only to be rewarded with a scrunched-up face, accompanied by a shrill scream.

"Josiah, hush." I glance around, praying I don't meet any judgmental eyes. The service hasn't started yet, of course, but the organist has started to play and Pastor Dunst is hovering near the front of the nave, checking his watch and fussing with his stole. I reach into the diaper bag, pull out one Josiah's teething rings, and offer it to him. He promptly grabs it and throws it on the floor, all the while continuing to scream. He's thrashing now, too.

I grit my teeth and fight the urge to scream myself. Before I can say another word, Eli reaches over and picks the baby up, bouncing him on his knee. Josiah instantly calms, clapping and giggling. *Traitor.*

I grab my bulletin and have barely opened it when Addison tugs at my skirt. "Mommy, I'm hungry."

I close my eyes and suck in a breath. After a short second, I open them and try to reason with my five-year-old. "You just had breakfast, Addy."

"But I'm starving!"

"You had five pancakes." I don't even try to keep the exasperation out of my voice.

"I know. Can I have a snack, though? Please?"

"Addison, you don't need anything else right now."

"But I'm hungry."

"Well, you'll just have to be hungry until church is over and it's time for lunch."

"But Mommy—"

"No, Addison."

Her lower lip slides out into a picture-perfect pout and her eyes well up with tears.

"Don't even start, young lady. Do you hear me? Or I'll take you out of here and give you something to cry about."

With a huff, she sits in the pew and crosses her arms. Shaking my head, I go back to the bulletin. Moments later, the bell tolls. Eli turns, Josiah in arm, and reaches for a hymnal. I pull one free myself and turn to "I Know My Redeemer Lives."

For the next fifteen minutes or so, I'm able to lose myself in the beauty of the service, despite the lily-induced headache. The hymns are uplifting, the liturgy familiar, the Bible readings no less beautiful and moving for having been heard time and again. By the time Pastor Dunst steps into the lectern to begin his sermon, I'm feeling almost light, and the closest to content I've been in a very long time.

"Mommy, I have to go potty."

The moment shatters, a gorgeous stain-glassed image now nothing more than shards of colored glass.

"So, go to the bathroom, Addison. You know where it is."

"But I want you to come with me."

I lean down, trying to keep my voice low. "Addison, you don't need me to come with you. You're perfectly capable of going to the bathroom by yourself. Just make sure you wash your hands and come straight back here when you're done, okay?"

"No, Mommy. I need you to come with me!" Her voice raises nearly two octaves on the "eee" of me. I shut my eyes and inhale deeply, fighting for composure.

"Roxy." Eli whispers to me over Addison's head. "Just take her to the bathroom." I meet his gaze as he cocks his head, raises his eyebrows, and minutely gestures with his head toward the front of the church. Seriously? Censure? Coming from him? Why can't he take her to the bathroom? Why do *I* have to miss the sermon?

I know the answer, of course. She's a girl, so I should take her; let's ignore the fact that it's a single, family bathroom. Moms take daughters, dads take sons. It's just the way it is, and who cares how fucked up it might be.

I bite my tongue, rise as inconspicuously as possible, and take my daughter by the hand. I spend the next ten minutes standing outside the door—because she wants me with her, but God forbid I actually *watch* her—waiting for her to poop, which she swears she has to do.

Finally, she comes out.

"Did you flush?"

"I didn't go."

"Excuse me? Addison, you said you had to go to the bathroom."

"I know. I thought I had to, Mommy, but I guess I didn't."

A picture of my hands around her throat flashes through my mind for the barest of split seconds before it passes, and I mentally shake myself. *She's five, Roxy. She's only five.* As every other parent has ever told me, better safe than sorry. I'd rather waste the ten minutes than have to clean up an accident in front of everyone.

We've barely made it back to the pew and sat back down when Eli's pager goes off. I look at him and raise my eyebrows as if to say, *"Really? Now?"* He can't help it, of course, and I know that, but seriously? Easter morning?

He ducks his head, climbs over me while simultaneously passing me Josiah, and heads for the back. Pastor Dunst has finished his sermon by this point, and the organist begins to play while a number of elders send fake gold-plated plates up and down the packed aisles to collect the offering.

A moment later, Eli returns, leans down, and whispers in my ear.

"I have to go."

I look up at him, my eyes wide with shock. "Are you kidding me?"

"No. Roxy, I'm so sorry. Amy Sharpe went into pre-term labor. Doctor Varrow says her placenta is ripping away from the uterine wall, and she needs emergency surgery. They're prepping her now."

"But what about the kids? It's Easter. What about—" I glance surreptitiously at Addison, who luckily isn't paying much attention, then turn back. "—Addy's basket?"

"Go ahead and let her have it. Don't change the plans just because of me. I'm not sure how long I'll be, and I want the kids to enjoy the day."

"What about me?" The petty question is out before I can stop it.

He purses his lips, and his eyes narrow. "Don't be like that, Roxy. Of course, I want you to enjoy the day, too. And you know I want to be there with you. I can't help the timing, and you know I have to go. It's my job."

I feel about two feet tall, and yet I still feel somewhat justified in my frustration. Unfortunately, Eli will only find one of those reactions acceptable.

"I know, Eli. I'm sorry. I just ..."

"I know. And I'm sorry, too." He leans in and kisses me lightly on the lips. "I love you, and I'll be home as soon as I possibly can."

I nod, then watch as he races out the back door.

"Where's Daddy going?"

"He has to go to the hospital, Addy."

"But it's Easter."

"I know. But one of his mommies is having a baby, so he has to go."

"But it's Easter."

Amusement wars with frustration. Oh, to once again have the logic of a child. "Yes, baby, I know. But mommies sometimes have babies on Easter. Just like Christmas."

She considers this for a moment. "Like me?"

"Yes, sweetie, just like you."

"So, you mean a doctor like Daddy had to be there when I was borned on Christmas?"

"Yes, Addy. And it's 'born,' not 'borned.'"

"Born on Christmas."

"Right."

"Did that daddy have kids like you and Daddy have me and Josiah?"

"He might have."

"And he had to leave them on Christmas. Just like Daddy's leaving us on Easter."

"Yes. Exactly."

She sits for a moment, lost in her own little world while the elders take the offering up front and Pastor Dunst begins the prayers. He's just finished when she tugs on my skirt again.

"Mommy?"

"What, Addy?"

"I guess it's okay Daddy has to go to work on Easter."

My heart swells with pride, and I lean down and hug her as close as I can while still holding Josiah.

"I love you, Addison."

She may drive me nuts the majority of the time, but it's worth every second for moments like this. She's smart as a whip and has a huge heart, and I love her for it.

I promptly forget that ten minutes later when, at the altar for communion, she reaches out for a small cup of wine—which she damn well knows she's not supposed to do—catches the elder off-guard, and causes him to drop the entire tray of wine.

Chaos ensues as glass shatters and spilled wine goes everywhere. My cheeks burn so hot, for a moment I have an irrational fear I'll actually catch fire. It passes quickly, and I drag Addy away as quickly as I can. Getting back to the pew, I pack up the diaper bag, tossing things in haphazardly, and with Josiah in one arm and Addy's hand in the other, I march out the back, exceedingly aware of dozens of pairs of eyes watching me go.

The ride home goes something like this: I scream at Addy for misbehaving. She starts crying because I yelled at her. Josiah starts crying because Addison is crying. I shout at them both to stop crying. Addy cries even louder. Josiah tries to top her. I briefly consider running the SUV into a telephone poll. Or off a bridge. That is, if there was a bridge in town. I turn the radio up. They pull an NPH—as in, challenge accepted. I scream at them to shut up.

Two minutes before pulling up to the house, they do. Because they're both asleep. Which means I now have to wake both of them up.

Putting the vehicle in park, I lean forward and bang my forehead against the steering wheel hard enough to have tears smarting in my eyes. *Dammit.*

Getting out of the car, I pull the back door open and nudge Addison awake. Immediately she starts to fuss. "I don't want to get out of the car. I'm tired."

"I know, sweetie. But we're home. We have to get out."

"I don't want to!"

"Do you want to go see if the Easter Bunny made it?"

She barely perks up at this, but the question does get a grudging "I guess." She unbuckles her seatbelt, slides off the seat, and drags her feet all the way into the house.

As soon as I jostle Josiah, he wakes up, and true to form, begins to cry. I settle him on my shoulder, bouncing and shooshing him. It does no good. By the time I reach the door, his half-hearted cries have turned into full-blown shrieks.

The horrible, exhausted part of me is tempted to set him on the floor, run into my bedroom, and lock the door. But of course, I can't do that, much as I might like to. Good mothers don't leave their children unobserved. I think about the other day, when Eli found me watching TV while Josiah cried. *They don't do it much, anyway.*

Setting the baby on his playmat, I head for the kitchen. Addy finds me there, preparing a bottle.

"Mommy, the Easter Bunny hasn't been here!"

"Give me just a second, Addy. Let me take care of your brother, and then we'll—"

"Daddy said he would come while we were at church. He promised. Daddy's a liar!"

"Addison Marie!"

I turn around and smack her lips. "You do not talk like that! Do you understand me? I will not tolerate it. I know what your Daddy said, and I am telling you, I need to take care of your brother, and then we'll figure it out. Got it?"

She doesn't say anything, just begins to sob.

"Knock it off. I didn't hit you that hard. I can give you something to cry about if you want."

"No!"

"All right then. Now, go into your room and I'll come get you in a few minutes."

She turns and heads out of the room, and I could almost swear I hear her murmur "I hate you" under her breath. But we don't use the word 'hate' in our house, so how would she know to say it? More likely, I'm channeling my own inner dialogue.

You shouldn't have hit her, Roxy. Bull. She shouldn't have talked to me like that. Calling her father a liar. That shit's not acceptable. *She's only five.* That's old enough. *She's tired, and probably missing Eli, and disappointed. It's normal.* I don't care.

Part of me is tempted to not give her the Easter basket Eli and I put together. Then again, that's probably just a bit harsh. Overkill. I smacked her, and that got her attention. It's enough.

Walking back into the living room, I lay Josiah flat and hand him his bottle. He pushes it away and continues to cry.

My headache is back in full force now, pain pulsing behind my eyes like the thumping bass in any run-of-the-mill nightclub. I fist my hands in my hair and pull, fighting the urge to scream. Inhaling deeply, I pick him up, settle him on my shoulder, and begin to sing.

It takes two and a half times through Phil Collins' "You'll Be In My Heart" from *Tarzan*, but he finally calms down.

"Good. Okay. Will you sit for a minute now, while I take care of your sister? Huh?" Josiah gurgles and giggles at me, lightly smacking my face. "Crazy child."

I bend over and set him on the floor. As soon as his butt hits the carpet, his face wrinkles and he hollers. I groan as I grab his stuffed bear from the couch and lay it next to him.

"Sorry, buddy, you're just gonna have to deal with it for a minute." Leaving him where he is, I head down the hallway toward Addison's room. I've gone two steps when she bursts out the door of my bedroom.

"Mommy, he came! The Easter Bunny came! Do you know where he left my basket? In your room, Mommy! It was just sitting there on your bed. He didn't do a very good job of hiding it. I mean, I barely had to look for it. Why did he put it in your room, Mommy? That's kind of silly, isn't it?"

In her hands is a bright pink basket, overflowing with springtime toys and Easter candy. My heart pounds and I feel my cheeks warming.

"Addison, what were you doing in my room?"

The tone of my voice obviously clues her in that something is amiss. She hesitates, shuffles her feet, and then says, "I was looking for you, Mommy."

"Were you supposed to be looking for me?"

"No."

"Where were you supposed to be?"

"In my room?"

"So why weren't you in your room?"

"I … I don't know."

"Didn't I tell you go to your room?"

"Yes."

"So why didn't you go to your room?!"

"I'm sorry, Mommy! I'm sorry!"

What started as a fairly calm conversation has led to me yelling at the top of my lungs and my daughter crying. Again.

Fuck.

Exhaustion washes over me. I'm too tired to fight with them anymore.

"Just take it into the living room, Addy."

"I can keep it?"

"Go, before I change my mind."

"Okay."

She tiptoes past me, then races into the living room, hollering over her shoulder. "Mommy, Josie's crying!"

I'm aware. And damn, I wish you wouldn't call him "Josie." I hate that nickname!

With slow deliberation, I turn and walk back into the living room. Addison is on the floor a few feet from Josiah, ripping through the Easter basket, throwing things every which way.

"Addison, honey, please try not to make a mess."

"Yes, Mommy." She doesn't look up. A jump rope flies past, followed by a butterfly-shaped container of bubbles.

"Addison. Quit throwing everything everywhere, or I'm going to take it away. Do you hear me?"

She looks up at me, her head ducked in what she hopes is chagrin, and very carefully places a bag of pastel M&Ms next to her lap.

Grabbing the remote, I flip the TV on and pull up Netflix.

"Can we watch *Daniel Tiger*, Mommy?"

"No, Addison. I'm turning on something for me."

"Aww ..."

I shoot her a glare as I flop into my recliner, and she immediately quiets, returning her attention to her basket. I'm two minutes into *Easter Parade* when I hear Addy yell.

"Josie, no! Stop it! Give me that!"

I turn in time to see her swipe a glow stick from Josiah's hands. A full second doesn't pass before he shrieks in anger.

"Addy!"

"Sorry, Mommy, but it's not his, it's mine."

"That doesn't matter, Addison. You don't need to be mean."

"Waaaaahhhhh!"

"Oh, Josiah, stop it."

"I didn't mean to be mean, Mommy. I just don't want him messing with my Easter stuff. He'll ruin it."

"Aaaaaahhhhhh!"

"He won't ruin it, Addison."

"But—"

"Waaaaahhhh!"

"Oh, good Lord, Josiah, shut up!"

I pull him roughly into my arms and bring his face to mine. "Just stop it, okay?" A stunned silence falls as both my children stare in response to my outburst.

"Mommy, you said …"

"Yes, Addison. I know what I said."

"But Daddy says we're not supposed to say …"

"I know, Addy. Just finish going through your basket, okay?"

She turns back to the array of goodies in front of her, remaining silent. Josiah leans sharply to the left, reaching for something on the end table beside my chair.

"No, Josiah." I hand him one of the numerous infant toys littered throughout the house. He promptly throws it on the floor, then leans toward the end table again.

"No!"

"I think he wants the jellybeans, Mommy."

"Well, he can't have the jellybeans."

"But maybe he likes them."

"He's too little for them, Addison. No, Josiah!"

I slap his hand, and again hand him a toy. He flings it across the room and screams. The toy hits a beer bottle Eli has left on the coffee table. The bottle topples, and stale beer spills out over the carpet.

"Dammit!"

I jump up, plop Josiah into the chair, and run for a towel. Racing back into the room, I sop up the spill. The bottle has rolled beneath the table, so I lean down to grab it. Coming back up, I knock my head on the table's edge.

"Shit!"

"No, Josiah! Stop it!"

He's slid off the chair, crawled across the floor, and is grabbing Addison's basket again. "Mommy, make him stop!"

"Dammit, Josiah!"

Letting the towel fall in a wet heap, I lean down to grab him and fight a wave of dizziness. I return him to the chair, then reach for the towel.

Crash!

Josiah is on his feet, one hand braced on the arm of the recliner, the other stretched out toward the bowl of jellybeans. *Eli and his damn jellybeans. Why couldn't he just leave them in the bag?*

The lamp, only moments ago on the end table, is now on the floor, the lightbulb shattered.

Suddenly, I can't do it anymore. I'm done.

"Fine. You want the fucking jellybeans? Have the fucking jellybeans!" I grab Josiah, plunk him on the floor, and set the dish of candy next to him. Then I head for the hallway. I stalk into my room, fling myself onto the bed, and stare at the ceiling.

My mind is a swirling twister of blankness. Nothing registers. Nothing matters anymore. I just lay there, unable—or maybe unwilling—to move.

Time passes. Hours … Minutes … I don't know. A portion of my mind seems to break free, and I can see myself stretched out across the bed, my eyes wide yet unseeing.

That small part of me hears Josiah coughing. It's a wheezing, wracking cough, almost as if he's struggling for breath.

You need to check on him, Roxy.

I can't.

Moments later, my bedroom door squeaks. The detached part of me watches Addison rush in, terror shining in her blue eyes, worry radiating from her waif-like body.

"Mommy, something's wrong with Josie!"

The coughing has stopped.

"Mommy, Josie's face is blue!"

I don't answer.

"Mommy! Get up!"

She grabs my arm with her small hands and shakes. I watch from above as she tries desperately to get me to respond.

Roxy, he's choking!

"Mommy, Josie needs help!"

Roxy, get up!

"MOMMY!"

Tears are streaming down Addison's face as she continues to shake me, her fingernails digging deep and leaving tiny crescent moons indented in my skin.

I don't move.

"Josie! Josie, wake up! Wake up!"

Addison has left the room, leaving me alone.

Yes. Leave me alone. I just need a fucking minute alone.

"Um ... My little brother needs help. I ... I don't know. He tried to eat a jellybean. He's little ... Um ... ten months. I think. No, nine. He's at work. He's helping a mommy have her baby. She's on the bed. She won't get up. I tried to get her up, but she won't. Please, my brother needs help. I don't know the address ... I'm sorry. Please don't be mad at me. Okay. No. No, I won't hang up the phone. Thank you."

She's such a big girl. My big baby girl. But she's still crying. I wish she would stop crying. I hate to hear my babies cry.

Sirens blare and a moment later, there's a knock on the door. I hear Addison open it.

Dammit, Addy. You're not supposed to open the door for strangers.

The sound of hurried activity comes from the other room.

"You did a good job, Addison. Where's your mommy?"

"Asphyxiation."

"One, two, three four." Pause. "One, two, three, four."

"He's gone."

The click of a door.

"What the hell's going on?"

"Sir, do you live here?"

"Yes. What's happening? Oh, God. Josiah? What happened to my son? Addy! Where's Addy?"

"Sir, please, I need you to calm down."

"I tried to get her up, Daddy. I told her Josie needed help. But she wouldn't come."

"Where is Mommy?"

"She's lying in bed."

"Sir, I need you to wait. Sir!"

I hear his pounding feet. "Roxy?"

I manage to turn my head, my eyes fixed on the door as it swings open. "Roxy."

The truth shines in my tear-sheened gaze as it meets his, and his knees give out. I hear the thud as they hit the floor, followed by a single word. It's my damnation.

"Roxanne."

The End

MIA'S EASTER BASKET

Mark Lukens

Mia hurried downstairs to the front door. The doorbell hadn't rung, no one had knocked, but she knew the Easter basket, with the package inside, would be waiting out there for her; just like it had the last three years on Easter morning.

She held the hem of her robe up a little as she shuffled quickly down the steps, trying to be as quiet as possible; she didn't want her seven-year-old daughter to wake up and see her with the Easter basket in her hand when she brought it inside—she didn't want Amy to ask why she had it, or ask what was inside.

The air was chilly as Mia stepped out onto her front porch. The sun was just peeking over the horizon, and her neighborhood street was still dark and quiet.

And there it was—just like she knew it would be: an Easter basket with one single object nestled down among the fake green grass. She was frightened to see it, yet she was sure she would have been much more frightened if it hadn't been there.

How many more Easter baskets would there be? How many more years would this go on?

Mia picked the basket up from the porch and hurried inside. She locked the door and glanced up the stairs to make sure Amy wasn't there, at the top, watching her.

She brought the basket into the kitchen and sat it down on a chair at the small kitchen table. She put some coffee on—she needed some coffee. She'd been awake most of the night, anticipating this morning, falling asleep a few hours ago only to be jolted awake by her alarm clock.

The coffee machine chugged to life, making loud gasps and sighs as the steaming liquid slowly filled the pot. Mia walked over to the Easter basket and stared down at the one plastic Easter egg inside—a pink one. Nothing else among the fake grass. No note. There was never a note.

She already knew what was inside the plastic egg.

Mia thought of her husband, Jerry. He'd been gone now almost five years.

They used to fight, a lot. Well, Jerry did all of the fighting. They had gotten along so well when they were first together, but after they were married, Jerry turned violent. First it was verbal abuse, then a few shoves and slaps. And then it got worse. Much worse. Even after Amy came along, Jerry didn't stop.

"You ever leave me and I'll kill you." Jerry's words echoed in her mind. "I'll hunt you down and find you. Then I'll kill you. And Amy, too. You hear me? I'll kill both of you."

Mia was trapped, living a lie, living in fear while everyone thought she had a great marriage. Of course Jerry controlled how much contact she had with people, especially her family.

Five years ago today, on Easter Sunday, it had gotten so bad Mia wondered if she wouldn't be better off dead. They had gone to her parents' house for a rare visit and Jerry believed that she had said something to her mother... some kind of secret plea for help. She'd said nothing to her mother—it was only his paranoid delusion. And it was just another excuse for Jerry to hit her, to hurt her.

They had stopped at a convenience store on the way home, so Jerry could get some beer (more fuel for the fires of his rage). Amy was only two years old then, crying in her car seat in the back because Jerry was yelling at Mia, smacking and punching her, as they sat in a parking space at the far end of the convenience store parking lot.

Mia was crying and cowering against the passenger door when Jerry got out and went into the store. She turned around and tried to get Amy to stop bawling.

A knock at her passenger window startled her. She turned to see an old man standing there in the fading light, the sun down behind the trees now. He was smiling and he had the kindest eyes that were full of concern. He made a roll-the-window-down gesture. The car was still running (Jerry knew she would never have the guts to drive away while he was in the store—it was like one of his tests) and she pushed the button to roll down the window.

"You okay, ma'am?"

Mia just nodded, wiping at her nose with a wadded-up tissue. The left side of her face was burning from Jerry's slap; there would probably be a bruise there tomorrow.

"I saw what happened," the old man said. "Do you need me to call the police for you?"

Mia's heart jumped in horror. "No. Please. I'm okay. Really."

She glanced at the store. She could see the checkout counter through the plate-glass windows, but Jerry wasn't there—yet.

Mia looked back at the old man, wishing he would go away before Jerry came back out and went ballistic. "Please," she croaked and managed a smile. "I'm fine."

She was ready to roll up the window on the old man, but there was something steely in his light blue eyes, something that held her there, almost hypnotizing her.

The old man glanced into the back seat at Amy, breaking into a wide smile. God, she wished Jerry smiled at Amy like that. "Hi, there," the old man said in a slightly higher voice—little kid talk—and he gave Amy a little wave of his fingers. His eyes darted back to Mia. "What's her name?"

"Amy."

Amazingly, Amy had stopped crying; it was as if she was fascinated by this old man, perhaps soothed by his voice and his smile.

Mia looked at the store again. Jerry was checking out now, a twelve-pack of Budweiser on the counter in front of him. He seemed like he was laughing, joking around with the cashier—a young female cashier.

"You know eventually he'll start hurting Amy, too," the old man said in his soft voice.

Mia looked back at the old man. His smile had slipped away. He had crouched down beside the car to get eye-level with her.

"Please. You need to go." She glanced back at the store windows. Jerry was still flirting with the cashier as she handed him his change and he grabbed the twelve pack of beer. And now he was coming this way.

"He won't stop hurting you," the old man said. "It will only get worse."

But it had already gotten worse. She had the scars on her body to prove it.

"Please, you need to go," she said again, a trembling finger resting on the button to roll the window back up.

"I can help you," he said, his words barely a whisper, yet they were so clear in her ears. He had produced a white business card with a shifting of his fingers, like a magician performing a trick. He dropped the business card into the car before she could get the window rolled all the way up.

Jerry was coming. Mia kept her eyes on him, while she slipped the business card into her purse before he saw her.

But Jerry wasn't watching her—his eyes were on the old man: a new target.

"Hey, buddy!" Jerry shouted at the old man. "You got a problem?"

The old man just stood there, near the sidewalk, in front of the store. He looked a little taller to Mia now, a little broader in the shoulders, a little more formidable.

"Get the hell away from my car!" Jerry yelled and Mia thought he was going to go after the old man, maybe attack him, or at least threaten him.

But he didn't.

The old man just smiled at Jerry, an enigmatic little grin, a secretive smile. He made a gun with his forefinger and thumb, and Mia read the word on his lips: "Pow." And then he walked away.

"Crazy old kook," Jerry said, as he got in the car. "Must've let him out of the loony bin a little too early."

Mia didn't say anything. She watched the old man walk away into the dusk.

"Was he bothering you?" Jerry asked. "Begging for money or something?"

"No," Mia whispered.

"I see you finally got Amy to shut up," Jerry grumbled, as he backed out of the parking space.

A week later, Jerry had unleashed one of his worst beatings, so far. Mia was afraid she had a cracked rib or two; or maybe an organ was punctured. There was a sharp pain in her side every time she took a deep breath.

He had burned her, too. He liked to burn her. He would use cigarettes, an iron, a hot frying pan, whatever was handy. He liked to burn her in places that she could hide with clothes.

It's only going to get worse. The old man's words echoed in her mind. Soon, Jerry was going to kill her, and then, he would be alone with Amy. She couldn't let that happen.

After Jerry went to work the next morning, Mia got the white business card out of her purse. The only thing on the card was a phone number.

The old man answered on the third ring.

"Hi, this is Mia. We met at a convenience store parking lot —"

"I remember you, Mia."

"You … you said you could help me."

"I can. And actually, you'd be helping me, too."

"How?" Mia asked, and then she couldn't help it—she broke down in tears, everything gushing out of her.

The old man waited patiently for Mia to stop crying. "I'll explain everything when we meet."

Mia met the old man at a park. They sat on one of the farthest benches, near the woods. Maybe it was dangerous, meeting a stranger in a remote location, but it would be even more dangerous if Jerry found out she was with some "guy" while he was at work.

The old man stared at her with his light blue eyes, such kind eyes. He looked like he was in his early sixties. Tall and thin, but he looked strong, somehow. A wave of tranquility seemed to emanate from him like heat from a radiator, soothing her jitters.

"I can make your problem go away," he told her.

"What do you mean?" But she was pretty sure she knew what he meant.

"You don't need to know the details. Sometime in the next few days, Jerry will just be gone. You don't need to know anything about it. The less you know, the better."

Mia wanted to think about it, but every time she took a breath, that sharp pain shot through her like a hot, twisted piece of sharp metal. The area where Jerry had burned her throbbed. Pretty soon, she would be nothing but scars and injuries—if she even lived that long. And she had to think about Amy.

This was for Amy.

"Okay," Mia said.

The old man smiled. "You're making the right choice. Every year, around this time, at Easter, I'll send you something to let you know that your husband will never hurt you again."

"Can I ask your name?"

"Just call me Peter."

And now, as Mia cradled a cup of coffee in her hands, she stared down at the Easter basket. She didn't want to open the pink plastic egg, but she knew she would have to.

She sat the cup of coffee down, and pulled out a pair of latex gloves from a box in the pantry. She had learned not to open the egg with her bare hands.

Inside the egg were two human ears, crusted with blood ... Jerry's ears.

Last year, it had been all of his front teeth and his tongue.

The year before that: several of his fingers and both of his thumbs.

The first year: some of his toes crammed inside the plastic egg like little sausages.

She closed the egg back up. She would have to bury it somewhere in the backyard. Bury it down deep. It's what she'd done with the other ones.

Mia could only imagine where Jerry was: caged or chained up in some dark place, kept alive by Peter, year after year, so he could slice off pieces of his body and send them to her every Easter.

"You said I would be helping you, too," Mia had asked Peter, during their meeting at the park that day. "How will I be helping you?"

Peter smiled at her, that kind smile that crinkled up the wrinkles around his eyes. "I used to be a doctor. I'd always wondered certain things about the human body ... and the mind. Thresholds. There were experiments I'd always wanted to perform, but they would be ... well, let's just say unethical, at the very least. You'll be providing me with someone to play with."

Play with. That was exactly how he had worded it.

Mia wondered what would happen once Peter was done "playing" with Jerry. Would Peter come after her? She had moved twice, but Peter had always found her—the Easter baskets were there every Easter morning, at her front door. She wondered if these plastic Easter eggs were a reminder of their agreement, a reminder that he would always know where she was and how to get to her.

The End

HE HAS RISEN

C.S. Anderson

Norman woke up handcuffed to a corpse.

Not the best way to start one's day.

His mouth felt dry and tasted like a sweaty construction worker had taken a dump in it, and his head was pounding like the clichéd, big bass drum. A hangover was just the universe's way to remind you that you are still alive.

And sometimes, that particular state of being kind of sucks.

"Do you remember what happened?" A voice asks gently from the shadows, the voice is empty and neutral. Whoever is asking the question already knows the answer and really doesn't care about the response that they get.

Norman wasn't all that sure that he did; he hadn't been a drinker before the zombie apocalypse hit, but in the last few months he had to admit that he had been hitting the booze pretty damn hard. Every time they went on a supply run, he was always on the lookout for stray bottles that he could snag. Yesterday he had found some tequila. He had meant to wait to start drinking it until he was off duty and back in his quarters. But he had talked himself into one small drink, followed by another and then one thing had just sort of led to another.

Like it tended to do.

He had been guarding a gate on the south end of camp, he remembered that much anyway. The bottle had been in his backpack; it was almost like it had been calling to him all morning. He had ignored that call for what had seemed like an eternity, holding his shotgun and dutifully scanning the terrain outside of the camp for any threat, be it zombies or raiders. He had ignored that call with what had felt like heroic resolve, all the way up to the point that he had given in and treated himself to what he had promised himself would be, just one quick drink.

Obviously, that promise, like so many others, both to himself and to others, had been a damn lie.

He recognized the voice; it belonged to the camp chaplain. Not that he had spent much time in the chapel, but the camp wasn't really that big. Sooner or later you met everybody.

"Father Gibbons? Is that you? I am sorry if I passed out on duty...again." Norman stammered as he tried to sit up on the bed.

He found that he couldn't. The wrist that wasn't handcuffed to the dead man lying next to him, was zip-tied to the bed frame of the infirmary bed he was on.

Shit, that couldn't mean anything good.

His mind whirled, trying to piece things together. He had started drinking, putting his shotgun down and sitting with his back against the guard shack, so that he was still able to scan the area, still doing his duty to the camp by standing guard. Hell, nobody had seen any zombies in over two weeks; it was ok to relax a little now and then.

Obviously something had happened,

They found me passed out on duty again, he told himself, that's all. It had happened before after all. The Commander had taken him out behind the meal hall and kicked his ass last time. Kicked his ass good and proper, and threatened him with worse if it happened again.

Apparently, it had happened again.

He was handcuffed to a dead guy; they were trying to scare him and yeah, it was working all right. Taking a deep breath, he told himself to calm down.

The priest stepped out of the shadows and stood over him... looking down at him with a sad but determined look on his face. He was holding an empty bottle in one hand.

"What the hell, Father? What's going on? Get me off this damn corpse!" Norman shouted up at him.

"That damn corpse was a living, breathing guard, who was killed trying to protect children from the zombies that got past your guard post while you were passed out in a pool of your own vomit." The priest told him this with a harsh edge to his voice as he shook the empty tequila bottle at him

Norman got a sick twisting in his gut, and as the priest's words began to sink in, he broke out in a cold sweat and started trembling a little.

"We scrounged some eggs and Sheri Anne mashed up some berries she picked to make a dye for them. She hid them all over the little field on the south-end of the camp, so that the children could have fun finding them. Just a little piece of normalcy from the old days, Norman. You no doubt went on Easter egg hunts yourself, when you were a boy. Back before the world began ending. Back before this terrible judgement came down on us all." The priest's voice was back to calm now, the harsh tone gone from it.

Norman closed his eyes, knowing that he had fucked up beyond any hope of forgiveness this time. If children had died because of his passing out at his duty post, the camp would exile his ass for sure. The Commander would do it without blinking an eye; he told him as much after the beating he had given him last time. That was a death sentence; he wouldn't last two days outside of the camp on his own. Loners who lived outside of camps had short, terrifyingly miserable lives. The only hope of staying alive was to join up with a camp.

If they tossed him out he would die, or even worse, he would die and turn into one of the damn zombies. It was the worst, most primal fear that he had: the fear that fuelled the drinking. Coming back as one of the rotting, mindless, shambling corpses, he had bloody nightmares about it sometimes.

"Please, Father, don't let them exile me! Please! I am begging you! I will never drink again, I promise you, please for the love of God, Father, don't let them exile me! I swear to God, Father, please help me!" He pleaded desperately with the camp chaplain. He hated hearing the pathetic whining sound of his own voice, but he had given up his pride about the same time as he had picked up the bottle.

The priest turned his back on him and didn't speak for a few moments. When he broke the silence, pain and grief colored his voice.

"Everyone was watching the children giggle and run around the field looking for the eggs. In the old days I never approved of such things, the whole Easter egg thing has always seemed a little too pagan to me. But you should have seen the joy on their little faces...until that joy was replaced by terror. Sheri Anne, did you know her? That brave woman covered a child with her own body, Norman. She lay down on top of the wee thing and tried to protect her. The zombies tore her to shreds and then tore the child to shreds. The guard, a recent recruit you probably hadn't even met yet, his name was Gibbitt, fired his gun until it ran empty and then he tried to hold off the zombies with a stick. With a stick, you cowardly piece of shit, with a damn stick! He got his throat torn out for his courage," continued the priest in the same strained tone.

Norman let out a low moan and started trying to free his hand from the zip tie holding him to the bed. It was no use however, they had attached it and had tightened it to the point where it was almost cutting off his circulation.

"Father, please talk to the Commander. He listens to you. Please, I am begging you, don't let him exile me! Talk to him, please! I beg of you please!" Norman sobbed as he jerked at his bonds.

The priest stared down at him for a long moment and in that gaze Norman saw no forgiveness, no mercy, no pity, no emotion of any kind.

"Five children are dead, Norman. Five precious souls that were our symbols of hope in this dying world. Five innocent children who paid with their fear, pain and blood for your weakness. They paid with their lives, Norman, as did Sheri Anne and Gibbitt here. The Commander himself gave the children the mercy of a shot to the head so that they wouldn't turn. I am surprised, honestly, that he didn't simply shoot you where you lay, soaked in your own vomit and piss. I stood there and waited for him to end your pathetic life. I would have done it, if I was him, Norman. Just to be clear, I would have cheerfully shot you in the head, then and there, and been done with it. But not the Commander. He said that he wasn't an executioner, and that a vote would be taken to decide your fate." The priest continued, his voice shifting now to a flat, empty tone as he tossed the empty bottle into a trash bin.

Norman twisted his head to stare at the dead guard that he was handcuffed to. Like the priest had said, most of the poor bastard's throat was gone. He closed his eyes and let out a shuddering breath.

"The camp voted to exile you, Norman. Overwhelmingly, they voted to give you a gun and a knife, and some basic supplies, and send you out into the wastelands. I prayed on it, and found that I couldn't live with that verdict. I prayed on it, and found that exile didn't square with what you let happened to those beautiful children. If you leave here as an exile, I will be denied the satisfaction of knowing what will happen to you. Exile means that I will be forced to miss your suffering. I have a different fate in mind for you my son, a different sort of penance. A little harsher than three Hail Marys or ten Heavenly Fathers, I fear." The Priest told him as he drew out a small chrome plated revolver.

The sound of the hammer being cocked was the single loudest thing that Norman had ever heard.

"Jesus Father, don't shoot me!" Norman screamed. He kicked his legs violently, but the priest was well out of reach.

"I won't, you snivelling little worm; well, at least not quite yet. I was supposed to shoot poor Gibbitt here, to give him mercy before he turned. Tell me, Norman, how long does it take for someone to turn after they have been bitten?" the priest calmly asked him, while taking a couple of extra steps away from the bed.

Norman looked at him as a gut-wrenching dread began to spread through him. The virus had been named 'Sundowners', because once bitten, you only had until sundown before you turned. Nobody had ever figured out how or why, but it was as regular as clock work. ,If bitten, you died and turned at sundown, whether that was ten minutes or twelve hours away.

Which led to a terrible question; namely, what time was it getting to be?

He looked out the window and saw that the sun was slowly beginning to set in the West. Turning his head again, he stared at the dead man's forehead which didn't have any bullet holes in it.

What that meant, sunk in almost immediately.

"Father, no!" he pleaded in a hushed, sick voice as, what the priest meant to do dawned on him. He began struggling with the zip tie again, desperately, even though he knew, that even if he managed to free that hand, he would still be handcuffed to the dead guard.

"I am going to leave you to your fate now, with a quote from a bible verse, Norman. It is Mathews 28:6," the priest told him grimly, the pistol pointed down at the floor.

Confusion showed on Norman's face. He had no idea what bible verse that would be. Even when he had been sober, he had never been a regular church goer.

Next to him, the torn-up guard began to twitch slightly, and a long low moan that slowly turned into more of a hungry growl, began to hiss out of the dead mouth.

"You should have attended a service or two; it may have saved even a weak sinner such as yourself. Mathews 28:6...He has risen." The priest told him, his voice shaking just a little, as he pointed a finger at the dead guard.

Norman began screaming as the zombie lurched into undead life and sunk its teeth into his shoulder. Blood sprayed against the window as the sun finished setting.

The Commander stood outside of the infirmary smoking a stale cigarette- his last one. He threw the empty pack onto the ground by his feet. The screaming went on for a little while, and then was followed by two gunshots. He had gotten here in time to intervene; he had listened to every word, telling himself that he would step in, before sundown came. Telling himself that he would end it, before it was too late.

He had surprised himself by choosing not to.

Sighing, he rubbed a weathered hand across his tired face. The priest had surprised him as well with this little mutiny. Every man had his breaking point and the slaughter of the children had apparently been the priest's. There had been old rage simmering in the chaplain's voice as he had talked to his prisoner. Lord knew how many other children the man had seen die, before he joined the camp as chaplain; or what other horrors he had witnessed, to make what he had just done to Norman seem like justice.

Hell, in this new dark and terrible world, maybe it even was justice. Who the hell was he to judge?

He crossed himself, said a quick prayer, then tossed the cigarette away and walked off into the darkness.

The chaplain could do penance for his own misdeeds, by cleaning up his own damn mess.

The End

THE ECHOES OF THE BUNNY-MAN

Steven Stacy

Kirby's house lay in a well-kept, suburban housing estate. Everyone took care of their gardens and around Easter, the daffodils began to bloom in their pretty shades of yellow and orange. It was dark now however, and although Kirby was asleep, her subconscious could hear the voices again. They whispered over and under each other in a haunting lullaby; but she was safe in the arms of unconsciousness. "When will she join us?"

"When will she become one with us?"

"We need her."

The voices of the dead sang, male or female, the gender was unidentifiable in the moonlit room, but the spirits stood in their ghostly apparitions around her bed, trying to see the sleeping girl. "Soon, soon, she will join us," one of them said, and this seemed to quieten the group for now. "Even if we have to push her a little…" The apparitions disappeared back into the moonbeams and their lullaby finished. Kirby stirred and turned over onto her back, she lay somewhere between sleep and awake. She went to move her arm and realised she couldn't. Her body seized with terror. Sleep paralyses again; it had been plaguing her since the deaths. She opened her eyes; bodies filled her bedroom. One lay over her: a boy, rotten and green in the bluish moonshine. Half of the stranger's teeth were visible through his rotting jaw. He stared at her in his death shroud. He was one of the twenty-four suicides that had beset the town within the last year. "Join us," he whispered, without moving his frozen jawbone. The muscle crawled with maggots. Kirby could do nothing but stare, in her sorry state, at the piles of victims strewn across her bedroom. All were in different stages of decomposition; all were dressed in their funeral clothes. Their Sunday best.

A thump hit against her bedroom window, causing Kirby's eyes to gaze outside. Her sister hung by the rope that had taken her life. Her dead face pressed against the window pane. Still pretty, even with the blanket of death on her greying flesh. Her eyes flew open and glared at Kirby. She jolted, desperate to move. "Join us Kirby, I miss you," Carlie whispered, in a ghostly voice that echoed in Kirby's head. Kirby's head moved and she turned it from the window. The suicide children disappeared from her room when she looked back. She looked at the window, and her sister was gone, also. She trembled, turned to her bedside dresser and grabbed a cold cup of coffee. She had had enough for one night. No more sleep paralysis.

Kirby lay on her bed holding a picture of her sister, Carlie, and her. It had been six months since Carlie had taken her life, and with it, she'd broken off a piece of the whole family's soul, that had been buried with her, to rot. Her mother was now a neurotic mess: she'd thrown herself back into Catholicism, and had started cooking like it was going out of fashion, though none of them ate much. Her father spent his nights home from work outside, fixing up an old car and drinking beer. Kirby hardly saw him. She rested her head on the pillow and as the watery morning sun rose, tears slid down her sun-kissed skin.

She showered and went for a run to clear her mind. She jogged through the forestry of Georgia Park, slowing near a bench where she and her sister used to stop and stretch together. Kirby could almost see them, laughing and talking about how cute Ryan Gosling was and how none of the boys had that old-fashioned charm anymore. She laughed aloud in the quiet park, remembering a joke, and her hand went straight to her mouth; she felt an immediate guilt for her laughter. *Had she laughed since Carlie's death?* If so, she couldn't remember. Carlie would never laugh again, Kirby thought bitterly. Guilt consumed her as she ran back to her home.

Kirby walked up the path, past her father's perfectly mown lawn, and unlocked the door. "Anyone home?" The house's silence answered with a resounding 'no' – she went to the kitchen, got a carton of milk from the fridge and glugged the ice-cold liquid back. She wiped away her milk-moustache and headed for the stairs. The phone rang as she placed her right foot on the first stair. She sighed and went back to grab the phone on the wall. She dreaded it being another journalist. "Hello?" Kirby's ear was met with a burst of static. She jerked the phone away, placed it back, and then listened to the sound. She was sure she could hear voices. A manic chant. "Join us, join us, join us..." Kirby clicked the phone off. She remembered her dreams. *I'm hallucinating from lack of sleep*, she told herself. On top of everything, her sleep paralysis was getting worse. She'd never experienced such bad bouts of it.

An hour later, there was a knock at her bedroom door. Kirby froze, looking at the handle as the person on the other side worked it.

"Hey honey, why did you lock the door?" It was her mother, Kara. Kirby opened it, to see her holding a laundry basket and smiling. It was a strained smile. She was mid-forties and attractive, with bright eyes and large curls of dark hair. "Oh, and this parcel was left on the porch for you." Kirby took the large, flat package that was wrapped in newspaper out of her mother's hand. She read a fragment of the story printed on the newspaper: *'Suicide cult' in Bridges Lock claims its 20th.'* That would make it two months old then.

"Nothing important," Kirby said, tearing open the paper. Inside was a white sweater, belonging to her, and some odds and ends with a note attached, reading; "I miss you, Cody xx." She groaned; it was her ex-boyfriend. They'd broken up after her sister's death. He couldn't handle the situation. She couldn't handle him not being able to handle it. "It'll be soup again, later," her mother said, picking up her laundry basket. "You haven't broken for Lent, have you?" Kirby looked up from her place on the bed.

"What? Oh, no, why?"

"Just checking; I think since Carlie...I just think it's important for us as a family to stay close to God. With everything that's happened in this town this year. There's a church service later tonight too. You didn't forget?"

"No, I didn't forget."

"Remember, whoever perseveres to the end will be saved." Since her sister's death, her mother's Catholicism was taking over every spare moment the family had. Kirby curled back up on her bed, she felt sick at the thought of the smell of incense and flowers, again.

The next morning, Kirby was up and dressed early. She needed to go for a run to clear her head, and the weather was nice. As she pulled open the door, she noticed a familiar red van outside. The door opened and Mary Wendice stepped out, her camera-man, David Reed, in tow. She was wearing a dark brown suit and black heels. Kirby hesitated on her porch, before walking down the steps. Mary ran up to her, beckoning her camera-man to follow. "Kirby, how are you?"

"Why do you care?" Kirby asked, nonchalantly. She stopped out of morbid curiosity. Mary Wendice worked for a local news channel, and like the Grim Reaper, wherever death was – so was she. "What do you want?"

"So, you haven't heard?" Mary pulled a face that just barely expressed human emotion. "One of your classmates, Morgan Davies, hanged himself last night." Mary searched Kirby's face as the girl gasped, her blue eyes widening.

"What?" asked Kirby. "I don't understand..." The world around her started to spin, all she could see was the red power-light on the camera. "Get that thing out of my face!" she screamed, stumbling back up her porch steps.

"That's bringing the total up, including your sister, to twenty-five," Mary continued. "Have you heard of or made a suicide pact with any of the local teens? Were you and Morgan close?" Suddenly her father's arm was around her, and she was being pulled back inside the house. Mary clicked her fingers and pointed to Craig, Kirby's father. The camera focused on his angry face. "Mr Vale, could I have a few words with you?"

"Leave us to grieve in piece!" The door was slammed shut. Mary stepped back and turned to David. She held back a smirk as they walked in unison towards the van.

"Please tell me you got the reaction shot…" Mary whispered. David nodded. "I don't know what's going on here, but I'm going to get to the bottom of it – and when I do, they'll make me a Dame…"

"Do you think she'll kill herself?" David asked, loading the equipment back in the van. He was tall and solid, a kind of body-guard for Mary, as well as a camera-man. *God knows she had her enemies.* Mary was deep in thought, her manicured hand trailing itself around her neck as she theorised.

"I'm not sure… she doesn't seem the type, but then – who does? They're so random, these suicides. No obvious correlation. Still, there has to be something connecting them," Mary got back in the front seat. She was desperate to get the scoop first.

Kirby sat at the kitchen table crying, as her father awkwardly hugged her, his Old Spice cologne, mixed with the scent of hyacinths, sitting in a vase on the table. "Daddy, what's going on?"

"Honey, I wish I knew, I really do." He pulled away from her and put his rugged hands together in prayer. "I wish Carlie was here," he said. "I just wish I knew where she was..." and suddenly he was sobbing. Kirby got up and hugged him from behind. She was a petite girl, and she felt even smaller around her father, smaller still whenever her dead sister was mentioned.

"Promise me you'll tell me if you ever feel like...like Carlie did," he said, his eyes closed.

"I promise," she whispered gently.

She took the back gulley out of the house to avoid 'Mean Mary,' as she liked to think of her. Also, 'Monstrous Mary' and simply 'bitch', depending on her mood. As she walked through the quiet, eerie labyrinth of gullies that led between the houses, she wondered if the ghostly voices had called to Morgan last night. *Had they convinced him to kill himself?* She hurried along the slim lanes between the houses, feeling like 'Alice in Wonderland,' until she reached the back of Conner's house. Conner was a close friend of her family.

Her sister had been her confidante whenever things got bad, before. Now, who could she talk to? She'd found Carlie, six months ago, hanging from the overhead fan in their connecting bathroom. *She* had found her. Who could she talk to about *that*? The school bloody counsellor? That was all she'd been offered. The doctor had given her *nothing*, not even for her insomnia, not even for her anxiety. In fact, he had already, against her wishes, started weaning her off the anti-depressant she'd been given initially.

She walked up the steep steps to Conner's back door and knocked. As she waited, she readjusted her grey camisole top and tight blue jeans. She could hear shouting inside, *arguing*, and then she saw Conner's mother at the window. She had raised Conner alone, as a single mother. She looked tired and old in the early spring light. She opened the door. "Kirby... I'm so sorry dear," she said. "I just saw you on the news." Kirby's hand went to her mouth in shock. She could have throttled Mary.

"They put that out already?" she asked stunned, walking into the kitchen and looking up at the TV where her shocked face stared back at her.

"I went to the local MP to try and get these blood-suckers stopped from interviewing you kids," Conner's mother said angrily, her fist clenched. "It's like a disease that's spreading. We need to cut off this flow of information."

Kirby nodded, looking up at the greying woman. But she didn't think this was as simple as teens copying each other. To her, that was ludicrous. Conner walked into the kitchen, wearing red pyjama's. He looked younger than his sixteen years. Kirby walked up and hugged him; she could see he'd been crying. Morgan had been his friend since childhood.

"Ma, we're going up to my room for a while," Conner said, taking her hand and leading her toward the stairs.

Normally, this would be his mother's cue to say, "Don't you two get up to anything I wouldn't do," with her eyes twinkling. She liked to tease and she often talked about how beautiful Kirby was; too beautiful for her geeky son. Kirby knew the mother and son didn't get along, but Conner had never told her why. He was quite the clam-shell when it came to his family matters. This wasn't the time for teasing though, and his mother must've seen that. Kirby's once-long hair had been cut short so she wasn't reminded of her sister every time she looked in the mirror. It was up in a golden-blonde quiff, held by clips and a lot of hairspray; like Sharon Stone's hair in her infamous 'Basic Instinct' interview. Kirby felt her beauty was a plump ripe peach, rotten inside, a bug squirming away, feeding on her fragile mind.

"What's going on?" Conner whispered, when they were out of ear-shot. "I've been on the web, everyone's covering it. It's crazy! I can't believe this about Morgan... he seemed fine yesterday, happy even." Conner's eyes were bloodshot. Kirby took the seat by his desk. Conner's room was covered in movie posters, mostly horror and thriller, a few of Spielberg's, such as E.T.

"I didn't know him like you guys, but yes, for what it's worth, he *seemed* happy."

Conner took a seat on his bed, near the window. "I spoke to Eric; he's gutted. They used to hang out a lot, even before *Cinema Club*."

Kirby winced at his choice of phrase. "Anyway, they're going to talk about him in the Easter service tomorrow."

"Have you experienced anything odd lately?" Kirby asked. "Or seen anything weird?"

"Strange question. No, why would you ask that? Have you?"

Kirby hesitated. "My sleep paralysis is getting worse and I'm seeing the most horrific visions. The teens that have killed themselves, and Carlie. Their bodies lay in heaps in my room, and I can't move, or even scream."

Conner sat forward. "Have you told your parents?"

"No." Kirby crossed her legs and folded her arms. "I shouldn't have told *you*. I feel crazy just saying it." She turned her head away, fiery tears burning behind her eyes. Conner kneeled in front of her and put a hand on her knee. She took it in her own hands.

"I believe you're seeing what you say," he said. His dark brown eyes looked gentle behind his glasses.

"Have you and your mother been fighting?" Kirby asked. She saw Conner instantly tense, and he took his eyes away from her. He was now staring at a picture of Eric, Morgan, Kirby, Leigh, and himself all smiling; a shot of them in cinema club.

"No," he said curtly, his cheeks flushing pink. He steered the conversation back to the subject at hand. "I can't see any connection among all the deaths," he said.

"What do *all* the suicides have in common? And what do they have in common with me and my sister?" She closed her eyes, trying to concentrate, but her mind was haunted with thoughts and images. She wanted to ask him about his mother, perhaps there was something she knew.

"I don't know about the others, but our parents were all in the same year in secondary school..." Conner began, thinking out loud. Kirby looked at him; *perhaps there were answers to be found at home.*

Eric lay on his bed in a half-awake state. He felt dizzy and lazy. Morgan had been his friend, and now he was gone; just another teenager's name on a long list in this town. Eric had type one diabetes and his blood sugar level was low. He could feel all his body's signs of a pending "hypo." The stress was too much, and he hadn't eaten. There was a bottle of Pepsi across the room, he needed to get to it. He usually carried a small bottle around with him, but the shock of Morgan dying had hit him hard. If he didn't drink some soon, he'd fall into unconsciousness, though. He'd left it on his computer desk last night while he was working. He tried to call out for help, but his voice was already useless. His saliva felt thick and gooey. Panic stirred in him. He'd have to roll off the bed and get to the Pepsi himself. He looked across the room and a worm of terror writhed inside his stomach: a man stood in a rabbit costume, white with startling red smears of blood. He had a noose draped around his neck, the frayed rope nearly touching the floor. He wore a mask with black whiskers bending every which way, and one ear flopped over. His eyes glowed red through the mask; and large off-white teeth curved around its chin. *It's just a hallucination, you need sugar*, Eric told himself. He was travelling into the arms of unconsciousness. The rabbit man just stood there, watching him. Eric used the extra adrenaline to roll off the bed, cracking his nose on the bedside cabinet. It started to pour blood.

"Why bother, Eric? You're just a burden to your family and friends." The rabbit-man's voice had a dream-like quality. "They have to watch you like a child. Your diabetes has made you little more than an infant. Why not just let your body do what it wants to? It wants to die, Eric…" Eric started to crawl towards his computer desk, his limbs impossibly heavy as they dragged across the carpet. His head dropped, leaving logic and reason, and hit the floor, leaving a blotch of dark red blood from his nose. "Your mother regrets giving you this life of pain and constant surveillance, did you know that?"

Eric lifted his head and tried to shake his head; he knew that wasn't true. *It wasn't*. "No," he managed to croak. The desk was just a small distance away now. The rabbit moved closer and dropped to his knees.

"Yes," he reasserted, his red eyes aflame. "Just close your eyes and fall asleep. You'll feel nothing, I promise." Eric was at the desk, finally, looking up to the lidless Pepsi. He reached up and touched the bottle. It fell to the ground. "*See*, fate is telling you to die, Eric. Why fight it?" The Pepsi was pouring out onto the grey-carpeted floor, staining it dark brown. Eric lost all sense and agreed to relax into the arms of unconsciousness.

"Okay...you're right..." Eric mumbled. The noose slid over his half-awake head and tightened as the rabbit threw it over the beam in Eric's bedroom and pulled him up. He suddenly found it hard to breathe. Eric watched his body get pulled backwards, then his feet left the floor. He felt like he was floating, except for the pain around his neck. He couldn't breathe now. A minuscule burst of panic occurred to his sleepy mind as he saw the rotting teenagers watching him; they appeared to be willing the rabbit-man on. "Join us!" they chanted repeatedly to Eric. His breath stopped and his eyes fluttered. Then, he joined them, and looked up at his own body hanging from his bedroom beam. He smiled in the arms of unconsciousness.

Kirby walked into her kitchen casually, tossing her keys on the table. "Oh, hey honey, do you want some pancakes?" her mother called from the kitchen.

"Mother, we've had pancakes for days... I like pancake day and everything, but it ended," complained Kirby.

"I've been making them for the Church fate tomorrow. Besides, I spread Nutella on them, with sliced strawberries and whipped cream." Her mother smiled, "They're delicious." Kirby pulled a kitchen chair out and sat down as her mother placed the pancakes on the pine table.

"What's this?" Kirby asked, pushing the plate aside and looking at a wicker basket filled with various Easter eggs, sitting on the table. She took a small one out. It was stained deep red. "What is this? It's an actual chicken egg, isn't it?"

"That's where Easter eggs come from, honey. People used to stain the eggs red for Easter. Dyed red to represent the blood of Christ, and the egg symbolizes the sealed tomb that Christ was placed in after he died. The cracking of the egg symbolizes his resurrection from the dead... it's all really interesting actually."

"Well, I think I'll stick to chocolate," Kirby said, picking out a regular Easter egg from the basket and ripping off the gold foil. She started breaking small parts off and stuffing them in her mouth. "Mum, I hate to bring it up, but did Carlie or I have any connection with the suicide teens?"

"Oh, Kirby..." Her mother cut her pancake, strawberry juice flowing onto the plate, and shook her head. "I've told you before, none that I can think of."

"I'm still having that terrible sleep paralysis. Seeing terrible things," Kirby said, her voice wavering.

"Honey, you've been under a lot of pressure lately."

Kirby stood up from the table. "I don't feel too good. Where did you get those Easter eggs? They taste... off."

"Someone left them on the front porch. It must be someone from church to make traditional eggs like that."

"And you let me eat one?!" Kirby's voice rose in pitch with every word, so that she ended in a near shriek. Her mother tutted and rolled her eyes.

"No one from church would do anything bad to us, Kirby." Kirby left the kitchen, her stomach queasy, and ran up to her bedroom, shrugging out of her jacket and pulling her sneakers off. Her eyes widened as a wave of dizziness swept over her. She felt her stomach clenching and throbbing along with her heartbeat. "Mother..." she tried to yell, her voice weak. She stood up and the room swam. She shivered violently. Quickly, she grabbed the wicker waste-paper basket, sat on the edge of her bed and pushed her fingers down her throat. A heaving lurch from her stomach sent up a brown liquid tinged with blood. She puked twice then breathed deeply, her eyes closed, bile dribbling from her lips. "What the hell..." she fell backwards onto her double-bed and stared up at the white ceiling. She could smell flowers in the humid room, from all the decorations her mother had been making for Church. The cracks and lines started to swirl and she closed her eyes, ashen-faced.

She was in her high school suddenly, and she realized she was unconscious. "The Easter egg," she whispered to herself, touching her lips. She walked down the main hallway of her school, as autumn leaves blew gently around her bare feet. She turned to see only darkness; there was no entrance or exit. She looked up at a huge banner painted in red and gold – "The Easter Dance 1985." The paper was old and as she passed it, one side of the banner tore and drifted languorously down. The doors to the classrooms were open and a flower-scented breeze that cooled Kirby's face drifted along the hallways.. As she passed by each door and looked in, she saw all the classrooms were empty, but on each blackboard was written her mother's recipe for pancakes.

"Kirby, you came…" a dreamy voice echoed. She looked over her shoulder to see a man wearing a mask and a filthy rabbit suit; a strangely distorted rabbit suit with blood all over its matted fur. Kirby gasped, whirling around and bursting into a sprint. She raced down the hallway, her feet smacking the cool tile flooring and crunching the crisp leaves. The walls were covered with more posters advertising the dance; these too were rippling from a faraway breeze. She could hear voices chanting rapidly: "join us, join us, join us." Something flew towards her from the ceiling and hit her full force in the chest, as she turned a corner. She landed on her back, skidding. She got up onto her elbows and looked skyward. A teenage boy hung from the tiled ceiling by a thick brown rope. She gasped at his limp, pale-blue limbs; he was long-dead, the smell alone told her that. The ceiling was slowly turning red. It crept along, like a sponge soaking up blood. It spread along the white tiles, towards her, and started to drip through. She screamed, as the warm liquid splashed onto her skin. The tiles gave way and over a dozen bodies came flying down, swinging by their necks. Her screams intensified, until she felt and tasted the thick blood dribble onto her lips. She snapped her mouth shut, whimpering. She could hear the creaking of the ropes that held the bodies and a distant laughter rattling down the hallways. She wiped the blood from her face. "No, no, no, this isn't real…I'm not here. I'm unconscious."

Her sister appeared at the other end of the hallway, holding out the noose that was meant for Kirby's neck, while Carlie's own noose held tight around her throat. "Join my ever-growing collection," the rabbit man's voice whispered to her through her sister's mouth. The words reverberated in her mind. She stood up and put her hands to her ears, backing away from it all. She skidded in the blood and hit one of the teenager's bodies, causing it to swing violently.

"We can always make it look like you joined the suicide squad," he said, laughing manically as the rabbit re-appeared where her sister had been.

Kirby turned to run, but another dead body plunged through the ceiling in front of her followed by a fresh gush of blood. It was her sister again. Kirby closed her eyes, her screams burning her sore throat. Her sister's eyes sprang open, gleaming white with a blue sheen of death.

"Join us, Kirby, it's peaceful here. All your pain just melts away... Besides, what do you have? No boyfriend anymore, no job anymore. You've lost everything: including me!" The corpse's skin turned more and more ashen, until fragments of it started to break off and turn to dust, drifting away on the breeze, leaving only a grinning skull.

"Enough!" she yelled, bursting into a race towards one of the large windows. Outside it was dark. Storm clouds gathered and drifted too quickly past the building outside. She shoved the window open and stepped up onto the window sill. She expected to see the grass below, but there was only mist swirling around in the black void. Suddenly, *he* was behind her. His red eyes shone like garnets in his Wonderland face. He offered her the noose. "I will never, *never*, do that! Do you hear me?" she screamed.

"They all say that, at first…." he said, through his thick bone-teeth. His face twisted and the school behind him started to fall apart, the bodies dropping like meat to the floor, as the ceiling crashed down. He shoved her abruptly, hard.

She fell backwards and plummeted through the mist, her legs pedalling air and her hands trying to grasp something. Her scream heightened, cutting through the darkness, turning into…

An ambulance siren. "We've got her!" a man shouted. "Kirby, can you hear me? Kirby?" The bright lights blinded her, momentarily. She got up on her elbows and found she was in an ambulance. Her mother was sitting just beside the shouting paramedic. Kirby looked around with drugged, half-open eyes; then she puked.

Kirby opened her eyes. She could hear the beeps of machines and her own heartbeat, the sound of people talking and the smell of disinfectant. Her mother was sitting by the bed. "What happened?" she asked groggily, with a voice which rasped from a red-raw throat.

"You took an overdose, that's what." Her mother glared at her. "How could you do that to me and your father, after this year from hell? I thought you were an individual, not a sheep that wants to follow the rest of this fucking town off a cliff." Kara closed her eyes, and gripped handfuls of her curly hair, elbows pointing towards the heavens.

"What about me, mother?" Kirby met her mother's eyes. "Do you honestly think that I would try to kill myself?"

"Well, then you tell me what happened!"

"Someone tried to poison me, mother. Those Easter eggs on the porch... I ate some, remember? The next thing I know I'm unconscious."

Kara looked up, still playing with her hair. Her eyes were glassy with tears. She reached out across the bed and took her daughter's hand.

"I'm so sorry, baby, but what was I supposed to think? How can I—"

"What happened at the High school dance of nineteen eighty-five? What did you do? And don't pretend you don't know what I'm talking about..."

Her mother's eyes widened in shock and her hands flew back to her thick hair, grabbing handfuls and squeezing. "How do you know about that?" she said breathlessly.

"The person that poisoned me, the person that killed Morgan and Carlie... They weren't suicides, they were set up to look like suicides by whoever he is. A guy dressed as a fucking rabbit! And I'm not talking thumper; he's hideous!"

Her mother got up and drew the curtain around the hospital bed. She turned back to her daughter, eyes sombre. "Brandon Conners was a gay kid at my secondary school... he came out at a time when none of us were used to gay people; when none of us knew how to accept it. The kids were cruel. ...I was vicious to him..." Kara turned away from her daughter for a moment, and when she looked back, she was crying. "I never told anyone that, not even Father Callahan...."

"What happened?"

"We had a school dance, most of the kids were nice to Brandon, well, nice to his face. When it came time for the announcement of the King and Queen of the dance -" Kara stopped, her breath coming out laboured. She'd kept this in for so many years. Only in her silent prayers had she admitted her wrongs to her saviour, Lord Jesus Christ. "He was the school football mascot – but the guys didn't accept him when he came out and so, I had this idea...' Another long, laboured breath. "He was voted Queen of the dance."

"Oh my God, how could you be so cruel?"

"That night he took his life, he – when his parent's found him, he was hanging from his bedroom light wearing his school mascot costume." She clamped a hand over her mouth, muffling the sobs.

"What was the school mascot?"

"A rabbit... a vicious rabbit for the rangers," Kara whispered. Then she sat up straight, clearing her throat and composing herself. "And that's the story of Brandon Conners. I've never forgiven myself. I don't expect you to. I gather your father told you..."

Kirby ignored her mother. *Let her have her self-pity*, she thought. *That's her problem*. Brandon Conners was *her* problem; hers and Conner's and Eric's and God knew who else. *He was out for revenge*. She had to stop him.

Leigh's mother told her about Kirby as soon as she got through the door. Leigh didn't hesitate. "I'm going to the hospital," she said and snatched her car keys back up. She'd lost too many friends this week to risk losing her best friend.

"What the hell do you think you're doing, young lady?" Kara demanded to know, as her daughter started yanking the monitors off her skin.

"I need to warn people. They're not suicides, Mum. It's Brandon." She ground her teeth and ripped the drip out of the back of her hand. She pulled too hard and blood jetted out, hitting the plastic curtain around the bed with a splish-splash. Kirby whimpered and then grabbed her folded-up clothes from the end of the bed and started dressing.

Kara took her daughter by the shoulders. "You need to stop this! You're in mourning, Conners is dead Kirby!"

Kirby ripped her mother's hands off her, and stared up at her angrily. "Were Conner's parents involved?" she asked. "With Brandon's death? Were they involved?"

"In a way," Kara said bitterly.

"What about Eric's?" Her mother turned from her, nodding her head.

"The other teens?"

"Yes and yes! God, Kirby, are you crazy!? Because it looks like you're suggesting Brandon Conner's ghost is killing people. Is that what you're suggesting? Actually, you know what? Don't answer!" She shook her head. "It's a tragic trend created by media hype."

"If believing that makes you feel less guilty. Go ahead!" replied Kirby, angrily.

Kara slapped her daughter. It was a sharp, precise slap, its noise startling within the quiet room. Kirby put a hand to her cheek and looked up at her mother, hurt but defiant - *always defiant*. Then she walked out.

Leigh was just about to park her Camaro, when she noticed Kirby rushing out of the hospital entrance. Her eyes narrowed in recognition. She caught up to Kirby and drove alongside her, winding down the window of the car. "Kirby, it's good to see you up and about!" she called. Kirby span around to see Leigh's car, she stopped running and smiled. "I heard you'd taken an overdose. I didn't believe it for a second," Leigh said.

"Thank God, somebody still has faith in me," Kirby said. Leigh pulled up along the roadside and Kirby climbed in. "It's great to see you," Kirby smiled. Leigh and Kirby had clicked years ago when Leigh's family had first moved to Bridges Lock. Leigh was the only black girl in school, her family the only black family in town; nevertheless, both girls got along like Betty and Veronica. Kirby being the Betty, Leigh being the Veronica. Leigh slowly drove down the deserted track that was covered in a canopy of willow branches, the lights to the vehicle lighting up the long road. The hospital lay in a secluded spot near the dense woodland surrounding most of the town.

"I need your help with something very important," Kirby said, coming straight out with it.

"Anything. What is it you need?"

"You wouldn't believe me if I told you," Kirby said. "That's the problem."

The car pulled to a stop. "Try me. There was a time you were the only person to give me the time of day here. I remember *that*," Leigh smiled sincerely, one glamorous hand tapping its manicured finger-nails against the steering wheel. Kirby looked at her friend. She had to tell *someone*.

"I know why these "suicides" are happening," Kirby told her friend in a conspiring tone.

"Before you go any further, I have to tell you some bad news," Leigh said, turning towards the window, which in the darkness only showed her own reflection. "Eric hanged himself today." Leigh and Kirby sighed heavily, the weight of the world on their shoulders. She had trusted Leigh would believe her, but she was scared. Still, she was desperate enough to take the gamble.

Leigh listened to Kirby's story with pity and horror; pity that the girl she called her 'bestie' might be so unhinged, and horror that the story might actually be true.

"So what do you plan to do about this... Brandon guy? That is his name, isn't it?" Leigh asked.

"I'm going to take myself to the brink of death, kill him, and come back out."

"What? Are you crazy! How're you going to do that?" Leigh's hand flew to her mouth, aghast.

"I'm going to hang myself until I get to him and then *you'll* resuscitate me before I die. I've checked – I'll have thirty seconds before I'm brain dead." She looked around the car, embarrassed, and feeling she probably should have kept that bit back. It was a lot of pressure for anyone.

"Brain dead?" Leigh looked at Kirby with wide, nervous eyes.

"I'll do it with or without you, I just think it'll be safer with you. I'm not sure if I could cut myself down after that long a time." In fact, Kirby knew she couldn't do this without her friend's help.

"...I'll do it because you're so fucked up," Leigh said with nervous laughter. "And because I think you're crazy enough to do it alone." Kirby smiled at her, tears making her eyes glassy. The girls smiled at each other in a tender moment. "But you better be right, and you better not die," Leigh said, her voice taut with tension. She started the car up, and the radio that sat above an old cassette player, came to life at the same time. A speaker started spurting out different voices and Leigh tuned it until she found a station. A female voice that Kirby recognized as the despised 'Monster Mary' boomed inside the car.

"And yet another teen suicide rocks the small town of 'Bridges Rock' tonight. Seventeen-year old Eric Saunders had no history of mental illness, or any affiliations with gangs; and so the question remains, why are so many local teens taking their own lives?" An upsurge of grief overtook Kirby, her already pale face becoming ashy, and the dizziness causing her to put her head in her hands. *Poor Eric. He'd been so scared of death.*

"I'm sorry Kirby, I had no idea it had hit the news. Are you okay?" Leigh put her hand on her friend's knee, clearly showing concern. She wasn't going to tell her about Eric yet. *Damn that bitch, Mary.* It had been hard enough for her to take.

"Yes," she said, the word coming out in a deep, melancholic sigh. Their hands found each others and intertwined. Leigh gave a reassuring squeeze.

Leigh bit her crimson lower lip, thinking. "Look, Kirby, I'll help you with this... I can't bury another friend. I'll be there to cut you down after thirty seconds. That way, you'll be as safe as you can be in these circumstances."

"I'm waiting for it," Kirby said, looking at Leigh with an eyebrow raised.

"Waiting for what?"

"The catch."

"I think we should record it on my phone," Leigh said, then placed a hand up to silence Kirby. "Look, if anything strange happens, we'll have it on camera. Besides, what if it *did* go wrong? I could end up in prison, Kirby." Leigh turned to her. "I'm your *best bet* as a reliable, trustworthy witness."

"You're right," Kirby said. She looked out at the cornfields whizzing past in the darkness. "I know you're right. I hope I still have enough time to save Conner."

"Worry about yourself, Conner and his family are probably at the church with most of the town. There's a tribute to Morgan. I wonder if they'll squeeze one in for Eric now, too," Leigh pondered aloud.

Kirby couldn't think about that. She needed to catch herself a rabbit.

Kirby unlocked her front door. Several lights were on, but when she called for her parents, there was no answer. "They'll be at church," Kirby said, letting her best-friend inside.

"Your mum still keeping up appearances?" Leigh asked, looking sombrely at Kirby.

"My mother never misses a church service, Leigh, it might look bad to the neighbours," she said. "You know the way; let's do this." They walked up the stairs, Kirby in her ankle boots, Leigh in her red high heels.

"Do you remember when we used to speed down these stairs on bean-bags?" Leigh laughed. "The good old days when we had no worries." Kirby laughed at the memory.

"And my mother would get so mad, saying we were going to break our necks," Kirby giggled. "I guess that literally *could* happen tonight." Suddenly, the mood turned sombre again, with the click of a finger; they were ripped out of their sweet memory.

"Where do you plan on doing it?" Leigh asked. Kirby looked up to her ceiling fan. It brought back horrific memories of her sister's limp, swinging body. *Brandon must have been behind that too – with her mother's part in his suicide, it made complete sense.*

"I need rope and a knife," she said. She could feel her grief being overtaken by a cold, incensed rage.

"I'll be waiting," Leigh called after her. She looked around the bedroom; it was all your usual teenage shit. Posters on the walls, Daredevil, Nirvana, Marilyn Monroe, a 'Scream 4' movie print. Her dresser was covered in various perfumes and lots of make-up; it appeared that Kirby didn't wear much at all, which meant, like Leigh, she was good at it.

"I can't believe we're doing this," Kirby said, walking back into her bedroom. She was carrying a kitchen knife and a long, thick, piece of rope. "Filming a snuff film would do your YouTube channel wonders though," Kirby winked.

"Don't even go there, girl! You're just lucky I trust you. Most people would call you foolish. It's Easter and you have a homo-repressed guy dressed as a bunny, bumping people off when they're unconscious. *Seriously*? If it were anyone else, I'd say they were crazy, and I was even crazier for getting involved," Leigh shook her head as she spoke.

"Don't you think it's strange that twenty-five people would kill themselves? All in the same *way*. All in the same *place*? All in the same *year*?" She lowered her voice to a whisper. "If I were a parent, I think I'd take solace in knowing that my child didn't choose to end their life."

"I think I'd feel worse knowing my kid got bumped off," Leigh countered, eyeing the rope.

"Turn on your camera, I'm not taking any chances with your life. You hold *no* accountability with this as far as anyone is concerned," Kirby said. She handed Leigh the knife and waited until Leigh adjusted the angle of the camera on her phone. The light illuminated Kirby's face.

"My name is Kirby Lane. I am of sound body and mind and I am -"

"That's debatable," Leigh said sarcastically. Kirby ignored her and continued.

"I am asking my best friend – Leigh Jacobs, to help pull me back from death. I am going to hang myself, and after I pass out, Leigh is going to cut me down and resuscitate me while filming the entire thing," Kirby turned to Leigh, ducking her head away from the camera. "You know CPR right?"

"Of course..." Leigh said, a roll of her eyes. Leigh adjusted the camera back onto Kirby's face.

"I'm asking her to do this. I'd have done it without her." Kirby shook her head. "God, it sounds so crazy when I say it aloud." She looked back at the camera, resolute. "But I'm fucking doing it."

They both looked at each other, and then after a moment's hesitation, Kirby pulled her desk chair out, climbed up, and started tying the rope around the static fan. Leigh watched with a cautious, fascinated face. Her hand felt clammy around the handle of the knife. She was scared. She didn't want to end up in jail. She wouldn't last a day with her big mouth and great legs. Mostly, she didn't want to watch her best-friend die.

Kirby looked down at her. The noose was itchy and rough against the tender skin of her neck. "If this goes wrong, I'm sorry dad," she said looking at the camera. Her hands closed into fists and, closing her eyes, she kicked the chair out from underneath her and dropped. Leigh jumped.

The noose tightened. Her hands immediately flew up to the rope, scrabbling at the hard, thick cord. Leigh, suddenly alarmed at this crazy thing they were doing, made a move to help her, but made herself stop. She looked at her watch, she'd time it from now, she decided. Kirby's bulging eyes looked up to the ceiling as she clawed at her neck. Her legs kicked as her lungs begged for oxygen. Her legs kicked, then jolted, then flexed. Her arms dropped. Then everything disappeared. '*Let's get unconscious honey. Let's get unconscious,*' Kirby could hear the sound of a beautiful woman's voice, singing, as she closed her eyes.

Kirby sat up and found herself in the same school hallway as last time. The crumbling walls and tattered posters; an apparition of a previous life. The breeze drifted across her skin and brought with it the laughter of children long lost, left or dead. Her bare feet crunched against dry, autumn leaves. Dust motes drifted in front of her face. "Brandon?" she called, and it echoed along the seemingly never-ending hallway. She looked up to see the banner advertising the school dance; it was back hanging just below the sagging ceiling. The school creaked and groaned in the dimming light. "Brandon Conners! I know who you are!" She walked towards a dust-covered rectangular box and broke the glass with her elbow. She took out a fire axe. It was still in the same place as years later, in her world.

"You came back to me," Brandon said, his voice echoing along the corridor. Stepping out from a hallway. He had a noose in his hand. "I see you won't be needing this." He tossed it to the floor.

Kirby ran at Brandon. He stood his ground, red eyes glowing. She reached him and threw the axe with all her strength, burying it within his shoulder. She yanked the axe back out and a foul-smelling dust, yellow in colour, burst out of the wound. "How can you kill someone who's already dead, you stupid child?" he taunted. Then he pushed her and, effortlessly it seemed, she went skidding down the decrepit hallway on her back, still clutching the axe. *What had she been thinking?* She got up and ran, her feet pounding the floor. She turned at a corner and started running up the large stairwell.

It's been ten seconds; I should cut her down... Leigh thought to herself. *No, I promised*. She was standing on the chair, her heels kicked off. Her shaking knife hand trembled precariously near the dense twine. She studied her friends face, wondering what was going on in her head. *How had she let her do this?* Leigh questioned herself. It was so irresponsible. So unlike either girl; but the town had gone crazy lately, and Kirby's story made sense in a senseless world.

Kirby made her way past several single-paned windows with sections of glass smashed out and a howling wind blustering through the openings. She started a slow jog into the darkness, turning a corner and coming face to face with a tall dark figure. She lifted the axe, her eyes wild.

"Wait!" Conner yelled, his hands up in defence.

"Conner, ...what the hell are you doing here?"

"I don't fucking know. I was eating an Easter egg, next thing I know, I'm here. What is this place?" Kirby stepped back and eyed him. He was wearing a black onesie. "Kirby, are you listening to me?"

"Shhh! Just stay behind me," she said. "We're in danger."

Suddenly, a large window on the second floor imploded and glass, paper and leaves flew at them. They crouched down, Conner wrapping an arm around her. Little strips of paper were gathering at their feet. "What the hell?" Conner picked one up and examined it. "It's to vote for the king and queen of the Easter dance. Nineteen eighty-five? Here..." he handed her one of the ballots. "Let me hold that," he said, reaching for the axe.

"It's okay, I got it," she said, reading through the ballets. Under Queen: Brandon Conners. Under King, Beth Easton. She picked up another, the same, and another. She turned to face Conner. He had stepped back into the shadows. "Your mother's name..."

"Beth Easton. Elizabeth Easton as you know her. My mother's a dyke, and my father was the queen of the dance, the belle of the ball. Surprise!" Kirby stared at him in disbelief. "He was gay, big deal, but that didn't stop my parents from wanting children. All it takes is a turkey baster, apparently." Kirby stumbled backwards, almost dropping the axe. "It's not very romantic, I know, but it proved they really wanted me, I guess," he continued, "and it did at least result in the conception of yours truly." He grinned nastily.

"How do you exist here?" Kirby asked.

"My father, my *real* dad, I believe you've met – Brandon. He came to me in a dream and pulled me in, just like you. Getting inside people's heads is a neat trick. Like Freddy on Acid."

"You're evil! You killed all those people," Kirby stared at him astonished.

"I did indeed," he said smugly.

"My sister?" She asked in a voice which was growing strong with anger.

He smiled and shrugged his shoulders. "Technically, they killed themselves."

"You were my friend!"

"I was never your *friend!*" he snarled. Your mother was a real mean girl, the original Regina George – she started the whole thing. Vote the gay guy the Queen and the Lesbian the King. Nothing hurt her more than seeing her daughter die though," he finished, an intimidating look on his face. She would never have thought it was the same person she'd been speaking to only hours earlier.

"So why not her instead?"

He smiled. "Oh, we'll get to her. They need to suffer first, like we've suffered. First they grieve, then they die."

"That's right," Brandon's voice agreed behind her. She spun around, axe raised. There they were. Demented father and son, and they had her cornered. Conner suddenly moved. Kirby was too slow. He punched her, hard, in the face. She fell backwards, hitting the wall and then the ground. Dust, leaves and ballots lifted into the air as she fell. Conner looked down at her, red light reflecting in his glasses.

Kirby licked the blood from her split lip, then tightened her hand around the axe handle. She burst into hysterical laughter, saying, "A gay bunny out for revenge?!" Suddenly, she swung the axe at Conner's left ankle, feeling the thud along her arms as it connected with bone, and came out the other side. Conner shrieked as he grabbed his leg that now ended in a stump, spurting blood. Then their world started to shake.

"No!" Brandon yelled, as Conner lay on the floor screaming. Kirby scrambled to her feet. She glared at Brandon, whose eyes were filled with dancing flames.

"Oh my God! She has a split lip!" Leigh gasped to the camera. "It's been twenty seconds. Screw thirty! I'm cutting her down..." She pressed the sharp blade into the rope and sawed, but it barely made a mark. She started sawing manically at the rope and little by little it frayed. "No, no, no!" Leigh cried out to the empty house. "Hang in there Kirby, don't you die on me!"

Kirby ran behind the moaning Conner, using him as an obstacle between her and Brandon. The old school was falling apart, shaking under their feet, dust and plaster falling from the walls. Brandon tore the rabbit mask off and ran to his son. He knelt down and held him. Then he looked up to Kirby with dark-brown eyes. The same eyes as his son's; and they were equally evil. "Haven't you and your family done enough?"

"...Silly rabbit," she said, with a wry smile that was full of sarcasm, and swung the axe again, burying it deep into Conner's throat, with a satisfyingly ensuing sound of bone and cartilage crunching. His head flopped sideways on his half-severed neck, blood spurting out of the main arteries and pouring out of his mouth. Brandon now screamed. He clutched his son's twitching body, trying to keep his head straight on his body by his hair, his face contorted with grief as fresh blood gushed onto his white fur suit, drenching it red. After a few moments of twitching, finally, Conner became still. Brandon let his body fall. He stood up and looked at Kirby murderously. She blinked and suddenly he was before her, his rabbit mask back on, as if he'd never taken it off.

"Now, you meet your sister!" He grabbed her by the throat and lifted her off the floor, snarling. His eyes were raging, burning with anger as she pawed uselessly at his strong grip, choking and spluttering, her eyes bulging...

Kirby's body dropped to the floor with a thud as the rope finally gave way. "Thank you Lord!" Leigh dropped to the floor next to her, threw her phone down, and kneeled over her body. Kirby's lips were blue, she looked dead. Leigh desperately loosened the rope around her neck, "don't you die on me! I swear to God. Oh Lord, please don't let her die," Leigh cried. The realization of everything fell upon her and she felt close to becoming hysterical. She started CPR, first she pressed her red lips to Kirby's pink and gave her oxygen, then she pounded urgently on her chest. Leigh's face crumbled when nothing happened. She bent to give her more oxygen.

Kirby thought that somewhere very far away she could hear Leigh's voice, and it brought her back to the fight with a start. She lifted both her heavy arms and pushed her thumbs into those glowing red eyes. She felt softness under her thumbs as she pushed down. The red glow started to dim. The bunny-man released his grasp, howling in pain, he dropped her. Kirby fell to her knees as Brandon stumbled backwards, paws to his face. Then she brought both hands together and pushed him hard. He tumbled backwards over his dead son's body. This was her chance. She got to her feet and ran for the window – it had been her escape route before, enough to wake her from this place. Plaster fell in great heaps as the world around her started completely caving in. *Without his son to ground him, would Brandon have any grasp on the real world?* She saw the window and jumped, knees up, arms over her face – her petite body flew out. Some shards of glass caught her side, but now she was falling in the darkness again. She could hear Leigh's voice, she tried to hold onto it. Hurtling through the air, the horrific idea that she might be trapped here entered her head. Legs kicking, arms flailing, Kirby continued to fall through the darkness wondering if she'd wake to see Leigh's face.

Leigh pulled her mouth away from Kirby's body. She looked down at her in horror, trembling as if a terrible fever had come across her. She'd been giving her mouth to mouth for what seemed like forever. "No, no, no – this can't be happening...." She leaned close to Kirby's ear, her black hair laid plastered to her skin in sweaty tresses. "Girl, you better get your act together and wake the fuck up!" Leigh screamed, leaning back on her knees. Then she lifted both hands, closed them together in a fist and brought them down on Kirby's chest with all her might. Kirby's body jolted, then fell back. "Come on!" Leigh screamed, and she brought her clamped- fist down again, twice, onto Kirby's chest.

A huge gasp of air raced through Kirby's body as her eyes shot open. Leigh burst into tears of joy. "Thank-you, Lord, thank-you," she cried, her voice broken with nerves. She bent over her friend and hugged her. As she felt Kirby put her arms around her back, she wept even more. "We are never, *ever*, doing that again," Leigh said, helping her friend to sit up a little. "Are you okay? You're not brain damaged are you?" Kirby's glassy, blood-shot, eyes took a while to take everything in.

"That matter's open to opinion," Kirby said with a raspy voice, and then Leigh knew she was safe and she allowed herself to laugh a little. "I feel like someone beat the shit out of me."

"Sorry...That would be *me*," Leigh said, helping her friend get the noose off her neck. "Oh Lord, I thought you were dead." Leigh took a deep breath and pulled her hair away from her face.

"I think I was," Kirby said, and both girl's embraced. They hugged each other hard and for a long time, like sisters.

The End

Author's Note:

Steven Stacy's story was inspired by actual events that took place in his life and in a nearby town. The traumatic loss of his sister, at the tender age of twenty-one, brought to the forefront of his mind the unbelievable events that had transpired during 2008, in the close town of Bridgend, South Wales; where twenty-seven young souls took their lives, all within the same year and, all but one, in the same way; by hanging. This is when the story is set.

An article in 'People Magazine' reported that by Feb 2012 seventy-nine people had committed suicide "in the area," again, all by hanging. These inexplicable events prompted an outcry of confusion and disbelief. None of the victims knew each other, and so it left people asking the question, why? The powerful role of the media was particularly brought into question.

Steven felt that if he could write a piece, and approach the subject in a delicate way, using his personal experiences, he could keep alive the memories of the victims and help their families by not letting their memories fade. Steven has a great amount of sympathy around this subject, losing his sister and two close friends to suicide within six months of each other.

If in some way this story helps to keep the victims' memories alive then he feels he has somehow helped the families and gained support for suicide victims everywhere. He and his family know all too well about the growing inclination within society towards suicide, and the lack of understanding of mental health issues in general. If, through his writing, he feels he can highlight the growing problem of mental health issues, and the lack of support to the people desperately suffering (in all backgrounds), and the victims' families; then he feels he has somehow helped raise awareness of the issue.

KILLER JELLY BEANS FROM OUTER SPACE

James Matthew Byers

A spacecraft, something like a jar,

Collided in a bank.

Beside its broken pieces stood

An empty, shallow tank.

Within its hull, the Tinies moved-

A color branded race.

No arms or legs, no, none at all-

They simply had a face.

They rolled about the wrecked debris,

Collecting all around.

Escaping from their enemies

Had forced them to the ground.

Inside the mind, they spoke in waves,

And as they made a line,

The Pink one made for higher ground.

The sun began to shine.

She called upon the Red and White,

The Black and Purple, too.

The Orange and the Green as well-
They had a job to do.
Collectively, they moved as one
Until they all agreed
A matter loomed above them all-
The Tinies had to feed!

The wreckage left them stranded there,
And where they did not know.
Beyond the hill and woodland flush,
The Pink one urged them, "Go."
A supermarket up ahead
With humans in and out
Compelling them to hesitate
Bombarded them with doubt.

A poster on the outer wall-
A smiling jelly bean-
Invited them to warble forth,
Embracing what was seen.
Perhaps they would find answers there-
Perhaps some of their kin.
The Tinies measured every move,
Deciding to go in.

The leader rolled, bereft of fear,

Sensations riding high.

Unnoticed by the moving crowd,

The Pink one glided by.

Her summons to the others heard

Inside their jelly minds

Propelled them to move such as she

And hopped beneath the blinds.

The window had been opened up,

And stealthily they moved.

As one by one, the Tinies dropped,

A single unit grooved.

Upon the second aisle, they roamed

Until they saw a bag

With multicolored jelly beans-

It made the Pink one gag.

The others followed suit with her,

Deciding that this place

Was home to some much worse than those

Who once had stuffed their face

With Tinies as a midday munch,

Or sometimes just a snack.

The Pink one popped up in the air

And landed by a sack.

Nobody moved inside the bag,
Nobody writhed or stirred.
When suddenly, a light bulb beamed-
A thought form had occurred.
The Pink one called the others round
To join her in her plan.
They hid behind an Easter sign
To scout this thing called man.

On her first glance, she thought it odd
So many of her kind
Had fallen prey, and bagged this way
Had died there in a bind.
Extensions from her pink gel shot
A tiny open slit
And searched for life inside the bag,
But suddenly, she quit.

Into the minds of those around,
She sent a message then:
"They are not Tinies! Not at all!
Just candy!" With a grin
Upon her face, the others joined,

As smiles, though rather brief,

Revealed a deeper rooted side-

Exposing razor teeth!

Now Tinies were a tiny lot,

And eaten, sure 'tis true.

But what the Earth had yet to learn

Is they eat me and you!

An Easter not forgotten when

A threat appeared in place-

Beware the Killer Jelly Beans

That hailed from outer space...

The smell of fresh blood pumping swift

In veins of every arm

Up reaching for that tasty treat

Became in way of harm.

The Pink one led her comrades in

The bag before them all.

A camouflage like none before,

They blended wall to wall.

A little boy snatched up their lot,

And in the buggy went

The Tinies with the jelly beans-

A poor three dollars spent!

They moved to where their eyes could see

Beyond their plastic cage-

Unbalanced in their wheeled domain,

The Tinies curbed their rage.

A smaller human female and

A teenager appeared.

Unlike the first encountered, these

Had unique skin they steered.

The tall one wore the color, black,

The smaller, something blue.

The Pink one noted with the rest

And planned what next to do.

The Tinies stayed extremely still

As over scanners slipped

The bag containing all of them.

Into the sack they dipped.

A rattle and a battled bump,

A dumping thud and then

The jelly beans and passengers

Embraced the tires' full spin.

The oldest girl boomed music out

As she drove them around.

The bags of groceries sat in back.

The Tinies, never found,

Removed themselves from in the pack

Of jelly beans to see

The who and what and where they were

Amid the car's debris.

The children had a tiny Pug

Who loved to ride along.

Upon the Tinies exodus,

They met his nosey song.

A bark and then a fitted growl,

Until the children fumed.

"Hey, Lance, just put a sock in it!"

But their dog was consumed.

He harped and howled and ran amuck

The whole way to their house-

And when the Pink one bit his nose,

He cowered like a mouse.

The smallest girl took notice then-

As drops of blood fell clean.

But now the stowaways eclipsed

And none of them were seen.

Into a room, the children strode

With paper sacks in tow.

And Lance ran past them to the back.

He didn't even slow.

The Tinies followed after him,

A hunger fit to roam.

When everything had settled down,

They sneaked around the home.

The mom and dad were both at work;

The oldest was in charge.

And with the milk and eggs put up,

The "Tinies" loomed at large.

As jelly beans went on a shelf,

A screeching sound was heard.

The boy and youngest girl ran in,

But offered not a word.

Beneath the chair, a matted fuzz

Encased in bloody ruts

Remained of what had been the dog.

Intestines, bone, and guts-

It seemed as if Lance had been food

To what they did not know.

The oldest grabbed a frying pan

Insisting they should go.

Around the corner came a thud,

And then a squishy splat.

The children, huddled up in fear,

Beheld their eaten cat.

Upon the dresser, open wide,

The bird cage emptied out.

And then the Tinies showed themselves

While feathers flung about.

"Those jelly beans! They- they're alive!"

The boy exclaimed in doubt.

His teenage sister swung her pan

And countered with a shout:

"Go with your sister! Go, go, go!

I'll hold them here, let's run!"

The little girl burst into tears.

This wasn't any fun.

The Pink one trilled an eerie sound

And Red and Purple jumped.

They bounced before the children's path-

The other Tinies slumped-

Removed from off the dresser's space

To nibble on the knees

Of all the kids now in a bind,

And begging, "Please! No, please!"

The multicolored terrors pressed

Upon the fearful lot.

A bunch of teeth and chomping gums

Careened and preened with rot-

As tattered flesh hung from each tooth

And blood from things they ate,

The children hugged and closed their eyes,

Prepared to meet their fate.

But something happened to avert

Catastrophe that day-

At once the roof blew off the house,

Removed and gone away.

The Tinies screamed and tried to flee,

But met their end in heaps.

The boy cried out triumphantly-

"We're saved by monster Peeps!"

The Pink and blue and purple beasts

Resembled chicks, indeed.

They pecked and prodded with each beak

And made the Tinies bleed.

In speed they gobbled up the crew,

And when at last were done,

Not even jelly beans remained-

No, they left not a one.

Now Tinies were a tiny lot

And ate their share of skin,

But greater things came after them

To wreak a deadly sin.

Though jelly beans might bite and munch,

There's something worse that creeps-

Beware marshmallows Easter Day-

Beware the killer Peeps!

The End

ROTTEN EGGS
Jeff Strand

"Oh no, don't eat me!" said seven-year-old Nicki, in a high-pitched voice, moving her chocolate bunny as if it were talking. "Don't eat my bunny ears!"

Brett, her little brother giggled and shoved some jelly beans into his mouth.

"It's not funny!" said Nicki as the bunny. "Please don't eat me! Noooooooo!" Nicki bit off the chocolate ears. "It hurts! It hurts!"

Their sister Rhonda, who was far too old for Easter baskets, looked away from her phone. "Eew! There's blood spraying everywhere!"

"No, there isn't," said Nicki.

"There is! Look at all that blood squirting out of your chocolate bunny's ears! It's getting all over everything! Eat it over the sink!"

"Mom!" Nicki called out. "Rhonda is doing gallows humor again!"

"Rhonda! Stop being morbid!"

"You were the one doing a funny voice while you ate its ears," Rhonda told Nicki. "Why are you amused by its suffering? Can you even imagine the sheer horror of having somebody chew your ears right off your head? Your action today is going to haunt your dreams for years."

"Mom! She's still doing it!"

"Rhonda! Save it for Halloween!"

"Fine, whatever," said Rhonda, looking back at her phone. "Why don't you eat its butt next?"

"I will!" Nicki did the high-pitched voice again. "Oh no, don't eat my fluffy tail! I'll do anything! Please! Nooooooo!" Nicki bit off the chocolate bunny tail, while Brett giggled some more.

Nicki and Brett, not known for their self-control, ate candy until they made themselves sick. Brett also ate a couple of strands of the plastic Easter grass that lined his basket.

"Aren't you guys going to do the Easter egg hunt?" Rhonda asked.

"Easter egg hunt! Easter egg hunt!" Brett shouted.

"The Easter Bunny went to a lot of work hiding all of them," said Rhonda. "If you don't look for them, he'll take it as a personal insult. You don't want to disrespect the Easter Bunny."

Nicki and Brett jumped to their feet. They ran around the house (wobbling a bit because of their queasiness) searching for the colorful eggs.

"We can't find any!" said Nicki, a few minutes later.

"What makes you think they're inside?" Rhonda asked.

The kids hurriedly ran outdoors to continue their search.

Mom walked into the living room. "Rhonda, thanks again for volunteering to hide the eggs. That was nice of you."

"Oh, sure, no problem. Happy to do it."

After about ten minutes, Nicki came back inside. "We can't find any of them."

"Did you even look?"

"Yes!"

Rhonda clucked her tongue. "The Easter Bunny doesn't like slackers. He went to all the trouble of setting up a fun Easter egg hunt for you, and you're spitting in his face. Is the problem that you *hate* the Easter Bunny?"

"No! We love the Easter Bunny!"

"You have a funny way of showing it. If I were the Easter Bunny— and you can thank baby Jesus that I'm not—I'd be devastated to find out that a little girl gave up on me so quickly. I'd cry bunny tears and I'd slink off to my dark, damp bunny hole and just sit there by myself, feeling lonely and unloved. I hope the Easter Bunny isn't a cutter."

"What's a cutter?" asked Nicki.

"That's enough," said Mom. "Rhonda's only teasing."

"Teasing? She eats the chocolate but doesn't want to do any of the work. She's in debt to the Easter Bunny for the candy she ate. Unless she wants him to take the chocolate back out of her stomach, she'd better get out there and find those eggs."

Nicki hurried back outside.

"I know it's fun for you to pick on your brother and sister," said Mom, "but I think you're taking the joke a little too far."

"They believe that a giant, magical rabbit gave them free candy. The joke had gone too far long before I got involved."

Mom smiled. "Fair enough. Just don't traumatize them, okay? I'm the one who has to pay the therapy bills."

"All right, all right, I'll behave."

Another ten minutes passed before Nicki and Brett came back inside. "We can't find *any* of them!" said Nicki.

"Not a single one?" asked Rhonda.

"Not one!"

"Wow. That's not going to make the Easter Bunny very happy. Did you even look?"

"We looked and looked and looked! It's not our fault!"

Rhonda shook her head sadly. "He's not a bunny you want to disappoint. But I'm sure he'll be okay with it, if you really did do your best."

"We did!"

"You're sure?"

"Yes!"

"Is the Easter Bunny sure he really hid the eggs?" Mom asked.

"Of course he is. The Easter Bunny isn't a total jerk. The eggs are out there, waiting to be discovered. It's just a shame that some children can't be bothered to look."

"We did look!" Nicki insisted. "We looked all over!"

"If the Easter Bunny gazes deep into your soul, will he believe you?"

Nicki and Brett went back outside.

"You did hide the eggs, right?" Mom asked.

"Yep."

"In *our* yard?"

"Yep."

"Do you think maybe you hid them too well?"

"Shouldn't we challenge them? What kind of adults will they grow up to be if everything is just handed to them?"

"I get what you're saying," said Mom. "But that's not really the point of an Easter egg hunt. If they've been looking for half an hour and haven't found a single one, you're not really being fair."

"Should I go out and tell them it was all a scam? End their childhoods early?"

"No. Maybe just give them some hints."

"They'll know that the Easter Bunny and I were in collusion. How do we explain that? How would I have that kind of information?"

"They're children, Rhonda. You can figure it out."

"All right. I accept no responsibility if their world becomes less filled with wonder." Rhonda got up from the couch and went out into the front yard, where Nicki and Brett were looking through some bushes. "Find anything?" she asked.

"No," said Brett.

"The Easter Bunny is getting madder and madder with every minute. Honestly, it makes me nervous to be around you. I hope he doesn't take it out on me, too."

"But we've looked *everywhere*!" said Nicki.

"Everywhere? Really? Are you telling me that you looked on the moon?"

"You know what I meant!"

"I do, but does the Easter Bunny? He's very literal."

"What does 'literal' mean?"

"Are you really going to waste time asking for definitions? My God, he could sink his fangs into your succulent flesh any moment now."

"He doesn't have fangs!"

Rhonda gave Nicki a very serious look. "Don't let him hear you saying that. He's very proud of his fangs."

"You're making all of this up. I'm going back inside."

Rhonda nodded. "You may be right. I may be playing a joke on both of you. And if you want to bet your lives on that... well, I understand. It's hard work, looking for Easter eggs. It's not worth the bother if you're one hundred percent positive that I'm making all of this up. I know that if I were absolutely, completely, *unquestionably* certain that somebody was playing a joke on me, I sure wouldn't be out here looking for eggs."

Brett began to cry.

"So what I'm saying is that, yes, I was just playing a joke, and probably nobody forced me to say that. You can call off the search. I'm sure everything will be fine."

Nicki and Brett glanced at each other, then resumed the hunt.

Three hours later, they'd found nothing.

"What if the Easter Bunny forgot to hide them?" asked Nicki, with a sniffle.

"Are you accusing the Easter Bunny of having Alzheimer's? Can you prove it?"

The door opened and Mom stepped outside. "Time to come in now."

"But we can't!" said Nicki.

"Yes, you can," said Rhonda. "I made it all up. The Easter Bunny doesn't care if you find his eggs or not. You guys are so dumb."

"He's going to sink his fangs into our flesh!"

"Did you hear that, Mom?" asked Rhonda. "They don't know how bunny teeth work."

"Enough," said Mom. "This has crossed the line. Nicki, Brett, your sister thought she was being funny, but she was just being mean. Everybody come in. It's time for dinner."

Nicki and Brett were still feeling sick to their stomachs from all the candy, but they managed to eat an acceptable portion of their ham. That night, they lay in bed in the room that they shared.

"I wish we'd found the eggs," said Nicki.

"Me too," said Brett.

"She was just trying to scare us."

"Yeah."

"I think."

"Yeah."

"We'd better sneak out and look some more. I don't want to go to sleep if the Easter Bunny is mad at me."

They quietly got out of bed and crept out of their room. Nicki picked up a flashlight and they very, very slowly opened the front door. They'd get in a lot of trouble if Mom caught them, but at least Mom wouldn't sink her teeth into their necks.

They searched for the eggs until Brett was so tired, that he couldn't stand up any longer. Why had the Easter Bunny made them so hard to find? Did he *want* to eat little children? Was he that hungry? Were they out of bunny food where he lived?

Nicki and Brett snuck back inside. Surely, the Easter Bunny would be impressed by how long they'd searched. He couldn't be mad, not when they'd put so much effort into playing his game, right?

Though Brett fell asleep quickly, Nicki spent the entire night staring at the ceiling, cringing at every sound. She thought she saw bunny ear shadows, darting across her bedroom wall, but decided that it was her imagination.

She was exhausted the entire next day at school. She even fell asleep once, snapping awake when Ms. Green whacked a ruler on her desk.

"I talked to the Easter Bunny," Rhonda told her that evening, when Mom was in the bathroom. "He's not happy."

"We looked!"

"I know you looked. That's why I put in a good word for you. But those eggs are out there, and as long as they go unfound, his rage will continue to grow. I asked if it was okay for Mom and I to help you, and he said no, absolutely not. In fact, he said that if you tell Mom you're still looking for them, he'll drag you into the pits of Hell."

"The Easter Bunny's from hell?"

"That's what he said. I don't believe him. You shouldn't, either. I'm sure you're not scared of Hell, anyway."

"There's nowhere left to look!"

Rhonda shrugged. "Those eggs are hidden somewhere on our property. If you want to give up, that's your choice."

Nicki chose to search.

Would the Easter Bunny have hidden them on the roof? Nicki couldn't imagine such a thing, but maybe she'd ask Rhonda to help her get the ladder out of the garage.

"They're not on the roof!" said Rhonda, later. "What are you, stupid? He doesn't want you to fall and break your neck! Jeez!"

Several days passed. Nicki didn't know what sanity was, but she could feel it slipping away. When Mom commented on the dark circles under her eyes, Nicki told her she was having nightmares, which was true, but she lied and said she didn't remember what they were about.

"It's been almost a week," said Brett, as they lay in bed unable to sleep. "He would've eaten us by now, wouldn't he?"

"Yes," said Nicki. And, she mostly believed that. But she didn't know what kind of schedule the Easter Bunny kept. If he only worked one night a year, that left a lot of free time. Maybe he was in no rush. Or, maybe, he had a lot of lazy children to eat.

On Friday night, Nicki was so tired that she almost walked into the wall. As she stumbled past Rhonda's bedroom, she heard her talking to a friend on the phone.

"My brother and sister are so dumb," she said. "You won't believe this..."

Nicki stood there for several minutes, getting madder and madder. When she heard Rhonda end the call, she hurried into her own bedroom.

At two in the morning, Nicki poked Rhonda in the chest with her index finger. "Get up," she whispered.

Rhonda sat up. "What do you want?"

"Come outside. It's important."

"Go back to bed."

Nicki shook her head. "We need your help."

Rhonda pulled the blankets over her head. Nicki tugged them back down.

"Fine, fine, whatever," said Rhonda. She got out of bed and quietly followed Nicki out of the house. Nicki led her to the backyard, where Brett was kneeling in the garden.

"We found them," said Nicki.

"Oh, yeah?" Rhonda grinned and walked over to Brett. "Nice... oh, God, those things *reek*!"

"You buried them," said Nicki. "All in one pile. I don't think that's very fair."

"Hey, don't blame me. The Easter Bunny must've—"

Rhonda pitched forward as Nicki shoved her from behind. She was able to break her fall with her hands, but now she was inches from the appalling odor, a smell so wretched it made her eyes water.

Nicki pushed her face into the pile of rotten eggs. The colorful shells cracked, slicing Rhonda's face as she plunged into the gooey mess. Watery egg slime went deep into her nostrils. She vomited, but didn't dare open her mouth.

"You made me scared of the Easter Bunny," said Nicki. "That wasn't nice."

Rhonda struggled to get free, but the smell was so overpowering that she thought she was going to pass out. A large piece of shell went into her right eye, and she let out a muffled scream that immediately made her suffering much worse.

"You should let her go now," said Brett.

"I will when I know she's learned her lesson."

"Mom's gonna be mad."

"I don't care," said Nicki, shoving Rhonda's face even further into the muck. Awful stuff went down her throat as a shell punctured her other eye.

Two minutes after Rhonda stopped moving, Nicki decided that her sister had learned her lesson.

The End

A TOWN CALLED EASTER

Kevin J. Kennedy

Nikki opened the picnic basket up and started setting out the various jams, marmalades, breads, cheese and crackers while Richard opened up the bargain basement bottle of bubbly they had bought for the occasion. They had been together for three months, each having spent a considerable amount of time single, recovering from their own bad relationships. It had been Richard's idea to get away for the day. He had never been the most romantic of men, and was trying to make sure that Nikki new how much he appreciated her, even though he wasn't the best at showing it all the time. Neither of them had much money, so this had seemed like a nice option.

"Did you bring any chocolate spread?" Nikki asked Richard.

"Uh, no. I thought we would act posh and have crackers n cheese and stuff like that," Richard said, grinning.

Nikki playfully punched him in the arm.."You're an idiot. Why'd you get all this stuff? You could have just got some crisps and some drinks and I'd have been happy," she told him, giving him her award winning smile. She was different from all the girls he had been with before. Nicer, less fake. He had never met anyone before, with whom he was so happy to spend so much time at home. They rarely left the house, anymore, other than to go to work.

"I thought you deserved a treat," Richard responded.

"Oh yeh, and what did I do to deserve this treat, might I ask?"

As she looked up at Richard from her seat on the tartan blanket they had laid down when they arrived, she could see he was no longer looking at her, but staring past her instead, into the distance. A quick glance over her should showed her nothing.

"Hey! Am I boring you?" Nikki asked, half joking, half annoyed.

No answer came straight away, but Nikki could see the look on Richard's face change.

"Get up! Get up now!" Richard urged, leaning forward and grabbing her around the wrist, and yanking her from her seat.

"Hey! What the fuck?" Nikki snapped, tugging her wrist back, but Richard didn't let her go.

"We need to run, Nikki! Now!" and with that Richard turned and started to run, pulling her with him. As Nikki started running, having no real other option as Richard had no intention of letting her go, she managed to look back over her should without falling and what she saw almost made her stop in her tracks. Although her mind filled with utter disbelief, she picked up her pace, and overtook Richard. Seeing that she was no longer fighting it, Richard let her wrist go, as she passed him, and picked up his own pace. The herd bearing down on them, was enough incentive for both to move at their top speed. Neither of them looked behind them as they sprinted towards the car that seemed to be their only protection.

Both Richard and Nikki crashed into the side of the car, not having slowed down enough on approach. Richard had already dug the keys out of his pocket but fumbled to get them in the lock.

"Fucking open it!" Nikki screamed, her voice high and whiny. "Quick! They're almost here!"

Richard grabbed her, and pushed her inside as he opened the door, diving in on top of her, and slamming it shut behind him. As the door slammed shut, there were three loud bangs, and the car shook with each. The animals smashing into the vehicle were roughly the same size and weight as wild boar, but looked completely different. They were covered in white fur, had pointy ears, and massive incisors. Other than the fact that they looked like they would tear most dogs apart, they looked pretty rabbit-like. Their legs were more like a dog's, but much more muscular, and their entire snouts were covered in scraggly looking whiskers. There was the sound of mental-bending as more of them smashed against the car, and the rattling of their massive nails, tapping the glass as some of them started to stand on their back legs, and look in through the side windows.

The engine roared to life, with Richard scarcely in his seat. It had been a struggle untangling himself from Nikki, the way they had jumped into the car, but he knew that time was of the essence. Jamming the gear stick into first gear, he stomped his foot on the accelerator, as he let the clutch up. The car began to wheel-spin in the still-damp grass, before catching and jerking forward. Just as the car stared to move, one of the giant rabbit-looking creatures came crashing through the back window. The glass erupted inwards, and covered both driver and passenger. Nikki screamed and Richard struggled to keep control of the car, as he headed back to the dirt track that brought them into the field.

"Nikki, do something. I can't let go of the wheel. There's a Maglite in your door." Nikki, having no idea what a Maglite was, and barely able to take her eyes of the monster that was halfway into the vehicle, nevertheless, quickly turned towards her door and looked in the tray. The only thing there was a massive metal torch. Nikki didn't give a fuck if it was the Maglite or not. She hurriedly wrapped her hand around the bottom of it, and turned back quickly. The beast was dragging itself further through the glass. Its white fur matted now, with red blood leaking out from where the broken window had cut it. Nikki quickly swung the torch as hard as she could, and connected with the front of its snout. She could feel the teeth crunch through the metal of the torch. The creature let out a horrific screech, before snapping at her. Several of its front teeth were now broken at awkward angles, but it just made it look all the more frightening. Nikki screamed as loud as she could but this time it wasn't high and shrill; it was filled with rage. She leaned further into the back of the car and started to repeatedly smash the torch down onto the thing's skull. The glass and bulb on the torch had broken with the first strike, but the solid metal was showing no sign of giving in. Her hand hurt, as she repeatedly struck the top of the creature's skull, but with each strike, it was receding back, out of the window. With one last mighty swing, she knocked the beast nearly unconscious, as it fell backwards through the glass; unable to keep its footing, it slid off the boot and into the grass, knocking over a few of the others who were following. As the animals howled and screeched, the car hit the dirt track and picked up speed, with the extra traction beneath the tires. Neither of them said anything as they sped back to the main road.

***

The two men stood, facing each other, in the middle of the military-style canteen. The compound was top of the range. Five of them had put up the cash to have it built, and moved in as soon as it was finished. The world was changing faster than ever and they were prepared for whatever came next. There were fifteen families, total, living there now. The compound had been built just a few miles from a little town, called Easter, with a population of just over two thousand. They rarely went into the town, but it was handy having it nearby, just in case. Most of what they needed was delivered in bulk, directly to the compound.

"What the fuck do you mean, 'they can't die'?" Tom, one of the initial five, asked Simon.

"We've been shooting them from the compound roof. They go down, but they get back up, in less than a minute. There were seven of us. Didn't take us long to put them down, but before we knew it, they were back up and attacking the gates. One of them was completely missing the top of its skull, and it was still throwing itself at the gate," Simon replied.

"I need to see this for myself. Let's go." And with that, they left the room.

***

Sam sat slumped in his chair, his back aching from years of bad posture. The local newspaper office was quiet, as always. Only the funding, from the town hall, kept them operational. There wasn't all that much news in a town the size of Easter, but the Mayor felt that every town should have a local paper, so it continued printing reports of who was pregnant, and who had died, even though everyone already knew before the paper hit the stands. He sipped at his frozen cold, strong black coffee as he stared out the glass front to the small office. The street outside was quiet as always, when the phone began to ring. *Wonder who's pregnant or dead this time.* Sam thought to himself. As the day progressed, the phone would continue to ring off the hook, long after Sam was dead.

***

"What the fuck do you mean, they just escaped?" Dr Arrivel, asked Winston.

"They got out boss. I'm sorry. It was my fault. It's…. you know…..
the Valium. My mind's so cloudy. It's my fault. I'm sorry," Winston
cowered in the corner, as he admitted his umpteenth fuck-up to his
boss. He knew the punishment would be severe; more so this time, than
ever. He knew it had taken Dr Arrivel years to perfect the Chaos Rabbits,
and now they were gone, all of them.

"Do you know what you have done, Winston? Letting those things
loose?" his boss said putting his head in his hands. Winston was
surprised that his boss hadn't struck him immediately, followed by a
sound beating.

"I'll get them back, boss. I promise. I just wanted to wait, and let
you know what's happened.

"Get them back! Do you know how many of them there will be
already? Do you know how quickly they breed? This town will be gone
by the morning, and then the next, and the next. We have to get out of
the country, and now!" and with that, Dr Arrivel turned, and left the
room quickly, leaving Winston standing alone, unsure of what to do.
After a few seconds, he rushed out of the room, quickly following his
boss.

***

"What the fuck *were* those things?" Nikki asked, in a panicked
voice, as they sped down the dirt track. She kept looking behind them,
but it didn't seem like the things were following.

Richard stared straight ahead, a look of determination on his face as he tried to keep the car on the track, driving a lot faster than anyone had in a long time on this narrow, half-road.

"I'm not sure they have a name, babe. They look pretty new. I think if they had been around for a while, Attenborough would have been all over that shit. Let's get back to town, and go straight to the police station."

"What, exactly, do you think old Bert is going to do about a hoard of killer rabbits, the size of dogs, Richard?" Nikki retorted, in a harsh tone.

"I don't fucking know, Nikki," Richard snapped back, then continued, "but *I* certainly don't fucking know what to do about them." It was the first time Richard had snapped at Nikki since they met and he regretted it, instantly, but the situation was far from normal and under the circumstances, he felt he shouldn't be too hard on himself. They were alive, and from the looks of things, they had escaped death. He would make it up to her as soon as they were out of this crazy situation.

***

"See, I told you." Simon, said to Tom, as the two men looked out at the compound gates. "They just keep attacking the fence. It may be reinforced, but eventually it's going to give. Doesn't really matter, now. Everyone is inside, and the place is on lockdown. They will never make it through the walls, even if they do get through the fence. The electricity running through the fence hasn't bothered them since we first shot them, but they seem to be learning. They have started to dig under the gate."

Tom took of his mirrored glasses, something Simon couldn't remember seeing before. The boss was one of those guys who wore his sunglasses in dark rooms. He looked towards Simon.

"I think this is the end of times, son."

Simon wasn't Tom's son. Tom called everyone 'son', even though he was only forty-eight himself.

"The end of times, boss?"

"There are giant fucking bunny rabbits attacking our electrified fence, some of which have parts of their skulls missing, with brains dripping out, and yet they still move. It's Easter fucking day and I've heard nothing of this on the news, which means this fucked-up situation started in a little town called Easter. Either somebody is about to make a fucking reappearance, or my name isn't Tom fucking McCallum."

***

Bazingo's friends all thought he was a bit mental. What was the point in being a clown in a town so small, with anywhere else so far away, that he would never make the journey? Bazingo, thought *they* were all mental, though. Clowns got a bad rap. Everyone thought they were creepy fuckers, scary; there were even people who had a phobia of them, what the fuck? Bazingo would make sure that, at least the kids of Easter town knew that clowns were people, just like everyone else. He spent more time online with his clown buddies these days, than he did in the outside world. His clown buddies understood him; he had even been invited to a few interesting clown circles that he never knew existed.

Backstage in the church hall, the only place in town that held any type of show outside of the town hall, he applied the finishing touches to his makeup. He always went with the predominately white face with a big red smile and rosy cheeks, no sad face or tears. He was a happy clown; he brought joy.

The church doors were never closed; the priest didn't believe in it. The church was for everyone, and he wanted people to know that. The rabbits' arrival went unnoticed by anyone. The church was still empty, other than Bazingo and the priest, but the priest had gone to search the rafters for some of the Easter props for the kids. Bazingo never heard the three oversized bunnies appear. Two still alive, saliva dripping from their massive incisors, the other was missing it's lower jaw, making it look even more terrifying than the others. It had no way to bite anymore but the massive bone-like claws, extending from its split paws were still deadly.

Bazingo, finishing applying the makeup, turned to see the three monsters standing in a semi-circle around him. The smile disappearing from his face barely showed through the makeup.

"What the fu……."

Bazingo's words were cut off by one of the live rabbits diving at him and burying it's teeth into his throat. The other two were on him before he hit the ground. The other live rabbit creature knowing at his innards as the dead rabbit moved through the church sniffing out the preacher. When the two live rabbits were finished with Bazingo, the sight he left was not one that would put a smile on children's faces.

***

The first rabbit, the one they had been testing on from the beginning sat hunkered in the cave. They had never been able to move it. It had given birth many times, each time to more deformed kits and most had been killed by the two humans that kept them. The last two litters had been much larger, both in number and size of the kits. All had survived and been caged by the humans. When they had seen their chance to escape, watched only by the buffoon assistant they had taken it. She was much larger than the others. She had survived for centuries in a cave on the coast of Scotland, happy in her life alone, often only visited by the gulls and sea creatures. She needed to eat rarely but when she did she would often be brought food by the passing wildlife. She was the mother of all known species in the Leporidae family, the first of her kind, the mother of them all. She needed no mate to breed, but when they started experimenting on her, that's when things had changed. They had inseminated her with all manner of animals and the results had been monstrous but it mattered not to her. She didn't understand modern values or religions or morals. She knew only that the kits were her children, her family and she needed as many of them to survive as possible. They had somehow sped up her cycle so she was almost constantly pregnant and with each new litter, the kits seemed to grow smarter. They grew to full size so fast and then they left her but she would have more, many more. As she went into labour, she could tell instantly that the newest batch of kits would be the largest yet.

***

Richard punched his foot down on the brake, causing the car to screech along the tarmac and stop only inches from the front of the small police office. He turned the engine off and jumped out of the car, leaving the door hanging open. "Come on." He said, waving Nikki with him as he burst thought the door, into the police office to find old Sam, asleep in his chair.

"Sam!" Richard shouted, causing Sam to sit up quick and spill his coffee all over his desk.

"For fuck sake, Richard! You'll give a man a heart attack. What in hells blazes has got you acting so crazy? You on drugs, boy?" asked the old cop, trying to look stern, while gathering his thoughts at the same time.

Just as Sam started to mop up the mess on his desk, the phone started ringing. He picked it up and Nikki and Richard watched as his face showed the confusion of what he was hearing.

"Giant rabbits, Mavis? Have you been drinking again?" he paused for a second and they could hear Mavis giving Sam the 'what-for' over the phone. "Okay Mavis, I'll be right over. Just you stay inside." And with that, he put the phone down. "Now, as you can see I'm pretty busy, so if you could just tell me why you came barging into my office like bats-out-of-hell, you can be on your way."

"We saw them, the rabbits. That's what we came here to tell you. There are loads of them and they are massive," said Nikki, rushing to get her words out. "They rammed our car."

"Rabbits rammed your car?" Sam asked, in a disbelieving voice. He pushed passed the young couple shaking his head, as he made his way to the door. "Maybe I'll catch myself some dinner on my rounds. Been a while since I had a nice rabbit stew." And he turned and pushed the door to the small office opened and was out on the street.

He had gone no more than two steps, when one of the creatures hit him, head height and took him to the ground. The beast landed on his chest and started ripping at his face, drowning out his screams as it tore the flesh from his face. Another joined it, quickly burying its maw in Sam's stomach and tearing his insides out. Soon, what little of Sam was left, couldn't be seen by Nikki and Richard, as there were at least fifteen of the monsters fighting for the scraps. It was quite a sight to behold. Some of the creatures had clearly been killed or badly wounded, but they moved amongst the others, their pace scarcely slowed. There was more variety among the herd, too. *Were they a herd or a pack?* Nikki wondered to herself. Some of the rabbit creatures were twice the size of the other German Shepherd-sized ones that they had seen earlier and while others were similar in size, they had less fur and it was darker. These were a lot more muscular than the rest, their tongues much longer too. Some of their tongues must have been a foot in length.

Just as Richard was wondering whether their best option was to lock themselves in a cell and wait for help, the creatures' heads all turned away from the window at once, obviously distracted by something outside. Like some mutated plague of monsters, hopping over cars and crushing the metal beneath their feet as they went, in a second they were gone.

Nikki looked at Richard with tears in her eyes. "We're going to die, Richard, aren't we?"

"Not if I have anything to do with it," he said, grabbing her hand and pulling her to the door. He peeked outside and could see the street seemed empty.

"Okay, when we get outside, just run for the car and don't stop for anything.

***

Easter town centre wasn't all that large. A few shops, a hairdressers, a small bank and a bar. In the middle of the day, though, it was where most of the townsfolk were, for one reason or another. When the creatures descended, it was all-out carnage. Men, women and children were run down in the street and torn apart in seconds. The rabbit monsters were everywhere; the larger ones had taken to jumping through store windows to attack those inside and allow their smaller kin entrance.

Some of the townsfolk fought back, using whatever came to hand as weapons, but there were too many of the creatures—there had to be hundreds. Those who fought, at best killed a few of the monsters, but they were quickly replaced by others and the rabbits that fell, got back to their feet only moments later. Some of the creatures were missing both eyes and yet they still went on, causing a path of destruction. Some of the creatures had most of the skin from around their mouths missing, causing the bone of their jaws to extend out; they looked absolutely horrifying. A few people made it to their cars and sped away, on route out of town or to pick up loved ones before leaving, but the rabbits gave chase, determined to leave no one alive.

***

Tom and Simon stood on the roof of the compound, surrounded by almost everyone else who lived there. Almost everyone there had their rifle amongst several other fire arms. When the rabbits had made it through the gates, they had started picking them off, but it was more for fun than anything else. The men knew the creatures couldn't get inside the walls, and they were only down for a few moments, before getting back up; obviously, the bullets didn't stop them. They had killed a few of them using grenades, but as more and more of the things kept turning up, they decided to hold onto their ammo for the time being.

At first they had all agreed against calling outside for help. They didn't want any government officials snooping around the compound but, after a while everyone agreed that they needed the outside held. They were entirely surrounded now by the things and the number seemed to keep growing. It seemed impossible, but the things seemed to give birth every few hours and the kits grew to full-size in an hour. It was unbelievable to watch. The call had been a hard one to make and the story was not pleasantly received, but they had done it. No one had come for them, though and there was no response from the other end, now. Could this be happening everywhere Tom wondered, as he looked out into the distance to watch more of the creatures lopping over the hill toward them.

***

Just outside the town limits, Richard pulled the car over to the side of the road, as the engine finally gives out.

"Oh my god! Richard, we can't stop here for fuck sake! We're in the middle of nowhere," Nikki said, with more than a little hint of fear in her voice.

"We've run out of petrol. I totally forgot. We were a bit distracted just trying to get out of there alive. I didn't have any more money for petrol. I spent the last of my cash on the picnic stuff. Although Nikki wanted to scold him, she also felt a little flutter in her heart. It lasted barely a second before the fear crept back.

"So what now?" Nikki asked.

"Well, I think we'd better start running. I don't know how much distance we put between them and us now, but it won't take them long to catch up. We need to find an old farm house or something because this car certainly wont keep them out."

"Fuck!" Nikki knew he was right. She just didn't want to believe it. Richard leaned over and pulled her in for a hug. With his arms round her he whispered in her ear. "Baby, I love you, but we need to go." And with that, they let each other go, got out of the useless vehicle and ran into the night.

***

As it got darker outside, everyone from the compound had vacated the roof and gone inside to either try and sleep, or get something to eat. Only Tom and Simon remained, looking out at what must have been thousands of the creatures lopping around and attacking each other. The number of variations was hard to count, but Tom could swear there were at least thirty different species or types of the creatures, and that wasn't including the ones that he was sure had altered looks due to their injuries or deformities.

"You know. I think we will be okay in here, at least for a while." Tom said.

"What do you mean?" Simon asked

"Well. It's the end. No one survives the end but I think we have a while left."

"The end. Like of times? Like you said earlier?"

"Yeh"

"You believe in all that Bible crap?"

"Na, I don't believe any of the religions have it right. I do think someone started all this mad shit that we call life, but I think He is probably a bit bigger than the stupid shit we attach to Him. He's back and He's pissed. Whether man made these rabbits or not it, was in His plan. He's not '*a*' god, He's the only God. The One who started it all and the One who's decided to end it now. It always had to end with us, I thought He would let us fuck it all up for ourselves, if I'm honest. We didn't have long left anyway, considering the way the world is going but He's obviously bored with our shit. Or maybe it was something else. Who knows? I can barely stand any-fucking-one. God only knows how He tolerated billions of us."

***

Dr Arrivel and Winston looked out to sea from the back of the ship. They had made their escape from the UK island, but they knew what they unleashed wouldn't stop there. They were only buying themselves time.

"You know Winston, I should have left you back there to die. You are the most useless excuse for a human being I have ever come across. I'm sure that those things will make it across the water somehow but if they don't I'm going to need you to help me with something."

"Yes boss, yes boss, anything." Winston replied quickly, nodding as he did.

"I've heard rumours that an old hunter who lives in the Appalachian Mountains has real proof that Bigfoot exists. Maybe if we can get to him in time..... Maybe..... Yes. We can create an army. That's it. I'll be a hero, the saviour of the human race."

Winston didn't like the sound of it. His boss's ideas always involved kidnapping someone or something and things always turned out bad. Still, what else was he going to do? He had no home to go back to. The UK would be decimated. If he had just never told his boss about the giant rabbit in the cave, none of this would have ever happened.

***

As the rabbits savaged the last residents of the little town called Easter, a man sat in the cave alongside the giant rabbit. His side pressed into the rabbit's soft fur, gently stroking it, with a contented smile on his face. They looked out into the night sky and appreciated the stars more than either of them had ever appreciated mankind.

The End

LORD OF THE DANCE

J. C. Michael

Blood ran from his wrists: thick, dark, warm. His hands raised above his head, it flowed quickly down his arms, before pooling momentarily on his shoulders, then coursing over his scarred, muscular, chest. As it continued to flow, he knew that the amount pulsing from his wounds was in excess of that which a normal man held within his body, but it had been a very long time since he had been such a man. In defiance of gravity, the blood on his shoulders began to flow upwards: tendrils at first, and then thick fingers around his throat and to his stubbled chin. As it reached his jaw, and began to cover the whole nape of his neck, he felt trickles of blood run down from his scalp; the droplets running down his face as if eager to join the mass that covered his broad shoulders. Soon, his naked body was awash with blood: blood that symbolised his own, blood that symbolised those he had killed—2,000 victims dead at his hands. Hands he now held in front of eyes stinging from the blood that washed over them. Hands that were the only part of his body that remained unstained, yet he felt he would never be able to scrub them clean.

***

It wasn't a new dream. He had dreamt it many times, and always more frequently at this time of year. A time of year dictated by his body and knowledge only he possessed, rather than the calendar decreed by the Church. His body was wet with a cold, sticky sweat and his clothes were sticking to him, making him feel all the more uncomfortable by the position he lay in; a position which gave him very little opportunity for movement. He'd been entombed beneath the greenhouse floor for a week now, his body stiff and aching from the lack of movement. He could shift himself enough, however, to begin un-wrapping the sodden bandages from his wrists. The wounds beneath looked fresh in the light of his head-torch, and he carefully removed the wadding filling the holes that punctured his wrists from front to back. How his hands worked despite the damage, he had little idea; it was but one of many things he had stopped trying to figure out. Besides, the wounds would soon be healed, and become little more than scars which would lay dormant for another year, before blooming into life once more at the time of his calling.

His wounds freshly dressed, he stuffed the old bandages in his waste bag, a black duffel full of bottles of urine and a Tupperware box of excrement. It was almost time. A dog barked. He heard voices approaching. He closed his eyes and lay still.

***

"Come in Alpha 1, Alpha 2 reporting in."

"Alpha 1 receiving, Alpha 2. Proceed with report."

"Area 3 clear. Now checking Area 4 for final sweep."

"Report received, Alpha 2. Complete the sweep and then return to HQ for final briefing. All operations are on schedule."

"Received Alpha 1. Alpha 2 out."

Two men walked the roof. Their uniforms, body armour, and peaked caps: all black and matched exactly, as did their equipment - light machine gun, stun grenades, pistols, and combat knives. The only difference was that one was holding the lead of an Alsatian, the other carrying a thermal camera.

"Do they really think somebody would be stupid enough to be up here?"

The second man sighed. His colleague was relatively new to the job; a good dog handler, but one of those men that always has a question ready on his tongue.

"Probably not, but that's because we check, isn't it? If we didn't set a perimeter, and didn't sweep the area, then some nutter would get the idea that they could hide away up here. The fact we check is what stops there being anything to find. Besides, there's always the off-chance that somebody would be stupid enough to give it a go."

"Sometimes I wish they would; give us a bit of excitement."

The sigh was louder this time. "Excitement? That's what you'd call it, if we came up here and found somebody with a gun, or a bomb? You wait until you've had some excitement, son, then you won't be so keen for a repeat."

"Come on, you can't say there isn't a bit of a thrill when things get hairy."

The second of the men, the older one now standing by the greenhouse with the thermal camera, grinned, "Aye, there is lad, but the paperwork afterwards is a fucking nightmare."

***

He could hear them walking above him. The dog was panting, claws scraping on the boards. They were talking about the plants and vegetables: how it wasn't a bad idea to have a little greenhouse so high up above the city and the pollution that sat heavy in the car-swamped streets, and where the sun wasn't blocked out by surrounding buildings. They started to walk away, and he eased his finger off the trigger of the gun he had held pointing toward them. It wasn't a surprise that they had missed him—they always did. It was part of the deal; part of the protection. People and animals had always looked the other way. Equipment always gave false readings. And luck always fell on his side, although luck could cut things pretty damn fine at times.

***

"It will soon be time."

The voice belonged to his own "Alpha 1", but he didn't need a radio to receive his instructions. Edging forward, he began to ease the concrete block out of the wall in front of him and slide it aside, toward the old pallets that the greenhouse had been built upon, and which had created the space he had inhabited since receiving the call to get ready. Blood was already beginning to show on his wrists, but the flow always increased around this time, and it was of no consequence. Soon, it would all be over. Soon, he could return to his comfortable house away from the modern world. He lived a life apart, despite the fact it was increasingly difficult to divorce himself from a world becoming ever smaller, and ever more invasive; but he wasn't of the modern world, and never would be.

The sunlight that shone into his hideout warmed his face for a moment, until he shimmied back into the darkness and began to set up his rifle in front of him. The weapon readied, he looked down the 'scope and swept it across the factory yard, far down below. A banner had been strung above the door – "Wood and Rose Welcome the President of the United States" – and he set the rifle at the centre of the doorway. As far as targets went, this was as big as they came, and would rank pretty highly amongst the 1,979 that had gone before. A small smile played at the corner of his mouth, at least this time it was someone he agreed needed to be killed. It was always harder when he didn't understand. When it was a child that had to die, in order to avoid fulfilling a dangerous destiny, or someone who, to all intents and purposes, looked like a good man, or woman. But it wasn't his place to question why; his purpose was to ensure that the target would die. And who was he to doubt the instruction he received? Had he not doubted at times yet seen the justification unfold following the event? The tireless celebrity charity worker cruelly stabbed by a mugger in a park, only to be outed as a predatory paedophile before the year was out. The billionaire philanthropist that the world mourned, along with half a dozen African leaders, who found it harder to come by the weapons they used to kill thousands of their own people after his death. There were times he worried the cycle would come to an end. Perhaps once he had killed 2,000? But he had thought that at 50, 100, and 1,000, too. At other times, he worried: perhaps, he had been duped, but then, he would see the evil in those who fell to him. He would see the justification in his purpose, and that, one day, he would ascend to Heaven for his deeds, and not be dragged to the pit of Hell. But, for the most part, he was content with his lot in life; he had lived enough lives to accept his role within a design he could never hope to understand. He was a tool, honed over centuries by the only Master one should follow in life – he was an instrument of God.

***

Forget what you have read; he was an eyewitness, and his story is untarnished by the thoughts and beliefs of those who have followed. Like many others, he had swarmed the streets to see Jesus taken to his place of execution. Like many of those in the crowd, he had been beaten back by the Roman soldiers, his nose broken by the hilt of a sword. Undeterred by the pain and the blood on his face, he had pressed through the crowd to see the man who he had believed would be their king, dragged through the streets of Jerusalem. Christ did not carry the cross. Christ did not stumble beneath the weight of the crosspiece, as he approached Golgotha. Those who wrote of such feats had their reasons, and knowing them, he understood their desire to embellish and enhance, but the truth was that Jesus of Nazareth had to be dragged, for He was all but dead before He reached the Hill of Skulls. His back had been whipped until only scraps remained, and the open wounds were sore from the heat and dirt. A barbed crown had been forced upon His head, the thorns puncturing His scalp so that His face was red with blood. His eyes were closed, swollen shut by fat, purple bruises matched only by the bruising that covered the rest of His body. Had they left Him in the street, He wouldn't have lasted out the day, but the Romans had to make their statement; even had He died on His way to the cross, they would still have nailed Him up for the carrion birds to have their fill.

Swept along in the crowd, he reached the outskirts of the city, and the sky above was clear and blue. On any other day, it would have been said that God was smiling on the Earth, for the beauty of the heavens was a direct contrast to the turmoil and grief below. As the crowd shouted and cursed, the Romans began their executions, saving Jesus of Nazareth until last. As the heavy iron nails were driven into his wrists, he never moved. Nor did he flinch, as the crosspiece was placed into position, and his ankles fixed to the upright by a single spike. Then, as Christ was hauled upright under the mid-day sun, the soldiers felt they had demonstrated their power over the man who had claimed to be the son of a God they didn't recognise, and they now needed to show their authority over those who remained. They drove into the crowd with clubs, swords, and shields, while centurions bellowed over the noise, that any who failed to disperse would be executed on the spot. The crowd dispersed, but as it did, Jesus of Nazareth raised his head to the heavens. Only a few saw it. That final breath of life. And he was one of them.

***

"They should pay for what they did to Him."

The cloaked figure spoke to him from the shadows, as he walked home that evening. His nose was throbbing, but the pain had been dulled by wine. He stopped and looked into the shadows, "I agree, but that is not what He taught."

"He was young, and those that are young have much to learn. His teachings would have developed over time, as the seed grows to become a tree. And when a tree is grown, it is akin to its father, for it takes the form of its father; a form stronger than the seed or the sapling. A form that understands the world around it, for it has grown in the only way it can, if it wishes to survive, and is a seed no more."

He nodded.

The figure approached. "Would his Father have turned the other cheek? Or are we not taught to take an eye when an eye is taken from us?"

"Who are you?"

The figure was up against him now, whispering, "I am a Father without a Son. I am a Father seeking one who will avenge Me. I am a Carpenter in need of an axe."

That was when he felt it. Blood running from his wrists, blood running from his scalp.

"The Roman who dragged your King through the streets like a dog, is patrolling but a street away. Take this."

A rock pressed into a palm, slick with blood.

"Cast this rock upon them and when they chase you, he will be the one to follow your trail, and you will be the one to make amends."

He stepped away "I am not a murderer; I am but a simple man."

The cloaked figure also stepped back, back toward the shadows, "This is not murder, My son, this is justice. You are sharing my Son's pain as you bleed and the only way for it to abate is to avenge His suffering. You are an angel now. So fly."

***

It had been as the man had said. The soldiers were on patrol, and the rock was thrown. They chased him through winding streets, until he felt his lungs would burst—his breathing encumbered by the damage to his nose—until... there he was, a single Roman soldier standing in front of him, his sword drawn. Turning back was impossible, as the rest of the soldiers were behind him. The one facing him, clearly having the foresight to cut him off. This one, so easily recognisable as one of those who had dragged Jesus through the dirt, who smiled between grimaces of exertion as he did so.

"I've killed one Jew today, now I shall add a second to my tally."

He had no idea what to do. No weapon with which to either defend or attack. Nothing to arm himself with, but a knife that sat on the windowsill to his right, next to a loaf of bread, cooling in the night air. He grabbed the knife as the soldier ran to him, and as his fingers closed around it, he felt the sword run into his side as the soldier ran into him, taking him down into the dirt. The pain swept through him, paired with a fury he had never felt before; a fury with which he drove the knife into the soldiers neck again and again and again. Blood spurted from the soldier's throat in bursts, as he gurgled curses, and, as he rolled the soldier off of him, he felt his wounds heal; both those on his wrists and the one in his side.

"You are Mine now. A killer. An instrument of My wrath. Was not David the slayer of Goliath? Did Moses not kill the Egyptian? To kill is not to sin when it is in My name, and I will call upon you to serve Me again."

There was nobody there. Just a voice. The soldiers never found him, and he returned to his home and the wife and children he would outlive. He would outlive everyone he would ever know.

***

Since then, he had been called upon every year to do God's bidding. The voice would give him instructions; a target, and guidance on how to eliminate it. In the days before the event, the stigmata would return, and only heal once the task was complete. Once, he had decided not to carry out God's bidding and had bled for a year. His crops had failed, his family died of pestilence, and his dreams were plagued each night by Angels cursing his failure. The next year was the first time he was called upon to kill a child—a test of his loyalty, just as Abraham had been tested through Isaac. This time, however, he wasn't called upon to kill his own son, nor was the child reprieved. And the man who had been spared the previous year? After avoiding the assassin's blade, he went on to butcher many: raping and slaughtering his way across Europe. At times, it felt as though all that blood was just as much on his hands, as those of the man who had committed the atrocities, for he had failed in his holy duty, and allowed those crimes to come to pass.

There had been one other occasion where his victim had survived his attempt to carry out the Father's will, and again he had bled for a month and suffered for his failure. The symptoms lifted when he suffocated the recovering woman in her hospital bed.

***

The voice had been the same for two millennia, as was the stigmata; and now, the time for reflection had passed. Looking down the 'scope he saw a line of cars approaching. Police outriders led the way, followed by bulky vehicles he would need far more than a rifle to damage. Over the years, he had come to be well-versed in the art of war—it was one of the few constants of human behaviour—he slowed his breathing as the cars came to a halt. He rested his finger on the trigger and waited, trying to clear his thoughts, but couldn't help wondering if this shot would spawn as many conspiracy theories as the shot he had taken in Dallas. The door of the largest, and most central, vehicle in the column opened. A young woman stepped out, less than half the age of the President and yet another symbol of a divided society – "he did right to trade in for a younger model," versus "he's old enough to be her daddy,"—such a divisive figure had never led the country, albeit a nation which was relatively young. A distinctive head began to rise up out of the car, the crosshairs lingered over it for a split-second as his own head began to tingle with trickles of blood running from his scalp, and then the President's head exploded as the high-impact round slammed into it from the back. The kill confirmed, he didn't wait to watch the Secret Service scurry around like ants; he would watch it all on FOX news, later. The items he had used—the bag full of piss and shit, the weapon, the food he had left over and the wrappers from what he had consumed—were all quickly stuffed into two duffel bags and pushed deeper under the pallets. There would be an investigation, but they would miss them. They always did. Putting his hand in his pocket, he removed a rosary, a rosary to which a piece of the true cross was attached. A genuine piece of the true cross, not one of the thousands of fakes that had surfaced during the Crusades. He raised it to his lips, kissed it, and noticed that his wrists were healed. He smiled, and as the sirens wailed, slipped away.

***

Inside the factory, Mr. Wood stood and looked out of the window at the pandemonium below. He was humming a tune, and then under his breath began to sing "Dance, Dance, Wherever you may be, For I am the Lord of the dance said he, And I'll lead you all wherever you may be, For I am the Lord of the Dance said he."

The End

EASTER GUNNY
Peter Oliver Wonder

Between his paws rested a bone, which he gnawed on with his sharp, yellowed-stained teeth. The miniature Australian Shepherd lay on the fenced-in porch of the mobile home. Pausing from the tedious chore of grinding against the bone with his teeth, he licked at the treat in appreciation. It wasn't often that he got to enjoy something that came directly out of a living being, but this ham bone was well worth the wait each year.

Or, maybe, that was just what he was made to believe by owners who would rather keep their dog tame.

Their dog, thought his little doggy mind, as images of wolves played on the box of light through the screen door. Gunny watched as it stalked its prey before grabbing it by the neck and giving it a violent shake.

What would his ancestors think? Somewhere inside his miniature frame was the blood of a wolf. Would a wolf be content to lay on a porch and be thrown scraps from a human family that was disinterested in him most of the time?

One of the human children came over and gave him a scratch between the ears before running his fingers down his back, through his long, soft coat—the orange, black, and gray hair all intermingling as he did so. "Happy Easter, Gunny," said the little human. Gunny loved the little human. Just as the thoughts about being something more than a pet were beginning to fade, the little human reached between his paws and removed the bone upon which he had been chewing.

"You want this, Gunny?" the young human teased. "Do ya want it, boy?"

Gunny stood from his comfortable lying-down position, and then placed his hindquarters on the wooden planks, orientating himself in a way that he would best be able to attack, should the young male not wish to return what rightfully belonged to him. He was unable to keep his tongue from lolling from his mouth, no matter how hard he tried.

"Go get it, boy!" shouted the little human, gleefully. Gunny began to race down the hallway, but stopped in his tracks after only a few paces. Ears high in the air, he waited to hear where it may have fallen. Perhaps it was the crowd of people causing too much noise, for him to be able to pinpoint the exact location of where it had fallen, or maybe...

The laughter of the small human caused Gunny to turn back around. He was now waving the bone in the air before him, taunting Gunny, as his tongue continued to lick at his flews where a faint taste of the ham still remained.

This is so wrong, Gunny thought. *All of this trouble for a bone with naught but the* taste *of meat. What I need is to get my teeth into some real meat.*

Of course, once the human finally threw the bone, instinct took over, and Gunny chased it down—his nub of a tail wiggling back and forth with glee as he did so.

"Are you kids ready for the hunt?" asked the older female that lived in the home. Cheers erupted from the young humans as they all ran out onto the porch, pouring through the front gate before going down the steps.

Not wanting to be away from his pack, Gunny was quick to follow. He playfully jumped his front paws up onto the little humans, only to be pushed away. It wasn't long before they had all dispersed in pursuit of their treasures.

With his animal instincts at full throttle, Gunny began sniffing around for what the others may be seeking. Out toward the far end of the lawn, there was a hint of something in the air that was not supposed to be there. There were other scents in the air—the smells of sugar, chocolate, and the copper disks the little ones seemed to think quite highly of—but what Gunny's nose was leading him to was something new.

The smell was accompanied by a sound. It was a sound he wasn't quite able to place. As he made his way toward the mystery, there was a spot on the grass some other canine had tried to claim for himself. Gunny wasn't about to let that slide, and so covered it with his own fresh batch of urine. There was only time for a quick squirt.

His nose was now full of the smell of whatever may be on the edge of the lawn. Gunny gracefully galloped over to the bushes and began sniffing around the front, and over to the side. Once he got to the reverse side, he found a long-eared creature unlike anything he had ever seen before.

The animal before him had Gunny in a bit of a quandary. Was this an invader? Was it a new member of the pack? It didn't take Gunny long to notice the very large incisors of this creature and took them to be a threat. He let out a growl to test the waters with this new animal. It refused to back down—its whiskers poked him in his left eye as it tried to sniff at him.

This would be its last mistake.

With its face right next to Gunny's mouth, it was nothing for him to open his jaw and clamp it down on the thing's neck, catching its long ears in his maw at the same time. Its hind legs kicked as it tried to get away, but a quick shake ended whatever resistance the thing may have thought to make.

Warm blood trickled down Gunny's jawline and flowed down into his throat. He continued to gnaw at the vertebrae inside the broken neck. The warm flesh and blood felt good on his gums and in his mouth. Proudly, he lifted the dead thing into the air and began to saunter back over to the humans, still chewing on the dead flesh.

As a scream issued forth from the once joyful front yard, Gunny stopped where he was. Because he was expecting praise, the quick kick to the ribs was all the more surprising. The grown human male, who lived in the house, was screaming something at him and slapped his nose, causing him to drop the small, dead thing.

Gunny knew the human's kick was held far back from what it could have been, so there was no serious bodily injury as Gunny whimpered off, back up the steps to the porch and through the still-open screen door. In the dining room, the door to his kennel was open. He walked inside, then got into his bed to think about what had just happened.

With his head resting upon his paws, he turned the events over in his head. The little humans were all happily searching in the yard for something, and he had found 'something'. There was an intruding creature on the property, and he had prevented it from attacking any of the humans on his watch.

Or maybe the humans wanted to keep the creature?

Maybe, they were looking to replace him.

Gunny's head popped up as the front door opened and the humans began to enter. Several of the little ones were crying. As they looked at Gunny in his kennel, they only started to cry more.

"You're a *bad* dog," said the grown female as she entered, holding the small child of the house in her arms.

When the grown human male of the house entered, he walked straight over to the kennel and grabbed Gunny's collar, then began to drag him toward the door. "Goddamn dog," he muttered as he jerked on the collar, cutting off his breathing and causing him to hack.

With a final tug, Gunny was thrown in front of the male human and out the door. Once the male was outside with him, the door was shut and the two were on the porch together. The gate that led to the stairs was still open, and a foot forced Gunny down the steps. His paws missed the first step and his lower jaw fell upon the edge of it, before he found his footing and avoided stumbling down the rest.

Bowing his head, Gunny tried to look submissive so the male wouldn't be too angry with him. "Go. Now," commanded the human as a foot shooed him toward the driveway. Gunny did as he was told, and continued to look back to make sure he was doing what was expected of him.

I'm nothing more than a pet. I have no will of my own. To do as I'm told, that is my lot in life. A wolf would never take this kind of treatment.

"Sit," the human snarled. Being the obedient pet he was, Gunny did as he was told, and took a seat on the driveway. He watched as the human unwound the hose from the side of the house, then cranked the little wheel above it.

A blast of cold water assaulted his face. The pressure was up much higher than it normally was when he was given a bath. The water hurt as it filled his nose and eyes. When he tried to turn away, the human followed him with it, attacking him ruthlessly with the intense stream of water.

"You killed the fucking bunny on Easter, Gunny," the man growled angrily. "You just might have ruined this holiday for the rest of these kids' lives!" The human moved closer with the hose, but dropped the stream from Gunny's face to his chest, washing the blood from the white of his coat.

A sneeze sent water flying from his snout, like a double barrel water gun. Despite the warm weather, the cold water in the shade made him start to shiver. The blast from the hose stung wherever it hit him. "Goddamn it! What has gotten into you?" the man asked, furiously. The hose was moved back to Gunny's face, causing him to inhale some of the water through his nose.

He snarled and bit at the water that was being used as a weapon against him. "What's the matter? Don't like that?" the human asked. "Well, I don't appreciate that you ruined the surprise for the kids!" A sustained blast of water was directed at his face once more.

A line had now been crossed. He would be a "g'boy" no more. Gunny lunged at the human, and sunk his teeth into his lower leg. The human let out a scream, before falling to the ground. As he did so, he released the hose, and the water finally stopped spraying.

"Son of a bitch! You are fucking dead!" The human reached for Gunny's collar, but his hand only found the sharp teeth that had penetrated his leg. His flesh was punctured again, as the fangs sunk in, between his metacarpals. Another scream escaped the man, as he reached over with his other hand.

Rather than snapping his jaws shut on the new hand, Gunny lunged toward the human's face. His lower teeth hooked under the human's jaw, as his top teeth came down just below his right eye. The good hand was pinned between the dog and his own chest as he tried to push the animal away.

The human managed to get some distance between himself and Gunny, but that only resulted in the animal's teeth tearing their way through his cheek. Scrambling to attack further, Gunny went for the throat this time, as he had seen the wolves in the light box do to smaller animals.

His teeth pierced the tube in the human's throat with little resistance before his jaw snapped shut. After a quick twist, Gunny pulled the tube away and watched, snarling, as the human grabbed at the area that had just been utterly decimated.

As he watched the blood drain from the human, who was steadily growing weaker, he heard something from behind him. It was faint at first, but began to increase as he continued to watch the red puddle spread across the driveway.

The sound was a tiny sob, coming from the little girl that lived in the house. Gunny turned his head, feeling the warmth of the blood, now thick in his chest fur, though the rest of his body remained cold from the blasts of water. Gunny began to take steps toward the child but, before he could get near, she let loose a scream of horror, then ran back indoors.

Gunny ran toward the steps, but before he could even get his hind legs up on the first one, more screams erupted from inside the home. He stopped in his tracks, contemplating his next move.

What have I done? Perhaps this was a step too far?

He looked back, behind him. The body was out of sight, around the corner, but the pool of blood was expanding to the edge of the driveway, and spilling into the gutter.

The sound of the door opening again caused him to snap his attention back in front of him. The grown female was bawling as she held the young female in her arms. Once she saw what was waiting in the driveway, she freed one of her hands from the young one, and covered her mouth with it. Her eyes widened and tears silently fell down her cheeks.

This is bad, thought Gunny, as he lowered his head in shame. The thick blood that was on his chest was quickly growing cold. Putting on his best 'sad puppy' face, Gunny walked up the steps with his head bowed.

"AHHH!" the grown female shrieked.

Gunny bolted back down the stairs, as the humans turned and headed back inside. After descending the final step, he made a sharp right turn and entered the hole that lead beneath the porch.

In his secret place, he lay down, and placed his head on his paws. He was terrified. All he had wanted to do was to be a good dog and partake in whatever sort of ritual his humans were taking part in.

He had so enjoyed killing the small thing with the long ears. It was so much fun, he couldn't help but get carried away when the human was mistreating him. Gunny thought they had been friends. Whenever the human was upset about something, Gunny was there to bring a smile to his face. Then he was punished for simply being a dog?

No, there was no excuse for his actions. He had killed his friend and made the other humans sad. He had been a very bad dog.

He wished he could take it all back. He wished he had never found that stupid creature and had, instead, just eaten some of the colorful eggs that the young humans had been seeking out. Sure, he still would have gotten in trouble, but no one would have been crying. No one would have been this upset due to a colorful egg having gone missing.

The door overhead opened, and Gunny could hear the young ones screaming and crying before it was slammed shut. Slow footsteps made their way down the stairs. He lifted his head and listened to the footsteps with his ears raised.

After the stairs, he could still hear her soft footsteps as they continued on in his direction. He could see the shadow as

it approached his secret entryway.

Her ankles were now in plain view. She stopped walking and just stood outside the hole in the siding. There were soft sobs coming from the human outside.

Gunny stood and walked over to his secret door. He poked his head outside and saw the human standing there with an unknown object in her right hand, and tears silently streaming down her cheeks.

She looked down at him and put the object near his head. Gunny closed his eyes and sniffed at it. The object had an unfamiliar smell, but it didn't last.

When he opened his eyes, the woman was gone, and so was the house and everything else he had expected to see. In its place was a beautiful field of grass with several of the creatures from earlier, hopping with their ears flopping around as they did so.

The cold wetness had disappeared from his head and chest. The guilt was no longer on his mind. In fact, the adult male was there beside him, petting the top of Gunny's head.

"You're a good boy," said the human. Gunny's attention once more went to the creatures in the field. "Go get 'em, boy!"

Gunny took off from the man in a prance—tongue hanging from the side of his mouth. He grabbed the first creature by the neck and gave it a violent shake. He could feel the neck bone snap in his mouth which filled him with a feeling of satisfaction.

"That's a good boy, Gunny! Get 'em all!"

The End

IT'S NOT ALL ABOUT BUNNIES AND CHOCOLATES

Veronica Smith

Jean stared in shock at her monitor. She usually hated and ignored those annoying ads that showed up on the sidebar of her Facebook feed; however, this one was different, and caught her eye. This one had a picture of a Hatch-A-Pet.

They were the latest craze to hit before Christmas, and her six-year-old daughter, Lillymairose, had dearly wanted one. Like many other parents, she wasn't able to buy it before it sold out. Searches on Ebay and other sites proved too pricey. They regularly went for about $40, but she only found them for $200-$300 each! She hated to let Lilly down, but as a single mother, there was no way she could afford that.

She quickly read it again, to make sure it wasn't just another scalper site, and was surprised to find it was local. She clicked on the link, and was navigated to a website with the bold statement:

Missed those Hatch-A-Pets at Christmas? Easter is this Sunday, and what better surprise in your child's basket, than a Hatch-A-Pet? Because of a warehouse overstock, we have 100 of these available for pickup. Click on the link, and reserve yours today. Once they are gone, they are gone!

She looked twice at the price, and immediately clicked on the "Reserve Now" button when she saw they were only $50.

Thank you. You are number 98. Please input your email address, and confirm this request with a reply email. Failure to comply within one hour will drop you from the list.

98? She had been pushing it; lucky she got in when she did. After following up with the email confirmation, she immediately received a response with an address to a local warehouse, to be there Friday, and the time. It also specified she bring cash. Slightly worried, she was beginning to think it was a black market thing, and was momentarily spooked. In the back of her mind she remembered the movie, 'Child's Play'. She remembered how that mother had gotten the Chucky doll, and what the ending to that was.

"Jean, you are being silly," she laughed aloud, then glanced around to make sure Lilly hadn't seen her computer screen. She'd have to take time off from work on Friday, but the look on Lilly's face, Easter morning, would be worth it. Already, she was thinking of what she needed to do: map the location, and take some money out of the ATM...

She was disheartened when she arrived at the location on Friday. There were a lot of people there, and the warehouse looked a little shady. The more she thought about it, though, the better she felt. It may have been a suspicious deal, but she'd be safe with so many people around. She realized that all of them, like herself, were clutching their printed confirmation numbers. Only those who responded to the ad would receive the Hatch-A-Pet.

She glanced at her phone, and saw it was almost time for it to begin. All conversation ceased when they saw a man open the door and step outside. He was handsome, wearing a three-piece suit, and looking very out of place in a dirty warehouse, but he just oozed confidence, and the crowd collectively sighed in relief.

"Welcome, everyone! I'm Dean Samuel, the CEO here!" he called out, effortlessly. His voice carried over the entire crowd, as though he'd had stage training. "I hope you all have your confirmation numbers. Only those with them will be rewarded."

Several people laughed and Jean thought to herself, *Rewarded? What an odd choice of words.* Her worry dissipated when she saw two men come out from behind 'Mr. Suit'. They were each holding several Hatch-A-Pets. She was going to walk away with one today!

Someone standing closest to them yelled out, "Why are they pink and blue?" It suddenly got very quiet. "They are supposed to be white, like an egg!"

All heads spun in Dean's direction, awaiting his response.

"Not to worry," he reassured, "these were made for the newest batch. The pink are female Hatch-A-Pets and the blue are male." He paused, before continuing, "I have a confession to make to you good people. These are not overstock. They are the first prototypes that we are planning to put out in a few months. We're testing the market here with all of you. Included in the box is a website address. After the egg has hatched, we want your opinions, and a there will be a short survey to take. *You* are our test audience for a brand new version of Hatch-A-

Pet! But it needs to be a secret. We didn't want scalpers to simply come buy a bunch of them, then put them up on auction sites. I hope you can all understand that."

Smiles and head nodding was seen everywhere. They loved the idea of being a part of something secret, something special. Many were already imagining their children's faces when the new Hatch-A-Pet cracked open.

"They are all programmed to begin hatching at noon, local time. Make sure your children will be up, and have that egg out of the package," he spoke, as he waved his hand behind him, and others brought out more boxes of Hatch-A-Pets, "Please have your confirmation and money already out, to speed up the process. Again, I thank you for your help in this. So, who's first?"

"Will the Easter Bunny come and visit tonight, Mommy?" Lilly asked, as Jean was tucking her in for bed.

"Of course," Jean replied, with a smile, "the baskets are in the living room waiting for him. I even left him a cookie, like you wanted."

Lilly smiled sleepily, an empty spot revealed where a front tooth had come out a couple days ago. She'd already had a visit from the Tooth Fairy; now the Easter Bunny. This house was just full of magical creatures this week! She snuggled down into her pillow and fell asleep before Jean had finished reading her her bedtime story. Closing the book and setting it on the bedside table, Jean tiptoed out of the room, closing the door behind her.

She smiled, as she visibly relaxed. It was her time now. She was going to fill the basket with the Hatch-A-Pet and the candy she'd bought later, but wanted to relax with a glass of wine right now. She picked out a movie from her DVR that Lilly was too young to watch, and settled in for some romantic comedy.

By the time the movie was over, the bottle of wine was empty. She upended the bottle and chuckled. When was the last time she drank an entire bottle in one sitting? It was delicious, though. She'd have to buy more of this one. She dropped the bottle in the garbage can, as she went into the kitchen to put the basket together. She had everything hiding in the cabinet, high above the sink where Lilly couldn't reach. Now, she had all the candy laid out on the counter, even those nasty Peeps that Lilly loved so much; bleh, too much sugar for Jean. The only thing left to get was the surprise. The Hatch-A-Pet had been pushed further back in the cabinet, and Jean needed a chair to reach it. She was a little unsteady as she stepped up, and realized how high she was. Maybe this wasn't the smartest thing to do after drinking the entire bottle! Her fingertips were touching the smooth edge of the box, and she wiggled them a couple of times, to pull it closer. Just as she had it in her hand, she wobbled on the chair, and almost screamed when the chair tipped. She righted it, keeping herself from falling, but the box still slipped from her fingers, and hit the kitchen floor.

"Oh, shit!" she loudly whispered, mindful of Lilly asleep, deeper in the apartment. She picked up the box, and set it on the counter. She took the egg from the box and set it in the pink and green Easter grass in the basket. Luckily, she'd managed to procure a pink one, although Lilly would've been happy with a blue one.

"Oh, no! I can't believe I did that!" There was a diagonal crack on the mottled surface of the egg. Briefly, she wondered why it had a rough surface, when they were supposed to be smooth, but she only worried about how to fix it. She frantically dug through her "junk" drawer to find some superglue. The crack was only on one side. If she faced it towards the back, and didn't let Lilly touch it until it hatched, maybe she'd never notice.

The hatching! Would the fall damage that part of it? Would it still hatch at noon like all the others? What if she ruined it, and it never opened? Lilly would be heartbroken. She was so mad at herself, and wished she had never drunk the wine. The alcohol was getting to her head, her emotions were getting the better of her, and she began crying. Without thinking, she picked up a Peep, and popped it into her mouth. Her mouth puckered at the intense sugar rush; she was still chewing it, when she saw the egg move. *What?* She swallowed a huge chunk of sugar and marshmallow, almost gagging from the thickness of it, and looked closely at the egg. It was wobbling slightly, and she could hear faint scratching coming from inside the egg. She looked at the clock in horror. Only midnight! 12 hours early. Oh God, she really screwed this up! What could she do? She quickly got her cell phone, and turned on the video. If Lilly couldn't see it hatch live, at least she could see it hatch on video. It was the best that Jean could do.

Since she wasn't sure how long the hatching would take, she pulled out the built-in stand that her phone case had - she didn't think she'd ever used it before - and propped it on the counter with the best view. Nervously, she pulled the chair closer to watch. She was tempted to go wake Lilly so she could watch, yet she hadn't finished filling the basket.

That's what I'll do! I'll fix it up, go get her, and tell her the Easter Bunny just left, but he told me that the egg was hatching early! Jean was excited with the idea, and artfully filled the candy around the egg in the basket. She was just pulling the eggs they had dyed out of the fridge, when she heard a loud crack.

She whirled around, and rushed back to the counter, glancing at the phone to make sure it was still recording. I should go get Lilly, before it completely hatches! She sat the dyed eggs on the counter, and took two steps away, when she heard a small, low-pitched growl.

What the hell was that?

Slowly, she turned, and picked up the egg. She watched the crack expand, as it grew and separated. Two little, glowing, pink eyes blinked at her. The eyes pushed closer to her, as a fuzzy, little nose pushed its way through the opening.

It's so cute!

She reached out, with a tentative finger, to touch the nose, when the top of the egg flew off with a louder crack. She pulled back her finger, in horror. This was not a cute, little Hatch-A-Pet! She didn't know what this was! It was small, only six inches tall, but had little pointed ears, with tiny tufts of fur on the ends, and glowing, pink, reptilian-shaped eyes! Its small snout was furred, with a cute, little black nose. When it opened its mouth, Jean saw that it was full of short, but sharp teeth. Its body was covered in black scales, which made the fur on its head look wild. A low growl rumbled from the back of its mouth, and as it reached for her, she saw four little arms with extra joints, ending in clawed hands that looked as sharp as its teeth. It also had four legs, with equally dangerous feet. She dropped the egg on the counter, and backed up too fast, smacking her butt into the counter on the other side. The little monster hissed and lowered its ears. Without warning, it pounced, landing on top of her head, its claws caught deep in her hair. She couldn't see what it was doing, but she could feel it! It was biting her; tearing small chunks out of her scalp!

She wanted to scream, but was afraid that Lilly would come out, and be attacked as well. Right now, there was a closed door between her and this creature, and she needed to keep it that way. Reaching up to grab it, she felt an agonizing pain in her left hand. She quickly pulled her hands down, and saw her left index finger was missing up to the first knuckle. Pain and terror turned into anger, and she steeled herself against the pain, as she reached up again and tore the creature from her head. She had both hands around its skinny torso and saw chunks of her scalp with hair hanging off, still clutched in its claws. It opened its mouth, and she was stunned to see how far it opened; it was as if the jaws of this monster came unhinged. She pulled back to throw it against the wall, and almost yelled, when it bit down on her wrist. She tried pulling it off, but its teeth were in deep. It began slashing at, her with all its claws, and sliced open her wrist in several places. Blood immediately sprayed, and she knew she was in deep trouble. All she thought of was Lilly, and what would happen to her if she died without killing this creature.

She took two steps to the fridge, and let go with one hand. The creature struggled even more, and she very nearly lost her grip on it completely. Before that could happen, she opened the refrigerator door, positioning the creature in the opening. With what little strength she had left, she slammed the door on the creature's head. It immediately stopped struggling, and wavered in her hand. Its teeth were still imbedded in her wrist and she felt it bite harder, so she slammed it again.

The little monster's head fell back, and its teeth slid out of her wrist. All the little arms dropped, and spread out on her hand like the drooping petals of a dying flower. Blood trailed down her arm, as she held it out away from her. She looked around, trying to figure out what to do with it. She looked back at the fridge, and had an idea forming. She opened the freezer and quickly dropped it inside. Listening for any sound inside, she found some dishtowels to wrap her wounds before going to get Lilly. She was feeling weak, and leaned against the sink while she ran her wrists under the water. Although the bite was small, only the size of a walnut, it burned like fire, and wouldn't stop bleeding. The missing finger seemed to hurt the least to her surprise. She still felt like she had the tip, and could swear she felt it bending. Her wrist was what worried her the most; she was pretty sure the beast tore open an artery. If she didn't get that taken care of soon, she would bleed to death. As she bent over the running water, she felt the blood from her scalp wounds trailing down her face. Her head could wait. She needed to get out of here.

Three dishtowels later, she was turning to go and get her daughter, when she heard a series of popping sounds. She looked back in time to see four little claws pushing through the seals on the freezer door.

No way!

She watched in horror as the sharp claws sliced up and down, until they separated the rubber. She couldn't move, as she watched the freezer door slowly open, long strips of the rubber sealing falling down, sliced into shreds. She saw the glowing pink eyes glaring at her, and her paralysis broke. She turned to run when it made a huge leap and landed on her face. It plunged one clawed hand into her right eye, and immediately all vision from that eye ceased. She almost screamed again.

Lilly, can't wake Lilly!

Her only thought was to run outside, putting the front door between Lilly and the creature. Stumbling into furniture, she felt the creature slice her face over and over. Her knees hit the coffee table, and she fell forward, arms outstretched, almost plunging them through the glass top on the table. Using her left hand to push herself back up, she used the right to pull the creature off of her face. With only a single grip on it, there was more chance for it to wiggle and the creature bent down and bit off half of the index finger on her right hand, right before her eye.

Well, at least they match now, she thought hysterically.

Once up, she used her left hand to increase her hold on the monster.

Gotcha!

It was getting harder to keep the monster in her hands, due to all the blood. She felt it getting loose, so she tried to adjust her grip, as she hurried to the door. Her eyes widened, as she saw the creature pop right out of her fist, like a banana squeezed from its peel. Again, it went straight for her face, and she felt the claws digging in her cheeks, her nose. Then, just before she reached the front door it tore out her left eye.

She was completely blind now, but she knew her front door was only a hand-stretch away. It didn't matter what happened to her, once she got outside, and the door shut behind her; only that Lilly was safe. She reached for the door, then felt a massive flare of pain in her throat. She tried to croak out a sob, but nothing came out. When she reached up, she only felt a gaping hole, with blood flowing freely. Her mouth moved silently, as she tried to say her daughter's name, but there were no vocal chords to set the word aloud; just the whistling, gurgling sound of her ruined throat.

She slowly dropped to the floor, as she couldn't hold herself up any longer. She slid down the door, landing hard on the carpet. Her fingers trailed down the hard wood of the front door, and she realized it was still closed. She was crying as she died, and her last thought was that of Lilly.

***

The apartment was quiet, and the only sound was the clock ticking in the kitchen; it read 7:59am. When it changed to 8:00am, a tiny "ding" sounded on Jean's computer, as she received an email.

Don't forget to get your cameras ready to record the hatching! Make it a family affair! Bring everyone to see it hatch. We want the world to know about it, and we want it to spread far and wide! Your Hatch-A-Pet will be the start of something big! Something new! Something no one will ever forget!

Although there was no one to see it, the email had been cc'd to everyone who had bought a Hatch-A-Pets at the warehouse.

Jean's cell phone played the theme song to "Game of Thrones" as the alarm she set for 8:00am had arrived. It played endlessly, and finally woke Lilly, who came out of her room. She stood in the doorway, rubbing the sleep from her eyes, "Mommy?"

The End

LAST SUPPER

Suzanne Fox

"...and Jez didn't say what was so important that he couldn't wait for us to arrive on Friday as planned?"

Mary shook her head. "No. Only that it was urgent and we should get there tonight. He sounded upset."

"I hope he appreciates how difficult it was for me to get tomorrow off work. Everybody wants time off at Easter. I had to kiss a lot of arse to get the extra day. I don't see what could be so important that it couldn't wait until Friday." He felt gentle fingers squeeze his thigh, and glanced across at his wife. Her face was relaxed, illuminated randomly by the lights of oncoming vehicles. Jesus, how does she manage to stay calm, whatever shit comes her way? He brushed her hand away. "Don't distract me. It's getting dark and we'll be leaving the motorway in a few minutes. You don't want the blame for making me drive off the road, do you?" A peevish satisfaction twitched the corners of his lips as he felt, rather than saw, her flinch back into the seat.

"I'm sorry, Jude. I didn't mean to distract you."

Jude shivered as her voice grated on his ears. Why the hell do I put up with her? he thought. I suppose spending a few days with Eve and Jez means I don't have to spend Easter weekend, alone, with her. Choosing to ignore her apology, Jude flicked a lever to indicate he was pulling off the carriageway. He slid the car around the curve of the road at speed, enjoying the knowledge that Mary would be anxious at the manoeuvre. She was the most nervous passenger he knew. Usually, a burst of speed or a sharp corner provoked a disapproving comment, but not this time. He guessed she was trying to avoid confrontation, not wanting to arrive at their friends' house under a cloud of tension. At the edges of his vision, he saw her fingers tighten on the edge of the seat and her foot push down an imaginary brake, and he swallowed down the urge to snap out a stinging comment. She annoyed him, but he could see the downside of having an argument before meeting their friends.

Jude drove along narrow rural roads, dropping his foot harder on the accelerator than necessary, and keeping his eyes fixed on the route ahead. His fingers reached for the volume button, and turned up the music, attempting to crush any conversation. Trees stretched their limbs across the lanes, reaching out to their neighbours, and deepening the shadows from a cold moon that splintered the black sky. The occasional flashes of other cars' headlights grew less frequent until, eventually, they left all other traffic behind. "Why the fuck did they have to move to the back of beyond?" Jude muttered.

"I sometimes think it would be nice to move out of the city," said Mary. "Buy a cottage, miles from anywhere. Grow our own veggies. We could get a dog."

Jude shook his head. "Do you have any idea how ridiculous you sound?" He swung the steering wheel hard right into a bend and heard

Mary draw in a sharp breath. "One week away from the restaurants, bars and shops, and you'd be begging to move back. I reckon in a couple of months, Jez and Eve will have this place back on the market, and be looking for a new city pad. Eve won't enjoy living in the wilderness." Before Mary could voice a reply, Jez turned the car through a dark gateway, and bumped along a rough drive. As they approached the large farmhouse, motion-sensitive lights illuminated the brooding building.

"What an ugly house," murmured Jez. "Give me a new-build, every time."

"I think it's charming," said Mary. "It looks full of character."

"I take it by character, you mean old and derelict?"

"It's not derelict, at all. Look at its charm. Can you see the iron crosses in the walls that hold the beams in place?"

"I can see them, and I'm probably going to end up knocking myself out on one of the fucking beams." Jude brought the car to a halt between Eve's Range Rover and Jez's Merc, and killed the engine. Within minutes they were approaching the solid wooden door.

***

Jez pushed up the sleeve of his sweater and glanced at his watch. They should be arriving at any moment and, as if they were tuned into his thoughts, a flicker of headlamps through the window announced the arrival of a car. He opened the door before they had time to knock. "Come in, come in. How was your journey?"

Jude and Mary entered the large oak-panelled hallway. "Whatever possessed you to move out of the city? There's not another house for miles. Thought I'd never find you," said Jude.

"Ignore him, Jez," said Mary. "He drove straight here, without any problems. I don't know how he did it. I'd have gotten lost. He's just getting urban withdrawal symptoms. This is a beautiful house."

Jez leaned in, and kissed Mary on the cheek. "Thanks. I'll show you to your room, so you can freshen up before dinner. It'll be ready in about twenty minutes."

Mary craned her neck to look past her host. "Where's Eve? I want to say hello first."

Jez stiffened. "Um, she's not here at the moment. You'll see her later, though, I promise." Avoiding further discussion, he picked up their bags, and started to mount the stairs. "I've put you in the larger bedroom at the back. The views are to die for. Of course, it's too dark to see anything now." He continued to make small talk, as he led the way to the guest room, before leaving them to unpack.

Fifteen minutes later, his guests joined Jez in the ample kitchen. "I must say, Jez," said Jude, as he cast admiring looks around the interior of the sleek and stylish, ultra-modern kitchen. "I wasn't expecting anything like this, when I saw the place from the outside. I imagined it was going to be like stepping inside the Addams family's house."

"I had the entire place remodelled before moving in. I kept some of the better, original features though. There's an amazing inglenook in the sitting room."

"I love the place," Mary smiled, then added, "When's Eve getting here?"

Jez filled generous wine glasses and passed them around. "You'll see her later. Come on, let's go through to the dining room. Supper's ready."

Jez led them through an arched doorway into a spacious dining room. A vaulted ceiling was the crown above a room that managed to blend ultra-modern with essences of past-times. The fusion was seamless.

"Wow," was all that Jude could muster. "This...This is not what I was expecting."

His host grinned. "This place is full of surprises. Take a seat I'll bring dinner through."

Mary touched his arm. "Let me help."

"No!"

Her hand recoiled, and she took a step back.

"I'm sorry." Jez reached out and pulled Mary toward him, in a hug. "I didn't mean to startle you. I just thought you must be tired after the journey. Please, sit down and let me bring the food in. I've been home all day, and I know you both had to work. Please?" His large blue eyes widened, along with his smile. He had a boyish charm that never failed to win her over. She relaxed and took a seat at the table.

"There's only three places set," said Jude. "Is Eve not joining us for dinner?"

"Er, no. She won't be able to make it in time." Jez glanced toward the kitchen. "I'll only be a moment. I don't want dinner to spoil." On cue, a timer buzzed in the other room. "It's ready. Top up the glasses, and I'll bring the food in." Jez closed the door behind him.

Through the door, came the sounds of shifting pans and rattling plates. "I wonder where Eve is?" remarked Jude. He took a large gulp of wine. "I get the feeling something's not right. I'm worried about her."

"Yes, I thought it was odd, her not being here. She's been dying for us to visit and see the new place," said Mary. "Did you notice her car was still in the drive?"

The door opened, and Jez appeared with plates of steaming food. He placed one before each of his guests, before returning to the kitchen to collect his own. Once they were all seated, he raised his glass. "Here's to the best two friends in the world. May we continue to enjoy... memorable times together and thank you, for coming at such short notice. I do appreciate that you're both busy people, and it must have taken a huge amount of brown-nosing to get extra days off work."

"You have no idea," Jude laughed. "I have never kissed so much arse in my life."

Jez raised one eyebrow. "Really? Never? Not even for pleasure?" His lips thinned in a parody of a grin

"Hey, steady on. How much did you drink before we got here?"

"I'm sorry. I didn't mean any offence." Jez put down his glass. "It's been rather stressful recently. Let's relax and eat this before it goes cold. I've spent all afternoon preparing it."

"It looks delicious. What is it?" asked Mary

"Salmon-en-croute. All the vegetables are locally grown. It's a gourmet's paradise living here. Plus, I've made a chocolate and hazelnut tart for dessert, with salted caramel ice cream."

"You should be taking notes, Jude," laughed Mary. "Eve's a very lucky girl. Jude can burn coffee."

"There's no need to cook at home," sneered Jude. "There are plenty of restaurants to take care of that."

"Well, I'm impressed, Jez." Mary cut a small piece from her salmon and popped it into her mouth. "Mm. This is delicious. Jude, try yours."

Trivial conversation peppered the course of their meal, punctuated by the sounds of silverware scraping against china. Jez watched with satisfaction as the plates were cleared of food. When the last morsel had been devoured, he gathered the plates. "Give me five minutes. I need to add the finishing touches to the tarts." He retreated to the kitchen once more.

"I'm worried about Eve," whispered Mary. "Jez hasn't offered any explanation as to why she's not here, and he doesn't seem...himself."

"He seems his usual self to me," Jude shrugged his shoulders. "But, I'll ask him about her when he gets back." He refilled their glasses.

Within ten minutes Jez returned, carrying a tray laden with desserts. "You've even iced our names on them!" Mary clapped her hands, before reaching to accept hers. "Look, Jude. He's iced 'Mary' across it."

"Yes, I can see. I'm not blind." He accepted the dish offered by Jez. "Thank you. Mm, this does look good." He placed a spoonful in his mouth, and his features relaxed as the rich chocolate melted on his tongue. "Wow. Damn, this is good. There's a flavour I can't quite put my finger on. What is it?"

Jez laughed. "Ah, the secret ingredient. I could tell you, but then, I'd have to kill you. I don't intend to reveal my culinary secrets to anyone."

Jude swallowed the final mouthful, closing his eyes as he savoured the sweet dessert. "Oh man, Eve is missing a treat tonight. I'm surprised she's not here, though. Has she gone away?"

Jez laid down his spoon, and pushed the remains of his pudding away. "There's no easy way to say this but, we're..." He took a long swig of wine. "We're no longer together."

Jude and Mary stared in silence at their friend. Neither of them had predicted this as a reason for her absence. Jude shattered the quiet. "What the fuck! She...she walked out? Did she say why? Jesus, man. Really?"

"Jude," hissed Mary. "Oh, Jez. I'm so sorry. Are you sure you want us here? Have you talked properly with each other? Maybe you can work it out."

Jez shook his head. "There's going to be no 'working it out.' It's too late for us. She's gone, and good riddance."

"You don't mean that." Mary reached out to take his hand, but he moved it away.

"I do." He stood up, clattered the dishes together, and stormed into the kitchen, leaving Mary and Jude open-mouthed.

"Jude, go after him."

"I...I don't think that's a good idea. I think we should leave. He obviously wants to be alone."

"And how would we leave? Both of us have drunk too much to drive, and we're miles from home. Besides, we can't leave him alone. Not like this."

Jude pulled his phone from a pocket. "I'll call for a cab."

"Don't you dare." She yawned, her mouth widening, and she raised a hand to cover it. "We are not going anywhere. Put that phone away."

Jude stifled his own yawn, and placed the phone on the table as Jez returned. "Who were you calling?" quizzed Jez.

Mary glared at Jude. "No one," he finally replied. "Do you want to talk about it." The words sounded bitter as they left his lips, and didn't welcome an answer, but Jez wasn't deterred.

"She's been having an affair." He paused, and studied their faces. Mary's shocked disbelief, and Jude's impassive stare. "It's been going on for ages. Turns out, that all those business trips she made, didn't involve a whole lot of business. Well, not of the kind I expected."

"I...I don't know what to say," stammered Jude. "Has she left you for him?"

"No. I don't believe she has." He refilled all their glasses. "Tired, Mary?"

"Oh, I'm so sorry," she answered, as she tried to stifle another yawn. "I don't know what's come over me. I feel exhausted."

Jude raised a hand to hide his own yawn. "I understand, if you don't want to talk. This is personal."

"I want to talk, though, and you're right, it is personal. Very personal." He looked from Jude to Mary and smiled. "You both look very tired, but I think you can stay awake a little longer while I talk. You're going to want to hear what I have to say."

Jude rubbed his eyes. "Perhaps we should talk another time. To be honest, I'm not feeling so good."

"I don't feel like myself, either," said Mary. "I think we might have picked up a virus or some other bug."

"You can go to sleep, soon," said Jez. "After I tell you what's been going on. A few months ago, I needed to speak to Eve while she was away on a work trip. Her phone had been playing up, and when I couldn't get an answer, I decided to call her office and ask them to get a message to her. Do you know what they told me?"

Both guests shook their heads, and Mary's mouth gaped, as another yawn overtook her.

"They told me she wasn't away on business. In fact, they told me she had taken a couple of day's holiday, and they had no idea where she was. Can you begin to imagine what I was thinking? No, don't bother to answer, just try to stay awake a little longer."

"I suppose I should have confronted her when she got home, but I was scared of what she might say. Cowardly, I know, but how does anyone know how they will react, when they suspect their wife of having an affair? I went through her phone. I read her emails. Nothing. She had covered her tracks well. Then, she announced another business trip, the week after Valentine's day."

Mary started to say something, but the words wouldn't form. Only gurgled sounds left her lips.

"Don't try to speak Mary, just listen. I decided to take some time off work, myself and follow her. I was hoping she was telling the truth, and I'd see her attending a conference or a meeting, but no. She drove to a hotel in Surrey. I followed her inside, at a distance, of course. She never saw me. There was somebody waiting for her in reception. A man. Can you guess who?"

This time, it was Jude's turn to try and speak, but the words melted, and dribbled down his chin.

"I know, Jude. You're sorry. You never meant it to happen. She was a scheming whore, who tempted you away from your own, dear wife."

A gagging, snuffling noise came from Mary. Jude tried to launch himself at Jez, but his legs refused to obey him, becoming tangled in his chair. He fell to the floor, where he lay sprawled, unable to get back up.

"I should have warned you not to try and stand. The tranquiliser I put in your desserts also works as a muscle relaxant. I had to be careful with the doses. I didn't want to accidentally kill either of you, hence my clumsy attempt at icing your names on the tarts. I had to be sure you ate the right ones. I'm sorry, Mary. You don't deserve any of this, but I can't let you stop me." Jez slumped back in his seat and waited, until Mary collapsed onto the table, and Jude lay snoring on the floor.

***

An aching weight attempted to keep Jude's eyelids shut. A dizzying sense of disorientation pervaded his mind, while nausea and pain swamped his body, and his limbs refused to co-operate. The cramps, that had settled deep into his muscles, threatened to tear him apart and the bite of tight ropes chewed at his wrists and ankles, with every clumsy attempt to move he made. A damp chill surrounded his nakedness. He tried to swallow, but his throat felt like he had ingested razor blades. With a final effort of will, he forced open his eyelids.

The lighting was dim, but not too dark to see by. Jude looked down, past his nakedness, and saw his mottled feet, strapped to lengths of wood. Slowly, to minimise the explosions firing through his brain, he turned his head to the left. His left wrist was similarly tied. A sluggish turn to the right, confirmed his right wrist was also restrained. A fifth rope was drawn around his waist, fully immobilising him to the cross-shaped structure. A clouded memory of a night surfing the seedier sites of the web rose through the darkness and he recognised what he was secured, spread-eagled to: a St. Andrews cross. A piece of equipment used by some members of the BDSM community. How had he come to be tied to such a contraption?

"I see you're waking up." The voice was distant, but when Jude turned to face the sound, he saw Jez was only a few yards away, resting against a bare brick wall.

Jude tried to speak, but his thirsty tongue refused to oblige, and all he could manage was a low mumble.

"I guess you need a drink." Jez pushed away from the wall, and picked up a bottle of water by his feet. He unscrewed the cap as he walked over. "Open wide, buddy." He tipped a hefty volume of water into Jude's mouth. The liquid hit the back of Jude's throat, and he gagged. Coughing and spluttering, he spat most of it to the floor.

"W...what have you done?" Jude rasped. His vocal cords were raw strings. Nothing made sense anymore. He had been eating dinner with the others, and then he was here. Except, that wasn't what had happened. Fragments of memory began to coalesce into the nightmare he found himself in. "E...Eve...?" he slurred.

"Eve? Eve, is your first thought? Surely you should be wondering what's happened to Mary, your wife. Remember her?"

Jude nodded, and groaned, "Where is she?"

"Mary or Eve?"

"M...Mary."

"That's more like it, Jude. You're learning. A little late, but you're learning. Mary's fine, if a little worse for wear." He pointed toward a corner of the room where, gagged and tied to a chair, slouched Mary. "Eve, on the other hand, well, she's not looking so good." Jez cast a glance to another corner, and Jude's eyes followed.

His scream ripped from his scorched throat and bounced off the bare walls. As soon as his breath was exhausted, he inhaled and screamed again. And again. He screamed until he was spent, panting for breath, as he hung from the cross.

"Let's hope that's out of your system. For a while at least." Jez walked over to the corner and picked up the disembodied head of his wife. "She's definitely not looking her best. I'm betting you don't want to fuck her anymore." He pried open her grey lips. "Tell me, do you still want to push your cock in there?"

Jude recoiled against the unyielding cross, as Jez thrust the head of his lover towards Jude's groin. *It's just a nightmare. I'll wake up soon. Please God. Let me wake up.* But the pain in his body reminded him that this was no dream. Jez had discovered what was going on between himself and Eve, and now Jez was going to make him pay. Sobbing from the corner drew Jez's attention, and he backed away.

"Don't be alarmed, Mary. I don't intend to harm you. You're as innocent as I am in this." He dropped his dead wife's head to the floor, where it bounced once, before rolling away. "I only want you to see your miserable husband for the lying, cheat that he is."

"F...For God's sake, let us go. Don't make it any worse for yourself." Jude was more awake, the actuality of the scene was growing, becoming brighter. This was real.

"Oh, Jude. I'm not making it any worse for me.. But you, on the other hand..." Jez stood with his face only inches away from Jude's. "It's going to get a whole lot worse for you. Unless you do exactly what I tell you to. Understand?" Jude nodded. "Good boy." Jez reached out, and ruffled his hair, like he would a small child's. "Now, I want you to tell me, exactly, what you and my wife did together."

Jude shook his head, "It...it was just sex. I'm sorry, Jez. I really am. I wish I could go back and do things differently."

"Tut, tut. Not good enough, Jude. I want details. I know you screwed the fucking bitch. I want to know exactly what you did with her. Did she blow you? Did you bend her over, and fuck her in the arse? She liked that, you know. Hold her by the hips, and force yourself deep inside her. Of course, you did."

"Now. Tell. Me!"

Sobs shook his body, and the rope cut deeper, as his body collapsed forward. Thin, warm trickles of blood snaked down his arms. "Yes. Yes. Yes. All of that. She wanted it all. Everything that you said."

"You haven't got it, have you? You are supposed to tell me what the two of you did together. Not just agree with what I say," Jez sighed, and walked to over to a small toolbox that sat on the floor, next to Mary's chair. "I was hoping it wouldn't come to this, but you leave me no choice." A muffled scream escaped Mary's gag, and the chair stuttered, as she tried to shuffle backwards, away from her approaching captor. He reached out, and stroked his hand down her cheek. "Don't worry, Mary. I'm not going to hurt you. You've already been hurt, just as much as I have, by what my wife and your husband have been doing. All you have to do is watch, and enjoy."

Grabbing the toolbox, Jez returned to the cross. He pulled out a handful of metal that clinked in his grasp. "Do you know what these are, Jude? No? Don't worry, you'll soon get to grips with them. They're nail spikes. Like the kind used on railways. They don't look friendly, do they?"

"F...For fuck's sake, Jez. This has gone far enough. Untie us both. Please." Tears spilled down Jude's face, as he pleaded.

His words went unheeded. Jez delved back into the toolbox, and drew out a hammer. "I thought the cross was a nice touch, with it being Easter. This cellar was one of the reasons we bought the place. Eve had been dying for us to have our own dungeon for ages." He laughed, "Dying. She never thought she would end up dead in here. She loved kink. Vanilla left her cold. She loved nothing more than being tied up and whipped, before a fucking. But you must know all about that. Hey, Mary. Did he ever tie you to the bed?"

"Jesus, Jez. Leave Mary out of this."

"It's a little late for you to be considering others. It's time you paid the price for your actions." He placed the point of one of the nail spikes on top of Jude's left foot. Jude tried to wriggle away, but the rope-binding was tight and unforgiving. Jez raised the hammer, paused for a second, and then swung it down.

There was the briefest 'chink', as the hammer struck the head of the nail, before the dark room filled with hoarse screams. Splatters of blood decorated Jez's pale face, and soaked into his shirt. He raised the hammer and struck the nail again, and again, until the head was flush with Jude's foot, and it became one with the cross. "Anything more to tell me yet?"

Jude screamed until all that he had left, were gulping sobs. "You...You bastard," he whimpered.

"Wrong answer, my friend." Jez picked up a second spike, and drove it into the other foot. Jude shrieked. His body twisted and bucked on the cross, but all his struggling did was tighten the knots of his restraints, and pump more blood from his wounds. "Anything to add, yet?"

Pain and fear robbed Jude of any ability to speak. Thick streams of snot dangled from each nostril, and tears streamed from blood-reddened eyes. The earthy, dark stink of shit blossomed, filling every corner of the gloomy room, and when Jude thought he couldn't scream anymore, he was proved wrong. Rigid steel pierced his wrists, driven by Jez's hammer. One blow missed the spike, smashing the bones in his hand but, for Jude, the hurt was swallowed into the agony that now formed his world. All thoughts of why he was nailed to the cross, were driven from his mind. No memory of Eve, her naked body, or of all the depraved things he had done to it, remained. All were driven out by his torture.

He had no awareness of Jez untying Mary. He didn't see Mary dragged, sobbing from the cellar. He didn't even notice when the light was switched off, and he was left, weeping and moaning, in total blackness. Time vanished, to be replaced by an eternity of torment. Minutes grew into hours, and hours grew into days. Moments of lucidity were interspersed with delirium, brought on by wounds that burned and festered. The poisons invaded his blood, and the rigours threatened to tear his flesh free of his prison. He cried. He moaned. He screamed. By the third day, he fell silent.

* * *

Jez stared out of the kitchen window and across the fields, in the direction of the nearest village. He imagined the ringing of the church bells, as they called the faithful to the Easter Service. The village was too far away for the chiming to be heard at the house. Superstitious cunts, he thought. He scorned anyone who chose to believe in the fairy tales pedalled by the church, and let themselves be controlled by the threat of eternal damnation. He knew there was only one life, and to get ahead, you had to be willing to do whatever was necessary.

His thoughts were interrupted by the muffled sounds of weeping. He had kept Mary locked in one of the bedrooms since the night he had dealt with her errant husband. Jez had never had any intention of harming her. No, his plan was to convince her that he had acted in both of their best interests and, if she worked with him, they could devise a convincing story to explain the disappearance of their adulterous partners. The problem with that being, Mary wasn't playing his game.

She was more traumatised than he had expected. He had anticipated tears and tantrums, but she had withdrawn, completely. His explanations and platitudes had either been ignored, or she hadn't been able to hear or understand him. She had scarcely moved from the corner of the bedroom where, she spent hour after hour, huddled and weeping. Jez was worried. He hadn't planned on having to remove Mary from the picture. Throughout all of his planning and forecasts, he had visualised her realising the consequences of her husband's philandering, and siding... with Jez, but he wasn't about to give up on her yet.

Jez mixed up some porridge in a bowl, and warmed it in the microwave. As soon as it pinged, he placed it on the kitchen table, along with coffee and orange juice, then climbed the stairs to her room. Although she had made no effort to escape, he, nevertheless, kept the door locked. He turned the key and entered. He discovered her cowering in the same position and corner that he always found her in. The sickly-sweet scent of unwashed skin filled the room. Mary's only trips to the bathroom had been to deal with bodily functions and not to bathe.

"Enough," said Jez. "Breakfast is downstairs, and one way or another, you are going to the kitchen to eat it. Are you going to stand, or do I drag you?" There was, predictably, no response. He walked over and grabbed her hands. Pulling her to her feet, she felt lighter and more fragile than he remembered. Could she have lost that much weight in a matter of just a few days? Not a morsel of food had passed her lips, since their last supper, with Jude. Sighing, he pulled her towards the door. She offered no resistance, and docilely followed.

Jez attempted to spoon-feed the porridge to Mary, but she wouldn't swallow, and now she sat with trails of porridge dripping from her chin, while the remainder congealed in the bowl. If he couldn't get her to co-operate with him today, he was going to have to rethink his plans. He had already left the bodies in the cellar for far too long. Mary's odour was bad, but it paled into insignificance next to the aura of decay and rot that was beginning to escape the basement.

"Mary!" Jez yelled, his mouth only inches from her face, but she didn't flinch. "For fuck's sake, Mary. Speak to me." He raised his hand, and the slap he delivered to her face sent her tumbling to the floor, where she lay, catatonic. He ran his fingers through his hair in frustration; the realisation of what would have to be done, became an urgent need.

He pulled open a drawer in one of the cabinets. It was stuffed full of all the random bits and bobs that every home has, yet don't warrant a special place of their own. He rummaged through the detritus until his hand settled on what he was after: the wire from a broken cheese slicer. He grabbed a couple of tea towels to protect his hands, and wound the ends around his fists. Kneeling next to Mary's prone form, he placed the wire around her neck. "I'm sorry, Mary. I never meant it to come to this, but you're forcing me to do this." His fingers flexed, and he drew in a deep breath.

"Jude?" Mary's voice was soft, yet it slammed into Jez like a juggernaut, and the garrotte slipped from his fingers. She pushed herself to her knees, and began a slow crawl across the floor. Jez followed at her heels. "Jude?" she called again, but this time her voice was louder, stronger. She had a purpose. Confusion clouded Jez's thoughts. Was this a good sign, or was Mary's mental state reaching a new low? He prayed to a God he didn't believe in, that it was a good omen.

He followed her until she paused, outside the door to the cellar, and pulled herself to her feet, like a baby learning to stand. The smell of death and decay burned stronger here. She pressed the palms of her hands and her forehead against the door, tilting her head to one side as if she were listening. "I hear you sweetheart. It's okay, I'm here."

Jez's heart sank. This was no good omen. It was clear that she was losing her mind, and he was responsible for pushing her to the edge of insanity. He had no choice anymore. Mary would have to go.

He froze. A prickling ran along his spine, and the hairs on the back of his neck rose to attention. From behind the cellar door, came the slow sounds of dragging footsteps. It's...it's not possible, he thought. Even if Jude's somehow managed to survive, there's no way he could escape the nails and rope fastening him to the cross. He reasoned that after four days without food or water, and with wounds that would be festering from lack of care – Jesus, he could smell the decay from where he stood – there was no way on earth that Jude could escape his fate. Yet, still, the muffled sounds continued.

"Rats!" he yelled. "It has to be rats." But, deep down, he knew that rats could never make such heavy, dragging sounds.

Mary's nails raked the door in frenetic desperation, as she tried to get past the wooden barrier. Her unexpected animation startled Jez. His hand flew out, connecting with the side of her face. She fell to the floor, screeching in pain and frustration. "You're going to join them down there, you bitch." He raced to the small bowl, where a mixture of keys lay, and pulled out a long, thin one. He returned to the cellar door, and slid the slender key into the lock. It turned smoothly, and he pulled open the door. A thick fog, of putrid flesh and excrement rising from the blackness, flooded his senses, as he turned to grab Mary.

She flew towards him like a banshee, arms outstretched, wailing as though her lungs would explode. She hit him like a wrecking ball, and he stumbled backwards. The ground disappeared from beneath his feet, and he was flying. For a brief moment, he recalled the old cartoons of his childhood, when the Roadrunner got the better of the wily old coyote. Then, with a crash, he returned to reality. The ground smashed against his limbs and his spine. Agonising pain erupted from his thigh, and he reached down to feel jagged bone and ragged flesh. He screamed.

Above him, framed by the light in the doorway, Mary grinned her lunatic smile before closing the door. Blackness surrounded and occupied him. Jez lifted his hands to his ears, to block out the shrieking, not realising it was he, who screamed. Whispers found their way through the cacophony, insinuating into his mind. He tried to push his way towards the stairs, scraping his fingernails against the rough concrete, but the splintered bone in his leg tore through his muscle. He collapsed onto his back.

The darkness thickened into a crushing weight against Jez's chest. He struggled for breath. The stench grew stronger, until it seemed to take on a physical form, and he could taste its ripeness deep in his throat, feeling its spongy putrefaction against his skin. Icy breath brushed against his ear, and dead voices whispered to him.

He opened his mouth to scream for mercy. Liquefied flesh oozed into his mouth, filling his throat and dripping into his nostrils. His screams reached a bubbling crescendo then...

Silence reclaimed the darkness.

The End

BUNNY AND CLYDE

Lisa Vasquez

Clyde was sitting very still on his bed, staring at the basket in the center of his floor. Mother had left it for him, like she did every year, for Easter. And every year, the baskets became a little more different. When he was younger, the baskets were dressed up in beautiful pastel colors. Plastic grass would cascade over the sides, topped with chocolate candy, a myriad of simple toys, and dyed eggs all arranged happily within its cellophane wrapping. At the very top she would tie a giant bow.

After his younger sister died, Clyde saw a change in his mother, too.

The change was mirrored by the appearance of the black woven basket sitting before him, filled with dirt. Not just any dirt. Dirt from his sister's grave.

It was still dark outside, and the half-light from the windows behind him, caused long shadows to appear along the walls. Clyde could feel the fear rising within him, as his heart kicked up the pace, bouncing around his ribcage, like a hummingbird.

"*Clyyyyyde.*"

The whisper preceded the screech of nails on glass. Her silhouette loomed, filling the window frame and darkening the room.

"Not again," he whispered. "Please? Not again."

"*Play with me.*"

A chill trickled down the young boy's spine, like ice water sliding over each vertebra, one at a time.

"Go away!" Clyde shouted over his shoulder.

"Get up, sleepy head," his mother whispered from the door. "It's Easter. Get up, and come down for breakfast."

Clyde jerked with a start, and looked over at his mother. Her dark hair hung like curtains, on either side of her slender face. The absence of glowing warmth, where the sun had once kissed her cheeks, was replaced by pasty alabaster skin. Once, her eyes were bright and loving, but now they were ringed in dark, bruise-colored circles. The contrast in color made them appear more menacing, and she was staring right through him, as if he wasn't there.

When she turned away, he climbed out of bed and tiptoed to the door. He watched his mother disappear down the hall and into the kitchen, before continuing to follow. He could smell the coffee brewing and hear her rummaging for a spoon in the silverware drawer. Turning back toward his room, he saw black fingers curling around the door jamb, and strands of matted hair, before the dark, oily shine of his sister's eye locked on him.

Clyde's lungs froze, and he backed up too quickly, bumping into the table of family pictures. The one of his sister fell over.

"*Play with me Clyde,*" she called softly to him, again. He could hear her faint and warbled voice, as if she was still under water.

Backing away, he shook his head before running into his mother's room. The curtains were still closed, leaving the room drenched in darkness. Even at eight-years-old, Clyde was still afraid of the dark ... especially now that he knew what lingered in it. He just wanted to be away from her. Running for the bathroom, he opened the linen closet, and climbed in behind the laundry basket, making himself as small as he could.

Closing his eyes, Clyde tried to control his breathing. It was coming in loud, frightened gasps, and his lungs worked overtime to bring oxygen to his brain.

Unable to find his own voice to call for her, he stayed frozen by fear, in the cramped fetal position. Every year that passed, his sister seemed to grow stronger. Her ability to manifest changed from a ghostly apparition and whispers, to appearing on the physical plane. There were even nights he woke to her sitting on his chest, with her long, dark hair tickling his cheeks. The smell of chlorine would be strong on her breath, and the feel of her skin was bitter cold; so cold it made him shiver.

When he tried to cry for his mother, nothing came out. *Just like now*.

***

After what seemed like a few hours, Clyde jerked awake. He had no way of telling how much time had passed, but the absence of light coming from beyond the closet door told him it must be night. He pushed the basket away with care, trying not to make a sound, then went to his knees, wrapping his fingers around the doorknob. Rotating it slowly, he cracked it open an inch and peered out.

There was no sound coming out of the darkness.

Pushing the door open wider, he emerged and crawled on all fours to the doorway leading to his mother's attached bedroom. With the help of the dimly lit lamp on her bedside table, he could see she was asleep. Lying there with such a peaceful look on her face, her chest rose and fell below the blankets. It made him sad to think he could not remember the last time he saw her this way.

Rising to his feet, he tiptoed to her bed and stared down at her, hoping to extend the moment. He reached out to touch her, but pulled back, afraid that it might wake her. *Let her sleep,* he thought, *She's been through so much.*

As he took a step back, his mother's eyes shot open and she sat upright. She looked around the room and then straight at him, but it was as if she could not see him. Looking straight through him, she called out in a voice still lost in a dream, "Who's there?"

"Momma it's ok, it's me."

Clyde reached out for her, but his mother's eyes drifted shut again and she sank back onto her pillow. The corners of his mouth turned down and he did his best to hold back his tears. When he turned to leave, he saw the bottles of pills lined up neatly on the bedside table.

"You didn't open … your basket," she whispered from her pill-induced coma.

"Sorry, momma," he whimpered. "I'll go right now and do it. I promise."

He waited for a response, but she was already gone from consciousness, once again. Wiping away his tears, Clyde left her there, and crept toward his room. The hallway seemed to grow longer, as he came nearer to the doorway where he'd last seen his sister appear. Plopping down in front of the basket, he let the tears fall freely onto his cheeks, stinging his skin with their salty heat. He wiped his sleeve under his nose, and reached for the basket. His eyes widened, as he watched water begin rising and spilling out of it.

Shoving himself back, his mouth dropped opened as a hand rose from where the water saturated the dirt, turning it to mud. The hand, whose fingers were balled into a fist, opened one finger at a time, stretching into the air. Inch by inch, it pulled itself up until the arm became an elbow and then, like a baby being pushed into the world, the head began to crown.

There was a gushing of water, and he watched on in horror, witnessing the basket fold open and his sister's shoulders begin to emerge. With one hand free, she pulled herself up from whatever Hell she came from. Her blackened fingers scratched and clawed at the floorboards. *The same scratching noise he always heard before she appeared.*

"Go away!" he shouted at her, huddling tighter to the wall behind him, "You're dead. Stay dead!"

The more his sister emerged, the more the water from the basket crept closer toward him. Her body turned, and she flopped onto her back like a breeching fish. Wet, black strands of hair covered her entire face except for the one, cloudy black eye always watching him. Her blue skin expanded and contracted in time with the opening of her mouth. *Was she trying to breathe?* Her body erected itself, and she stared down at her estranged sibling, before she collapsed. Her body flopped to the other side with a loud thud, pulling her other arm out. With both arms free, she used them to escape from the invisible grasp on her.

Reaching out to Clyde, she opened her mouth. Dirty water, soiled with algae, leaves and knots of her hair came spilling out. She was trying to speak. Her little lips moved and he expected to hear his sister's voice. Instead, the voice that came out was monstrous and sent chills through his already trembling body.

"*Clyde. Please... help.*"

Shaking his head, he shut his eyes tight and cried. Fear wore him down. He could no longer bring himself to run and hide.

"Bunny, I can't. You're ..." his words hitched in his throat and he choked out a sob before he could finish the sentence, "You're dead."

Bunny rolled onto her stomach and pressed her face against the floor, her nose and mouth submerged by the water. Clyde crawled toward his sister, unable to fight against all the warnings screaming in his head. When he was close enough, she reached out and took hold of his wrist. He smiled for a split second, feeling the touch of his sister's hand. It was real. As frightening as her appearance was, he never equated with the monster being *her*. But when her fingers tightened on his wrist, his smile melted into a grimace. He could feel the flow of blood stop and the sensation of pins and needles creeping through his fingers.

"Bunny, you're hurting me! Let go!"

With a sharp pull, Clyde's body slid against the floor, his pajama bottoms soaking up the water as she began to drag him toward her. Panic swelling within his chest, he thrashed against the unnatural strength of her grip. Bubbles appeared around her face, which was tilted slightly so she could stare at him, like always, through the part in her hair, as she continued to draw him closer.

Letting out a scream, Clyde used his free hand to strike at his sister, filling him with guilt with each blow he landed against the back of her head. After the fourth or fifth one, her grip released and he bolted out of the room. He ran as fast as he could until he crashed into the wall next to the sliding glass door. Wanting to put as much distance between his sister and him, he slid it open and ran out. He could still feel her breath tracing against the exposed skin of his neck.

Clyde turned his head to look behind him, and tripped when his foot was caught by the leg of one of the patio chairs. He watched the sky pass overhead as he fell into the pool, neglected since the day Bunny drowned in it.

When his body hit the water, his head slammed against the concrete deck, sending lightning bolts of pain throughout his skull and forcing his mouth to open wide. Bubbles of air escaped and rolled to the surface. Looking up, he saw Bunny standing there, silhouetted by the porch light behind her.

With a mouthful of water, and blood seeping from his cut, Clyde tried to swim up for air but his clothes were too loose and tangled around him, making it hard to move. He felt something hook onto his foot and looked down to see it was Bunny. Her fingers hooked into his pant leg and she began to pull him toward the bottom of the pool with her.

His lungs burned and his oxygen was depleted; *he was going to die*. Clyde kicked at his sister's hand with wild abandon, but her hold was too strong. Unable to hold his breath any longer, he released it and felt the cool intake of water rush in.

Lucy smiled as she listened to her two children at play, running through the yard and chasing one another. She peeked out the window and saw Bunny was bouncing through the grass, a blue ribbon on her dress floating on the wind behind her. Following her was Clyde, reaching out for the end of it in his best Sunday suit.

"Don't get dirty!" she called out, with a laugh, "We have church in thirty minutes!"

"OK, momma!" Clyde called back, amidst the fit of giggles.

The breakfast dishes were washed and dried, and she was putting them away, when the phone rang. She looked out the window one more time before she picked it up.

"Hello?"

"*Hey, Lucy. It's me,*" her husband said on the other end.

Lucy's smile dropped, along with the color in her face, and her eyes welled with tears, "Bill?"

With the static on the other end, she could barely hear him speak. Pressing the phone into her ear, she used her finger to plug the other, hoping it would help.

"Bill, I—I can't hear you," her voice was shaking, as she leaned into the receiver, "C—can you speak up, Bill? Where are you?"

The other end of the line seemed to go dead. Lucy covered her mouth, as she pressed her back against the wall and slid down. Unable to hold back, she let out a sob, and tried to blink away her tears. Behind them, the world seemed to be under water and blurry. When the tears would not clear, and she could not breathe, she clawed at her eyes and throat with one hand, while still gripping the phone in the other. The static on the line grew louder, followed by a sudden, high pitched screech. The noise was so loud, Lucy pulled the receiver away from her ear.

Dropping it on the floor, she felt instant relief as air filled rapidly into her lungs, and then used it to scream out, "Bill!"

An angry dial tone chopped through the small speaker of the earpiece. Lucy reached for it again then froze at the voice on the line.

"Lucy! The children! Save the children!"

She let out a scream, and scrambled to her feet, realizing she had not heard Bunny and Clyde's laughter the entire time she'd been on the phone. When she got to the sliding glass door, she threw it open and looked around. She couldn't see either one of them.

Lucy's stomach dropped, and her lungs constricted so they felt like they were squeezing her heart toward her throat. The pressure against the pounding muscle caused her chest to ache and her head to swim. Adrenaline jolted through her veins flicking on the switch turning "helpless" into "action", and she ran toward the pool. When she looked down she could see the cover of the pool had fallen in.

"No!" she screamed, falling to her knees. Leaning closer, she peered into the murky water and saw a shadow. "Clyde? Oh my God, Clyde! Give me your hand!"

She reached out toward him, drawing herself nearer, until she could see his face. His big, brown eyes were open, but the light was gone from them. He was floating there, still and serene, as if suspended in time. For a moment, she felt like he was cradled in a state of serenity, waiting for her to save him.

"It's OK, baby. Give me your hand," she sobbed, "Momma's here...Give me your hand, Clyde!"

There was a sudden jerk of his body, and a split second of awareness, before his final breath left his body, forcing a trail of bubbles toward her. When his body went limp again, he floated down, lost to the black-green depths, out of range to the sounds of her screams, echoing above.

The scream from the dream was dragged out along with Lucy and into the darkness of the room where she was sleeping. It had been three years since she lost her children. They kept telling her it would get easier, but it didn't. It only got harder.

After her husband died, and left her with two small children, and then to lose them three years later, she could only fall asleep with the aid of the medicine her doctor prescribed. It didn't stop the reoccurring nightmares, which were progressing, and becoming more real. She focused on her breathing, a technique used to calm her down, when she felt a chill creep across her arm. Looking down, she could see by the light of the lamp on her bedside table, the fine hairs standing straight up. Her skin had dimpled to the drop in the air's temperature.

Though she was afraid to look, she forced her head to turn. She could see them. They were real. A set of dirty footprints. By the size of them she could tell they were from a small child, and they lead into her room from the hallway, where her children's room remained untouched.

Leaning over, Lucy looked down. The footsteps ended next to her bed.

The End

MAGIC AWAITS

Christopher Motz

Steve looked at the sign, and buried his head in his hands.

"You can't be serious," he whined. "A scavenger hunt? I'm twelve years old; I'm too big for all that stupid kid stuff."

His father stopped the car in the turnout at the end of the driveway, and turned to his son in the back seat. "Larry asked us to bring our children, so here you are," he said.

"Why does Larry get to tell you what to do?"

"He's my boss, you know that. He wants to have a special day for all of his employees' kids, since he doesn't have children of his own. Can't you at least pretend to have fun?"

His mother turned around in the passenger seat and looked at him sternly. "There will be kids here that are your age, and it'll only be for a few hours. You need to get out of the house more, you're too pale."

"Oh my God," Steve groaned. "Whatever."

He hopped out of the car and gave his parents a final irritated glance. Slamming the car door, he walked to the front of the immense, brick mansion, and looked up at the brightly colored sign hanging from the porch.

HAPPY EASTER FROM LARRY & BARRY THE BUNNY

SCAVENGER HUNT - TODAY ONLY

GAMES AND PRIZES

PREPARE TO ENJOY THE SPIRIT OF THE SEASON

MAGIC AWAITS

"Gimme a break," Steve muttered.

The front door opened, and a skinny old man in a lame Easter sweater walked onto the porch.

"Little Stevie Appleton," he exclaimed. "I'm so glad you could make it."

Steve eyed him warily, as he did with all strangers. Larry, with his hunched back, thick tufts of silver hair sprouting from his ears, and sporting a pair of thick-lensed glasses, looked ninety years old. His fake teeth – dentures that had turned a muddy shade of yellow – protruded from behind thin lips.

Steve turned, and watched his father's Mercedes slowly bounce down the driveway. His mother stuck her hand out the window, and gave a final wave, as the taillights disappeared around the bend. Steve was alone. Steve, and Larry, and Barry the friggin' bunny, and whatever bunch of kids were unfortunate enough to waste their night in some old creep's house

My parents are assholes, he thought.

"Come, come," Larry said, waving Steve onto the porch. "Come inside, meet the other guests, sample the treats I've laid out for you.

You like cake, don't you?"

"I guess," Steve mumbled.

"Of course, you do. What kid doesn't like cake? You go right on in." Larry laid a gnarled hand on Steve's shoulder and nudged him toward the door. The old man turned and scanned the driveway. Everyone had arrived. Steve was the last.

Larry stepped inside and closed the thick, oak door behind him.

***

"I know you're all excited to get started," Larry croaked, "but, every game needs rules. If you give me one more second of your time, we can get that out of that way."

Steve watched as a man in an obnoxious bunny suit entered from the side of the room, carrying a tray of plastic cups full of what looked to be orange juice. *So, this must be Barry the Bunny*, Steve thought. *His suit is stained and smells like old mothballs. Where'd they get this guy*?

A few of the younger kids jumped in their seats, reaching out and petting the soft fur of the suit. Barry took it all in stride, handing them their orange juice, walking down the row as the kids poked and prodded his legs and stomach. Steve took his orange juice, and put the cup beneath his chair. He didn't like orange juice, especially orange juice from a stranger, delivered by a six-foot asshole in a stinky bunny suit.

Larry coughed and spread his arms at the front of the long room. It may have once been a dining room, but the table had been removed.

A large chandelier hung from the ceiling; most of the little bulbs were missing or burned out. A massive fireplace stood at the far end of the room; the mantle was covered in faded, framed portraits. Steve noticed twelve names written on index cards, and taped in a row on the wall, six on each side. His name was closest to the fireplace.

"Listen up, boys and girls," Larry called over the children's shrill chatter. He waited until the room quieted, and looked at each of them with a smile. He seemed like a nice enough old man. Maybe Steve was being too critical of the whole thing. He shrugged and watched Barry join Larry at the front of the room. Steve wanted to laugh out loud. The man in the suit looked ridiculous.

"Are we gonna be finding Easter eggs?" a girl squealed. She looked to be about seven years old, and she had two little, pastel-colored bows in each of her pigtails.

"We'll be finding all kinds of neat things," Larry replied to scattered applause and cheers, "but first, I need to tell you how the game is played." More clapping and excited shouts. "This isn't your typical scavenger hunt, boys and girls, this is a *magical* scavenger hunt. All over my house, I've hidden packages. Boxes wrapped in brightly-colored paper with a photo of Barry the Bunny on them." Barry waved, and the younger kids waved back, in awe of the giant, gray rabbit. "When you find a package, bring it back to this room, and place it on the floor beneath your name. Never look in the boxes, or you'll be disqualified from the chance to win the grand prize."

"What's the grand prize?" a boy asked.

"That's a secret," Larry said. "We'll all find out together, when the packages are found, and returned to this room. One box will have a special item. The person who finds that box will be the winner of the grand prize, but don't worry, everyone will go home with something they'll never forget! Everybody wins!" The room erupted with cheers again. Steve and another boy about his age were the only two not clapping. They looked at each other and nodded, sharing their disinterest in the entire silly show.

"There are several locked doors in the house," Larry continued. "These doors are not to be meddled with. Those rooms are off-limits, and anyone seen trying to enter those areas will be disqualified. That's all you need to know," he said. "No locked doors and no peeking in the boxes. That's as easy as it gets, boys and girls."

More cheers.

"Are you ready?" Larry asked.

Cheers.

"Are you sure?"

Cheers.

"Then, good luck, and happy hunting," he yelled. "Go!"

The younger kids scattered like cockroaches, exiting through two doors, one on either side of the room. Steve and the other boy walked toward each other: two strangers seeking comfort in an uncomfortable situation.

"I'm Steve," he said to the boy.

"Paul," the other boy replied.

"You want to do this together?" Steve asked.

"Sure. At least it won't be totally lame if we have each other to talk to."

"Right?"

"I guess we'd better go," Paul said. "That stupid rabbit is watching us."

Steve looked over, and saw that both Barry and Larry were watching them. Creepy bastards. "Yeah, I guess so."

They exited the dining room side-by-side, walking slowly down a long hallway with doors on each side. Several were closed. A little boy with a mop of red hair stood at one of the closed doors, turning the knob, back and forth in his hand.

"I wouldn't do that if I were you," Steve warned.

The kid looked at him, startled. He poked his tongue between his lips, flipped them the middle finger, and ran down the hall, and around the corner. Paul looked at Steve and laughed. It was all they needed; they were instant friends. Suddenly, this stupid party was tolerable. At least they had each other to complain to.

***

Steve and Paul crept down the long hall, carefully dodging the younger kids intent on bringing back their multi-colored packages. Some were scarcely the size of ring boxes, while one was so large, the young girl who found it had to push it across the floor. Steve felt a smile come to his lips, suddenly feeling like this might not be so bad, after all. He nudged Paul's arm, before entering a small bathroom on the right. There weren't many places in there to hide anything. Steve opened the large cupboard beneath the sink and found his first package-pink paper with a frilly, yellow bow. He laughed and held it in front of him, showing it to Paul.

Paul shrugged, and opened a door into a small linen closet. On the top shelf, partially hidden by clean, fragrant towels, was another box, just a bit larger than the one Steve had found, with blue and purple polka dots, no bow.

"Who wrapped these things?" Paul asked. "They're totally ugly."

Steve laughed and nodded. "Yeah, they are, but maybe one of us will win the prize."

"A *secret* prize," Paul added. "What kind of idiot has a contest, and doesn't tell us what we're playing for?"

"The idiot hanging out in the living room, with a man in a bunny suit."

They erupted into laughter.

It took a second for Steve to realize that Paul was no longer laughing. Steve quieted, then followed his new friend's gaze. Standing in the hall, watching them, was Barry the Goddamn Bunny. He didn't move, didn't speak. Steve wasn't sure he was even breathing.

"Oh, hey," Steve said, "we're sorry, man. I was just kidding."

Barry said nothing. Slowly, his arm moved, pointing down the hall, toward the dining room, from where the anxious squeals of children filled the hall.

"I think he wants us to take our boxes to the dining room," Paul said.

Barry nodded his head, as a pair of tattered bunny ears bobbed along. *They could have at least bought a new suit*, Steve thought.

They walked back to the dining room, careful not to be run down by frenzied children. Colored boxes were scattered on the floor, beneath the individual names on the wall. One little boy already had six boxes, while another had none. The room was organized chaos. Steve and Paul took their small boxes to the designated place on the floor, watching old man Larry at the end of the room, grinning, hands folded in front of him. His bunny-suited cohort stood directly to his left, fuzzy, gray arms crossed.

Steve shuddered, as a chill suddenly came over him. That damn bunny gave him the creeps.

He turned to leave the room, as Paul joined him and nearly bumped into Barry the Bunny, standing at the room's entrance. "What the hell?" Steve said. He spun around, and saw Larry standing exactly where he'd been before, watching over his guests with rheumy, blue eyes. Barry wasn't there - Barry was *here*. There's no way he could have crossed the room, and gotten in front of him, that quickly. What kind of game was this old man playing?

"Come on," Paul said, "we can look upstairs. I didn't see any kids going up there. Probably scared of the boogeyman."

"Or the bunny-man," Steve uttered.

"What?"

"Nothing, let's go."

Once upstairs, Steve saw that Paul was right in the assumption that kids weren't coming up here. The house was quiet. Doors yawned open on either side; dim light from the setting sun bathed the floor in patches of reddish-orange. The voices from the first floor had become distant and whispery, but high-pitched. If Steve didn't know better, he'd think those voices were screaming instead of laughing.

"Look!" Paul exclaimed. "In here."

Steve followed him into a large bedroom, painted a drab shade of green. A dusty bed sat in the center of the room, and resting on the pillow was another colorful box.

"These things are everywhere," Steve said. "We can clean house up here."

Paul opened the closet door and pointed. "Another one." He grabbed it, and placed it on the bed, next to the other. "I think we should see what's in them."

"That's against the rules," Steve whispered. Why did the rules suddenly seem important to him?

Paul saw the look on Steve's face and chuckled. "What? Are you scared, now? I thought you didn't care about this stupid game."

"I don't," he huffed.

"So, what's the big deal? No one's going to see us."

Steve walked to the doorway, and looked down to both ends of the hall to make sure they were alone. He closed the bedroom door, and joined Paul at the edge of the bed. Something inside him screamed to keep the boxes closed, but his curiosity slowly took over. Paul put his fingers beneath the lip of the box's lid, and lifted ever so slowly. He bent and squinted. His tongue poked between his lips, and he bit down on it, as he peeked through the widening crack between the box and its lid.

His eyes and mouth popped open simultaneously, a comic look of surprise and shock etched into his features.

"Ohmygodholyshit," he blurted.

"What, what is it?" Steve cried. "What's in the box?"

Before Paul could answer, the doors to an antique wardrobe were flung open, and Barry the Bunny jumped out with a grunt.

"How the hell did you get in there?" Steve shouted. "How are you everywhere all at once?"

Paul backed toward the door, his new friendship forgotten. His only thought was of getting out of the room, out of the house, running five miles home if necessary, and never setting eyes on this place again.

Paul grabbed the doorknob and pulled; the door opened a few inches before Paul felt warm, fuzzy arms wrap around his chest from behind. He tried to scream, as he was dragged back, but Barry the Bunny clapped a musty, furry hand over his mouth before he could make a sound.

"What are you doing?" Steve shrieked.

Barry turned, and glared at him with fake, painted eyes as he pounded Paul on the back between his shoulders. Paul dropped to the floor with a thump.

"You're not allowed to look in the boxes," Barry said. His voice was deep, gravelly, muffled by the fabric of the costume.

Steve trembled with fear, yet couldn't help but be surprised that Barry had spoken. There was a real man under all that dirty fabric.

"Show me your face," Steve demanded, choking back a sudden urge to cry. "What do you look like under there?"

Barry grabbed the costume head and lifted.

Steve took one look, and screamed, his stomach suddenly roiling with acid and undigested Easter cake.

He ran for the door, tripped, scrambled back to his feet, and bolted through the opening into the hall.

"Where do you think you're going?" Barry called. "There's no leaving here. Trust me. I know."

Steve ran, and ran, and ran, down twisted hallways, up flights of stairs leading to dead-ends, and solid walls; he tried locked doors, peered through windows into absolute darkness, feeling the gaze of invisible eyes looking back.

He slid beneath an ancient-leather, cigar sofa and covered his mouth with his hands. The dust was so thick, it clung to his clothes and moist skin in fat clumps. He couldn't hear voices from the floor below, as if the kids waited silently for Barry to find Steve, and reunite them all for the reveal of the day's grand prize.

The door screeched open, an inch at a time, allowing a shaft of dim light into the room.

Steve saw Barry's fuzzy feet enter.

He held his breath.

"I know you're under there," Barry said. "I always know where the kids are hiding."

Steve exhaled harshly, and started crying. "What do you want? What's going on here?,

"Larry will explain everything, once the game is over. Why don't you come out now? If I have to drag you out, I'm not going to enjoy it, but I *will* do it."

Steve slid from beneath the couch and looked up at the man in the bunny suit. The costume head was back in place.

"Why are you doing this? Why did you hurt Paul?"

"Listen carefully," Barry said. "I've been doing this for ten years; ten *long* years. I was just like you—just another boy—whose parents thought this would be a fun little party; an exciting evening at the boss's house. My time is up. The magic holds for ten years, before the old man needs more."

"Needs more *what*?"

"Energy. Power. Whatever essence he drains from them. Every ten years, one is chosen."

"You're crazy," Steve screamed. "Insane!"

Steve bolted for the door, but Barry stepped in front of him, blocking his only way out.

"We can do this the easy way, or the hard way," Barry said. His voice sounded tired, old, drained. "Either way, you're coming back to the dining room with me. Time is short, and the old man doesn't like to be kept waiting."

Steve spun in a circle, frantically looking for another way out, another door, a window, anything. He was trapped. Barry came closer, wrapped his arms around him, and Steve went still in his grasp. He dragged him down the hall, down a flight of stairs, and into the dining room where the children—including Paul—sat in their chairs silently, staring ahead blankly, as Larry stood and spread his arms.

"Now we're all here," Larry exclaimed. "Time to announce the grand prize."

A cheer went up in the room, robbed of all enthusiasm, or emotion. Dull. Monotone.

Steve's eyes fluttered open, as he was dragged to the front of the room, and dumped on the floor at Larry's feet. He felt like he'd been drugged; his body wouldn't cooperate. He tried to move his legs but couldn't. He felt saliva dribbling down his chin, but couldn't reach up and wipe it away.

"Don't worry, son," Larry said. "You'll get the feeling back in no time at all."

The old man was right. Already, his fingers and toes were coming back to life.

"Behold," Larry exclaimed, "the grand prize winner."

Voices once again joined in a monotonous drone of a cheer. Steve watched them clap lifelessly; emotionless automatons, running on autopilot. He tried to shout, but his voice was little more than a faint breath. Paul stared at him without recognition, stared through him.

Larry walked over to the spot on the floor where Steve had deposited the few small packages he had found. He picked one up, opened it, and pulled out a gold ring with a large black stone. Strange symbols were etched into the ancient band.

Barry the Bunny quickly reached down and rubbed at his hand. The ring was gone. The ring he'd been forced to wear for ten years was now held up in Larry's gnarled hand. He exhaled a long, shaky breath, and barked a single, short laugh. It was the first time he'd laughed in a decade. Barry removed his costume head, and the room gasped in a single voice. Barry was a thousand years old, a million; an ageless mummy wrapped in thin, brown skin that tightly hugged his skull. A few thin wisps of gray hair stuck up from his desiccated flesh; his eyes had turned completely white, and had sunk into his head. Lips retreated from rotten teeth, like a fetid tide revealing green and corroded pilings below the waves.

"Barry is going to leave us now," the old man said. "His job is done."

"Where's he going?" a young girl asked.

"Where all good bunnies go, of course." Everyone nodded, as if this explained everything. "Say goodbye to the boys and girls," Larry said.

Barry waved, smiling, as the skin around his mouth cracked and split. The room lit with a brilliant green glow and the bunny costume crumpled to the floor, empty.

"What you've all been part of today is something that has been happening for thousands of years," Larry said calmly. "I'm older than your parents, older than your grandparents." Kids gasped and giggled, covering their mouths to hide their laughter. "I'm older than your cities, and older than your race. I've always been here."

"What's in the boxes?" a boy of eight asked.

"You," Larry said plainly. "Every time you lay your hands on one of these packages, a little piece of your essence is held inside. You won't even miss it."

"But, why?" another boy asked.

"Well, to keep the Bunny alive, of course. Being the Easter Bunny is hard work, and he needs your energy to see him through."

The room flashed with the same green light, and when their eyes adjusted, they saw Steve now standing in the ragged costume. He felt like he weighed a thousand pounds. He could barely move in the thick suit; he was sweating within seconds. He tried to yank the suit away from his neck and hissed in pain. It wasn't going anywhere. It was part of him. It *was* him.

Steve blubbered quietly. This wasn't normal. Whatever the old man was telling them, was a lie.

"Put your head on," Larry ordered. "The kids want to see their new bunny."

"Put it on. Put it on. Put it on," they chanted.

Larry grabbed the costume head from the floor and handed it to him. "You have to put it on yourself, kiddo. That's how this works."

"I don't want to," he whispered. "I don't want to be the bunny-man."

"But, you will," Larry said.

Slowly, Steve raised the head, and placed it over his own. He could see the room through thin pieces of cloth that acted as the bunny-man's eyes, could see the children watching with innocent wonder. Steve sniffed back tears, and smelled the musty, sour stink inside the mask. Barry had lived in this suit for ten years. How many had come before him?

Larry opened one of the boxes and Steve's legs began to tremble, as he felt immense power rush into every molecule of his being. One by one, the brightly-colored packages were opened, and Steve was imbued with the energy the old man had stolen from all the children. He didn't understand why; he didn't understand anything. His memories were slowly beginning to blur. He couldn't seem to recall his mother's face, or the name of the girl he had his first crush on.

"Why me?" he croaked.

"It could be anyone," Larry said. "You're not special, Steve. You're just the one who was chosen. I've given you the power—their power— to keep you alive for the next ten years. I'll teach you everything I know, show you things no living human has ever seen. You'll be filled with wonder every day of your life, until you're replaced."

"I don't understand," Steve whimpered. "I don't understand any of this."

"You don't have to understand it," Larry said. "Do as you're told, and one day you'll follow Barry into the clearing in the forest. Your essence, combined with the essences I've given you, will keep me alive for the next decade, will allow me to feed while our plans grow closer and closer."

"Feed? You're going to eat me?"

"In a sense, but you won't feel a thing."

"What plans?"

"For my race to return, of course!" Steve was more confused than ever, but, as his body became one with the suit, he grew numb.

Larry wasn't human. Every ten years he charged a new human battery and fed on it, sucked it dry, until it was time for another. Larry's will was already exerting force over Steve's mind, and the boy was powerless to resist.

Steve had no idea what Larry was, what his plan was, or what happens next. He only knew he had to obey.

"Okay, kids," Larry said. "Time for everyone to meet their parents outside."

One by one, the kids filed outside, through the front door, into a world that Steve would never see again. As Paul walked past, Steve grabbed his arm, and stopped him. The old man nodded, allowing just this one, final question.

"What did you see in the box?" Steve asked.

"You," the boy replied. "I saw you, locked up in a cage. You were screaming."

Paul pulled his arm from Steve's grip, and exited.

Larry walked to the front porch, and watched the kids join their families. Not one of them would remember Steve the Bunny-man, in the morning. He spied Steve's parents, sitting patiently in their Mercedes, along the edge of the driveway. Steve's mother looked up at the man, her eyes opening a bit wider. Larry nodded and relayed the message wordlessly. Steve's mother hung her head briefly, and nodded back. The children's parents knew; they always knew, and they were reimbursed handsomely for that knowledge. Amazing what a person, what a parent, was willing to overlook, for a suitcase full of hundred-dollar bills.

Larry closed the large front door, and shuffled into the dining room, where Steve stood motionless, quietly crying.

"Don't worry, my boy," Larry said. "It won't hurt a bit, I promise. Your parents will be taken care of, and you'll live by my side, until the time comes to move on."

Steve felt his head nod. He looked down at the gold ring around his finger, a magical shackle that tethered him to his new body. He knew no matter how much he tugged, he could never remove it.

"You didn't answer me," Steve said.

"There will be a time for questions and answers," Larry explained. "I'll let you have one more."

Steve cleared his throat and looked Larry in the eye. "Why a fucking bunny?"

"Simple," Larry replied. "Everyone trusts the Easter Bunny."

***

HAPPY EASTER FROM LARRY & STEVIE THE BUNNY

SCAVENGER HUNT - TODAY ONLY

GAMES AND PRIZES

PREPARE TO ENJOY THE SPIRIT OF THE SEASON

MAGIC AWAITS

"Oh, come on, mom," the boy whined. "I don't want to be part of some stupid scavenger hunt.

"How do you know it's stupid, if you're not willing to go inside and see?"

The boy huffed, and exited the car, his shoes crunching on the loose gravel of the driveway. The house was huge. He listened as the faint strains of other voices echoed from inside.

"We'll be back for you at nine o'clock," his father said.

"Don't be late," the boy said. "I don't want to be here any longer than I have to."

"You might have fun," his mother said. "Who knows? Maybe you'll never want to leave."

"Your mother's only teasing," called his father.

The boy frowned. His mother giggled, as the car pulled away.

His skin broke out in goosebumps.

"Here, boy," a deep, raspy voice called from behind. "The party is inside." He walked up the steps to the porch and stopped. "I'm Larry and this is my home."

The boy shrugged and sighed deeply.

"There's cake inside," Larry laughed. "Everyone loves cake."

The two entered the house together. Larry scanned the driveway and smiled.

Larry closed the heavy door behind him and muttered, "Magic awaits."

The End

AN EASTER PRAYER

Weston Kincade and David Chrisley

Author's Note:

For fans of my Amazon bestselling A Life of Death series, there are a few Easter eggs spread throughout this story. The official re-release of the entire trilogy will be this May. Happy reading!

The first day of the Tranquil Heights Easter Festival began with the sounds of blaring horns, kazoos, exploding balloons, and children exclaiming over cotton candy and carnival rides. Within the town's closed streets, sidewalks were lined with portable booths, vendors shouting about their wares, and signs advertising everything from plush stuffed animals to kettle corn and funnel cakes. A tall, lanky woman with untamable red curls sat on a stool outside one stall teaching three children how to paint Easter eggs. Multiple dunking booths were stationed at either end of the street, one manned by a local priest—who looked wetter than a drowned raccoon in a wedding tuxedo—and the other occupied by the local superintendent of schools. A scarily large, portable waterslide even graced the park on the far end, looking like an elephant squatting for photos, its spiraling trunk-slide towering upwards. The morning sun beat down upon the glistening water, parents out for a stroll, and drenched children running from the base of the waterslide up the steps to the top. Each journey sent them past a cotton candy stand, lemonade cart, mobile hot dog vendor, and even an outdoor video arcade, where the sound of pinball machines and 80s arcade games *dinged* away, adding to the odd cacophony. It was a thrilling time for the residents of the small mountain town, but not for everyone. Between the covered video arcade and the cotton candy stand sat a rusting claw machine full of encapsulated toys.

Within the machine, amidst the milieu of childhood thrills and chaotic splendor, Lorenzo squeezed his oversized eyes shut then opened them, staring up at his surroundings. The bumpy ride had left him unconscious for most of the trip. All he could remember beyond the darkness of their packing boxes was the fall into his new home, tumbling and bouncing against the clear shell of his prison. Now, gazing through it, he was astounded by the number of creatures in their own prisons above and below. Everywhere Lorenzo looked, arms, legs, and oddly shaped faces plastered themselves against the clear walls. Lifting a chubby, neon-green arm, he pressed against the solid bubble. It didn't budge, but giving it more force caused his entire cell to teeter and fall forward, stopping when it lodged against six others. Gravity shifted until his green, octopus-like body settled against the side, what was now his new floor. The red, acorn-like bottom walled off the area behind him, but everything else was still visible. It was a world unlike anything he could have imagined. A move in the wrong direction could send him tumbling down the mountain of enclosed creatures.

A pink octopus like himself gazed up at him from below, blue eyes peering out with sorrowful, large, square irises. "Help," she mouthed. "Please help."

Something dug at Lorenzo's insides as he peered down at her pleading eyes. She was a stranger like everyone else he could see, but that something unsettled him. Uncertain of how he'd gotten here, where "here" was or why they were imprisoned, Lorenzo banged on the wall nearest her. "I will," he cried. "I'm not sure how, but I will." The words seemed hollow, infused with a lack of confidence.

Turning to look up and around him, past countless creature-filled bubbles, a large metal claw shifted far overhead. Three metallic limbs jiggled back and forth as the claw moved left then right, adjusting ever so slightly toward the end. Suddenly it stopped, hung for a moment, lowered. Its arms clutched at a nearby bubble with a blue bottom. A yellow creature with orange bumps and a trumpet bell for a mouth jumped around frantically as the silver arms encircled him, picking his cell up and carrying him off. Lorenzo stared, open-mouthed, at the abduction. The trumpeteer pleaded with them all, panic filling his eyes until the claw opened and he fell, disappearing beyond the mountain of imprisoned creatures.

Cries went up from those near the abyss he'd dropped down. "He's gone!" "Kidnapped!" "Bastards!"

Lorenzo gaped. *It's only a matter of time! They're coming for us.*

His gaze returned to his pink fellow octopus. Trapped beneath him, she couldn't have seen, but the voices were enough to drive away any hope she may have retained. She lay curled at the bottom of her cell like a rejected child's toy, face hidden beneath her many legs.

The cries from others in the vicinity continued. Enormous shapes passed by outside, nearly as large as Lorenzo's new home, all titans compared to him. The multitude of tall, two-legged creatures sent his head spinning. Icy dread leaked into the depths of his green stomach when he realized what covered the titans' bodies—skins... skins of other creatures in a variety of colors and patterns.

Lorenzo's eyes widened as the claw overhead began moving again, coming his way. His mind summoned a titan like those he'd seen, this one wearing a neon-green skin—his skin.

No, can't be. No one would do that, he tried to reassure himself.

Lorenzo held his breath until the claw whizzed past. Relief passed through him, replaced a second later by a feeling of shame as another acorn capsule was lifted away. Screams erupted from all over this time. Everyone knew what was coming. A brown critter with beady eyes and whiskers scampered around the cell overhead, rocking it to and fro within the machine's grasp. A dramatic intake of breath echoed through the four-walled world as the transparent cell lodged between two claws. Panicked, the critter rushed the same side of his cell, spinning the bubble like a hamster wheel until it lodged once more, this time the majority of it hanging out from between two metal fingers. The hush disappeared as voices filled the air from their own cells, cheering him on. If the brown, four-legged creature could escape the clutches of this new world, it meant they all had a chance, including Lorenzo. For the first time since waking, hope filled his heart and soul. The giant claw was nearly over the hole. At the last second, one final attempt sent the yellow-topped bubble tumbling end over end back into the collection below, barely missing the gaping abyss. Cheers echoed from the transparent cells.

This time muffled shouts erupted in the world outside. A two-legged creature wearing a tie-dyed shirt that read "Easter Bunnies Must Die!!!" bellowed in anger, throwing his hands into the air.

Lorenzo tried to make out the many giants lined up behind the frustrated one, when something dawned on him. They were lining up to do more than kidnap him and the others. "Nooooo! They want to kill us," he shouted, trying to alert his fellow creatures. "Look at the skins! They are out to kill bunnies and all creatures!"

A large voice interrupted his warning, booming, "Happy Easter, everyone! Welcome to this year's festivities. Step right up and try your chance at winning one of many cute, bouncy animals. Take them home, throw them at the wall. Some even stick! It's hours of fun for only a quarter."

Where the booming voice came from, Lorenzo had no idea. However, this was clearly no place for him. A glance down brought the pink octopus to mind again, the only other creature like him he'd seen thus far. She was still huddled in place, shuddering with fear. Even at this distance, with two transparent walls separating them, he could make out glistening tears. His heart sank to the tips of his tentacles until a *thud* echoed from above. Turning his attention up, he was surprised to find nothing out of the ordinary, if you call being stuck in this fiberglass box and terrorized by a world of titans ordinary. Just then another *thud* came. Lorenzo's gaze focused on the cause, eyes widening. The yellow creature with a trumpet bell for a nose was plastered against the side of their small world—face, nose, and eyes bulging against the glass wall like a SpongeBob pizza. The trumpeteer was abruptly pulled back, his face lingering a split second too long before he was flung away.

We're nothing but toys to them, puppets on strings. Lorenzo looked around at the hundreds of assorted creatures like and unlike himself. Bolstered by the temporary escape moments before and the bubbling anger boiling up from within, Lorenzo came to a decision. *I have to do something. I* have *to.*

At that very moment something hummed to life, a sound he hadn't noticed before. The claw resumed its route overhead and countless eyes tracked its progress from below, dreading where it would stop. However, this time something gleamed within the depths of Lorenzo's square pupils—determination.

Thrusting down the fear that threatened to rise into his throat like an inflated blowfish, Lorenzo listened and watched the claw's motions. He began associating the sounds with the metallic creature doing the bidding of the giants outside. Each time it stopped, the hum changed. In the mechanism above the claw, a chain spun to life, turning one way then another with each adjustment. Like a monkey with a lightbulb, Lorenzo had an epiphany. He watched, planning his escape with each movement of the mechanical hand of god overhead, wincing each time another fellow creature unsuccessfully dropped into the far hole.

Time, he whispered silently. *More time. Just give me time… Time, that's what I need.* Each second the metal hand spent over his head gave Lorenzo pause, and the chant began again more intensely in his mind.

Another creature was lifted into the air, squealing, its clear cage clutched between the tips of all three metal appendages. The cell flexed, popping the purple bottom off and allowing the magenta pig to fall free. The entire mountain of creatures inhaled as they watched the scene play out overhead. Lorenzo's gaze didn't waver, until the claws closed tight, gripping the squealing creature before it could escape and impaling it with all three pointed ends. The squeal turned into a bloodcurdling scream as the pig struggled futilely.

"Oh no," a voice whispered sympathetically from someone afar, while another said simply, "That ain't good."

Lorenzo's eyes dropped, but a moment later he forced them skyward. The claw had continued moving and reached the hole. This time when the dreadful fingers opened, they stuck momentarily inside Mr. Pig, his insides flexing until they finally gave way. The metal appendages separated, but the creature remained impaled by one, hanging off the end. Magenta goo spread over Mr. Pig's large gut, leaking down and dropping into the abyss. *Drip… Drip… Drip.*

The wounded creature's cries echoed over them, and the titan at the controls outside began banging on the glass wall, shouting, "Let go, piggy. You're mine now."

The pit of Lorenzo's stomach bottomed out as though the claw had torn him open, leaving his own insides to gush away. A glance down reassured him that wasn't the case, but the feeling of uncertainty and fear could not be shaken. His gaze drifted past his own tentacles to find the pink lady who had captured his attention so completely. She was still huddled below, but her eyes held him without moving.

"What happened?" she asked.

Although unable to hear her voice, Lorenzo knew what she said. A shake of his head was all he could muster. No words would come, and he could not hold her gaze for a moment longer than he had to. *We have to get out.*

While the scene playing itself out above was horrifying, it was almost unbelievable. Something from the past filtered into his mind... *Easter... He said this was an Easter festival,* remembering the announcer's words from earlier.

Mr. Pig's eyes closed and his struggles dwindled to nothing. His silent body slowly slid off the claw and plummeted into the blackness below.

As the gears turned in Lorenzo's little green head, another giant stepped up to the controls, this one smaller. An anxious face with long hair, a daisy flower barrette, and an oversized forehead peeked through the glass like a wide-eyed puppy, barely tall enough to see in. Her small hand manipulated the joystick. The claw hummed back to life. A hush descended on the claw machine's world, followed by whimpers and a few panicked screams from below.

The claw moved steadily toward the mountaintop. Creatures all around Lorenzo flew into a frenzy, scrabbling at their transparent cells and trying to pop the colored bottoms off with all their might, to no avail. Panic set in as Lorenzo's heart plummeted to join his stomach.

"Not happening!" he shouted, leaping forward, unable to stop himself. He had to gain the claw's attention. Using every tentacle, Lorenzo pulled himself forward. The cell resisted at first, teetering before rolling under the octopus's weight. In seconds the prison was tumbling down the mountain of creatures. The claw stopped, shifting up then right as it attempted to intercept him.

As the circular cell tumbled around Lorenzo, a thought came to him, *Am I insane...? That thing's coming for me now.*

The consequences of his actions dawned on him just as his acorn-style hamster ball bounced into the valley of identical capsules then momentarily started to roll uphill. The edge of the gaping hole came into sight in front of him. Lorenzo's eyes widened in shock. All eight arms shot out, attempting to stop the capsule's momentum. Another bounce off a pink-bottomed cell sent Lorenzo forward. His arms flailed, trying to reverse the spin. He had to stop before it was too late. Finally the momentum halted, but the abyss loomed large below him as he teetered on the very edge.

"Carefully," he whispered to himself, plotting every move of his tentacles like a neon-green ballerina who just encountered a land mine, slowly reversing until the abyss wasn't directly below his see-through cell.

A second later, the slow movement stopped as the capsule lodged in a divot between three other cells. Lorenzo breathed a sigh of relief and slumped to the lowest point, releasing the tensed energy from his body.

It was only then that the voices and sounds around Lorenzo filtered into his mind. In his panicked state, everything outside had ceased to exist like a horse with blinders. Now, as though slowly lifting his head out of water, the sound of screamed warnings blared to life. "Look out!" "It's coming." "Run!"

There was no escape, nor could Lorenzo summon the energy. After bouncing down the mountain and the subsequent near fatal fall, he was exhausted. He felt like a pile of limp noodles left at the bottom of a ramen bowl, like his muscles were full of goo.

"I c-can't," was all he could muster. "Can't do it… Just can't."

His pounding heart slowed to a steady *thu-thump, thu-thump*. Furry, scaled, and slick arms waved within transparent cells all around and below, trying to get Lorenzo's attention.

"C-can't…" He tried to wave back; a weakened tentacle lifted drunkenly then fell to the floor. The other captives were safe for the moment. That was all Lorenzo could think about, his mind sluggish. Muted voices echoed around him, but he was too weak to listen.

Seeing his predicament, Lorenzo's new neighbors took matters into their own hands as the claw descended from above, aiming directly for Lorenzo's prison. "Ahoy, you!" a brown, hairy ape grunted, pointing at a dachshund some distance opposite him. Lorenzo had come to a stop between them. "Pin him," the ape continued.

A nod and yelp answered back as the small dog leaped into action, bouncing over the few capsules between them. The ape started his own toward Lorenzo, waving at a third creature. It trundled forward too. The three built up speed, each creature's gaze moving from Lorenzo to the descending claw overhead repeatedly.

It was a race.

The claw hummed as it lowered, the metal cord unraveling inch by inch. Three acorn prison capsules trundled toward Lorenzo. But the claw beat them, encircling Lorenzo just as the others crashed against his transparent cell. The three creatures applied as much pressure as they could as the claws closed, but the pressure was too much. Lorenzo's bubble popped, the metal fingers digging in and flexing the transparent cell now that it had detached from the red bottom. The claw lifted his clear cell up and over as it caught between the three metal digits. They grazed Lorenzo's prone form. He tried to roll away, pushing at the metal fingers, but he had never been one for feats of strength. One end of a claw caught in Lorenzo's tentacles as it lifted. His eyes widened into orbs, square irises clearly visible as he was lifted into the air upside down.

"Help!" he tried to shout, but his voice was weak.

Voices and shouts of concern began to filter up to him. An aged, gray rhinoceros with a permanent tear etched on its cheek sat beneath the scuffed shell of its cell, head bowed Eeyore-like. Her soft, gruff voice resonated from a whisper.

She chanted low, "Tis the day, of my kin. Tis the night, when we may win. Will you come and help, Señor Dones a Dios?" building with each short phrase.

The sound sifted through the air, reverberating in the four-walled world until Lorenzo's breathing calmed. His half-hearted screams dwindled to nothing and he focused. One arm after another, he unwound himself from around the large claw. It gouged into him time and again, but he simply grimaced and glared at the rebelling tentacle until it did as it was ordered. He had never before been this tired, but an unknown willpower forced him onward as the rhinoceros's sad words echoed to Lorenzo, chanting in prayer to the gifting gods. A special connection exists between toys and the gifting gods, or *Dones a Dios*. It goes back to time immemorial.

As Lorenzo was lifted higher and dragged through the air toward the abyss, he finally unraveled himself and dropped below. Momentum carried him so far that he landed with an "umph," tumbling over voices and extended hands plastered against their own transparent cells. He came to a stop with tentacles spread barely an inch from the drop-off. The metal hand retreated to its corner overhead, dropping his transparent top down the abyss. Lorenzo let out a sigh of relief.

"Tis the day, of my kin," the rhinoceros repeated. "Tis the night, when we may win. Will you come and help, Señor Dones a Dios? We beg of you." Her bass voice was even louder now in the small environment.

The chant settled on Lorenzo like a warm blanket—until the metal claw jolted back to life. Another titan was at the controls. Lorenzo's eyes slowly lifted, watching through the haze of her words. The mechanical abductor stopped and turned, heading away. He watched, lost in the sensation created as other voices picked up her words. As though it could hear her, the claw closed the distance between them then lowered directly over the sad rhinoceros's head.

When Lorenzo realized, he rose. *No, they can't.*

The crane came down slightly off target, but a far claw scooped her capsule closer, pushing her within its grip.

He moved forward with one suctioned leg then another; however, too much distance remained. Picking up speed would not be enough. Having closed less than half the distance in his weakened condition, he watched her drift upwards, her words jittering with the shaky movement but persisting nonetheless... until her bubble was dropped down the abyss.

No, why? What did we ever do to you?

But of course, nothing answered his silent question. Instead, cries echoed from those around Lorenzo as the rhinoceros's words drifted to nothing. The chant that had picked up mere moment before dwindled immediately, and the sensation coursing through Lorenzo's body seemed to ripple to his tips and disappear. Everything—every creature he encountered—was vanishing within seconds.

Suddenly the words gripped his stomach, seeping up through him and into his mind. Words he couldn't forget. Words that needed release. "Tis the day, of my kin," he began. "Tis the night, when we may win. Will you come and help, Señor Dones a Dios?" Lorenzo asked standing in the valley of imprisoned creatures. His voice grew louder, impassioned, and others picked it up once again. At the same time, he was drawn to the edge of their world, limping as green goo seeped from his wounds.

His words faded as in front of Lorenzo, just a few feet outside, a small pink bunny hopped into sight beneath the hot dog cart, its belly bleached white. Its pink nose twitched as it stood on white hind legs. For all intents and purposes, the colors reminded Lorenzo of the toys around him, but the creature was somehow outside, free. Peering out the nearest glass wall, the black, opalescent eyes caught his attention. The creature was devoid of the light, boisterous energy one would expect from such a stuffed animal. The nose twitched as it gazed back.

The chant continued behind Lorenzo, and as he watched he picked back up, muttering the words under his breath and finishing with, "We beg of you."

Nose twitch.

Just then he could swear the small creature grew an inch taller, its pink ears now touching the bottom of the hot dog cart. However, through the rivulet-covered transparent wall, it could just have been his imagination. The animated toy rabbit sniffed the air then lowered itself to the cement sidewalk, seemingly searching for food.

The chant continued, growing, building, inhabiting every space, nook, and crannie as Lorenzo's words grew louder, but something was missing. The claw sprang back to life again, moving, turning, and plucking one plastic prison from many, dropping it down the abyss and going for another. A second fledgeling creature vanished from sight, arms pawing at the sides of its cell, then a third and fourth. Each vanishing toy ate at Lorenzo. Something more had to be done.

"You can do it," he mumbled. "You can do it."

As the claw started again, he gathered himself, gauged the distance to the likeliest target, and ran toward it. The yellow top was sticking up, its inhabitant hidden below.

Lorenzo reached it with time to spare and began pulling at the lid, attempting to pry it off with all his might without endangering the creature inside. It didn't budge, even when he wrapped tentacles around the base of the clear cell and squeezed. Instead, the claw descended and it was all Lorenzo could do to shove away before he was lifted too. What turned out to be a St. Bernard fell down the hole with a muffled yelp and whine. Lorenzo's heart sank lower than even a deep-sea sub could reach.

Something tickled the back of his neck, just beneath his green skin; Lorenzo knew extreme measures would have to be taken. Defeated, he wandered back to the wall, the claw busily working overhead. He gazed at the rabbit as it shuffled around beneath the cart, sniffing the walkway. The voices repeated the chant, now supported by an emotional fervor. The rabbit hopped out from under the cart, considerably larger. There was no question. As the voices rose, it became the size of a small poodle, then a collie, rottweiler, and finally even as large as a washing machine, its tufted tail twitching. The creature halted in place, black eyes peering down into the claw machine and straight at Lorenzo.

The itch at the back of his neck was clear. The absence of emotion or a soul in the rabbit's eyes contrasted with its pink and white, fluffy exterior. This would not be enough. Even now the titans simply walked around the enormous bunny, peering at it like some new Easter entertainment. The claw continued overhead, screams interspersed with the chanting voices. Lorenzo had to do more. It was required to get the desired effect... the deserved effect.

"Señor Dones a Dios," he began, this time speaking from the heart, "we need your help."

Lorenzo turned from the world outside and strode up to the nearest acorn cell. A red squirrel peered out at him with a tail like a chinese folding fan and blinking blue eyes that pleaded silently. His face remained blank, emotionless. Wrapping tentacles around the plastic cell holding the squirrel, he squeezed. This time he couldn't consider the welfare of the creature inside. It didn't matter. Summoning all the strength he could muster, Lorenzo's suction-cup arms slowly clenched. The transparent shell didn't budge at first, only swiveling with his weight. Lorenzo held tighter, biting his lip and praying to any of the gifting gods that would heed his call. The transparent cell creaked then cracked, another split following as it collapsed under Lorenzo's weight, but he didn't stop. Other creatures watched as his tentacles wrapped around the red squirrel, pressing the plastic shards into its fur. Using a free tentacle, he snapped off a sharp piece and brought it to the squirrel's throat.

The overwhelming voices around him stopped as dozens of faces stared, uncomprehending.

"Señor Easter Bunny, we beg of you. These giants are seizing us with every second that passes. Please save us. These creatures are devils. To you, Easter Bunny, I pledge this sacrifice in your name." Sliding the shard across the struggling squirrel's neck, stuffing spilled out in tufts and the shine in the creature's blue eyes dimmed. Lorenzo stood, shard still clutched in a green tentacle. "A sacrifice of one to save the many!" he shouted.

Grey clouds began forming in the sky above, filtering out and coating the area, turning it from a dazzling Easter Sunday to dreary, overcast night. Gusts of wind picked up, blowing through the building-lined corridors and carrying cotton candy wrappers, bags, and papers along for the ride. The gusts became more intense, rocking the machine, and the claw machine's inhabitants chorused in unison, phrase after phrase. Those that had been watching lost interest as an earthquake rocked their world, tipping it to the extreme. The titans outside screamed as lightning crackled overhead and sheets of water cascaded down. Only the toy creatures could hear the chorus of wet voices falling from overhead, carrying on like a siren's call answering their prayers. The giant people quickly jogged under overhangs and into shops, holding newspapers and jackets over their heads as temporary protection from nature's surprise attack.

The vertical machine fell, slamming into the cement ground with a horrendous crash that shattered two glass walls. Acorn capsules tumbled out onto the sidewalk. Hostile freezing rain pelted the clear, plastic orbs like tribal drums, the cold fogging each and making them brittle.

The large ape who saved Lorenzo minutes before beat against the wall of his cell until the plastic spiderwebbed. A moment later his hairy hand plunged through the transparent wall and a guttural scream echoed out, "Free!"

Other creatures did the same, finding the freezing temperature adversely affected their plastic prison cells. Some managed to pop the bottoms off, while others followed the ape's example and simply beat their way out.

Lorenzo pushed up from beneath a pile of encapsulated creatures, all struggling to free themselves. Standing, he stumbled down the pile to the ground, his gaze moving skyward. The rain pelted him but did not carry with it the freezing cold that had affected their cells. He squinted under the wet barrage, inhaling and taking in the first sensation of freedom he'd ever encountered. *Yes, Ape, freedom!*

Around him, the giants were fleeing. Angry, bearded clouds roiled overhead as a giant boot came down. Spotting it at the last second,

Lorenzo dove to the side, but not quickly enough. As the foreboding shadow momentarily paralyzed him, Lorenzo covered himself in fear. Something quickly shuffled all about him. He spotted glimpses of pink and white tufts through his tentacles. Then the giant went sprawling into the cotton candy machine with an "umph" and a drunken scream filled with pain. Lowering his arms, Lorenzo was astounded to see that the Easter Bunny had doubled in size. Its great head peered down from the side, the onyx eye still devoid of any kind of sunny disposition. In its place, a fire lit the black orb from within, barely visible. The drunken giant wore a tie-dyed shirt that Lorenzo recognized. His blood boiled as he read the partial text still visible from beneath the overturned cart, "Easter Bunnies Mu…" A glance to where the tie-dyed miscreant's head should be made Lorenzo's eyes widen to orbs the size of small disco balls. There was nothing there, no head, nothing. It was then he realized the colorful shirt was splattered with red blood, arterial veins still gushing out onto it. The sight was shocking, but after a moment he pulled himself together.

Part of him was still uncertain beneath the layers of anger building within his core. He reminded himself, *They deserve this.*

Lorenzo stood and stared at the world around him. The Easter festival had turned into a feast, but nothing these great titans would enjoy. Stuffed animals hanging from the vendors' stalls were plucking themselves from their hooks, trying to elude the few vendors who had not run. They lunged for the stuffed animals, trying to stop their animated escape. The creatures crawling out of the acorn capsules ran free, attempting to find cover. Some had been squashed by stampeding feet as the titans fled from nature's wrath.

Turning back to the giant pink and white Easter Bunny with blood dripping from its oversized buck teeth, Lorenzo inclined his head. A shiver ran through him momentarily. "Thank you, Señor Easter Bunny," he said heartily. "We are in your debt." Shame crept through him as the memory of what he had done—to summon this gifting god to its full height flashed back to life. The red squirrel's blue eyes had shown with life, glowing like two lighthouses, a life he had extinguished more completely than any fire extinguisher could. The magic had freed them, but the memory would haunt him till his dying day.

Instead of turning and leaving like Lorenzo expected, the Easter Bunny nodded then lowered its head and shoulders to the ground, mere inches from the toy octopus. The implied meaning was clear, and Lorenzo's mouth dropped open.

"Really?" he asked.

The Easter Bunny said nothing. His enormous nose simply twitched as though to say "Yes, really. Get a move on!"

Seizing pink tufts of hair, Lorenzo climbed up the gifting god's furry cheek and settled down between the large, pink and white ears. A sigh of relief drifted from his lips. He still felt the exhaustion that had consumed him before, and the climb was enough to bring it to his attention again. The Easter Bunny rose onto huge, white hind legs. Lorenzo could feel anticipation quivering through the creature, but it didn't move.

"Let's go," the little, green octopus said.

The pink head looked left then right, but did nothing more.

Gazing over the nearby carts, through the pounding sleet and rain, Lorenzo had a much better view of the festival. The streets were nearly vacant except for fleeing animals, and most of the murderous titans were settling themselves along the sidewalks on park benches, curbs, or standing beneath store awnings. The giant children began to play in clustered circles. Adults stood around conversing, yammering about the weather, work, and whatever else might be on their minds. The whole scene was unsettling. After everything that had happened— the abduction, abuse, and even murder of his fellow creatures—the titans would go on to have a wonderful Easter, even if it would be more wet than they anticipated. It frustrated Lorenzo. The red squirrel's pitiful face appeared in his mind once more, and now frustration turned to anger. The small, cuddly creature had been sacrificed for this, a momentary reprieve.

Suddenly a pink, eight-tentacled body like his own caught Lorenzo's attention far below, plastered to the lined asphalt street. She wasn't moving. Another defenseless creature had succumbed to the mob of enormous people, murdered beneath their feet without care or concern. The anger spread, engulfing every inch of Lorenzo's green body, inside and out, shoving concern for his own personal welfare away yet again. She had been like him but was mowed down without a thought.

"This isn't over," he shouted. "Toys, to me!"

A slight nod of approval from the Easter Bunny reassured him that he was on the right course. Emboldened by the gifting god's approval, Lorenzo pushed himself to stand and gripped one edge of both ears in separate tentacles to steady himself. Pink fur cushioned him like comfortable house slippers. Memories of the brown rat-like creature, the sad chanting rhinoceros, and so many others disappearing into the abyss flashed before his eyes, only for the creatures to wind up abused, forgotten, or even thrown into walls. The final image of the yellow trumpeteer plastered against the glass wall infuriated Lorenzo, sending his anger into a volcanic fury that overlapped its edges. Rage poured into his body like superheated lava flows.

"No mercy," he mumbled to himself.

A nose twitch and gentle nod beneath came in response. Summoning the courage to give the order as toys and stuffed animals alike gathered at the rabbit's enormous feet, Lorenzo's gaze settled on the crowds of people lining the sidewalks. Some were pointing their way, at the massing toys and enormous rabbit. However, it seemed to be curiosity more than fear or trepidation that prompted them.

"Too many of us have died this day!" Lorenzo shouted.

At first the sound of muttering voices drifting from below persisted, but as his words echoed over them, the toys quieted.

"Far too many!" he continued. "We have all watched friends and strangers carried off to be murdered. To be slaves, accepting every kind of abuse. To be treated as less than the sand encrusted in my tentacles. To be treated worse than any living creature should be."

A roar of shared anger swept through the crowd of creatures.

"This ends today!" Lorenzo shouted. "No more!"

Thousands of gathered toys took up his cry. "No more! No more! No more!" was chanted throughout the streets, the syllables reverberating through rain and air like drum beats. More of the titans began looking their way.

Lorenzo's words built in volume and hatred as his gaze turned to the pedestrians lining the streets. "Fight for your friends, your fellow creatures, your lost loved ones. Fight for the right to live. But *fight* nonetheless. *Fight!*" Giving the rambunctious crowd a moment to take the words in, Lorenzo smiled as the furious chant of "No more!" carried to the titans. Far more were taking notice of the miniature creatures filling the street now. Raging masses will do that, even from creatures so small.

"Charge!" he cried from atop the huge bunny.

The mass of creatures spread out, targeted the nearest people. Stuffed animals climbed the titans with vigor, hungry for blood and revenge. The claw machine toys spread over the wet asphalt like a flood of ants, covering anybody unlucky enough to be close.

When Lorenzo spotted stuffed animals decorated as striped Easter eggs but with chicken legs scratching and flailing at one of the vendors, he laughed aloud. "Onward, Señor Easter Bunny," he ordered with anticipation. "We will summon everything we can and destroy these giants."

In response, he was surprised when one of the Easter Bunny's ears dipped halfway, pointing at the great waterslide that looked like a posing elephant. It sprang to life, pulling metal poles up and swinging its blue tube slide around like a trunk. Lorenzo cheered when a huge plume of water gushed from its trunk, hitting the crowd of people lined along the sidewalk and slamming them into storefronts. Glass windows shattered, slicing at the people below. Those to the sides were swept off their feet onto the cement, sending them sliding down side streets and alleys. It all happened so quickly that it wasn't until seconds later that Lorenzo heard the great titans' bloodcurdling screams. A malicious grin spread over his green, pudgy face.

"Now it's on," he said, glee dancing in his square irises. Pushing forward on the Easter Bunny's ears, the creature pounced, crushing a nearby storefront beneath it. People ran from the ruins scattered beneath them, and the magic rabbit's razor-sharp buck teeth plucked one from below, severing its torso. Lifting its head, the bunny swallowed the top half of the man, then perused the ground for another. A second later the rabbit had decimated a woman in a yellow sundress, now splattered in red.

The huge gifting god had no mercy, and Lorenzo howled with delight as retribution was dealt to the humans.

A short time later, the creatures had vanished into the trees and vacant lots scattered across Tranquil Heights. Shouts echoed across the ruins of what had been a thriving street with children and parents talking and joking over a wonderful Easter weekend. People called for missing relatives and family members, shouting excitedly when a survivor would stumble out of a ruined booth or storefront, running and enveloping them in relieved hugs.

A man of moderate height in a brown duster pulled himself from the rubble at the far end of the street, dusting off a matching fedora on his pants leg, then straightening and slapping it on his head. With both hands on his lower back, he stretched and groaned as something snapped back into place.

"Dad, where are you?" echoed one of many voices, but this was one voice the man knew.

Taking a stiff step forward, he raised a hand and called, "Right here, Jamie!" He looked around at the devastation and shook his head. Fishing in his pocket, he brought out a billfold attached to a newly dented Tranquil Heights police badge. Slapping it across his other hand, he muttered, "I don't look forward to writing this report."

The End

TRYING TO WRITE A HORROR STORY

Andrew Lennon

I don't even know what it is I'm doing here. Writing a story? Yeah, right. I've been avoiding picking this laptop up all morning. There's always something else that can be done. The dishes need washing, there's food shopping that needs to be done, there's all that important news on Facebook that I need to check. Avoiding getting things done is something that I'm particularly good at. A master of procrastination one might say. In fact, it's taken me four attempts to write this much. Am I even at one hundred words yet? I don't know, I try to avoid checking that word counter. It leads to obsession, and a tendency to fill a story with rubbish; just padding it to hit a word count, isn't going to make for a good story.

What even does make a good story? I say that like I know what I'm talking about, but in fact, I'm completely clueless. I just write down things as they come into my head. Sometimes they turn out to be a story. If what readers tell me is true, then it turns out to be a pretty good story. Well, most of the readers. There are some that don't care for my work, but I've learned to accept that as perfectly natural. It is impossible to write something that is liked by all. Everyone has different tastes. 'Art is subjective', as they say. (Whoever 'they' are!)

So, why am I sitting here, babbling away like this is some sort of diary entry? Well, truth be told, this is a habit I developed a while back. If you're struggling to find words to make a story, then just write down any old words. Once you get into the flow of things, a half-decent idea will come along, and those words will begin to have substance. At least, that's what I hope. There're no guarantees, of course. With my poor attention span, it's quite possible that I'll set this laptop down while I go to make a cup of coffee, and then not come back to it at all. It'll just be another unfinished story, before it even got started.

Right, focus, come on. You need to get this done. All morning I've been sitting here now, and I'm still no further into the story. I did have an idea this morning; it seemd good at the time. I woke from my nightmare full of excitement. That's where most of my ideas come from, nightmares. I often wake, screaming and fighting shadows that aren't really there. I have this tendency in which I wake up, and can still see my dreams, but I don't know they're dreams. I think they're real. It seems logical to me that, if you are awake, and you can see something, then it has to be real, right? Unless you've been taking some form of drug, you have no reason to doubt your senses. So, I freak out at the sight of these demons' shadows for a few minutes; sometimes I even jump from the bed, and fight nothing for a while. After several seconds, I become fully awake. No longer in that weird crossover of dreamland and the real world. It's at this point I realise those visions were not actually there, but they would make for a damn good story. So I grab my moleskin notebook from the headboard, and I scribble them down. I usually fall back to sleep pretty quickly after that. It's weird really. I freak out so much, but it doesn't take much to calm down, at all. Anyway, I've learned not to question the process; I just accept that I will continue to have nightmares until the day I die, but those nightmares are the muse for all my stories. I'm also willing to accept that they're not really a bad thing; they can't hurt me, after all.

What was I saying? See? This is the problem I was telling you about. My attention span is awful. I had to stop writing for a moment to answer the door. From there, I decided to take a toilet break, go and get a drink, make something to eat, then boom-there's an hour gone. Now, I find myself having to read back through this, to figure out exactly where I was going.

Ah, story ideas, that was it. Well, as I was saying; usually, I can thank my nightmares for giving me the fuel for my stories. Those dark dreams are the birthplace of my messed-up ideas. Except for last night's nightmare. When the morning sun lit my bedroom up with its bright gaze, I overflowed with excitement. I knew that last night's dream was a real doozy. It would make for a fantastic story. That is, until I read my scrawl from the middle of the night.

There's a reason that my story idea seemed to be so good. Would you like to know what that reason is? Because it wasn't my idea! You cannot understand the frustration that came over me, when I read through my notes to find very in-depth ideas for a story about a killer clown who was terrorising a town, and killing off people one by one. A clown named Pennywise. Yes, my fantastic idea that I scribbled in the middle of the night, was none other than 'IT', by Stephen King. How I didn't notice at the time of making my notes, I will never know. Perhaps, I was blinded by excitement, or I was still half asleep and just didn't pay attention. Whatever the reason, my plans for the day quickly unraveled when I read those notes. Damn, I can't even begin to imagine what King felt when he wrote that story. If I was so excited at the concept of someone else's idea, then the actual creator must have been ecstatic. I can only imagine the kind of messed-up dreams that he has. They must be a hell of a lot worse than mine.

Hang on a second, there's a knock at the door.

Okay, I'm back. I have just been chatting with a very cheerful postman. Well, truth be told, he didn't look very impressed at all; he looked like he wanted to escape. Of course, I kept him talking for as long as I could. Anything to keep me away from this godforsaken laptop.

Amongst a bunch of letters, which I threw on the side, the postman gave me a very neatly wrapped red parcel. It had been tied with yellow string, and a label hung from the side.

Let's have a look, and see who it's from.

Dear Andrew,
I hope you have a lovely Easter.
Love from your number one fan.
Becky Narron.

Wow, that really is totally unexpected! She lives in Indiana, USA; it must have cost her a fortune to send this to me. I don't like that she calls herself a "fan", though. I'm not comfortable with that word; it makes me feel weird. I don't have fans; celebrities have fans, and I am certainly not a celebrity. I have readers, and truth be told, I feel bloody lucky to have those readers; especially ones as loyal as Becky. There are some readers that get every single piece of work that you write. You can't buy that kind of loyalty. It's really humbling at times, and I don't know exactly what I did to earn this, but I am thankful for it every day. As if being a constant reader wasn't a big enough gift, Becky has now gone and sent this to me. Let's get it opened, and see what's inside. I'm really excited now.

Well, this really is a lovely surprise. Becky has sent me a massive Easter egg. I know it's not actually Easter for another couple of days, but I'm going to eat it now. First though, I need to drop a message to her to say thank you.

Hi Becky,

Thank you so much for your lovely gift. That was totally unexpected!

I've been struggling a little bit today, so you have no idea how good your timing is. I'm going to tuck into this straight away.

Thanks again

Andy

Ps: how did you get my address?

Well, I must tell you, this is really good chocolate. I have no idea what brand it is, there's no label or anything. It came in a plain, white box, and if I didn't know better, I'd say it was homemade. The problem now is I can't stop eating it. It's always been a problem of mine with chocolate: once I start, I can't stop until it's all gone.

Okay, okay, come on, Andy. Concentrate, now. You've almost spent an entire day sitting in front of this stupid screen, and haven't made any progress, at all, with this story.

I'm finding it harder to focus, now. My vision is beginning to blur; perhaps I need to take little break. I know I haven't made progress with my story, but that doesn't mean I haven't been staring at the screen for too long. And, truth be told, I've felt a little bit sick since eating that chocolate egg. It's my own stupid fault for eating the whole thing in one sitting. My punishment for gluttony will be an upset stomach, by the looks of it. I am starting to feel a little faint as well; maybe I should go and get a glass of wat....

Time to panic! I don't know what the hell happened, but I've somehow managed to get from the couch in my living room to my bed upstairs. I don't know who has done this or how, but I'm strapped to the bed. I can't move my legs or body at, all. The only thing I'm able to move are my hands and wrists, which are securely tied to the laptop. Hence, how I'm able to type this.

Of course, my first instinct was to log onto the internet to try and summon help. My captor obviously anticipated this move, as the internet has been disconnected. I've tried screaming, but there's been no response. I'm not surprised really; double-glazed windows are rather good at sound proofing. The house next door is attached to mine, so they would have been able to hear me, if they hadn't moved out last week. We're still waiting for the new tenants to move in.

For God's sake! On any other weekend, I'd have my wife and kids here with me. They asked me to come with them to Wales, camping for the weekend, but no, I thought the solitude would be good for my writing. If only I'd known that writing would be the only thing I'm able to do, because I can't bloody move! I should have just taken the break, like my wife said. What's so wrong with a nice weekend of fresh air, and walks on the beach? My God, I would kill to be breathing in that crisp sea breeze right now! That weird cold, but burning, sensation you get from walking along the shore; that would be heaven. Instead, I'm lying here in bed, alone and scared.

I can hear someone downstairs. I've tried calling to them, to ask what they want. I've even kept quiet, to see if I can identify what it is they're taking, or breaking. But, the only thing I can hear, is the sound of pots and pans in the kitchen. And, judging by the smell that's rising up the stairs, they're cooking. What kind of person breaks into someone's house, ties them up and then cooks dinner?

Okay, I can hear someone coming. Time to find out what's going on.

Well, now, we have some more information. Believe it or not, "number one fan" Becky Narron has taken me hostage! I have no idea

382 | TRYING TO WRITE A HORROR STORY

how long she's been in this country, or how the hell she figured out where I live, but she's here now, and the crazy bitch has tied me up.

A woman of about 5"7, with reddish brown hair, entered my room, talking with a southern American accent. She was highly offended when I asked who she was, and why the hell I was tied up. She looked at me in shock, like I should know. "Becky," she said. "Becky Narron. How do you not know who I am? I'm your biggest fan."

Well, besides the fact that she lives on the other side of the world, and, as far as I'm aware, she doesn't have any pictures of herself on Facebook (which is how we connected in the first place), so, I had no possible way of knowing what she looked like. Jesus Christ, for all I know, this woman could have been following me for weeks, months even.

She stormed out of the room, after I explained that I hadn't recognised her, leaving a plate of food at the foot of the bed. I couldn't tell you, exactly, what that food was; it's all mashed together. I'm guessing that she planned on spoon-feeding me, unless she was going to untie me to enable me to eat. I've got to be honest; I kind of hope she does, because I'll smash this laptop right across her head. Wishful thinking, eh?

It's been a while, now. I've been calling Becky's name, and apologising, but there's been no answer. God! I'm starving, as well. Even that ridiculous mush, at the end of the bed, looks appealing now. My wrists are hurting, from trying to struggle out of these binds; my head hurts and I'm thirsty. God, please, someone, just help.

I'm fed now; but, I feel sick with fear. Becky is far more unstable than I'd originally thought; she is completely crazy.

Entering the room, she asked me, "Well, are you going to acknowledge your number one fan, now?"

"Yes, Becky." I said. "I'm really sorry, I was just so surprised to see you here."

After scolding me about paying more attention to my readers, she fed me the mashed food. I'm not entirely sure what it was, to be honest. Some form of potato, carrots and ham perhaps? It was hard to tell, the whole thing was drowning in a weird sauce.

Anyway, I asked her why she was doing this to me. If she loved me as much as she said she did, then surely punishing me like this was a contradiction to that love. She said that she wanted me to write a special story, for her. Well, of course, I tried to explain to her, that it wouldn't be possible for me to write under these conditions—kidnapped and tied to my bed—it was just ludicrous!

"Well, perhaps you could use this situation as an inspiration for your story. I could be your muse," she smiled.

"Sorry to break this to you, Annie Wilkes, but Stephen King already did that, you crazy cow."

The irony of almost stealing one of his stories earlier today did cross my mind, but I kept quiet about that.

"Oh, yes." Becky flashed a sinister grin. "You're right. Well, perhaps I'll break your ankles the way she did; that really motivated that writer didn't it!"

And then she stormed out again. Now, I'm waiting in terror for her to re-appear with a goddamned hammer in her hand, or something comparable. This is absolutely crazy. Things don't happen like this in real life. I mean, okay, if it actually did happen to Stephen King, then you could understand it, but not me. Pretty much everyone in the world could pass me in the street, and be totally unaware that I write books. I'm not good enough at this game to deserve this next-level, crazy-ass shit; it's not fair!

I can hear her rustling about, downstairs. I swear to God, I heard the sound of knives being emptied out the drawer. What is this woman going to do to me?

I've opened a new Word doc, so it looks like I'm working on a story for her. It also means I can hide this log of events. I've got three different passwords set up on this laptop. All three have to be entered, to get far enough, to reach the Word docs. If the moment comes that she tries to finish me off, I'll hit the power button, then this doc can be evidence used against her. At least someone will know who did this to me.

Oh God. What's going to happen when my family arrives home? I don't want them finding me dead in bed. I've already lost my dignity; the yellow stain appeared in the middle of the sheets a while ago. Becky had ignored my cries for a bathroom trip.

She's coming. I can hear her thumping up the stairs. If this is it, then tell my wife and kids that I loved them very much. I hope I made you proud in my short stay on this world. And please just….

Well, I wasn't able to finish that last paragraph, but I feel that it should be left in, so you can understand how quickly everything happened. Here's what happened next:

Becky rushed into the bedroom, holding a large sledgehammer. I shit you not; she had a hammer just like the one that was used in 'Misery'. It's like she took that book as the inspiration for this whole thing. Well, she was bright red in the face; you could almost see the rage seeping from her pores. She screamed things at me; I don't even know half of what she was saying. It was all blurred into to some rambling gibberish. Spittle flew from her mouth. I flinched as it continually showered me in the face and eyes. I could see her physically shaking with rage.

I wailed, "What have I done to make you hate me so much?"

"Hate you?" she asked, calming for just a moment. "I'm not doing this because I hate you. I'm doing this because I love you."

Her face once more turned bright red, and she began swinging that horribly huge hammer. I couldn't bear watching it, so I shut my eyes tightly, and thought to myself

This is it.

"I love you more than anyone in the wo...." Her voice fell silent and she slumped to the floor.

"Not as much as me, bitch." My wife, Hazel, looked down at my fallen captor. She had a candle burner in her hand. I recognised it as being the one from the window in the hallway. It was an extremely heavy, ceramic burner. I thought about just how heavy it was, as my wife repeatedly slammed it into Becky's head. She didn't stop until she was breathless and unable to continue.

"Oh my God!" Tears streamed from my eyes. "I'm so happy to see you. I thought she was going to kill me. Quick let me out, we have to call the police."

"Not just yet." Hazel smirked, "First, you have to finish writing me a story; use this as inspiration."

And then she walked out of the room!

So, here I am. And here is my story.

Please, pray that she likes it.

Please....

The End

HATCH

Christina Bergling

"What is that?" my mother asked.

Her eyes narrowed at the corners, the way they did when she scrutinized me for a lie. Or a half truth, as I often tried to sell them. The skin on her nose twitched subtly as she attempted to temper her reactionary disgust.

"It's an Easter egg," I said.

"Jeremy, that is not an Easter egg."

"Yes, it is, Mom. Look at the painting."

She tried to lean closer to the offending orb, while keeping a safe distance from it. Her pupils bounced against her irises as she brought her eyelids up and down in examination.

"Who would paint an Easter egg gray and brown? It looks like it has been pooped out. Easter eggs are supposed to be pretty, in pastel colors, with stickers. I don't know what this is supposed to be. Where did it come from?"

"From inside a chicken."

"Boy, I will find a wooden spoon in this kitchen." She tried not to laugh behind her hollow threat.

"I found it."

"You brought some strange, ugly, poop-colored egg into my house?"

"Our house."

"Boy," she said again. "You have no idea where it has been. You don't know what it is."

"Mom, it's an Easter egg."

"It is not an Easter egg. Ugly thing."

"Yes, it is."

"Well, whatever it is, I don't like it."

"But can I keep it?"

She stood up, from leaning on the counter beside me, and took a step back. I watched the corner of her mouth fold, as she started to nibble on the back of her lips, the way she did when she wanted to tell me no, but lacked the justification to win the fight.

"Fine," she finally replied. "But I want it out of my kitchen. I want you to wash it. And your hands. And keep it out of my sight."

"But what if the paint comes off?"

"Wash it and your hands, or it goes in the disposal right now."

"OK, OK. Thanks, Mom!"

I felt the unmitigated smile on my cheeks as I scooped up my new, homely treasure. My chest fluttered with victory at the undeniable rush of persuading a grown up, rare as it was intoxicating. My footsteps banged on the floor, as I bounded up the stairs.

"I don't hear water!" my mother shouted up after me.

It was like she had eyes in the back of her head or hidden cameras in every hallway. I turned on my heel and dashed into the bathroom. If she did not hear water in seconds, there would be another holler up the stairs at me. If she had to climb up to me, my egg was as good as gone.

I tugged the hand towel from the rack and folded it into a pile beside the sink, perching my precious little egg on top of it like a display pillow for its distant Faberge cousin.

I cranked the knob to turn the water on high, so my mother could hear it with her supersonic spy hearing downstairs. As I absently rolled my fists under the spray, I bent down to bring my eyes near the egg's strange shell.

My mother was right, another rarity; it did not look at all like a traditional Easter egg. Where there should have been the streaked application of dye that fizzled out from a tablet, I could make out fine and meticulous brush strokes. The brown and gray that my mother found so unsavory formed crisp lines in tiny, alternating triangles. The shapes expanded around the full waist of the egg then faded smaller as they climbed toward either end.

Who could have painted something so small and detailed? And why? The ugly and unappealing mystery fascinated me.

The water temperature climbed against my skin until my nerves shrieked at the burning edge and yanked me away from my examination.

"Don't worry," I whispered to my egg. "I'm not going to wash you."

I sloppily dabbed my hands on the towel then hastily cradled the egg in my palm. The shell felt warm to me, even as my hands recovered from my distracted scalding. The egg felt right in my hand, at home, natural. I wanted to pull it closer still and let it caress against my cheek, but something in that impulse felt eccentric.

I could hear the mumble from the television floating up the stairs. I knew my mother had collapsed onto the couch, still in her nurse's scrubs. She might have had a beer bottle keeping her company, but it would be the only one after a long shift. She said more than that when I was home would be inappropriate and too much like my father. Wherever he was.

In any case, she would be immersed in her decompression time, and it would be better for all of us if I just took my precious egg to my room with me. I was sure it wanted to play video games with me, anyway.

I took a shirt—a clean one from the drawer, not even one of the scattered dirty ones littering my floor—and created a makeshift nest for my new friend on the dresser beside my bed. Something in the pit of my stomach seemed to know the egg wanted to be upright, a difficult enough task for such a shape. I coiled the cloth tightly to prop it up and keep it warm, just as its assumable chicken mother would have—had it still been alive under all that precise paint.

My fingers danced over the controller in learned and skilled patterns, and the Navy Seals on the screen moved at my practiced whim. My mind wandered off, abandoned the thin rails of my prepubescent body, and climbed into that screen—inside the skin of my avatar that pushed to traverse the uncanny valley. If my mother ever granted me enough hours, I felt like I could disappear entirely into that other world, which looked more realistic with each game release.

Then the egg moved.

Or, I thought it moved.

Out of the corner of my peripheral vision, just at the edge of the flickering light, I thought I saw the egg twitch or, maybe, hop just slightly. I paused the game and turned to face the small perch. I stared at the painted shell in the glow of the television. I held my eyelids back until my eyes began to dry. Nothing. Yet the egg was no longer upright, either. It had slumped to the side since I began my game.

I laughed to myself and reached forward to adjust the egg. Nothing could be alive inside after so many nights in the spring snow outside. But, had it not felt warm in my hand?

The break in my campaign allowed me to feel the weight of my eyelids, the lethargy spreading through my muscles. My mother must have dozed off in front of the television to allow me so much uninterrupted play. Deciding to call it a night, I flipped off the television then light and slid myself under the covers.

Then, in my last fleeting minutes of consciousness, I reached out in the dark and drew the egg in with me.

In the middle of the night, still half embedded in a dream, I woke startled and in a cold sweat. Heat radiated and throbbed from my body as the air outside my blanket cocoon licked icy tendrils along my forehead. My head swam disorientated, somewhere between a twisting dream and the stagnant room around me. Then I felt it—a steady thump, almost like a heartbeat—beside me.

My egg.

Panic popped my brain out of the sleepy fog, like a buoy. In the darkness, I pawed frantically around my sheets, feeling for the smooth edge of the crafted paint. Under the flattened corner of my pillow, I found the egg cradled safely.

I gathered the egg into my hands and, without thinking, brought it up against my cheek. I closed my eyes, to make the black around me a shade darker still, and dropped my breathing into a relaxing trance.

And I waited.

In the suspended moment, I nearly slipped back across the line into swimming unconsciousness. Then I felt the gentle press against my cheek. A throb, just like the sound, a tap maybe. I snatched the egg away from my face and stared at it, through the dark, in disbelief.

The shell expanded slightly against my fingertips, and I could hear the pulsing in my head again. I must have been dreaming. I had to be dreaming. Yet the world around me felt so thin, the way only the waking world could be so shallow.

The quiet pumping inside the egg mesmerized me. The sensation enlivened the egg, made it something else. It was no longer a coffin encasing what could have been a chicken. It was holding something. Something alive.

Sleep won, though. The same way it did when I would try to sneak hours of gaming after my mother went to bed. It reached its heavy hand up over my brain and pressed my eyelids down.

My alarm shattered the persistent echo of the heartbeat in my dreams. I found the egg still cradled in my immobile palms. I had not moved the entire night, locked in a drowsy paralysis. The eggshell stuck to the curve of my palm, but in the daylight, it looked decidedly not alive, decidedly not as animated as it had felt in my hand in the night.

Maybe it all had been just a dream.

"Jeremy, you better be out of that bed!" my mother bellowed through the door.

I shrugged to myself then placed the egg back in its t-shirt nest on my dresser. Without a second thought about it, I threw on questionably-clean clothes and sprinted down the stairs.

"J. Hey yo, J!"

I heard Aiden's voice swim up through the steady thumping that still echoed in my ears. The bell sliced through the air around us as I lazily swung my head in his direction.

"You in there, J?"

Aiden cocked his head to the side and opened his eyes expectantly at me. Even at the desk right next to me, he felt so far away, like he was talking to me from the end of a long hallway. I tried not to take too long responding, blinking hard and shaking my head to clear the eerie, throbbing fog between my ears.

"Yeah, yeah, sorry, man." I stumbled on my words.

"What? Did you stay up late sneaking in some campaigns last night, or what?"

"Nah," I said, reaching under my chair to gather up my books. "Something way weirder, dude."

We stood up from the blue plastic chairs, wrapped with smooth desk surfaces, and began shuffling down the aisles towards the classroom door.

"Well, then what?" Aiden asked, as we approached the hallway.

I opened my mouth, intending to tell Aiden all about my strange new egg with the intricate, morbid Easter paint and the pulsating warm shell.

"Mr. Ramirez," Ms. Clark interrupted. "Hang back a moment, please."

Aiden gave me another wide-eyed stare, popping his eyebrows for emphasis, then disappeared out into the teeming stream of passing students. I walked up to Ms. Clark's desk, struggling to suppress the undulating sound gaining volume against my skull again. I tried to orient myself by staring at the gouged edge of her desk.

"Jeremy, are you ok? You seem distracted today."

"Yes, Ms. Clark. I'm fine. Just tired. I did not sleep well last night."

"I wanted to talk to you briefly about your essay."

"What's wrong with it?"

"Oh, it is not that it is wrong, just not finished. As always, your writing was quite impressive. Your vocabulary is always stunning. However, past your vocabulary, I'm not sure what you are really saying. The assignment is to decide whether the witches' prophecy drives Macbeth to madness. I want you to give me another draft, and I want you to really concentrate on your argument. What are you trying to convince me of here?"

I floundered under her words, which seemed to wash over me in waves—tides to the rhythm of that egg's steady heartbeat. I knew she stared at me, in anticipation of either a gracious acceptance of her critique or an outraged rebuttal. I grasped onto the sentiment that she wanted me to make an argument. I could remember that.

Make an argument. About Macbeth.

"I can do that, Ms. Clark. When do you want the revision?" I asked.

"Friday. Just have it on my desk by Friday."

"Will do. Thank you, Ms. Clark."

The school day vanished in a blur. The voices around me fell distant, and the volume of their sounds rolled in swells. While my teachers droned on about algebra or biology, the strange intruder perched in a crumpled shirt beside my bed consumed my thoughts. I saw every brush stroke in the gray and brown paint, felt their texture against my fingertips. I felt the warmth and movement of the shell against my cheek. I was so fixated on the small orb that I did not even think that my thoughts shifted in strange patterns or worry about what those patterns might mean.

I could not dash up the stairs of my house fast enough. I leaped, taking the stairs two at a time, feeling the reach along my groin to make each stride. I felt an almost claustrophobic fear that my egg would be gone. Or that it had fallen and broken. Or that it had hatched and left.

I flung the door open to my room to find the egg perched exactly where I left it, silent and unmoving atop the folds of fabric. I felt the smile stretch my face, possessed and unnatural across my cheeks. Like a foreign emotion embedded in my brain. Yet, I snatched the shell into my palm, closed my eyes, and traced the shape over the curve of my cheek.

The distant anxiety that had nagged on the edges of my nerves all day faded with contact with my egg. Even though I found the shell cool and dormant, its presence snapped me back to the surface of my brain, quieted the steady rhythmic thumping in my head.

I rolled the egg back and forth between my hands, watching it bump and sway along the shapes of my fingers. Then I noticed something in the previously perfect paint. I brought the shell close to my eye and scrutinized it in the afternoon light breaking through my window. Below the lines of gray and brown, a black vein snaked along the surface. As I turned the egg over, there were more veins. The branches of black lines drew a strange map around the gentle curves of the shell.

That had certainly not been there the previous night, before or after I had examined it with my mother. She would have noticed and told me how very disgusting it was. It would have been dumped straight into the disposal.

I caressed the surface with my fingertips, attempting to trace out the lines, but I only felt the brushstrokes in the paint. As I brought the egg closer to my eye, a distinctive tap shook the edge of the shell. My body startled so hard I nearly dropped my new treasure. I pulled it back from my face and froze anxiously on my bed.

Tap again, harder this time. The egg jostled against my hand, and the pulsating sound returned to my ears, echoing against the canals and into my brain. I stopped breathing.

Tap! Beneath the sound of the tiny impact, I thought I heard the slightest crack. I frantically turned the egg round and round through my fingers, searching for the perforation. The surface remained immaculate. The egg fell dormant again as I stared desperately for the next movement.

"Jeremy Anthony!" My mother's voice severed my trance.

She was home from her shift and brandishing my middle name. I felt the tickle of panic run cold down my back, and I set my egg safely on my makeshift nest before hurrying down the stairs to face my fate.

"Jeremy," my mother said again, when she made eye contact. "What in the hell happened here?"

"What?"

"What do you mean 'what'? You left the back door wide open. Then you just trailed all your crap through the house. Your backpack is just dumped in the kitchen."

"Oh, yeah." I leaned around to look at the trail I had left. I had not even noticed in my pursuit of my egg. "Sorry." I shrugged.

"Sorry? Baby, what happened?"

"Um," I stumbled. "Well, Ms. Clark is having me rewrite my essay."

"Why? You always do so well in her class."

"She said my writing is fine. That my vocabulary is impressive, but I did not make an actual argument."

"What are you supposed to be arguing?"

"I'm supposed to be arguing whether the witches' prophecy drove Macbeth mad and is the root of everything he does after."

"And what does your essay say?"

"She's right. It doesn't really say anything. I pretty much give a nice little summary of the prophecy and what Macbeth does, in eloquent ways."

"That's my little wordsmith, but what do you think?"

"I don't know. Can you really blame a bunch of awful decisions on some suggestion? Just some old women planting ideas in your head?"

"Ideas are powerful, baby. But are they a cause or an excuse?"

"In both cases, wouldn't it drive him to act?"

"That's what you have to decide. Did the prophecy lead to the actions, or was he going to do them even without the idea?"

"Maybe the idea could have infected him, could have unlocked some malicious intent in him."

"See, you know what you think. Now, you just have to write it. Well, baby, you better get to it. I know you'll do just great. You've always been my smart cookie. Did you get some dinner?"

"Yes?" I fumbled on the word in my mouth, my mind struggling to connect thoughts.

"No, you didn't. Here, let me make you a quick sandwich. Fuel for your essay writing."

With a heaped plate, I hustled back up the stairs, leaving my mother to her quiet, uninterrupted trance in front of the TV.

When I opened my door, I could only hear the steady, and now deafening, pulsing of the egg. My eyes found the small shape, increasingly darkened by the spreading of the eerie black veins, and became transfixed. They were ensnared, trapped as I discarded my entire meal to my desk, beside my untouched Macbeth essay. I slapped behind me until my arm found the door to close it behind me.

As I stared at the strange orb, I realized it was moving, vibrating against the cloth nest. In the dim light from my desk lamp, it twitched and jostled.

Something was hatching.

I crawled across my mattress like a tentative cat, and wrapped my fingertips around the edge of the dresser, bringing my face against my paled knuckles.

The egg rocked side to side, rolled with the movement beneath the shell. The veins began to ripple the surface of the shell, throbbing against containment. The sound of the heartbeat climbed to a crescendo, filled my head, overflowed from my ears, undulated against my skin.

The crack split my world as the shell fractured open. The pulsating sound disappeared. Even the egg finally froze.

I lost my breath again. My respiration disappeared somewhere beneath the terrifying swell of my anticipation. Some terrible blend of excitement and disoriented terror.

The egg remained still long enough for my pulse to start knocking on my eyeballs, begging me to gasp in a breath. I did not dare gulp at the air. I surrendered to slowly suck in the oxygen through the side of my mouth, soft and gentle and immobile. My eyes began to dry from being fixated on the shell. The cracks spread across the surface, adding routes and intersections across the black veins, making the world more complicated.

I nearly gave up. I almost resigned myself that the hatching was as far as it would go. Then another, louder crack echoed against my bedroom wall. A large chunk of the shell at the very apex of the shape popped up and tumbled to the cloth nest below.

With my heart seized in my chest and curled up against my ribcage, I leaned forward to peer inside. Before my eyes could even cross the plane of the shell, a thick black liquid began to ooze from the hole. The same color as the veins on the outside, the goo began to pour out of the egg like an oil well.

The liquid was thick and shiny. It looked so sticky, the way it dripped and clung to the egg shell, pooling tightly around the base and over the folds of the nest. Something inside my quivering heart told me not to touch it, but I had to know how it felt. The ooze seemed to speak to me in a strange, unintelligible language that sounded just like that sick pulsing in my head.

I could not resist. I extended a trembling finger and slowly moved towards the hatching egg. The liquid seemed to respond to me. The swell reached out and climbed into the air toward me, almost expanding in an identical shape to my fearful digit.

Our movements were slow at first, my own and the slime. The two of us moved toward connection in a near frozen moment. Then the goo contacted my skin.

The black liquid was slimy and alarmingly warm. It bubbled so hot that my skin tried to retract away from the burn. Yet before I could withdraw my finger, the ooze surged. I let out a startled scream and leaped back, pulling my trapped finger with me. Yet the liquid clung to me, wrapping around my entire hand.

Below the goo's writhing and warbled surface, I felt the vivid bite of pain at the tip of my introductory finger. I wanted to rip the slime from my hand, but I was too terrified to spread it to my free hand. With panic welling in my chest and through a barrage of struggled outbursts, I shook my arm as hard as I could, hoping to fling the ooze off me with sheer force.

I swung my arm with all my might, feeling the gravity in every joint from my shoulder to my hidden fingers. I felt my tendons stretch and whine, yet the liquid stuck, unaffected, as it climbed over my wrist.

It was going to swallow me whole. How did so much goo fit in such a tiny, ugly egg?

The pain exploded on my fingertip again. I yelled out and went to draw the injury to my body. The sensation rooted at my nail, as if the nail itself ripped up from the bed. I thought I could hear the crack of the nail and the rip of the skin below. When the tearing reached a climax, any awareness of my nail vanished; it was lost below the pain.

Then the liquid appeared to recede in a strange sensation of pressure. It drew down from my wrist, climbed away from my palm. The awful pushing feeling only grew more concentrated as the slick liquid disappeared.

It was not until the base of my fingers reappeared that I realized the goo was disappearing into me, drawing into my fingertip under my fingernail.

Sheer fear, cold and sharp, sent spires out through my limbs, paralyzed me in dumbfounded contortion. I wanted to scream for my mother. I wanted to snatch the tail end of the ooze, before it vanished into my flesh. Yet, I just gaped, wide-eyed and stupid.

The last of the bubbling slime slurped under my nail. The throbbing sound dissolved. The ripping pain under my nail dissipated back across my nerves. The lights in the room even seemed to brighten. The entire experience vanished so completely I could have been convinced I hallucinated the entire mess.

Then I looked down at my nail. The whole thing, cuticle and all, was completely black, the consuming color of that awful goo.

Tentatively, I reached toward it, drawing my hand back before touching the infected finger.

The blackened digit felt like mine. My nerves reacted normally, informing me my other fingers were running over it, suspiciously. My skin maintained its normal pigment. I tapped on the nail itself. It even responded normally, yet the discoloration unnerved me to my core.

Still cradling my now traitorous fingertip, I looked up at the egg. As I watched, the shell disintegrated in front of me, rolling into a pile of dust on the makeshift nest.

As if nothing had ever happened. As if it had never mesmerized me, at all.

"What happened to your finger, Jeremy?" my mother exclaimed, as she heaped scrambled eggs on my plate. "Your nail is completely black."

"Oh, I slammed it in my desk drawer last night. Got it really good, I guess."

My entire body felt heavy. I had slept under a shifting haze of disorientating nightmares. Every cell suffered the adrenaline aftermath that now felt like just one of the fading dreams.

"Oh, honey. Did you get your essay redone?"

"No, I actually fell asleep after the finger smashing. I'll try to get it revised in study hall today."

"Sounds good. Now, eat up. You're moving like molasses today." My mother looked at me out of the side of her eye, the way she did when she was examining me. Then she smiled gently before moving to wash the pan in the sink.

The exhaustion continued to pile on my forehead, as the hours ticked away at school. At my desk, the classroom stretched out and thinned into oblivion around me, as I stared at my alien nail. I tapped it on my book, feeling the impact reverberate through the stain and along my nerves. Everything felt dull and far away, except that black color.

"Hey J, let's ditch study hall today," Aiden said, bumping his backpack against mine, as we walked down the hall.

"I can't today. I have to rewrite my Macbeth essay for Ms. Clark."

"You never have homework to do in study hall, man. You always get it done days in advance. What the hell is going on with you this week?"

"I have had some weird things happen to me this week, Aiden."

"What weird things? Let's cut out, and you can tell me what the hell is up, man."

We stopped alongside my locker, and Aiden moved to look me in the face.

"Whoa," he said, taking a step back.

"What?" I floundered. My eyelids felt like they were lined in lead.

"Dude, your eyes." Aiden leaned forward and squinted at me, horrified.

"What? What about my eyes? What's wrong with them?" I instinctively reached a hand up to the edge of my eyelid.

"I don't know. They're like gray, man."

"My eyes are brown, Aiden."

"No, no. Not the colored part. The white part. It's all gray and kind of, I don't know, veiny."

I immediately saw a flash of the black veins snaking over the shell of my cursed little egg. I poked at my eyeball to only feel the usual wet and squishy orb. Aiden leaned forward, squinting at me curiously, almost alarmed.

"Stop it, Aiden. You're freaking me out." I took a defensive step back, feeling the cool metal of the locker on my shoulder.

"You're freaking *me* out, dude. I don't know. Maybe you should go see the nurse. Your eyes just don't look normal, man."

My heart knocked against my clavicle, bringing the throbbing sound back to my ears. The pulsing of the egg coming from inside me. It felt like an auditory intruder, like a black thorn in my brain, puncturing the tissue to release the black goo beneath.

Despite Aiden's pestering, I did not go to the school nurse. I told him I would. He waved to me as I walked in the direction of the front office. Yet, once he was out of sight, I dashed toward the back of the school and slipped off campus as the security guard dozed in his golf cart.

I burst through the door of my house, again leaving the door ajar behind me, and again abandoning my backpack and coat in a trail behind me. Ragged breaths chapped my lips, as my heart continued to hammer against my chest until it felt bruised. I rushed up the stairs through my exhaustion, and flung myself toward the mirror.

Aiden was right; my eyes did not look normal. I leaned into the reflective glass, examining the tainted spheres closely. The white meat of my eyeball was tinged an awful gray: a sickly and unnatural color. I saw the thin spiderweb of veins Aiden had noticed. I pushed closer to the mirror, turning my head to expose more eyeball. As I tugged my eyelid down, a pulsation flared from my black fingertip up my arm and into my face. When that sensation reached my eye, the thin veins popped and snaked black like those in the egg, branching out under my conjunctiva.

Another wave of horror flared over me. The stranger in the mirror swayed and wobbled, before blackness bled out of the corners of the world and swallowed me whole.

The hard tile floor dug pressure points into my joints, but the discomfort was not what woke me. My skin was on fire, crawling with a teeming and relentless itch. A cold sweat dripped from my forehead as my flesh writhed at the surface. My hands clawed at the sensation, but my fingertips flinched away from the lumpy texture of my own body.

I slapped desperately at the light switch, then squinted back against the glare. I dropped to the floor to avoid the deranged and terrified stranger inside the mirror. I almost did not want to look at my skin. The painful prickle on my nerves told me it was serious. I did finally force my disgusting eyes down.

I found my skin welted and puckered. Lumps sprouted up over my hands, my arms, every visible part of my body like enflamed gooseflesh, making the skin look distended and deformed. At the peak of each bump, something wispy peeked through my flesh, something barely visible. I brought a finger to investigate and felt the protrusion ruffle against my touch.

My brain seized. Thoughts dissolved into chaos. What was happening to me? What was that black goop that had forced itself under my nail? What was it doing to me? My black nail, my black veined eyes, now this distortion of my own skin.

Why was my mother working late tonight? How could I even tell her what was happening to me, what that egg, she so instinctively hated, was doing to me? Even in my fear, I did not want to have to tell her how right she had been.

My head swam, somewhere between terror and exhaustion. My heart could not go on beating this hard in my chest. I did not know what to do; so I went to bed. I did not look at my own reflection. I did not touch my own skin. I burrowed beneath my blanket and told myself I would wake up myself again.

I did not wake up myself again.

I heard my alarm squawking from far away, at first. Then, the sound seemed to climb into my ears, penetrating my blanket and piercing into my brain. As my consciousness spread back out into my body, my nerves began sending an assault of garbled messages. All of pain, discomfort, confusion, and panic. I awoke in the exact same disaster I had fled hours before.

When I moved my eyelids to open my eyes, it felt like they dragged over sandpaper. The veins bulged so sharply they changed the texture of my eye. My skin ached the way only a fever could inflame it, where every cell on the surface and every layer stacked beneath pricked with extra, terrible sensation. I was aware of my entire flesh suit, and how very unhappy it was.

As I shifted my limbs under the covers, my skin caught and dragged on the fabric. The blankets and sheets clung to me as if I were tangled in the fibers. I did not want to touch my own skin; I did not want to know.

Every movement hurt. My eyeballs ached, encased in those horrid black veins. My flesh pulled taut and suffered a terrible and constant ripping sensation. My skeleton, itself, felt foreign beneath my sack of fatigued muscles. I took a deep breath through my cracked lips and brought my fingertips to my forearm.

I bristled at the sensation of my own arm, the same way the texture of my arm bristled against me. The lumps managed to rise, even further engorged than the night before. I let my finger trace the incline of one bump to find the projection at its summit. Whatever jutted out of my enraged skin had grown longer. The spire stuck out stiff yet flexed and folded at my touch. It felt familiar, which made it even more alarming.

When I heaved my broken and distressed body from the mattress, I managed to ache more. I found it awkward and near impossible to stand normally. When I attempted to straighten my spine, stack my shoulders above my hips, my back rounded in protest. My chest pushed forward unnaturally; my legs bent severely, bringing me down closer to my thighs and to the ground. My arms refused to hang at my hips; instead, they hovered and near flapped at my sides. I went to take a step, and my entire body undulated in a strange movement, my chest swaying up and back, my legs lifting high into my belly, my head bobbing in aftermath.

Hot tears burned down out of my hideous eyes. A crushing sensation of panic overtook the foreign body in which I now found myself trapped. My mother could be right all she wanted. She could be right until the end of time. I just wanted her to put her arms around my ugly, lumpy shoulders and tell me it would be all right.

She was still working. Since she said she saved lives for a living, I was only permitted to call her at work in case of a "real emergency." This definitely felt like it shattered the very definition of emergency.

"I need to speak to Yolanda Ramirez," I squawked into the phone. My voice felt strange in my throat and came out as unrecognizable as I felt.

"I'm sorry. She's just gone into a trauma. Can I take a message and have her call you back?"

"Oh. Um. Could you tell her to call her son?"

"Jeremy, is that you?"

"Yes. Hi, Linda."

"Oh, honey, I didn't recognize your voice. Is everything OK?"

"Yes. I mean, no. I'm really not feeling well. I think I might need her help."

"Sweetheart, do you need me to go get her? I can tag her out if it's serious."

"No, no. I'm OK for now. But could you please have her come home after the trauma?"

"Yes, of course, Jeremy. You hold tight. OK, kiddo?"

"Thanks, Linda."

When I hung up the phone, the tears rained down my face again. I imagined they were black, just like the veins.

All the pain in my body began to concentrate. It climbed up my limbs and out of my eyes, drawing to a terrible peak in the center of my face, pressing and stretching behind my nose. I forgot about the weird plumes exploding out of my pores or the rotten-looking veins mapping my eyeballs. My awareness tunneled down and reduced to the tip of my face.

An intense pressure erupted from the back of my skull. Something tried to split my face open and escape. Perhaps the living thing rolled into the black tar of that dreaded egg. As the sensation culminated, I thought I could hear the cracking and popping of my cartilage breaking, the shredding of my very skin.

I moved to sprint to the bathroom, to see what was being unearthed through my face, yet I became tangled in the new awkward movements of my body. Instead of taking sprinting strides, my feet popped up in a flapping march. My chest contracted down toward each rising knee. My head pecked forward and back in jerking motions hard enough to knot my muscles, if they even were my muscles anymore. I felt myself receding, falling back away from the skin and the eyes that were no longer mine. Disappearing beneath the black ooze-infected body.

I bobbed and weaved through the hallway, scarcely noticing when my fingertips winged hard against the wall or when I slammed my toes against a corner. I managed to toss myself into the bathroom and stand before the mirror.

I could not believe my eyes or the foreign eyes that stared back at me. The black veins had receded. A giant orange iris, consuming my entire eyeball like a bloody sunset, stared back at me. The black pupil in the center darted waywardly. I had to struggle hard to focus on anything. The world became glimpses and flashes back and forth.

The swollen pimples along my flesh had blossomed, full feathers unfurling from the misshapen skin. My own skin vanished under the interlocking layers of white and brown feathers. They moved individually, ruffling in waves with my panic. Even in the small mirror, I could not recognize the shape into which my form now contorted.

I leaned closer, bringing my twitching amber eye near the glass, striving to lock onto my nose. As I stared, another burst of pain throbbed up from my center and out of where my nose used to be. A spatter of blood dropped into the sink. I reached my fingertips out from the feathers and explored the protruding shape.

The point curved slender and firm, the surface slick under my blood. The end hooked downward before parting into two snapping pieces. I went to scream, and the two points parted. A distressed squawk exploded from my lungs. My body descended into a flurry of unfamiliar hopping and flapping movements. With each alien sound and gesture, I felt myself falling farther away, becoming less the boy who picked up an ugly Easter egg he found outside.

Far in the distant downstairs, behind the bathroom door, I heard my mother's worried voice calling me. Her footsteps slammed frantically through the house as they ascended closer. I never once called her home from work. She must have been terrified. When she burst through the door, her breath panted audibly.

"Oh my God." Her words fell heavily on the floor between us.

She did not move to gather me in her arms. She did not crouch to comfort me. She stood frozen and flinching in the doorway, locked in shock I could understand, all too well.

She found me perched on the floor on a nest of crumpled towels. When she finally did take a step forward, I felt my hackle swell. She wanted to take my egg. She wanted to destroy it, just like she hated the last one. I could not let her. My neck began to jerk violently as my wings waved aggressively.

My mother released a terrified yowl, as she turned to flee, but my new body was too fast for her. Before she could clear the hallway, I landed on top of her. She rolled over, frantically slapping and batting her arms against me. Somewhere lost at the very edge of what was left of me, I watched my beak peck and plunge into her face and neck until the blood erupted and she stopped moving.

I wanted to cry, yet the punctured version of my mother just seemed to fall farther away, receding into the bloodied backdrop. My thoughts became shorter, simpler. I felt less, in every damning second after. Eventually, I could only think of one thing: my egg. The squawk that escaped my dripping beak almost sounded natural. With a ruffle of my feathers, I hopped up and returned to my perch on top of my precious egg.

The End

SULPHUR

Mark Fleming

There's the kid next door, rolling eggs along the path, giggling while she races after them, to the point where each one strikes the garage wall. All the noise is disturbing my hangover, and the stench of the white mush hangs in the air, kneading my guts. It smells like sulphur.

I stand abruptly, the chair crashing to the floor. Moments later, I'm marching through excoriating sunlight. For a moment, I consider that I should really speak to a parent – Charlotte and I have only been here a couple of weeks and we've yet to be introduced to our new neighbours. But when you're still drunk from the night before, you have a free pass to subvert etiquette.

"Hey, you!" I snap through the privet. "Enough with the Easter eggs, yeh? Have you ever watched 'Children in Need'? Kids your age are starving in..." Here I consider the countries where kids her age are starving. Is it still Ethiopia? "Africa."

I can't be sure if she heard or even understood; my voice is slurring badly. But her laughter alters, developing a sadistic edge. I glower through the branches and glimpse movement. Then her face materialises among the foliage, lips curled into a sneer, eyes boring into mine, before vanishing so abruptly, I wonder if I imagined it. Ever crazier hallucinations are a symptom of my increased bingeing. Stumbling backwards, I only realise I'm still clutching a glass when, it slips from my fingers and shatters on a paving stone.

Staring at the amber fluid snaking along the cracks, I hear a triumphant cackle. I *definitely* heard her that time. But my fury wanes: she's only a child; judging by the bicycle propped by their front door the day we arrived, maybe eleven or twelve?

Next thing, I'm rifling through drawers and cupboards like a burglar. "Where's that other bottle, Charlotte?" I roar. *"Charlie, you still here?"* The only noise is another egg trundling to its doom. "That brat next door is doing my fucking head in with her stupid Easter eggs. I was watching her earlier, sitting in her garden, painting them … taking ages to create intricate patterns … only to smash them to bits. Hey, you in, Charlie? I'm popping into the village."

When I seize the car keys from the mantelpiece, my toe catches a fold in the Persian Rug. I thrust an arm out. Charlotte's expensive Chinese vase dashes onto the hearth. I steady myself against the wall, dislodging a picture that tumbles face forward, glass splintering. Scarcely giving either a second glance, I negotiate the tricky steps down into the kitchen.

My drinking has spiralled out of control, but yesterday was particularly bad. I've no memory of whatever blazing row culminated in Charlie launching a photo album at me. Its contents are strewn over the tiles like the aftermath of a looting. I woke among this debris at half past four, feeling as if I was being stretched on a rack.

I claw a fistful of photographs. Here is a microcosm of our lives together: our wedding, various birthday and anniversary occasions, the pair of us in ski suits or snorkelling attire. My gaze lingers on an image of me grinning behind the wheel of my previous BMW, the gleaming white 5 series.

My reverie is destroyed when two eggs strike the French windows. The harder I blink, I realise my bleary vision has conjured two of them. Yolk slithers down the glass.

Incensed, I seize the handle and barge outside again. Overly hasty, I slide across the grass and crumple in a heap, my face scraping across stones. But the kid has made good her escape, and my demise is greeted with sniggering from the far side of the hedge. This stokes my anger ten-fold. I yell: "I'm going to take every last one of your stupid Easter eggs and *smash them all to pieces!*" This provokes another chuckle, and no wonder: smashing them all to pieces seems to be collusion rather than punishment.

The privet hedge forms a tangled barrier between our two houses, running along a wall adjoining her parents' garage. The brickwork requires pointing, but the wall's weatherworn façade was obviously ideal for her fleeing. It will allow me even swifter access.

Digging my toes into the cracks, I grunt with the effort of climbing upwards, branches stabbing at my enflamed cheeks. As I heave myself higher, until I'm level with a skylight above the garage, the stink of sulphur grows more acrid. Pausing for breath after the unfamiliar exertion, I gaze through the murky pane. Cobwebs mask the gloomy interior. I glimpse the ground level, twenty or so feet below, where a space is large enough to accommodate a 4x4.

Searching for my nemesis, I scan the shrubbery. A burgeoning rhododendron bush sprawls beyond the hedge, its pink blossoms almost translucent. Aside from their stirring against the gentle breeze, I notice more purposeful movement. I freeze, fighting against the alcoholic film causing my eyes to stream in the harsh daylight. Grinding a knuckle into my eye sockets, I concentrate. Creeping beneath the bush, she'll be clutching another fragile grenade.

I hunker down, ready to spring from the wall, choosing a landing position among an expanse of grass. Shielding my eyes, I also notice the point where her Easter eggs have been getting pulped all morning: just in front of the garage; so close that, the odour of sulphur catches the back of my throat.

Inadvertently, I belch; the horrid taste of regurgitated whisky corroding my tongue. Screwing my eyes shut, I fight against the onset of nausea. But, the hardboiled eggs are overpowering my fragile stomach. I take deep breaths to no avail. My guts heave, and a foul concoction bursts forth, forcing me to cough, splutter, and spit a disgusting mess overboard. Struggling to breathe, my fingers dig into stone, hands quivering with the effort of maintaining this precarious balance, while my body is wracked with further spasms.

Thoughts of the malicious kid abandoned, pain gnaws at my arms. The ground seems even further away. Aware of traffic flowing by, I am struck by how ridiculous I must look. But, another queasy wave overpowers me, and I hurl down my shirt. Then, just as swiftly as the sensation came over me, it recedes, leaving overwhelming relief. My lungs suck cool air, banishing the acidic bile with a verdant aroma of flowers. Purged of sputum, my body craves more whisky to cleanse my bitter palate. Just as I am relishing the recovery, my peripheral vision catches the bush rustling. An egg cracks into the side of my head.

The glutinous innards slither down my chest, adding to the mess already staining the cotton. Shock having tempered my rage, I now focus on the rhododendron, preparing to pounce on the upstart. I glance towards my neighbours' house, in case her vindictive acts have at last attracted a parent's attention. Curtains drawn, they remain oblivious to the commotion in their garden.

Because my head is now recoiling from the impact, my position has become even more hazardous. My initial bravado has also evaporated. If I simply leap down now, I'm liable to sprain an ankle. Instead, I begin the process of squirming around, turning my back on my assailant so that I can grasp the top of the wall, then gradually lower myself, relinquishing my hold at the last instant. Once on terra firma, I'll hunt her down, seizing the scruff of her neck, and dragging her over to the house, where I'll rap on the door and demand retribution for their daughter's actions.

Swivelling around, inch by painstaking inch, I'm now facing our garden. I feel the egg white soaking into the puke down my front, and I shake my head at what a trail of destruction being set in motion by such a young child. I'm about to begin the descent when, I hear her cackling again. It sounds as if she's right at the foot of the wall. I jerk my head around in time to see another egg taking flight. The impact drenches my face in sticky goo that blinds me. Her laughter now hysterical, I feel the wall rocking beneath my grip until, my hands give way, and I'm pitching forwards, face-first, tumbling into our garden, the sudden violence inspiring a cacophony of blackbird alarm calls from surrounding treetops.

For drawn-out moments, I remain paralysed. As the screeching recedes, I consider the possibility that my ungainly fall has caused serious damage. Whether or not I have cracked any bones, I know my skin will be florid with bruises. Hesitantly, I reach out, gaining purchase, probing into the soil. I wriggle around onto all fours, then push myself up; the effort drawing tears. It feels like there could be blood coursing down my face. Standing as laboriously as a weightlifter, I lurch away from the wall; retreating from the sulphurous bouquet, that seems to cling to the squat outhouse in an invisible mist.

"I'll deal with the fucking brat later," I mumble. "First things first. More fucking drink is required ... more than ever."

Walking by the French doors, I glare at the windows, failing to see which one of the shining panes was impacted with the egg. I barge back into the house, unbuttoning my shirt, crumpling it into a ball. Padding upstairs, I seize a replacement from its hanger, then trip again and plummet all the way down to the ground floor, where my head cracks the bannister. More determined than ever, to put as much liquor as possible between this entire trauma and myself, I lock the front door and crunch across the drive to our garage.

Clambering into the black BMW, I generate a whole new series of aches that pummel my muscles. My fingers pulse when I grip the steering wheel. The cloying sulphur seems to have followed me into this confined space inside the car, contaminating my clothes. Shutting my eyes, I focus on the plush scent of leather and plastic. My lids grow heavier.

I squint towards the garage door, but it's shimmering ... I try to focus, until I'm no longer seeing the metal door at all, but am staring intently at the wild scene beyond the windscreen, while the white bonnet hurtles along winding country roads... I'm way above 50, edging towards 60... I nudge the brakes each time the tyres clip the verge, then I stomp more furiously as I round a sharp bend. The noise of the squealing brakes brings my head up, and my eyes snap open.

Drinking has turned day into night; during the day, I continually nod off this way, lapsing in and out of these lurid dreams. At night, I spend hours tossing and turning, and staring into the dark.

I've dropped the keys. Fumbling around at my feet, my fingers brush a bottle. I tug it out and beam like a kid on Christmas morning: it's a three-quarters-full bottle of *Jim Beam*. How long it has nestled so tantalisingly beneath my grasp, is a mystery. Unscrewing the lid, I take generous mouthfuls, my tongue rolling around my lips, as I savour the sweet taste. I relish the burning sensation melting through me, its afterglow evaporating each niggling pain, every last anxiety. Now I'm sinking into a huge marshmallow ...

I wake again, my forehead cracking the wheel. I know this narcolepsy will persist unless I get moving. Glancing at the bottle, I'm fleetingly impaled with shame. I've become a slave to this in such a short time. But, what I *do* know is this: one bottle won't see me through 24 hours. My need to restock my supplies before the weekend is urgent, particularly since the village shop refuses to deliver. Apparently, I was abusive to their driver a few days ago.

I dig the fob from my other pocket, aiming it, squeezing until the door judders upwards. Blinking against the invasive light, I switch on the engine. Puffs of exhaust ghost by. Taking another slug, my trembling palms caress the dashboard. Fatigue washes over me ...

... the airbags envelop us, smothering the ugly duet of our screams. After an age, I finally turn to Charlotte, caressing her cheek. "I'll get help, Charlie." Unclipping my belt, I extricate myself from the dented white chassis, glancing in both directions. The road is deserted, the only sounds: rooks cawing from a field. I teeter over to her side, wrenching open the passenger door, shock exaggerating my shambolic movement. After unclipping her, I heave her limp body over my shoulder, and carry it awkwardly by the buckled tree trunk, struggling through the undergrowth to the opposite side, then shoving her into position beneath the airbag, and twisting her fingers around the wheel. Retracing my steps, I finally slump into the passenger seat, thumb 999, bark at the voice at the other end, then wait, feeling Charlotte's warmth in the seat. An alcoholic haze envelops me, dragging me into a fitful slumber before I hear the sirens.

The accident happened last Sunday afternoon. Monday's tabloid headlines were predictably salacious: 'EASTER HORROR ON COUNTRY ROAD' ... 'MP's WIFE CAUSES DEATH CRASH.' As the unwitting passenger, I was portrayed as the victim of a terrible event, my widower status inspiring widespread messages of condolence. The opposite was the case for Charlotte. Despite her fatal injuries, the small amount of alcohol in her bloodstream condemned her as a drunk driver. But her vilification demonstrated exactly what would've happened to me had I not had the courage to make that split-second decision. In my profession, a ruthless streak is one of the attributes separating greatness from mediocrity; the leaders, from those they lead. Had I not apportioned blame in that way, a rising Westminster career would have been destroyed, and the country, as a whole, would've lost out. I wasn't going to end up like Ted Kennedy: forever tainted by the crash at Chappaquiddick Bridge.

When I return to the House, after the Easter recess, and the end of my compassionate leave, I'll book into rehab. Everyone will sympathise - constituents, journalists, colleagues, opponents. I anticipate remaining the centre of attention for all the effusive well-wishers, especially the many eligible women, who've been sending cards, photographs and phone numbers; as an aphrodisiac, power and heartache are a potent combination.

I'm about to disengage the handbrake, when I realise I've inadvertently shut the garage doors. Exhaust smoke swirls below the level of the windows. My liquor-addled mind pictures the walls closing, as if I'm trapped inside a cave, like Jesus was; like that circumstance celebrated by all that nonsensical, fucking egg destruction.

"Thankfully, I don't need divine intervention to be released," I announce, patting the seat beside me for the fob. It isn't there. Black clouds envelop the enclosed space. I try snatching a breath, but imagine my ribcage being constricted by some horridly thick serpent. My unravelling thoughts add glistening scales to the terrible vision. Then a brief fissure in the murk reveals a face. A palm slaps the windscreen, the sudden jolt hauling me back from lethargy, and inspiring a vicious coughing fit.

"Who's there?" I must've nodded off again. The noxious fumes are conspiring with the alcohol. Desperately, I twist the key to kill the engine, but my fingers are quaking so erratically, it snaps in the ignition. Sapped of energy, I hack and splutter, each attempt to breathe like shears, lacerating my chest. I feel consciousness ebbing.

Mesmerised by the dense fog, I flashback to the moments after the crash. Before I went to Charlotte, I staggered over to the tiny figure entangled in a crumpled bicycle, ashen-faced and blinking up at me. When I'd jerked the wheel, too late to avoid the collision, her head had whipped round, her white eyes locking onto mine. She saw *me* at the wheel. So, before swapping Charlotte over, I had to do this. I bowed to her paralysed body, placing my palm over her nose and mouth. She hardly twitched, as I starved her of oxygen. After agonising minutes, while every sense bristled for the sound of oncoming traffic, I probed her neck, checking that her pulse had gone. Her glazed expression seemed to follow me for a second, before fixating on the beautiful blue sky. Incongruously, I touched her lids shut.

When I made my way round to the passenger side, I noticed a wicker basket, attached to the front of the bicycle with yellow ribbons; eggs were strewn over the tarmac, their shells painted in myriad colours. Perhaps she was on her way to the village church. No wonder I keep having phantom visions of Easter Sunday, fantasising about being egged, and smelling eggs. Conversing with a deceased loved one is natural, when you're grieving; being haunted by a mischievous poltergeist I put down to the D.T.s.

Among the shifting veils of gas, the face appears again. The girl's gleeful expression gloats over the sight of my wilting body; her harsh laughter escalating at each of my pathetic attempts to struggle with the handle. Yet another hallucination. What the fuck else could it be?

The mirage is aural, too. I hear a faltering voice. *"This is how mummy and daddy did it … after the policemen came to my house to tell them what happened to me …"*

"No!" I gasp. *"Leave me alone!"*

"When the police found mummy and daddy in the garage, one said to the other, he would never forget that smell, the smell the exhaust made, 'cause the engine was running so hot … he said it reminded him of rotten eggs …"

I no longer have the strength to escape, or to deny, the stark realisation that the vile darkness clogging my trachea isn't going to stop; and the sulphur has nothing to do with Easter eggs or car fumes, but can only be the stench of Hell ...

The End

PAYING IT FORWARD

Jeff Menapace

1

Good Friday
Bucks County, Pennsylvania

The waiter brought their check with two fortune cookies, one for each of them. Julie took her cookie and cracked it open, pulling the small strip of white paper out and discarding the rest.

"You gotta eat it if you want it to come true," Darren told her.

Julie wrinkled her nose. "I don't like them. Besides, I haven't even read it yet." She raised the little strip of paper and squinted in an attempt to read the tiny print.

Darren reached across the table and plucked the fortune from her fingers.

"*Hey.*" She tried snatching it back.

"Doesn't work that way," he said. "Gotta eat the cookie blind to what the fortune says. There's risk involved."

"What if it tells me I have to go down on you right here and now?"

"Then this is the greatest Chinese restaurant ever."

Julie smirked, huffed, and then shoved both halves of the fortune cookie into her mouth. "Happy?" she mumbled, mouth still full.

Darren handed the fortune over. "Only if it says what you proposed it might."

She laughed, crumbs flying and hitting the table, causing her slap a hand over her mouth and laugh some more, before washing the cookie down with water. Finished, she let out a final chuckle, straightened herself up, and squinted again as she read: *"Be kind to strangers."*

"That's it?"

"That's it." She tossed the fortune on the table.

Darren picked it up and read it himself. "Lame."

"What's yours say?"

Darren cracked his cookie, and pulled out the little strip of paper.

"Gotta eat it first," she warned.

He winked at her and then did as she'd done, shoving both halves into his mouth at once before reading.

"Ooh...what if it says you have to go down on *me*?" she teased.

He, too, spoke with his mouth full, crumbs flying. "Then it means you picked up the wrong cookie."

Julie laughed again. Only six months they'd been together, and yet it seemed like forever. The good forever, not the prison sentence. As if everything before Darren was from some past life, not worth remembering.

"So, what's it say?" she asked again.

Darren read it and laughed.

"What?"

He handed it over. Julie read it, frowned, then read it aloud. "*Be kind to strangers.*" She glanced up him. "Weird."

"I think the people here write the fortunes, themselves," he said. "This is their way of angling for a big tip."

"Maybe it's a sign," Julie countered.

"What do you mean?"

"I don't know—like a cosmic sign or something."

Darren snorted and sipped the last of his tea from the little white cup.

"I'm being serious."

He smiled and shook his head. "Yin and Yang, we are. I swear."

Yin and yang indeed. But they made it work. Julie's forever optimism more than enough to compensate for his indomitable skepticism.

Julie matched Darren's smile with a grin, reached across the table and took one of his hands in both of hers. "I have an idea."

He groaned.

She ignored him. "You ever hear of 'paying it forward'?"

The waiter approached again, glanced down at the small black vinyl folder that held their bill and spotted no cash or credit card poking out just yet. He asked if they'd like something else.

"Can you give us a few more minutes please?" Julie asked.

The waiter eyed them cautiously for a moment before leaving. They were a nice-looking couple, but they were young—Darren twenty-two, Julie twenty-one. Young couples sometimes found it amusing to eat and run. Julie, however, had something else, entirely, in mind.

Julie leaned in and asked again. "Have you ever heard of it?"

"*Paying it forward?* Yeah, it's like do something nice for someone in hopes that they'll pass the act on to the next person, and so on, and so on, right?"

"Exactly." Julie leaned in further, getting excited. "I just read about this one where this lady was buying groceries with her kids, except she forgot her wallet at home. So, she's like all embarrassed and about to turn around to put all the stuff back, but this guy behind her offers to pay for her groceries—and there were *a lot*—on the condition that she pay it forward and does something nice for some stranger the next chance she gets. Isn't that awesome?"

"So awesome."

She squeezed his hand. "*Stop.* I think we should do it."

"Go to the supermarket and wait for someone to forget their wallet?"

"Do it here. Now."

Darren frowned and looked around the restaurant. It was modestly filled. A few families with kids, an older couple, a man sitting by himself. "There's like ten people here. What are the odds someone forgot their money?"

"That's not what I'm suggesting. I'm saying we just pay for their meal."

Darren pulled a face. "Meh—I'm not sure most people would go for that, Jules. I mean forgetting your money is one thing, but offering to pay for their meal..."

"No, you don't offer, you just do it. We would bring the waiter over, tell him we'd like to pay for someone's meal, but tell him not to say anything until *after* we're gone. That way, they can't object. We can also leave a little note on the check telling them to pay it forward next chance they get." She grinned like a kid.

Darren released yet another groan. A defeated groan. A groan Julie knew well. She let out a little squeak of excitement and bounced in her seat. "I love you," she said.

"I know." He scanned the restaurant again. "So who's getting a free meal?"

Still grinning, Julie scanned the restaurant, too. She immediately stopped on the man sitting by himself. Julie guessed him in his late forties. Salt and pepper hair cropped short to mitigate the thinning in front. He seemed of average build and height from his seated position by the far corner of the restaurant near the storefront window, its neon "open" sign casting a flickering red across his tablecloth. He was staring absently out the storefront window as he ate, everything about him seemingly in slow motion, the way he chewed, the way he swallowed, even the way he blinked, which was not seldom in his constant gaze out the window, though when he did, each blink was followed by a slight startled expression, as though shocked to find himself siting in a Chinese restaurant. The man did indeed look lonely, but more so, he looked lost. To Julie, there was a difference. Loneliness could be fixed, as she so wonderfully found with Darren just six months ago. Lost was...lost could be anything.

"Him." She gestured subtly to the man by the storefront window.

Darren looked. "Why him?"

"He looks—I don't know, sad kinda. Lost."

"And our buying his food is going to fix him?"

Julie gave a frustrated, yet undeterred, sigh. "The *gesture* is. Kindness begets Kindness. Pay it forward."

"Lest the fortune cookie gods strike us down."

Julie grinned again and called the waiter over.

2

"At least he didn't eat much," Darren said on the drive home. "Two egg rolls. Who goes to a Chinese restaurant and orders just egg rolls?"

"I told you, the food doesn't matter; it's the gesture. When the waiter goes over and tells him what we did, he'll be just as touched as if he'd ordered a ten course meal."

Darren snorted. "You *do* know the way to a man's heart is through his stomach, don't you?"

She leaned over and stroked the inside of his thigh. "I thought it was this."

Darren took his eyes off the road for a tick. She was looking up at him with the contradictory, yet exquisite, combo of innocently naughty eyes.

"Any chance we can pretend one of those fortune cookies actually said what you thought it might?" he asked.

Still the hand on the thigh, still the innocently naughty eyes. "We can't; we're not in the restaurant anymore."

"The location doesn't matter; it's the *gesture*," he said, ridiculously pleased with himself for recycling her own words, especially at a time when blood to the brain was funneling south.

Julie laughed. Slid her hand further up his thigh.

"Wait, stop—*stop*."

She stopped. "What?"

Darren didn't reply. His gaze was fixed on the rearview mirror. Julie spun in her seat and looked out the back window to see for herself. Someone was riding their tail big time.

"Who is that?" she asked.

"No idea," Darren muttered.

Boom—high beams now. Darren squinted into the rearview and cursed under his breath.

"Just slow down and let them pass," Julie said.

Darren did. The car behind slowed with them, the high beams now flickering, accompanied by bleats of the horn.

"Maybe you've got a flat and they're trying to tell you," Julie said.

"We'd *know* if we had a flat."

"Well, pull over and see what they want then," she said.

The absurd suggestion spun his head her way. "*Are you nuts?*" He was suddenly angry—angry at the car behind them, and angry at his girlfriend's naiveté. What would she have done if he wasn't here? "It could be a fucking *psychopath* behind us," he said.

Still the flashing high beams, still the horn, and goddam if the sonofabitch's bumper wasn't nearly touching theirs.

"What if they're hurt?" she asked.

"They can't be that hurt if they can drive a car. If it's an emergency, they can go around us. I slowed down for them, you saw it."

"Pull over at the next stop then," Julie said.

"Where?"

There *was* no next stop. Bucks County dabbled in affluent, but its heart would always belong to rural—dark back roads that seemingly (now especially) went on forever.

The car suddenly cut into the oncoming lane, gunned its engine and pulled up alongside them. Both Darren and Julie instantly looked left. The interior of the car was black, nothing but a faint silhouette behind the wheel. No one in the passenger seat or in back.

Darren gave a demonstrative splay of the hands. *What the hell do you want?* it clearly read.

The car's interior light clicked on. The driver came into view.

Julie leaned left. "*It's him!* The man from the restaurant!"

Darren winced from her yell. "I see that."

The man continued driving next to them in the oncoming lane. The sick irony that no oncoming cars had since approached during the whole ordeal was anything but lost on Darren.

"So then what's he doing?" Julie asked, sounding somewhat less panicked, as if paying for this man's food had somehow given them immunity to any wrongdoings from the guy should he turn out to be Ted Bundy.

The man's passenger side window slid down. He then made a rolling gesture with his right hand, urging Darren and Julie to do the same.

Darren obliged but only cracked his window a few inches, just enough to hear. They cruised next to each other at just under twenty-five miles an hour now. Still no approaching cars in the oncoming lane.

"Why did you do that?" the man called through his passenger window. "Why did you pay for my meal?"

"Geez, you're welcome, buddy," Darren muttered to Julie. Then, through the crack in his driver's side window: "Just being friendly, that's all! Be careful, man." Darren gestured towards the oncoming lane.

The man ignored Darren's gesture, kept right on cruising in the oncoming lane. "Being friendly?" he called over. "Like being good to your fellow man at your own expense?"

"Are you kidding me?" Darren muttered again. "This guy's gonna fucking kill someone."

"You think we offended him?" Julie asked. "Maybe he's one of those guys who's proud to a fault, you know?"

Darren knew the type well. His old man. He remembered the first time he'd tried to buy his father a beer, how excited he'd been. A rite of passage of sorts for any newly crowned twenty-one-year-old boy— buying his old man a beer. His father had instantly refused, and with none too much disgust. He'd buy his own goddamn beers, he'd told his son.

The thought of his father poked Darren's temper. He called out the window: *"What's your problem, man!?"*

Julie leaned over Darren's lap. "We were just trying to pay it forward!"

The man suddenly cut right, slicing into their car. Sparks flew up the driver's side window. Julie screamed. Darren fought the wheel and ended up stomping the brakes in panic, the car fishtailing before swerving off the road and stopping just shy of rolling over the wooded embankment.

The man stopped his own vehicle about twenty yards ahead of them.

A moment of surreal pause as Darren and Julie sat motionless in the idling car, rapid breathing their only capable sounds.

Finally, in barely a whisper, Darren asked: "Are you okay?"

The white of the man's reverse lights came to life up ahead. He was coming back.

Darren threw the car into reverse, hit the accelerator, and the tires spun uselessly in the muddy ridge above the embankment.

"*Turn the wheel!*" Julie cried.

He did. Left then right then left again, each crank as useless as the last. Darren opened the driver door and hurried out.

"*What are you doing!?*"

"*I've got to push! Get behind the wheel!*" He glanced over his shoulder. The man's car continued to back slowly towards them. "*Hurry up!*"

Darren put his body behind the front bumper and pushed with every ounce of strength he had, the tires continuing to spin uselessly as Julie kept her foot on the accelerator.

Darren looked over his shoulder again. The car was upon them now, the white reverse lights clicking off, leaving only the red glow of the brakes. The driver's side door opened.

Darren rushed back to the driver's side door of his own car. "*Lock the doors and call 911!*" he yelled to Julie through the glass. "*OKAY!? LOCK THE DOORS AND CALL 911!*"

Julie nodded, locked the doors, clicked on the overhead light, spun in her seat, and began frantically digging throughout the car for her cell phone. She spotted it on the passenger side floor and instantly snatched it up.

Two small explosions outside made her scream and jerk bolt upright.

She turned off the overhead light and peered through the windshield and into the dark beyond. She saw only the man's idling car straight ahead. No Darren. No man.

Julie cracked the driver's side window an inch. *"Darren!?"*

The passenger side window exploded. Julie screeched and made a frantic climb into the back seat. The man reached in, groping for her.

"HELP ME!!!"

The man's entire torso had now wormed its way into the car.

Julie frantically kicked at his attempts to snatch her ankles.

"SOMEBODY, PLEASE!!!"

The oncoming lane finally shone headlights of an approaching car in the distance. Julie's face clicked from terror to hope. She whipped her head back towards the man, and they stared at one another for an odd spell, neither flinching.

The approaching lights grew stronger. Julie turned towards them once more, turned back and the man was gone.

Julie did not hesitate. She opened the back door and fell out onto the road. Scrambled to her feet and immediately ran to the oncoming lane where she began jumping, screaming, waving at the oncoming car.

The car swerved right around her and kept on going.

Julie spun after it. *"WAIT! COME BACK!!!"*

The sound of someone approaching from behind now.

Julie slowly turned, and of course it was him. In his hand was a gun. Behind him, Julie could just make out the silhouette of Darren's body face down on the side of the road. Moonlight caught and reflected its shine in the small black pool encircling his head. She put a hand to her mouth to stifle a cry.

"It's okay," the man said with a reassuring smile. "I understand everything. I really do." He gestured to the fleeing car's shrinking lights in the distance. "You see? That's all the proof you need. It truly was meant to be, Mary."

For a brief moment, Julie's confusion overrode her fear. She frowned. "*Who?*"

The man brought the gun down onto the side of Julie's head, dropping her cold. Stewart Paul then tilted his head skyward, closed his eyes, breathed in the night air, and smiled lovingly towards the heavens.

This was the one. He was sure of it.

When the waitress had told Stewart his check had been paid for back at the restaurant, he'd all but flipped the table darting after the couple. Witnesses, sure, but Stewart was sure that if this was indeed to be the one, He would protect him, just as He protected him only moments ago when the car had refused to stop. Besides, the restaurant didn't have Stewart's name on file from the debit card in which he'd intended to pay.

He'd been paid forward.

Stewart bent and dragged Mary back to his car. Loaded her into the trunk along with His body. Not a single car drove by during the process. What more proof did he need?

Easter Sunday

Somewhere in rural Pennsylvania

Stewart Paul descended his basement stairs, humming the hymn he'd heard that morning at church. He'd so badly wanted to tell everyone what he had waiting for him at home, but simply couldn't risk it, just yet. And, truth be told, a hint of selfishness tugged at his reasoning for secrecy too: he'd wanted to be the first to bear witness. Well, he and Mary Magdalene, of course.

Despite his wanting to bear witness, there was a part of Stewart that hoped he would descend and find himself in an empty basement. The casket open and vacant, Mary no longer bound in her chair at the foot of the casket, the two of them gone. Yes, to witness his life's purpose come to fruition before his very eyes, would have been breathtaking indeed, but there was something magical about the prospect of it all happening in his absence, stirring memories of Christmas morning as a boy, the base of the tree brimming with gifts, when it was bare as could be only the night before. All of it happening in his absence as he slept.

Except Santa Claus was not real. His Lord and Savior was. And this Easter morning, Stewart Paul would watch his Lord and Savior Jesus Christ rise from the dead, his faithful companion, Mary Magdalene, at his side. And it would be glorious.

Taking the basement stairs two at a time now in his eagerness, Stewart was both disappointed and relieved to find Mary still bound and gagged in her chair at the foot of the casket, the casket lid still closed.

Disappointed: something magical had not happened in his absence.

Relieved: something magical would now happen in his presence.

Mary lifted her head slowly upon Stewart's arrival. She gave a weak moan through her gag. The fear and exhaustion in her eyes tugged at Stewart's heart.

"I know it's been tough," Stewart said, "I do." He placed a hand on her head, and brushed a lock of hair from her face. She was too weak to fight it. "But, the time has now come. I assure you, I will convey your loyalty to Him, during this ordeal. Think of how pleased He will be." Stewart stroked her cheek. This time she flinched. Stewart smiled. "I understand. You are as eager to begin as I am, aren't you?" Stewart positioned himself alongside the casket, beamed and said: "Well then, I believe the expression is, *without further ado*?"

Stewart opened the casket and peered inside. His eager smile dropped. He quickly reached inside and inspected His body. Placed two fingers to His neck. No pulse. Worse still, the gunshot wounds to the head and body were still there, the surrounding tissue already beginning to decay. And the smell...

Stewart slammed the casket lid shut, draped his body over the lid, and wept.

4

Dusk had just begun to gray the light, when Stewart finished. He patted the soil flat with the back of the shovel, then checked the sturdiness of the two makeshift crosses he'd inserted at the head of each grave. They held firm.

His back and shoulders aching from the day's effort, Stewart trudged his way back to the house, thinking about what might have been. He'd been so sure.

Giving one final glance back towards the dozens of crosses erected and spread out across his land (some far more weathered than others; they would need replacing soon, he took note), Stewart refused to let this year's experience deter him. When the time did come, his Lord and Savior would reward him for his perseverance. His patience. His faith.

Tired as he was, Stewart managed a smile and an optimistic nod of the head. He went inside to clean up.

The End

AFTERWORD

Kevin J. Kennedy

After the success of Collected Christmas Horror Shorts, I kept getting asked by both readers and authors if I planned on doing another antho. In truth I had no idea. I had thought about doing another Christmas one, a year down the line, but that was about it. The question kept popping up though. After a bit of back and forth with it, I asked a few authors what they thought about doing an Easter antho and this book was born.

I had looked at the feedback from the last book and although there were very few negatives, one that came up a few times, was that some of the stories could have been longer, so the minimum word count was raised. To give the authors some room to work, the max word count went up too, which is why this book is much bigger than the last one. That's why it's so important to leave reviews, both authors and publishers do listen. I hope you enjoyed the book. I'm obviously a little biased. I get to read all the stories and put the ones I like the most into the book.

I never set out to publish anthologies and I'm not sure if I will continue. Like everything in life there are good points and bad points. For every great story you accept you have to reject another for one reason or other and I don't enjoy that part in the slightest. I don't imagine many people do. While I write this, I'm also sitting here with no idea how well the book will do. I know I like it and that was pretty much the formula for the last book so I hope I have got it right again. It sometimes feels like a lot of pressure knowing that all the authors involved have put their faith in you and taken the time to write a story for your book. I suppose if I didn't worry about it I couldn't really care all that much.

There are a lot of anthologies coming out these days so I'm truly thankful you have given ours a try. The authors in the book are all personal favourites of mine and I can only hope you enjoyed their stories as much as I did. Almost every author in the book has provided contact details so if you loved their story why not drop them a message and tell them? I'm sure it would make their day. I'd love to hear your thoughts too so feel free to say hi.

AUTHOR BIOS

Amy Cross is the author of more than 100 horror, paranormal and fantasy novels. Her books include Asylum, The Farm, The Bride of Ashbyrn House and The Haunting of Blackwych Grange. She has also written three collections of horror short stories, titled Perfect Little Monsters, Twisted Little Things and The Ghost of Longthorn Manor.

Her website is www.amycross.com.

Lex H Jones is a British cross-genre author, horror fan and rock music enthusiast who lives in Sheffield, North England.

He has written articles for websites the Gingernuts of Horror and the Horrifically Horrifying Horror Blog on various subjects covering books, films, videogames and music. Lex's first published novel is titled "Nick and Abe", and he also has several short horror stories published in anthologies. When not working on his own writing Lex also contributes to the proofing and editing process for other authors.

https://www.facebook.com/LexHJones
https://www.amazon.co.uk/Lex-H-Jones/e/B008HSH9BA

Latashia Figueroa gives two good reasons for her love of horror: her childhood home was believed to be haunted and Stephen King often told her bedtime stories. Pet Cemetery was the first.

She began a career in New York City's fast paced fashion industry, ignoring the voice in her head that whispered, Writer. Though the job was exciting, it was not fulfilling, and when the opportunity arose she returned to her childhood love.

Latashia embraces her fascination of the dark and macabre through her writing. Her stories have been described as "psychological thrillers with a dash of horror." She attends writing classes often, adores music, the outdoors, the arts, and yoga. She also has an obsession with heights and roller coasters.

Latashia Figueroa is the author of THIS WAY DARKNESS, and IVY'S ENVY (Want & Decay Trilogy,#1) Her short story, OUT FOR A HUNT, is featured in Dark Futures Annual 1 Anthology. She lives on the east coast with her very supportive husband.

https://latashiafigueroa-author.com/

Mark Cassell lives in a rural part of the UK with his wife and a number of animals. He often dreams of dystopian futures, peculiar creatures, and flitting shadows. Primarily a horror writer, his Steampunk, Dark Fantasy, and SF stories have featured in numerous anthologies and ezines. His best-selling debut novel, The Shadow Fabric, is closely followed by the popular short story collection, Sinister Stitches, and are both only a fraction of an expanding mythos.

Website: www.MarkCassell.co.uk

Briana Robertson excels at taking the natural darkness of reality and bringing it to life on the page. Heavily influenced by her personal experience with depression, anxiety, and the chronic pain of fibromyalgia, Robertson's dark fiction delves into the emotional and psychological experiences of characters in whom readers will recognize themselves. Her stories horrify while also tugging at heartstrings, muddying the lines of black and white, and staining the genre in multiple shades of grey.

In 2016, Robertson joined the ranks of Stitched Smile Publications. Her solo anthology, "Reaper," which explores the concept of death being both inevitable and non-discriminatory, debuted in early 2017. She also has stories included in "Unleashing the Voices Within," by Stitched Smile Publications, "Man Behind the Mask," by David Owain Hughes, Jonathan Ondrashek, and Veronica Smith, and "Collected Easter Horror Shorts" by Kevin Kennedy.

Robertson is the wife of one, mother of three, and unashamed lover of all things feline. She currently resides on the Illinois side of the Mississippi River, with a backyard view of the Saint Louis skyline, and is a member of the Saint Louis Writers Guild.

Website: www.brianarobertsonwri.wix.com/brianarobertson

Mark Lukens has been writing since the second grade when his teacher called his parents in for a conference because the ghost story he'd written concerned her a little. Since then, he's had several stories published and four screenplays optioned by producers in Hollywood— one of which is in development to be a film. He's the author of many bestselling books including: Ancient Enemy; Darkwind: Ancient Enemy 2; Sightings; The Exorcist's Apprentice; and What Lies Below. He's a proud member of the Horror Writers Association. He grew up in Daytona Beach, Florida. But after many travels and adventures, he settled down near Tampa, Florida with his wonderful wife and son ... and a stray cat they adopted.

He loves to hear from readers! You can find him at:
www.amazon.com/Mark-Lukens/e/B00G8GYUUG

www.marklukensbooks.wordpress.com

C.S Anderson is one of the founders of Alucard Press and is the author of The Black Irish Chronicles, The Dark Molly series, The Zombie Extinction Event Novels and Sin City Succubus. He resides in the soggy Pacific Northwest with his lovely wife and long suffering editor Gail. He loves to hear from fans and can be reached at alucardpress@yahoo.com

https://www.facebook.com/Alucardpressblackirish/?ref=bookmarks

Steven Stacy has always had a love for media of all kinds, especially horror. He finds his influences through his life experiences, his love of the horror and thriller genre, and his nostalgic view of media of all types. He finds joy in escapism and creating other worlds into which others can escape.
Swiss, Swedish and Dutch bloodlines run through Stacy's blood, but he was brought up in the busy City of Cardiff, Wales. A keen rower and tennis player, Stacy thought his first career would be in singing, but writing always stayed with him. He has written since a child, filling his notebooks with stories and poems in school. He has written for numerous horror magazines, such as 'Gorezone' and 'Scream', and interviewed horror icons such as Robert Englund, Heather Langenkamp, Neve Campbell, Matthew Lillard, Dee Wallace, Wes Craven and Sigourney Weaver.

He also loves graphic novels, 'Hush' by Jim Lee and Jeph Loeb & 'Selina's Big Score' by Ed Brubaker & Darwyn Cooke – he's a huge fan of Catwoman, and has a treasure trove of Catwoman memorabilia, making him a true geek; working in a comic book shop for years never helped.

Steven graduated First Class Honors from Bath University in 'English Literature & Creative English.' His favourite writers include Stephen

King, Kathleen Winsor, Oscar Wilde and Ira Levin. He is currently working on his first major novel. A huge fan of Cats, Stacy works voluntarily with the 'Cat's Protection League', and lives at home with his pet Bengal cat's, Isis and Amber, and his snow Bengal, Marnie.

"Here's to the ones who dream, foolish as they may seem.
Here's to the hearts that ache, here's to the mess we make."

Facebook: @stevenCJstacy
Twtter: blondarrow

James Matthew Byers resides in Wellington, Alabama with his wife, kids, a dog named after an elf, and two tortoises. He has been published in poetry journals and through Jacksonville State University in Jacksonville, AL, where he received his Master's in 2010. His epic poem, Beowulf: The Midgard Epic, is out now from Stitched Smile Publications, LLC in both Kindle and special edition paperback. James designed and illustrated the cover and interior art for his debut novel at SSP, where he works as an in house illustrator. He also has a short story featured in their latest release, Unleashed: Monsters Vs. Zombies. James has recently won three Prose Challenges at www.theprose.com. His poems, "More Gravy," "The Raven Redux," and "Nativity Nuance" all took first place. His poem, "The Dinner Fly," will be published in "Weirdbook Magazine" issue 35 in May, 2017. He continues to write prolifically, supporting anyone who wishes to place their hammering fingers to the keyboard anvil, becoming a polished wordsmith in the process.

Find James Matthew Byers at:
Twitter: www.Twitter.com/MattByers40
Facebook: https://m.facebook.com/Mattbyers40/

Jeff Strand is the author of over 30 demented books, including PRESSURE, DWELLER, DEAD CLOWN BARBECUE, A BAD DAY FOR VOODOO, and WOLF HUNT. He lives in Tampa, and loves hot dogs, sushi, and yogurt. Visit his Gleefully Macabre website at www.jeffstrand.com.

Kevin J Kennedy is a horror author and publisher from Scotland. He fell in love with the horror world at an early age watching shows like the Munster's and Eerie Indiana before moving on to movies like the Lost Boys, the original The Hills Have Eyes and Nightmare on Elm Street. (The eighties was a good time to grow up.)

In his teens he became an avid reader when he found the work of Richard Laymon. This furthered his love of horror and introduced him to many of the authors you will find in this very book. At the age of thirty four Kevin wrote his first short story and it was accepted by Chuck Anderson of Alucard Press for the Fifty Shades of Slay anthology. He hasn't stopped writing since. Look out for his new novella 'You Only Get One Shot' co-written with J.C. Michael.
Kevin lives in a small town in Scotland with his beautiful wife Pamela, his step daughter and two strange little cats.

You will find links to all of Kevin's pages through his website. www.kevinjkennedy.co.uk

J. C. Michael is an English writer of Horror and Dark Fiction. He is the author of the novel "Discoredia", which was released by Books of the Dead Press in 2013, and has had a number of short stories published since then. These have included "Reasons To Kill" in the Amazon bestselling anthology "Suspended in Dusk" and "When Death Walks The Field Of Battle" in "Savage Beasts" from Grey Matter Press.

Taking his inspiration from Stephen King and James Herbert his writing frequently explores the dark side of human nature where moral boundaries are questioned, and the difference between good and evil is far from clear.

For more information on his writing please find him on Facebook, or take a look at his author profile on Amazon.

https://www.facebook.com/james.c.michael1
https://www.amazon.com/J-C-Michael/e/B00AX8BFIK

Hidden in a remote location in California lives a man that responds to the name **Peter Oliver Wonder**. Though little is known about him, several written works that may or may not be fictional have been found featuring a character of the same name.
Devilishly handsome, quick witted, and as charming as an asshole can be, Peter has come a long way since his time in the United States Marine Corps. Making friends wherever he goes, there is never a shortage of adventure when he is around.
The works that have been penned under this name are full of horror, romance, adventure, and comedy just as every life should be. It is assumed that these works are an attempt at a drug fueled autobiography of sorts. Through these texts, we can learn much about this incredible man.

http://peterowonder.wix.com/peteroliverwonder
https://www.facebook.com/PeterOliverWonderAuthor/
@PeteOWonder

Veronica Smith lives in Katy, Texas, a suburb west of Houston. Her first full length novel, Salvation, was just published in December 2016. She self-published a short story, Last One in the Chamber for You, My Love to Amazon. Her first novella, Chalk Outline, was originally self-published but is the process of being re-released. She also has over a dozen short stories published in anthologies and e-Zines. In addition to writing, she's a co-editor for two anthologies. Follow her to get the latest on her works.

www.facebook.com/Veronica.Smith.Author
https://kvzsmithwordpresscom.wordpress.com/

Suzanne Fox is a writer of both horror and erotic fiction who is lucky enough to be able to live and work in the beautiful county of Cornwall with her partner and three pussies (cats!). She loves the challenge of combining both genres in her writing. Her work has been published in both print and online magazines, and has also been included in several anthologies. Besides writing, she loves to dance and drink wine.

She had great fun writing her story, "Last Supper," and she hopes that you had as much fun reading it. Please join her on her Facebook page.

https://www.facebook.com/suzannefoxerotica/?ref=aymt_homepage_panel

By design, **Lisa Vasquez** creates horror with vivid, dark, words and twisted images that not only drags the reader in between the pages, but onto the covers that house them. When she releases her grasp, readers are left alone to sort through the aftermath those images leave behind; each one becoming a seed rooting itself within the soft confines of their psyche.
Lisa takes this passion for writing horror and uses it to mentor other authors and volunteers as the Publisher's Liaison for the Horror Writers Association.

She is the CEO of Stitched Smile Publications and owns her own book cover design company, Darque Halo Designs.

You can read Lisa's work in several anthologies, or by purchasing her newly released novel, "The Unfleshed: Tale of the Autopsic Bride" (www.books2read.com/unfleshed). For more information and updates on Lisa's work, you can find her at: www.unsaintly.com or on Facebook (facebook.com/unsaintlyhalo), Twitter (@unsaintly), Instagram (unsaintly)

Christopher Motz was born in 1980 in a small town in Pennsylvania. From a young age he began writing tales of the supernatural to show his parents. Christopher is an avid reader of all things horror and science fiction, following in the footsteps of some of his favorite authors: Stephen King, John Saul, Peter Straub, Ray Bradbury, H.P. Lovecraft, Brian Keene, and others. His first novel, "The Darkening" was released in 2016 with "The Farm-A Novella" released shortly after. His latest novel will be available in 2017, along with a novel in collaboration with author Andrew Lennon.

https://christopher-motz.com/
https://www.facebook.com/authorChristopherMotz/

David Chrisley lives in many places. His body may reside in the comfort of Appalachia's New River Valley, but his mind is rarely there. In his mental wanderings, he has become a student of life and a porch-swing philosopher. He enjoys relating his imagined travels to anyone who will listen.

Weston Kincade has helped invest in future writers for years while teaching. He is also a member of the Horror Writers Association. His works include fantasy and horror novels which have hit Amazon's bestseller lists. His non-fiction works have been published in the Ohio Journal of English Language Arts and Cleveland.com, his fiction published by Books of the Dead Press and in anthologies by Alucard Press, Kevin J. Kennedy's bestselling Christmas Horror Shorts, and TPP Presents. When not writing, Weston makes time for his wife and Maine Coon cat Hermes, who talks so much he must be a speaker for the gods.

To find out more about Weston Kincade, visit http://kincadefiction.blogspot.com and sign up on his email list to find out about upcoming releases, special deals, and giveaways. No spam, I promise.

Andrew Lennon is the bestselling author of Every Twisted Thought and several other horror/thriller books. He has featured in various bestselling anthologies, and is successfully becoming a recognised name in horror and thriller writing. Andrew is a happily married man living in the North West of England with his wife Hazel & their children.

Having always been a big horror fan, Andrew spent a lot of his time watching scary movies or playing scary games, but it wasn't until his mid-twenties that he developed a taste for reading. His wife, also being a big horror fan, had a very large Stephen King collection which Andrew began to consume. Once hooked into reading horror, he started to discover new authors like Thomas Ligotti & Ryan C Thomas. It was while reading work from these authors that he decided to try writing something himself and there came the idea for "A Life to Waste"

He enjoys spending his time with his family and watching or reading new horror.
For more information please go to www.andrewlennon.co.uk

Colorado-bred writer **Christina Bergling** sold her soul early into the writing game. By fourth grade, she knew she wanted to be an author, and in college, she actively pursued it and started publishing small scale. However, with the realities of eating and paying bills, the survivalist in her hocked her passion for dystopian horror for a profession as a technical writer and document manager, even traveling to Iraq as a contractor. Bergling is a mother of two young children and lives with her family in Colorado Springs.

Learn more about Christina Bergling at http://christinabergling.com

Mark Fleming lives in Edinburgh. A writer of fantasy, horror and contemporary fiction, his stories have been published in numerous outlets, including The Big Issue, The Leither Magazine, Front and Centre (Canada), pulp.net and anthologies such as the Picador Book of Contemporary Scottish Fiction.

He is currently working on The Wolfslayer Series, a saga set in Dark Ages Britain, featuring druids and werewolves. Book 1 of the series, Wolf Warriors, is available to read on Inkitt.com. Book 2, Wolf Slaves, is due for publication later this year.

Aside from creative writing, his main passion is loud rock music: he plays guitar and keyboards in Scottish post-punk band Noniconic. He insists their music is catchy, but also ideal for horror movie soundtracks.

www.markjfleming.net

Jeff Menapace

A native of the Philadelphia area, Jeff has published multiple works in both fiction and non-fiction. In 2011 he was the recipient of the Red Adept Reviews Indie Award for Horror.

Jeff's terrifying debut novel Bad Games became a #1 Kindle bestseller that spawned two acclaimed sequels, and now all three books in the trilogy have been optioned for feature films and translated for foreign audiences.

His other novels, along with his award-winning short works, have also received international acclaim and are eagerly waiting to give you plenty of sleepless nights.

Free time for Jeff is spent watching horror movies, The Three Stooges, and mixed martial arts. He loves steak and more steak, thinks the original 1974 Texas Chainsaw Massacre is the greatest movie ever, wants to pet a lion someday, and hates spiders.

He currently lives in Pennsylvania with his wife Kelly and their cats Sammy and Bear.

Jeff loves to hear from his readers. Please feel free to contact him to discuss anything and everything, and be sure to visit his website to sign up for his FREE newsletter (no spam, not ever) where you will receive updates and sneak peeks on all future works along with the occasional free goodie!

www.jeffmenapace.com

Made in the USA
San Bernardino, CA
23 November 2017